# THE SISTERS-IN-LAW

A NOVEL OF OUR TIME

GERTRUDE ATHERTON

1st WORLD
LIBRARY
Literary Society

# The Sisters-In-Law

## Gertrude Atherton

© 1st World Library – Literary Society, 2004
PO Box 2211
Fairfield, IA 52556
www.1stworldlibrary.org
First Edition

LCCN: 2006902700

Softcover ISBN: 1-4218-1832-9
Hardcover ISBN: 1-4218-1732-2
eBook ISBN: 1-4218-1932-5

Purchase *"The Sisters-In-Law"*
as a traditional bound book at:
www.1stWorldLibrary.org/purchase.asp?ISBN=1-4218-1832-9

1st World Library Literary Society is a nonprofit
organization dedicated to promoting literacy by:

- Creating a free internet library accessible from any
computer worldwide.
- Hosting writing competitions and offering book
publishing scholarships.

Readers interested in supporting literacy
through sponsorship, donations or
membership please contact:
literacy@1stworldlibrary.org
Check us out at: www.1stworldlibrary.ORG
and start downloading free ebooks today.

***The Sisters-In-Law***
*contributed by Tim, Ed & Rodney*
*in support of*
*1st World Library Literary Society*

TO DR. ALANSON WEEKS OF SAN FRANCISCO


Several people who enter casually into this novel are leading characters in other novels and stories of the "California Series," which covers the social history of the state from the beginning of the last century. They are Gwynne, his mother, Lady Victoria Gwynne, Isabel Otis and the Hofers in ANCESTORS; the Randolphs in A DAUGHTER OF THE VINE; Lee Tarlton, Lady Barnstable, Lady Arrowmount, Coralie Geary, the Montgomerys and Trennahans in TRANSPLANTED and THE CALIFORNIANS; Rezánov in the novel of that name, and Chonita Iturbi y Moncada in THE DOOMSWOMAN, both bound in the volume, BEFORE THE GRINGO CAME; The Price Ruylers in THE AVALANCHE.

# BOOK I

## CHAPTER I

I

The long street rising and falling and rising again until its farthest crest high in the east seemed to brush the fading stars, was deserted even by the private watch-men that guarded the homes of the apprehensive in the Western Addition. Alexina darted across and into the shadows of the avenue that led up to her old-fashioned home, a relic of San Francisco's "early days," perched high on the steepest of the casual hills in that city of a hundred hills.

She was breathless and rather frightened, for although of an adventurous spirit, which had led her to slide down the pillars of the verandah at night when her legs were longer than her years, and during the past winter to make a hardly less dignified exit by a side door when her worthy but hopelessly Victorian mother was asleep, this was the first time that she had been out after midnight.

And it was five o'clock in the morning!

She had gone with Aileen Lawton, her mother's pet aversion, to a party given by one of those new people whom Mrs. Groome, a massive if crumbling pillar of San Francisco's proud old aristocracy, held in pious disdain, and had danced in the magnificent ballroom with the tireless exhilaration of her eighteen years until the weary band had played Home Sweet Home.

She had never imagined that any entertainment could be so brilliant, even among the despised nouveaux riches, nor that there were so many flowers even in California. Her own coming-out party in the dark double parlors of the old house among the eucalyptus trees, whose moans and sighs could be heard above the thin music of piano and violin, had been so formal and dull that she had cried herself to sleep after the last depressed member of the old set had left on the stroke of midnight. Even Aileen's high mocking spirits had failed her, and she had barely been able to summon them for a moment as she kissed the friend, to whom she was sincerely devoted, a sympathetic good-night.

"Never mind, old girl. Nothing can ever be worse. Not even your own funeral. That's one comfort."

## II

That had been last November. During the ensuing five months Alexina had been taken by her mother to such entertainments as were given by other members of that distinguished old band, whose glory, like Mrs. Groome's own, had reached its meridian in the last of the eighties.

Not that any one else in San Francisco was quite as exclusive as Mrs. Groome. Others might be as faithful in their way to the old tradition, be as proud of their inviolate past, when "money did not count," and people merely "new," or of unknown ancestry, did not venture to knock at the gates: but the successive flocks of young folks had overpowered their conservative parents, and Society had loosened its girdle, until in this year of grace nineteen-hundred-and-six, there were few rich people so hopelessly new that their ball rooms either in San Francisco or "Down the Peninsula," were unknown to a generation equally determined to enjoy life and indifferent to traditions.

Mrs. Groome alone had set her face obdurately against any change in the personnel of the eighties. She had the ugliest old house in San Francisco, and the change from lamps to gas had been her last concession to the march of time. The bath tubs were tin and the double parlors crowded with the imposing carved Italian furniture whose like every member of her own set had, in the seventies and eighties, brought home after their frequent and prolonged sojourns abroad: for the prouder the people of that era were of their lofty social position on the edge of the Pacific, the more time did they spend in Europe.

Mrs. Groome might be compelled therefore to look at new people in the homes of her friends - even her proud daughter, Mrs. Abbott, had unaccountably surrendered to the meretricious glitter of Burlingame - but she would not meet them, she would not permit Alexina to cross their thresholds, nor should the best of them ever cross her own.

Poor Alexina, forced to submit, her mother placidly impervious to coaxings, tears, and storms, had finally compromised the matter to the satisfaction of herself and of her own close chosen friend, Aileen Lawton. She accompanied her mother with outward resignation to small dinner dances and to the Matriarch balls, presided over by the newly elected social leader, a lady of unimpeachable Southern ancestry and indifference to wealth, who pledged her Virginia honor to Mrs. Groome that Alexina should not be introduced to any young man whose name was not on her own visiting list; and, while her mother slept, the last of the Ballinger-Groomes accompanied Aileen (chaperoned by an unprincipled aunt, who was an ancient enemy of Maria Groome) to parties quite as respectable but infinitely gayer, and indubitably mixed.

She was quite safe, for Mrs. Groome, when free of social duties, retired on the stroke of nine with a novel, and turned off the gas at ten. She never read the society columns of the newspapers, choked as they were with unfamiliar and plebeian names; and her friends, regarding Alexina's gay disobedience as a palatable joke on "poor old Maria," and sympathetic with youth, would have been the last to enlighten her.

# III

Alexina had never enjoyed herself more than to-night. Young Mrs. Hofer, who had bought and remodeled the old Polk house on Nob Hill - the very one in which Mrs. Groome's oldest daughter had made her début in the far-off eighties - had turned all her immense rooms into a bower of every variety of flower that bloomed on the rich California soil. It was her second great party of the season, and it had been her avowed intention to outdo the first, which had attempted a revival of Spanish California and been the talk of the town. The decorations had been done by a firm of young women whose parents and grandparents had danced in the old house, and the catering by another scion of San Francisco's social founders, Miss Anne Montgomery.

To do Mrs. Groome full justice, all of these enterprising young women were welcome in her own home. She regarded it as unfortunate that ladies were forced to work for their living, but had seen too many San Francisco families in her own youth go down to ruin to feel more than sorrow. In that era the wives of lost millionaires had knitted baby socks and starved slowly. Even she was forced to admit that the newer generation was more fortunate in its opportunities.

Alexina had not gone to Mrs. Hofer's first party, Aileen being in Santa Barbara, but she had sniffed at the comparisons of the more critical girls in their second season. She was quite convinced that nothing so splendid had ever been given in the world. She had danced every dance. She had had the most delicious things to eat, and never had she met so charming a young man as Mortimer Dwight.

"Some party," she thought as she ran up the steep avenue to her sacrosanct abode, where her haughty mother was chastely asleep, secure in the belief that her obedient little daughter was dreaming in her maiden bower.

"What the poor old darling doesn't know 'll never hurt her," thought Alexina gayly. "She really is old enough to be my grandmother, anyhow. I wonder if Maria and Sally really stood for it or were as naughty as I am."

Alexina was the youngest of a long line of boys and girls, all of whom but five were dead. Ballinger and Geary practiced law in New York, having married sisters who refused to live elsewhere. Sally had married one of their Harvard friends and dwelt in Boston. Maria alone had wed an indigenous Californian, an Abbott of Alta in the county of San Mateo, and lived the year round in that old and exclusive borough. She was now so like her mother, barring a very slight loosening of her own social girdle, that Alexina dismissed as fantastic the notion that even a quarter of a century earlier she may have had any of the promptings of rebellious youth.

"Not she!" thought Alexina grimly. "Oh, Lord! I wonder if my summer destiny is Alta."

# CHAPTER II

I

She was quite breathless as she reached the eucalyptus grove and paused for a moment before slipping into the house and climbing the stairs.

The city lying in the valleys and on the hills arrested her attention, for it was a long while since she had been awake and out of doors at five in the morning.

It looked like the ghost of a city in that pallid dawn. The houses seemed to have huddled together as if in fear before they sank into sleep, to crouch close to the earth as if warding off a blow. Only the ugly dome of the City Hall, the church steeples, and the old shot tower held up their heads, and they had an almost terrifying sharpness of outline, of alertness, as if ready to spring.

In that far-off district known as "South of Market Street," which she had never entered save in a closed carriage on her way to the Southern Pacific Station or to pay a yearly call on some old family that still dwelt on that oasis, Rincon Hill - sole outpost of the social life of the sixties - infrequent thin lines of smoke rose from humble chimneys. It was the region of factories and dwellings of the working-class, but its inhabitants were not early risers in these days of high wages and short hours.

Even those gray spirals ascended as if the atmosphere lay heavy on them. They accentuated the lifelessness, the petrifaction, the intense and sinister quiet of the prostrate city.

Alexina shuddered and her volatile spirits winged their way down into those dark and intuitive depths of her mind she had never found time to plumb. She knew that the hour of dawn was always still, but she had never imagined a stillness so complete, so final as this. Nor was there any fresh lightness in the morning air. It seemed to press downward like an enormous invisible bat; or like the shade of buried cities, vain outcroppings of a vanished civilization, brooding menacingly over this recent flimsy accomplishment of man that Nature could obliterate with a sneer.

Alexina, holding her breath, glanced upward. That ghost of evening's twilight, the sad gray of dawn, had retreated, but not before the crimson rays of sunrise. The unflecked arc above was a hard and steely blue. It looked as if marsh lights would play over its horrid surface presently, and then come crashing down as the pillars of the earth gave way.

Gertrude Atherton

## II

Alexina was a child of California and knew what was coming. She barely had time to brace herself when she saw the sleeping city jar as if struck by a sudden squall, and with the invisible storm came a loud menacing roar of imprisoned forces making a concerted rush for freedom.

She threw her arms about one of the trees, but it was bending and groaning with an accent of fear, a tribute it would have scorned to offer the mighty winds of the Pacific. Alexina sprang clear of it and unable to keep her feet sat down on the bouncing earth.

Then she remembered that it was a rigid convention among real Californians to treat an earthquake as a joke, and began to laugh. There was nothing hysterical in this perfunctory tribute to the lesser tradition and it immediately restored her courage. Moreover, the curiosity she felt for all phases of life, psychical and physical, and her naïve delight in everything that savored of experience, caused her to stare down upon the city now tossing and heaving like the sea in a hurricane, with an almost impersonal interest.

The houses seemed to clutch at their precarious foundations even while they danced to the tune of various and appalling noises. Above the ascending roar of the earthquake Alexina heard the crashing of steeples, the dome of the City Hall, of brick buildings too hastily erected, of ten thousand falling chimneys; of creaking and grinding timbers, and of the eucalyptus trees behind her, whose leaves rustled with a shrill rising whisper that seemed addressed to heaven; the neighing and pawing of horses in the stables, the sharp terrified yelps of dogs; and through all a long despairing wail. The mountains across the bay and behind the city were whirling in a devil's dance and the scattered houses on their slopes looked like drunken gnomes. The shot tower bowed low and solemnly but did not fall.

Gertrude Atherton

## III

As the earth with a final leap and twist settled abruptly into peace, the streets filled suddenly with people, many in their nightclothes, but more in dressing-gowns, opera cloaks, and overcoats. All were silent and apparently self-possessed. Whence came that long wail no one ever knew.

Alexina, remembering her own attire, sprang to her feet and ran through the little side door and up the stair, praying that her mother, with her usual monumental poise, would have disdained to rise. She had never been known to leave her room before eight.

But as Alexina ran along the upper hall she became only too aware that Mrs. Groome had surrendered to Nature, for she was pounding on her door and in a haughty but quivering voice demanding to be let out.

Alexina tiptoed lightly to the threshold of her room and called out sympathetically:

"What is the matter, mother dear! Has your door sprung?"

"It has. Tell James to come here at once and bring a crow-bar if necessary."

"Yes, darling."

Alexina let down her hair and tore off her evening gown, kicking it into a closet, then threw on a bathrobe and ran over to the servants' quarters in an extension behind the house. They were deserted, but wild shrieks and gales of unseemly laughter arose from the yard. She opened a window and saw the cook, a recent importation, on the ground in hysterics, the housemaid throwing water on her, and the inherited butler calmly lighting his pipe,

"James," she called. "My mother's door is jammed. Please come right away."

"Yes, miss." He knocked his pipe against the wall and ground out the life of the coal with his slippered heel. "Just what happened to your grandmother in the 'quake of sixty-eight. I mind the time I had getting her out."

Gertrude Atherton

IV

It was quite half an hour before the door yielded to the combined efforts of James and the gardener-coachman, and during the interval Mrs. Groome recovered her poise and made her morning toilette.

She had taken her iron-gray hair from its pins and patted the narrow row of frizzes into place; the flat side bands, the concise coil of hair on top were as severely disdainful of untoward circumstance or passing fashion as they had been any morning these forty years or more.

She wore old-fashioned corsets and was abdominally correct for her years; a long gown of black voile with white polka dots, and a guimpe of white net whose raff of chiffon somewhat disguised the wreck of her throat. On her shoulders, disposed to rheumatism, she wore a tippet of brown marabout feathers, and in her ears long jet earrings.

She had the dark brown eyes of the Ballingers, but they were bleared at the rims, and on the downward slope of her fine aquiline nose she wore spectacles that looked as if mounted in cast iron. Altogether an imposing relic; and "that built-up look" as Aileen expressed it, was the only one that would have suited her mental style. Mrs. Abbott, who dressed with a profound regard for fashion, had long since concluded that her mother's steadfast alliance with the past not only became her but was a distinct family asset. Only a woman of her overpowering position could afford it.

Mrs. Groome's skin had never felt the guilty caress of

cold-cream or powder, and if it was mahogany in tint and deeply wrinkled, it was at least as respectable as her past. In her day that now bourgeois adjective - twin to genteel - had been synchronous with the equally obsolete word swell, but it had never occurred to even the more modern Mrs. Abbott and her select inner circle of friends, dwelling on family estates in the San Mateo valley, to change in this respect at least with the changing times.

# V

Alexina had washed the powder from her own fresh face and put on a morning frock of green and brown gingham, made not by her mother's dressmaker but by her sister's. Her soft dusky hair, regardless of the fashion of the moment, was brushed back from her forehead and coiled at the base of her beautiful little head. Her long widely set gray eyes, their large irises very dark and noticeably brilliant even for youth, had the favor of black lashes as fine and lusterless as her hair, and very narrow black polished eyebrows. Her skin was a pale olive lightly touched with color, although the rather large mouth with its definitely curved lips was scarlet. Her long throat like the rest of her body was white.

All the other children had been clean-cut Ballingers or Groomes, consistently dark or fair; but it would seem that Nature, taken by surprise when the little Alexina came along several years after her mother was supposed to have discharged her debt, had mixed the colors hurriedly and quite forgotten her usual nice proportions.

The face, under the soft lines of youth, was less oval than it looked, for the chin was square and the jaw bone accentuated. The short straight thin nose reclaimed the face and head from too classic a regularity, and the thin nostrils drew in when she was determined and shook quite alarmingly when she was angry.

These more significant indications of her still embryonic personality were concealed by the lovely curves and tints of her years, the brilliant happy candid eyes (which she could convert into a madonna's by the simple trick of lifting them a trifle and showing a lower crescent of devotional white), the love of life and eagerness to enjoy that radiated from her thin admirably proportioned body, which, at this time, held in the limp slouching fashion of the hour, made her look rather small. In reality she was nearly as tall as her mother or the dignified Mrs. Abbott, who rejoiced in every inch of her five feet eight, and retained the free erect carriage of her girlhood.

Alexina, with a sharp glance about her disordered room, hastily disarranged her bed, and, sending her ball slippers after the gown, ran across the hall and threw herself into her mother's arms.

"Some earthquake, what? You are sure you are not hurt, mommy dear? The plaster is down all over the house."

"More slang that you have learned from Aileen Lawton, I presume. It certainly was a dreadful earthquake, worse than that of eighteen-sixty-eight. Is anything valuable broken? There is always less damage done on the hills. What is that abominable noise?"

The cook, who had recovered from her first attack, was emitting another volley of shrieks, in which the word "fire" could be distinguished in syllables of two.

Mrs. Groome rang the bell violently and the imperturbable James appeared.

"Is the house on fire?"

"No, ma'am; only the city. It's worth looking at, if you care to step out on the lawn."

Mrs. Groome followed her daughter downstairs and out of the house. Her eyebrows were raised but there was a curious sensation in her knees that even the earthquake had failed to induce. She sank into the chair James had provided and clutched the arms with both hands.

"There are always fires after earthquakes," she muttered. "Impossible! Impossible!"

"Oh, do you think San Francisco is really going?" cried Alexina, but there was a thrill in her regret. "Oh, but it couldn't be."

"No! impossible, impossible!"

Black clouds of smoke shot with red tongues of flame overhung the city at different points, although they appeared to be more dense and frequent down in the "South of Market Street" region. There was also a rolling mass of flame above the water front and sporadic fires in the business district.

The streets were black with people, now fully dressed, and long processions were moving steadily toward the bay as well as in the direction of the hills behind the western rim of the city. James brought a pair of field glasses, and Mrs. Groome discovered that the hurrying throngs were laden with household goods, many pushing them in baby carriages and wheelbarrows. It was the first flight of the refugees.

"James!" said Mrs. Groome sharply. "Bring me a cup

of coffee and then go down and find out exactly what is happening."

James, too wise in the habits of earthquakes to permit the still distracted cook to make a fire in the range, brewed the coffee over a spirit lamp, and then departed, nothing loath, on his mission. Mrs. Groome swallowed the coffee hastily, handed the cup to Alexina and burst into tears.

"Mother!" Alexina was really terrified for the first time that morning. Mrs. Groome practiced the severe code, the repressions of her class, and what tears she had shed in her life, even over the deaths of those almost forgotten children, had been in the sanctity of her bedroom. Alexina, who had grown up under her wing, after many sorrows and trials had given her a serenity that was one secret of her power over this impulsive child of her old age, could hardly have been more appalled if her mother had been stricken with paralysis.

"You cannot understand," sobbed Mrs. Groome. "This is my city! The city of my youth; the city my father helped to make the great and wonderful city it is. Even your father - he may not have been a good husband - Oh, no! Not he! - but he was a good citizen; he helped to drag San Francisco out of the political mire more than once. And now it is going! It has always been prophesied that San Francisco would burn to the ground some time, and now the time has come. I feel it in my bones."

This was the first reference other than perfunctory, that Alexina had ever heard her mother make to her father, who had died when she was ten. The girl realized abruptly that this elderly parent who, while uniformly kind, had appeared to be far above the ordinary weaknesses of her sex, had an inner life which bound her to the plane of mere mortals. She had a sudden vision of an unhappy married life, silently borne, a life of suppressions, bitter disappointments. Her chief compensation had been the unwavering pride which had made the world forget to pity her.

And it was the threatened destruction of her city that had beaten down the defenses and given her youngest child a brief glimpse of that haughty but shivering spirit.

# VI

Alexina's mind, in spite of a great deal of worldly garnering with an industrious and investigating scythe, was as immature as her years, for she had felt little and lived not at all. But she had swift and deep intuitions, and in spite of the natural volatility of youth, free of care, she was fundamentally emotional and intense.

Swept from her poor little girlish moorings in the sophisticated sea of the twentieth-century maiden, she had a sudden wild access of conscience; she flung herself into her mother's arms and poured out the tale of her nocturnal transgressions, her frequent excursions into the forbidden realm of modern San Francisco, of her immense acquaintance with people whose very names were unknown to Mrs. Groome, born Ballinger.

Then she scrambled to her feet and stood twisting her hands together, expecting a burst of wrath that would further reveal the pent-up fires in this long-sealed volcano; for Alexina was inclined to the exaggerations of her sex and years and would not have been surprised if her mother, masterpiece of a lost art, had suddenly become as elementary as the forces that had devastated San Francisco.

But there was only dismay in Mrs. Groome's eyes as she stared at her repentant daughter. Her heart sank still lower. She had never been a vain woman, but she had prided herself upon not feeling old. Suddenly, she felt very old, and helpless.

"Well," she said in a moment. "Well - I suppose I have been wrong. There are almost two generations between

Gertrude Atherton

us. I haven't kept up. And you are naturally a truthful child - I should have - "

"Oh, mother, you are not blaming yourself!" Alexina felt as if the earth once more were dancing beneath her unsteady feet. "Don't say that!"

The sharpness of her tone dispelled the confusion in Mrs. Groome's mind.
She hastily buckled on her armor.

"Let us say no more about it. I fancy it will be a long time before there are any more parties in San Francisco, but when there are - well, I shall consult Maria. I want your youth to be happy - as happy as mine was. I suppose you young people can only be happy in the new way, but I wish conditions had not changed so lamentably in San Francisco....Who is this?"

# CHAPTER III

I

As Alexina followed her mother's eyes she flushed
scarlet and turned away her head. A young man was
coming up the avenue. He was a very gallant figure,
moderately tall and very straight; he held his head
high, his features were strong in outline. But the
noticeable thing about him at this early hour of the
morning and in the wake of a great disaster was his
consummate grooming.

"That - that - " stammered Alexina, "is Mr. Dwight. I
met him last night at the Hofers'."

The young man raised his hat and came forward
quickly. "I hope you will forgive me," he said with a
charming deference, "but I couldn't resist coming to
see if you were all right. So many people are
frightened of fire - in their own houses."

"Mr. Dwight - my mother - "

He lifted his hat again. Mrs. Groome in her chastened
mood regarded him favorably, and for the moment

Gertrude Atherton

without suspicion. At least he was a gentleman; but who could he be?

"Dwight," she murmured. "I do not know the name. Were you born here?"

"I was born in Utica, New York. My parents came here when I was quite young. We - always lived rather quietly."

"But you go about now? To all these parties?"

"Oh, yes. I like to dance after the day's work. But I am not what you would call a society man. I haven't the time."

Mrs. Groome was not usually blunt, but she suddenly scented danger and she had not fully recovered her poise.

"You are in business?" She disliked business intensely. All gentlemen of her day had followed one of the professions.

"I am in a wholesale commission house. But I hope to be in business for myself one day."

"Ah."

Still, all young men in this terrible twentieth century could not be lawyers. Mrs. Groome knew enough of the march of time to be aware of the increasing difficulties in gaining a bare livelihood. Tom Abbott was a lawyer, like his father before him, and his grandfather in the fifties. It was one of the oldest firms in San Francisco, but she recalled his frequent and bitter allusions to the necessity of sitting up nights these days if a man wanted to keep out of the poorhouse.

And at least this young man did not look like an idler or a wastrel. No man could have so clear a skin and be so well-groomed at six in the morning if he drank or gambled. Alexander Groome had done both and she knew the external seals.

"Is Aileen Lawton a friend of yours?" she asked sharply.

"I have met Miss Lawton at a number of dances but she has not done me the honor to ask me to call."

"I think the more highly of you. Judge Lawton is an old friend of mine. His wife, who was much younger than the Judge, was an intimate friend of my daughter, Mrs. Abbott. Alexina and Aileen have grown up together. I find it impossible to forbid her the house. But I disapprove of her in every way. She paints her lips, smokes cigarettes, boasts that she drinks cocktails, and uses the most abominable slang. I kept my daughter in New York for two years as much to break up the intimacy as to finish her education, but the moment we returned the intimacy was renewed, and for my old friend's sake I have been forced to submit. He worships that - that - really ill-conditioned child."

"Oh - Miss Lawton is a good sort, and - well - I suppose her position is so strong that she feels she can do as she pleases. But she is all right, and not so different - "

"Do you mean to tell me that you approve of girls

- nice girls - ladies - painting themselves, smoking, drinking cocktails?"

"I do not." His tones were emphatic and his good American gray eyes wandered to the fresh innocent face of the girl who had captivated him last night.

"I should hope not. You look like an exceptionally decent young man. Have you had breakfast? Alexina, go and ask Maggie, if she has recovered herself, to make another cup of coffee."

## II

Alexina disappeared, repressing a desire to sing; and young Dwight, receiving permission, seated himself on the grass at Mrs. Groome's feet. He was lithe and graceful and as he threw back his head and looked up at his hostess with his straight, honest glance the good impression he had made was visibly enhanced. Mrs. Groome gave him the warm and gracious smile that only her intimate friends and paid inferiors had ever seen.

"The young men of to-day are a great disappointment to me," she observed.

"Oh, they are all right, I guess. Most of the men that go about have rich fathers - or near-rich ones. I wish I had one myself."

"And you would be as dissipated as the rest, I presume."

"No, I have no inclinations that way. But a man gets a better start in life. And a man's a nonentity without money."

"Not if he has family."

"My family is good - in Utica. But that is of no use to me here."

"But your family *is* good?"

"Oh, yes, it goes 'way back. There is a family mansion in Utica that is over two hundred years old. But when the business district swamped that part of the old town it was sold, and what it brought was divided among six. My father came out here but did not make much of a success of himself, so that he and my mother might as well have been on the Fiji Islands for all the notice society took of them."

He spoke with some bitterness, and Mrs. Groome, to whom dwelling beyond the outer gates of San Francisco's elect was the ultimate tragedy, responded sympathetically.

"Society here is not what it used to be, and no doubt is only too glad to welcome presentable young men. I infer that you have not found it difficult."

"Oh, I dance well, and my employer's son, Bob Cheever, took me in. But I'm only tolerated. I don't count."

The old lady looked at him keenly. "You are ambitious?"

He threw back his head. "Well, yes, I am, Mrs. Groome. As far as society goes it is a matter of self-respect. I feel that I have the right to go in the best society anywhere - that I am as good as anybody when it comes to blood. And I'd like to get to the top in every way. I don't mean that I would or could do the least thing dishonest to get there, as so many men have done, but - well, I see no crime in being ambitious and using every chance to get to the top. I'd like not only to be one of the rich and important men of San Francisco, but to take a part in the big civic movements."

Mrs. Groome was charmed. She was by no means an

impulsive woman, but she had suddenly realized her age, and if she must soon leave her youngest child, who, heaven knew, needed a guardian, this young man might be a son-in-law sent direct from heaven - via the earthquake. If he had real ability the influential men she knew would see that he had a proper start. But she had no intention of committing herself.

"And what do you think of what is now called San Francisco society?" she demanded.

He was quite aware of Mrs. Groome's attitude. Who in San Francisco was not? It was one of the standing jokes, although few of the younger or newer set had ever heard of her until her naughty little daughter danced upon the scene.

"Oh, it is mixed, of course. There are many houses where I do not care to go. But, well, after all, the rich people are rather simple for all their luxury, and as for the old families there are no more real aristocrats in England itself."

Mrs. Groome was still more charmed. "But you were at Mrs. Hofer's last night. I never heard of her before."

"Her husband is one of the most important of the younger men. His father made a fortune in lumber and sent his son to Yale and all the rest of it. He is really a gentleman - it only takes one generation out here - and at present he's bent upon delivering the city from this abominable ring of grafters...There is no water to put out the fires because the City Administration pocketed the money appropriated for a new system; the pipes leading from Spring Valley were broken by the earthquake."

"And who was she?"

Mrs. Groome asked this question with an inimitable inflection inherited from her mother and grandmother, both of whom had been guardians of San Francisco society in their day. The accent was on the "who." Bob Cheever, whose grandmother had asked or answered the same question in dark old double parlors filled with black walnut and carved oak, would have muttered, "Oh, hell!" but Mr. Dwight replied sympathetically: "Something very common, I believe-south of Market Street. But her father was very clever, rose to be a foreman of the iron works, and finally went into business and prospered in a small way. He sent his daughter to Europe to be educated...and even you could hardly tell her from the real thing."

"And you go down to Burlingame, I suppose! That is a very nest of these new people, and I am told they spend their time drinking and gambling."

He set his large rather hard lips. "No, I have never been asked down to Burlingame-nor down the Peninsula anywhere. You see, I am only asked out in town because an unmarried dancing man is always welcome if there is nothing wrong with his manners. To be asked for intimate week-ends is another matter. But I don't fancy Burlingame is half as bad as it is represented to be. They go in tremendously for sport, you know, and that is healthy and takes up a good deal of time. After all when people are very rich and have more leisure than they know what to do with - "

"Many of the old set in Alta, San Mateo, Atherton and Menlo Park have wealth and leisure-not vulgar fortunes, but enough-and for the most part they live quite as they did in the old days."

His eyes lit up. "Ah, San Mateo, Alta, Atherton, Menlo Park. There you have a real landed aristocracy. The Burlingame set must realize that they would be nobodies for all their wealth if they could not call at all those old communities down the Peninsula."

"Not so very many of them do. But I see you have no false values. You. Must go down with us some Sunday to Alta. I am sure you would like my oldest daughter. She is very smart, as they call it now, but distinctly of the old régime."

"There is nothing I should like better. Thank you so much." And there was no doubting the sincerity of his voice, a rather deep and manly voice which harmonized with the admirable mold of his ancestors.

# III

Alexina appeared. "Breakfast is ready for all of us," she announced. "We cooked it on the old stove in the woodhouse. I helped, for Maggie is a wreck. Martha has swept the plaster out of the dining-room. Come along. I'm starved."

Young Dwight sprang to his feet and stood over Mrs. Groome with his charming deferential manner, but he had far too much tact to offer assistance as she rose heavily from her chair.

"Are you really going to give me breakfast? I am sure I could not get any elsewhere."

"We are only too happy. Your coming has been a real God-send. Will you give me your arm? This morning - not the earthquake but those dreadful fires - has quite upset me."

He escorted her into the dark old house with glowing eyes. He had seen so little of the world that he was still very young at thirty and his nature was sanguine, but he had never dared to dream of even difficult access to this most exclusive home in San Francisco. Its gloom, its tastelessness, relieved only by the splendid Italian pieces, but served to accentuate its aristocratic aloofness from those superb but too recently furnished mansions of which he knew so little outside of their ballrooms.

And he was breakfasting with the sequestered Mrs. Groome and the loveliest girl he had ever seen, at seven o 'clock in the morning.

He looked about eagerly as they entered the dining-room.. It was long and narrow with a bow window at the end. The furniture was black walnut; two immense sideboards were built into the walls. It looked Ballinger, and it was.

It was heavily paneled; the walls above were tinted a pale buff and set with cracked oil paintings of men in the uniforms of several generations. The ceiling was frescoed with fish and fowl. There had been a massive bronze chandelier over the table. It now lay on the floor, but as James had turned off the gas in the meter while the earthquake was still in progress the air of the large sunny room was untainted, and the windows were open.

The breakfast was smoked but not uneatable and the strong coffee raised even Mrs. Groome's wavering spirits. They were all talking gayly when James entered abruptly. He was very pale.

"City's doomed, ma'am. Thirty fires broke out simultaneous, and the wind blowing from the southeast. A chimney fell on the fire-chief's bed and he can't live. People runnin' round like their heads was cut off and thousands pouring out of the city - over to Oakland and Berkeley. Lootin' was awful and General Funston has ordered out the troops. Pipes broken and not a drop of water. They're goin' to dynamite, but only the fire-chief knew how. Everybody says the whole city'll go, Doomed, that's what it is. Better let me tell Mike to harness up and drive you down to San Mateo."

Mrs. Groome had also turned pale, but she cut a piece of bacon with resolution in every finger of her large-veined hands.

"I do not believe it, and I shall not run - like those people south of Market Street. I shall stay until the last minute at all events. The roads at least cannot burn."

"This house ought to be safe enough, ma 'am, standin' quite alone on this hill as it does; but it's a question of food. We never keep much of anything in the house, beyond what's needed for the week, and the California Market's right in the fire zone. And the smoke will be something terrible when the fire gets closer."

"I shall stay in my own house. There are grocery stores and butcher shops in Fillmore Street. Go and buy all you can." She handed him a bunch of keys. "You will find money in my escritoire. Tell the maids to fill the bathtubs while there is any water left in the mains. You may go if you are frightened, but I stay here."

"Very well, and you needn't have said that, ma'am. I've been in this family, man and boy, Ballinger and Groome, for fifty-two years, and you know I'd never desert you. But no doubt those hussies in the kitchen will, with a lot of others. A lot of stoves have already been set up in the streets out here and ladies are cookin' their own breakfasts."

"Forgive me, James. I know you will never leave me. And if the others do we shall get along. Miss Alexina is not a bad cook." And she heroically swallowed the bacon.

## IV

James departed and she turned to Dwight, who was on his feet.

"You are not going?"

"I think I must, Mrs. Groome. There may be something I can do down there. All able-bodied men will be needed, I fancy."

"But you'll come back and see us?" cried Alexina.

"Indeed I will. I'll report regularly."

He thanked Mrs. Groome for her hospitality and she invited him to take pot luck with her at dinner time. After he had gone Alexina exclaimed rapturously:

"Oh, you do like him, don't you, mommy dear?"

And Mrs. Groome was pleased to reply, "He has perfect manners and certainly has the right ideas about things. I could do no less than ask him to dinner if he is going to take the trouble to bring us the news."

# CHAPTER IV

I

That was a unique and vivid day for young Alexina Groome, whose disposition was to look upon life as drama and asked only that it shift its scenes often and be consistently entertaining and picturesque.

Never, so James told her, since her Grandmother Ballinger's reign, had there been such life and movement in the old house. All Mrs. Groome's intimate friends and many of Alexina's came to it, some to make kindly inquiries, others to beg them to leave the city, many to gossip and exchange experiences of that fateful morning; a few from Rincon Hill and the old ladies' fashionable boarding-house district to claim shelter until they could make their way to relatives out of town.

Mrs. Groome welcomed her friends not only with the more spontaneous hospitality of an older time but in that spirit of brotherhood that every disaster seems to release, however temporarily. Brotherhood is unquestionably an instinct of the soul, an inheritance from that sunrise era when mutual interdependence was as imperative as it was automatic. The complexities of civilization have overlaid it, and almost but not wholly replaced it by national and individual selfishness. But the world as yet is only about one-third civilized. Centuries hence a unified civilization may complete the circle, but human nature and progress must act and react a thousand times before the earthly millenium; and it cannot be hastened by dreamers and fanatics.

All Mrs. Groome's spare rooms were placed at the service of her friends, and cots were bought in the humble Fillmore Street shops and put up in the billiard room, the double parlors, the library and the upper hall. Some forty people would sleep under the old Ballinger roof that night - dynamite permitting. Mrs. Groome was firm in her determination not to flee, and as James and Mike were there to watch, she had graciously given a number of the gloomy refugees from the lower regions permission to camp in the outhouses and grounds.

II

Alexina spent the greater part of the day with Aileen
Lawton, Olive Bascom, and Sibyl Thorndyke, out of
doors, fascinated by the spectacle of the burning city.

The valley beyond Market Street, and the lower
business district, were a rolling mass of smoke parting
about pillars of fire, shot with a million glittering
sparks when a great building was dynamited. All the
windows in those sections of the city as yet beyond the
path of the fire were open, for although closed
windows might have shut out the torrid atmosphere,
the explosions would have shattered them.

"Oh, dear," sighed Olive Bascom, "there goes my
building. The smoke lifted for a moment and I saw the
flames spouting out of the windows. A cool million
and uninsured. We thought Class A buildings were
safe from any sort of fire."

"Heavens!" exclaimed Alexina naïvely, "I wish I had a
million-dollar building down in that furnace. It must be
a great sensation to watch a million dollars go up in
sparks."

"I hope your mother hasn't any buildings down in the
business district," said Aileen anxiously. "I've heard
dad talk about her ground rents. She'll get those again
soon enough. I fancy the old tradition survives in this
town and they'll begin to draw the plans for the new
city before the fire is out. It used to burn down
regularly in the fifties, dad says."

"I don't fancy we have much of anything," said

Alexina cheerfully. "I think mother has only a life interest in a part of father's estate, and I heard her tell Maria once that she intended to leave me all she had of her own, this place and a few thousand a year in bonds and some flats that are probably burning up right now. I gathered from the conversation that father didn't have much left when he died and that it was understood mother was to look out for me. I believe he gave a lot to the others when he was wealthy."

"Good Lord!" Aileen sighed heavily. "It won't pay your dressmakers' bills, what with taxes and all. I won't be much better off. We'll have to marry Rex Roberts or Bob Cheever or Frank Bascom - unless he's going up in smoke too, Olive dear. But there are a few others."

Alexina shook her head. Her color could not rise higher for her face was crimson from the heat; like the others she had a wet handkerchief on her head. "There is not a grain of romance in one of them," she announced. "Curious that the sons of the rich nearly always have round faces, no particular features, and a tendency to bulge. I intend to have a romance - old style - good old style - before the vogue of the middle-class realists. There's nothing in life but youth and you only have it once. I'm going to have a romance that means falling wildly, unreasonably, uncalculatingly in love."

"You anticipate my adjectives," said Aileen drily. "Although not all. But let that pass. I'd like to know where you expect to find the opposite lead, as they say on the stage. Our men are not such a bad sort, even the richest - with a few exceptions, of course. They may hit it up at week-ends, generally at the country clubs, but they're better than the last generation because their fathers have more sense. I'll bet they're all down there now fighting the fire with the vim of their grandfathers....But romantic! Good Lord! I'll marry one of them all right and glad of the chance - after I've had my fling. I'm in no hurry. I'd have outgrown my illusions in any case by that time, only Nature did the trick by not giving me any."

"Don't you believe there isn't a man in all San Francisco able to inspire romance." If Alexina could not blush her dark gray eyes could sparkle and melt. "All the men we meet don't belong to that rich group."

"Bunch, darling. Where - will you give us the pointer? - are to be found the romantic knights of San Francisco? 'Frisco as those tiresome Eastern people call it. Makes me sick to think that they are even now pitying 'poor 'Frisco.' "Well? - I could beat my brains and not call one to mind."

"Oh!"

"What does that mean, Alex Groome? When you roll up your eyes like that you look like a love-sick tomato."

"Mortimer Dwight was most devoted last night," said Sibyl Thorndyke. "She danced with him at least eight times."

"You must have sat out alone to know what I was doing," Alexina began hotly, but Aileen sprang at her and gripped her shoulders.

"Don't tell me that you are interested in that cheap skate. Alexina Groome!

You!"

"He's not a cheap skate. I despise your cheap slang."

"He's a rank nobody."

"You mean he isn't rich. Or his family didn't belong. What do you suppose I care? I'm not a snob."

"He is. A climbing, ingenuous, empty-headed snob."

"You are a snob. You ought to be ashamed of yourself."

"I've a right to be a snob if I choose, and he hasn't. My snobbery is the right sort: the 'I will maintain' kind. He'd give all the hair on his head to have the right to that sort of snobbery. His is" (she chanted in a high light maddening voice): "Oh, God, let me climb. Yank me up into the paradise of San Francisco society. Burlingame, Alta, Menlo Park, Atherton, Belvidere, San Rafael. Oh, God, it's awful to be a nobody, not to be in the same class with these rich fellers, not to belong to the Pacific-Union Club, not to have polo ponies, not to belong to smart golf clubs, to the Burlingame Club. Not to get clothes from New York and London - "

"You keep quiet," shrieked Alexina, who with difficulty refrained from substituting: "You shut up." She flung off Aileen's hands. "What do you know about him? He doesn't like you."

"Never had a chance to find out."

"What can you know about him, then?"

"Think I'm blind? Think I'm deaf? Don't I know everything that goes on in this town? Isn't sizing-up my long suit? And he's as dull as - as a fish without salt. I sat next to him at a dinner, and all he could talk about was the people he'd met - our sort, of course. And he was dull even at that. He's all manners and bluff - "

"You couldn't draw him out. He talked to me."

"What about? I'm really interested to know. Everybody says the same thing. They fall for his dancing and manners, and - well, yes - I 'll admit it - for his looks. He even looks like a gentleman. But all the girls say he bores 'em stiff. They have to talk their heads off. What did he say to you that was so frantically interesting?"

"Well, of course - we danced most of the time."

"That's just it. He's inherited the shell of some able old ancestor and not a bit of the skull furniture. Nature often plays tricks like that. But I could forgive him for being dull if he weren't such a damn snob."

"You shan't call him names. If he wants to be one of us, and life was so unkind as to - to - well, birth him on the outside, I'm sure that's no crime."

"Snobbery," said Miss Thorndyke, who was intellectual at the moment and cultivating the phrase, "is merely a rather ingenuous form of aspiration. I can't see that it varies except in kind from other forms of ambition. And without ambition there would be no progress."

"Oh, can it," sneered Judge Lawton's daughter. "You're

all wrong, anyhow. Snobbery leads to the rocks much oftener than to high achievement. I've heard dad say so, and you won't venture to assert that *he* doesn't know. It bears about the same relation to progress that grafting does to legitimate profits. Anyhow, it makes me sick, and I'm not going to have Alex falling in love with a poor fish - "

"Fish?" Alexina's voice rose above a fresh detonation, "You dare - and you think I'm going to ask you whom I shall fall in love with? Fish? What do you call those other shrimps who don't think of anything but drinking and sport, whether they attend to business or not? - their fathers make them, anyhow. And you want to marry one of them! They're fish, if you like."

The two girls were glaring at each other. Gray eyes were blazing, green eyes snapping. Two sets of white even teeth were bared. They looked like a couple of belligerent puppies. Another moment and they would have forgotten the sacred traditions of their class and flown at each other's hair. But Miss Bascom interposed. Even the loss of her uninsured million did not ruffle her, for she had another in Government and railroad bonds, and full confidence in her brother, who was an admirable business man, and not in the least dissipated.

"Come, come," she said. "It's much too hot to fight. Dwight is not good enough for Alex - from a worldly point of view, I mean," as Alexina made a movement in her direction. "We should none of us marry out of our class. It never works, somehow. But Mr. Dwight is really quite all right otherwise. I like him very much, Alex darling, and I don't mind his being an outsider in the least - so long as he doesn't try to marry one of us.

Gertrude Atherton

He's *too* good-looking, and his heels are fairly inspired. No one questions the fact that he is an honorable and worthy young man, working like a real man to earn his living. It isn't at all as if he were an adventurer. He has never struck me as being more of a snob than most people, and I don't see why I haven't thought to ask him down to San Mateo for a week-end."

"You'll certainly have a friend for life if you do," said Aileen satirically. "Fall in love with him yourself if you choose. You can afford it."

"No fear. I've made up my mind. I'm going to marry a French marquis."

"What?" Even Alexina forgot Mortimer Dwight. "Who is he? Where did you meet him?"

"I haven't met him yet. But I shall. I'm going to Paris next winter to visit my aunt, and I'll find one. You get anything in this world you go for hard enough. To be a French marquise is the most romantic thing in the world."

"Why not Elton Gwynne? It's an open secret that he's an English marquis. Or that young Gathbroke Lady Victoria brought last night?"

"He's a younger son, and he never looked at any one but Alex. And Isabel Otis has preëmpted Mr. Gwynne. And I adore France and don't care about England."

"Well, that is romantic if you like!" cried Aileen, her green eyes dancing" "You have my best wishes. Doesn't it make your Geary Street knight look cheap - he boards somewhere down on Geary Street."

"No, it doesn't! And I'm a good American. French marquis, indeed! Mr. Dwight comes of the best old American stock from New York. He told mother so, I'd spit on any old decadent European title."

"I wish your mother could hear you. So - he's been getting round her has he? Where on earth did he meet her?"

Alexina, with sulky triumph, reported Mr. Dwight's early visit and the favorable impression he had made.

Aileen groaned. "That's just the one thing she would fall for in a rank outsider - superlative manners. His being poor is rather in his favor. I'll put a flea in her ear - "

"You dare!"

Aileen lifted her shoulders. "Well, as a matter of fact I can't. Tattling just isn't in my line. But if I can queer him with you I will."

"I won't talk about him any more." Alexina drew herself up with immense dignity. She had the advantage of Aileen not only in inches but in a natural repose of manner. The eminent Judge Lawton's only child, upon whom, possibly, he may have lavished too much education, had a thin nervous little body that was seldom in repose, and her face, with its keen irregular features and brilliant green eyes, shifted its surface impressions as rapidly as a cinematograph. Olive Bascom had soft blue eyes and abundant brown hair, and Sibyl Thorndyke had learned to hold her long black eyes half closed, and had the black hair and rich complexion of a Creole great-grandmother. Alexina

Gertrude Atherton

was admittedly the "beauty of the bunch." Nevertheless, Miss Lawton had informed her doting parent before this, her first season, was half over, that she was *vivid* enough to hold her own with the best of them. The boys said she was a live wire and she preferred that high specialization to the tameness of mere beauty.

IV

Said Alexina: "Sibyl, what are you going to do with your young life? Shall you marry an English duke or a New York millionaire?"

But Miss Thorndyke smiled mysteriously. She was not as frank as the other girls, although by no means as opaque as she imagined.

Aileen laughed. "Oh, don't ask her. Doubt if she knows. To-day she's all for being intellectual and reading those damn dull Russian novelists. To-morrow she may be setting up as an odalisque. It would suit her style better."

Miss Thorndyke's face was also crimson from the heat, but she would not have flushed had it been the day before. She was not subject to sudden reflexes.

"Your satire is always a bit clumsy, dear," she said sweetly. "The odalisque is not your rôle at all events."

"I don't go in for rôles."

And the four girls wrangled and dreamed and planned, while a city burnt beneath them; some three hundred million dollars flamed out, lives were ruined, exterminated, altered; and Labor sat on the hills and smiled cynically at the tremendous impetus the earth had handed them on that morning of April eighteenth, nineteen hundred and six.

They were too young to know or to care. When the imagination is trying its wings it is undismayed even by a world at war.

# CHAPTER V

I

That night Alexina knew that romance had surely come to her. She shared her room with three old ladies who slept fitfully between blasts of dynamite. But she sat at the window with no desire for oblivion.

On the lawn paced a young man with a rifle in the crook of his arm. He was tall and young and very gallant of bearing; no less a person than Mortimer Dwight, who had been sworn in that morning as a member of the Citizens' Patrol, and at his own request detailed to keep watch over the house of Mrs. Groome.

He had not been able to pay his promised visits during the day but had arrived at seven o'clock, dining beside Mrs. Abbott, and surrounded by old ladies whose names were as historic as Mrs. Groome's. The cook had deserted after the second heavy shock, and, with her wardrobe in a pillow case, had tramped to the farthest confines of the Presidio. It was not fear alone that induced her flight. There was a rumor that the Government would feed the city, and why should not a hard-working woman enjoy a month or two of sheer idleness? Let the quality cook for themselves. It would do them good.

James and the housemaid had cooked the dinner, and Alexina and her friends waited on the table. Then the girls, to Alexina's relief, went home to inquire after their families, and she accompanied Mr. Dwight while he explored every corner of the grounds to make sure that no potential thieves lurked in the heavy shadows cast by the trees.

He had been very alert and thorough and Alexina admired him consumedly. There was no question but that he was one of those men - Aileen called it the one hundred per cent male - upon whose clear brain and strong arm a woman might depend even in the midst of an infuriated mob. He had an opportunity that comes to few aspiring young men born into the world's unblest millions, and if he made the most of it he was equally assured that he was acting in strict accord with the instincts and characteristics that had descended upon him by the grace of God.

## II

There was no physical cowardice in him; and if he would have preferred a life of ease and splendor, he had no illusions regarding the amount of "hustling" necessary to carry him to the goal of his desires and ambitions - unless he made a lucky strike. He played the stock market in a small way and made a few hundred dollars now and then.

He would have been glad to marry a wealthy girl, Olive Bascom, by preference, for he had an inner urge to the short cut, but he had found these spoiled daughters of San Francisco unresponsive...and then, suddenly, he had fallen in love with Alexina Groome.

His past was green and prophylactic. He was moral both by inheritance and necessity, and his parents, people of fair intelligence, if rather ineffective, stern principles, and good old average ideals, had taken their responsibilities toward their two children very seriously. People who talked with young Dwight might not find him resourceful in conversation but they were deeply impressed with his manners and principles. The younger men, with the exception of Bob Cheever, who respected his capacity for work, did not take to him; principally, no doubt, he reflected with some bitterness, because he was not "their sort."

He never admitted to himself that he was a snob, for something deep and still unfaced in his consciousness, bade him see as little fault in himself as possible, forbade him to admit the contingency of a failure, impelled him to call such weaknesses as the fortunate condemned by some one of those interchangeable terms with which the lexicons are so generous.

But if he would not face the word snob he told himself
proudly that he was ambitious; and why should he not
aspire to the best society? Was he not entitled to it by
birth? His family may not have been prominent to
excess in Utica, but it was indisputably "old."
However, he assured himself that the chief reason for
his determination to mingle with the social elect of San
Francisco was not so much a tribute to his ancestors, or
even the insistence of youth for the decent pleasures of
that brief period, but because of the opportunities to
make those friends indispensable to every young man
forced to cut his own way through life. Even if his
good conscience had compelled him to admit that he
was a snob he would have reminded it there was no
harm in snobbery anyway. It was the most amiable of
the vices. But he thought too well of himself for any
such admission, and his mind had not been trained to
fish, even, in shallow waters.

Nor did he admit that if the lovely Miss Groome had
been a stenographer he would not have looked at her.
He would indeed have turned his face resolutely in the
other direction if she had happened to sit in his
employer's office. Fate forbade him a marriage of that
sort, and dalliance with an inferior was forbidden both
by his morals and his social integrity.

But that Alexina Groome should be beautiful, as
exaltedly born as only a San Franciscan of the old
stock might be, with a determinate income, however
modest, with a background of friendly males, as
substantial financially as socially, who would be sure
to give a new member of the family a leg-up (he liked
the atmosphere and flavor of the lighter English

novels), and, above all, responsive, seemed to him a direct reward for the circumspect life he had lived and his fidelity to his chosen upward path.

III

He was free to fall in love as profoundly as was in him, and during that early hour of the agitated night, with that pit of hell roaring below to the steady undertone of a thousand tramping feet, he felt, despite the fact that all business was moribund for the present and his savings were in the hot vaults of a dynamited bank, that he was a supremely fortunate young man.

Moreover, this disaster furnished a steady topic for conversation. He was aware that he contributed little froth and less substance to a dinner table, that, in short, he did not keep up his end. Although he assured himself that small talk was beneath a man of serious purpose, and that no one could acquire it anyhow in society unless addicted to sport, still there had been times when he was painfully aware that a dinner partner or some bright charming creature whose invitation to call he had accepted, looked politely bored or chattered desperately to cover the silences into which he abruptly relapsed; when, "for the life of him he had not been able to think of a thing to say."

Then, briefly, he had felt a bitter rebellion at fate for having denied him the gift of a lively and supple mind, as well as those numberless worldly benefits lavished on men far less deserving than he.

He felt dull and depressed after such revelations and sometimes considered attending evening lectures at the University of California with his sister. But for this form of mental exertion he had no taste, keenly as he applied himself to his work during the hours of business; and he assured himself that such knowledge would do him no good anyway. It did not seem to be prevalent in society. If he had been a brilliant hand at bridge or poker, the inner fortifications of society would have gone down before him, but his courage did not run to card gambling with wealthy idlers who set their own pace. On the stock market he could step warily and no one the wiser. It would have horrified him to be called a piker, for his instincts were really lavish, and the economical habit an achievement in which he took a resentful pride.

IV

On this evening he had talked almost incessantly to Alexina, and she, in the vocabulary of her years and set, had thought him frantically interesting as he described the immediate command of the city assumed by General Funston, the efforts of the Committee of Fifty, formed early that morning by leading citizens, to help preserve order and to give assistance to the refugees; of rich young men, and middle-aged citizens who had not spent an afternoon away from their club window for ten years, carrying dynamite in their cars through the very flames; of wild and terrible episodes he had witnessed or heard of during the day.

His brain was hot from the mental and physical atmosphere of the perishing city, the unique excitement of the day: when he had felt as if snatched from his quiet pasture by the roots; and by the extraordinary good fortune that had delivered this perfect girl and her formidable parent almost into his hands. Under his sternly controlled exterior his spirits sang wildly that his luck had turned, and dazzling visions of swift success and fulfillment of all ambitions snapped on and off in his stimulated brain.

Alexina thought him not only immoderately fascinating in his appeal to her own imperious youth, but the most interesting life partner that a romantic maiden with secret intellectual promptings could demand. Her brilliant long eyes melted and flashed, her soft unformed mouth wore a constant alluring smile.

A declaration trembled on his tongue, but he felt that

he would be taking an unfair advantage and restrained himself. Besides, he wished to win Mrs. Groome completely to his side, to say nothing of the still more alarming because more worldly Mrs. Abbott. *She* was a snob, if you like!

# V

At nine o'clock, after he had given the inmates of the house and outbuildings stern orders not to light a candle or lamp under any circumstances - such was the emergency law - he bade Alexina a gallant good-night, and betook himself to the lawn within the grove of sighing eucalyptus trees, to pace up and down, his rifle in his arm, his eyes alert, and quite aware of the admiring young princess at the casement above.

He did his work very thoroughly, visiting outhouses at intervals and sharply inspecting the weary occupants, as well as the prostrate forms under the trees. They were all far too tired and apprehensive to dream of breaking into the house that had given them hospitality, even had they been villains, which they were not.

But they did not resent his inspection; rather they felt a sense of security in this watching manly figure with the gun, for they were rather afraid of villains themselves: it was reported that many looters had been stood against hissing walls and shot by the stern orders of General Punston. They asked their more immediate protector questions as to the progress of the fire, which he answered curtly, as befitted his office.

# CHAPTER VI

## I

MRS. ABBOTT entered Alexina's room and caught her hanging out of the window. She had motored up to the city during the afternoon, and, after a vain attempt to persuade her mother to go down at once to Alta, had concluded to remain over night. The spectacle was the most horrifyingly interesting she had ever witnessed in her temperate life, and her self-denying Aunt Clara was in charge of the children. Her husband had driven himself to town as soon as he heard of the fire and been sworn in a member of the Committee of Fifty.

"Darling," she said firmly to the sister who was little older than her first-born, "I want to have a talk with you. Come into papa's old dressing-room. I had a cot put there, and as there is no room for another I am quite alone."

Alexina followed with lagging feet. She had always given her elder sister the same surface obedience that she gave her mother. It "saved trouble." But life had changed so since morning that she was in no mood to

Gertrude Atherton

keep up the rôle of "little sister," sweet and malleable and innocent as a Ballinger-Groome at the age of eighteen should be.

II

She dropped on the floor and embraced her knees with her arms. Mrs. Abbott seated herself in as dignified an attitude as was possible on the edge of the cot. Even the rocking-chairs had been taken down to the dining-room.

"Well?" queried Alexina, pretending to stifle a yawn. "What is it? I am too sleepy to think."

"Sleepy? You looked sleepy with your eyes like saucers watching that young man."

"Everybody that can is watching the fire - "

"Don't quibble, Alexina. You are naturally a truthful child. Do you mean to tell me you were not watching Mr. Dwight?"

"Well, if I say yes, it is not because I care a hang about living up to my reputation, but because I don't care whether you know it or not."

"That is very naughty - "

"Stop talking to me as if I were a child."

"You are excited, darling, and no wonder."

Maria Abbott was in the process of raising a family and she did it with tact and firmness. Nature had done much to assist her in her several difficult rôles. She was very tall straight and slender, with a haughty little head, as perfect in shape as Alexina's, set well back on

Gertrude Atherton

her shoulders, and what had been known in her Grandmother Ballinger's day as a cameo-profile. Her abundant fair hair added to the high calm of her mien and it was always arranged in the prevailing fashion. On the street she invariably wore the tailored suit, and her tailor was the best in New York. She thought blouses in public indecent, and wore shirtwaists of linen or silk with high collars, made by the same master-hand. There was nothing masculine in her appearance, but she prided herself upon being the best groomed woman even in that small circle of her city that dressed as well as the fashionable women of New York. At balls and receptions she wore gowns of an austere but expensive simplicity, and as the simple jewels of her inheritance looked pathetic beside the blazing necklaces and sunbursts (there were only two or three tiaras in San Francisco) of those new people whom she both deplored and envied, she wore none; and she was assured that the lack added to the distinction of her appearance.

But although she felt it almost a religious duty to be smart, determined as she was that the plutocracy should never, while she was alive, push the aristocracy through, the wall and out of sight, she was a strict conformer to the old tradition that had looked upon all arts to enhance and preserve youth as the converse of respectable. Her once delicate pink and white skin was wrinkled and weather-beaten, her nose had never known powder; but even in the glare of the fire her skin looked cool and pale, for the heat had not crimsoned her. Her blood was rather thin and she prided herself upon the fact. She may have lost her early beauty, but she looked the indubitable aristocrat, the lady born, as her more naïve grandmothers would have phrased it.

It sufficed.

# III

By those that did not have the privilege of her intimate acquaintance she was called "stuck-up," "a snob," a mid-victorian who ought to dress like her more consistent mother, "rather a fool, if the truth were known, no doubt."

In reality she was a tender-hearted and anxious mother, daughter, and sister, and an impeccable wife, if a somewhat monotonous one. At all events her husband never found fault with her in public or private. He had his reasons. To the friends of her youth and to all members of her own old set, she was intensely loyal; and although she had a cold contempt for the institution of divorce, if one of that select band strayed into it, no matter at which end, her loyalty rose triumphant above her social code, and she was not afraid to express it publicly.

Toward Alexina she felt less a sister than a second mother, and gave her freely of her abundant maternal reservoir. That "little sister" had at times sulked under this proud determination to assist in the bringing-up of the last of the Ballinger-Groomes, did not discourage her. She might be soft in her affections but she never swerved from her duty as she saw it. Alexina was a darling wayward child, who only needed a firm hand to guide her along that proud secluded old avenue of the city's elect, until she had ambled safely to established respectability and power.

She had been alarmed at one time at certain symptoms of cleverness she noticed in the child, and at certain enthusiastic remarks in the letters of Ballinger

Groome, with whose family Alexina had spent her vacations during her two years in New York at school. But there had been no evidence of anything but a young girl's natural love of pleasure since her début in society, and she was quite unaware of Alexina's wicked divagations. She had spent the winter in Santa Barbara, for the benefit of her oldest, boy, whose lungs were delicate, and, like her mother, never deigned to read the society columns of the newspapers. Her reason, however, was her own. In spite of her blood, her indisputable position, her style, she cut but a small figure in those columns. She was not rich enough to vie with those who entertained constantly, and was merely set down as one of many guests. The fact induced a slight bitterness.

## IV

She began tactfully. "I like this young Mr. Dwight very much, and shall ask him down, as mother desires it. But I hope, darling, that you will follow my example and not marry until you have had four years of society, in other words have seen something of the world - "

"California is not the world."

"Society, in other words human nature, is everywhere much alike. As you know, I spent a year in England when I was a young lady, and was presented at court - by Lady Barnstable, who was Lee Tarlton, one of us. It was merely San Francisco on a large scale, with titles, and greater and older houses and parks, and more jewels, and more arrogance, and everything much grander, of course. And they talked politics a great deal, which bored me as I am sure they would bore you. The beauty of our society is its simplicity and lack of arrogance - consciousness of birth or of wealth. Even the more recent members of society, who owe their position to their fortunes, have a simplicity and kindness quite unknown in New York. Eastern people always remark it. And yet, owing to their constant visits to the East and to Europe, they know all of the world there is to know."

"So do the young men, I suppose! I never heard of their doing much traveling - "

"I should call them remarkably sophisticated young men. But the point is, darling, that if you wait as long as I did you will discover that the men who attract a girl in her first season would bore her to extinction in her fourth."

"You mean after I've had all the bloom rubbed off, and men are forgetting to ask me to dance. Then I'll be much more likely to take what I can get. I want to marry with all the bloom on and all my illusions fresh."

"But should you like to have them rubbed off by your husband? You've heard the old adage: 'marry in haste and repent - '"

"I've been brought up on adages. They are called bromides now. As for illusions, everybody says they don't last anyway. I'd rather have them dispelled after a long wonderful honeymoon by a husband than by a lot of flirtations in a conservatory and in dark corners - "

"Good heavens! Do you suppose that I flirted in a conservatory and in dark corners?"

"I'll bet you didn't, but lots do. And in the haute noblesse, the ancient aristocracy! I've seen 'em."

"It isn't possible that you - "

"Oh, no, I love to dance too much. But I'm not easily shocked. I 'll tell you that right here. And I 'll tell you what I confessed to mother this morning."

# V

When she had finished Mrs. Abbott sat for a few moments petrified; but she was thirty-eight, not sixty-five, and there was neither dismay nor softening in her narrowed light blue eyes.

"But that is abominable! Abominable!"

And Alexina, who was prepared for a scolding, shrank a little, for it was the first time that her doting sister had spoken to her with severity.

"I don't care," she said stubbornly, and she set her soft lips until they looked stern and hard.

"But you must care. You are a Groome."

"Oh, yes, and a Ballinger, and a Geary, and all the rest of it. But I'm also going to annex another name of my own choosing. I'll marry whom I damn please, and that is the end of it."

"Alexina Groome!" Mrs. Abbott arose in her wrath. "Cannot you see for yourself what association with all these common people has done to you? It's the influence - "

"Of two years in New York principally. The girls there are as hard as nails - try to imitate the English. Ours are not a patch, not even Aileen, although she does her best. But I hadn't finished - I even powder my face." Alexina grinned up at her still rudderless sister. "After mother is asleep and I am ready to slip out."

"I thought you were safe in New York under the eyes of Ballinger and Geary, or rather of Mattie and Charlotte. They are such earnest good women, so interested in charities - "

"Deadly. But you don't know the girls,"

"And I have told mother again and again that she should not permit you to associate with Aileen Lawton."

"She can't help herself. Aileen is one of us. Besides, mother is devoted to the Judge."

"But powder! None of us has ever put anything but clean cold water on her face."

"You'd look a long sight better if you did. Cold cream, too. You wouldn't have any wrinkles at your age, if you weren't so damn respectable-aristocratic, you call it. It's just middle class. And as out of date as speech without slang. As for me, I'd paint my lips as Aileen does, only I don't like the taste, and they're too red, anyhow. It's much smarter to make up than not to. Times change. You don't wear hoopskirts because our magnificent Grandmother Ballinger did. You dress as smartly as the Burlingame crowd. Why does your soul turn green at make-up? All these people you look down upon because our families were rich and important in the fifties are more up-to-date than you are, although I will admit that none of them has the woman-of-the-world air of the smartest New York women - not that terribly respectable inner set in New York - Aunt Mattie's and Aunt Charlotte's - *that* just revels in looking mid-Victorian....The newer people I've met here - their manners are just as good as ours, if not better, for, as you said just now, they don't put on airs. You do, darling. You don't know it, but you would put an English duchess to the blush, when you suddenly remember who you are - "

Mrs. Abbott had resumed her seat on the cot. "If you have finished criticizing your elder sister, I should like to ask you a few questions. Do you smoke and drink cocktails?"

"No, I don't. But I should if I liked them, and if they didn't make me feel queer."

"You - you - " Mrs. Abbot's clear crisp voice sank to an agonized whisper. For the first time she was really terrified. "Do you gamble?"

"Why, of course not. I have too much fun to think of anything so stupid."

"Does Aileen Lawton gamble?"

"She just doesn't, and don't you insinuate such a thing."

"She has bad blood in her. Her mother - "

"I thought her mother was your best friend."

"She was. But she went to pieces, poor dear, and Judge Lawton wisely sent her East. I can't tell you why. There are things you don't understand."

"Oh, don't I? Don't you fool yourself."

Mrs. Abbott leaned back on the cot and pressed it hard with either hand.

Gertrude Atherton

"Alexina, I have never been as disturbed as I am at this moment. When Sally and I were your age, we were beautifully innocent. If I thought that Joan - "

"Oh, Joan'll get away from you. She's only fourteen now, but when she's my age - well, I guess you and your old crowd are the last of the Mohicans. I doubt if there'll even be any chaperons left. Joan may not smoke nor drink. Who cares for 'vices,' anyhow? But you haven't got a moat and drawbridge round Rincona, and she'll just get out and mix. She'll float with the stream - and all streams lead to Burlingame."

"I have no fear about Joan," said Mrs. Abbott, with dignity. "Four years are a long time. I shall sow seeds, and she is a born Ballinger - I am dreadfully afraid that my dear father is coming out in you. Even the boys are Ballingers - "

# VI

"Tell me about father?" coaxed Alexina, who was repentant, now that the excitement of the day had reached its climax in the baiting of her admirable sister and was rapidly subsiding. "Mother let fall something this morning; and once Aileen...she began, but shut up like a clam. Was he so very dreadful?"

"Well, since you know so much, he was what is called fast. Married men of his position often were in his day - quite openly. Yesterday, I should have hesitated - "

"Fire away. Don't mind me. Yes, I know what fast is. Lots of men are to-day. Even members of the A. A."

"A. A.?"

"Ancient Aristocracy. The kind England and France would like to have."

"I'm ashamed of you. Have you no pride of blood? The best blood of the South, to say nothing of - "

"I'm tickled to death. I just dote on being a Groome, plus Ballinger, plus. And I'm not guying, neither. I'd hate like the mischief to be second rate, no matter what I won later. It must be awful to have to try to get to places that should be yours by divine right, as it were. But all that's no reason for being a moss-back, a back number, for not having any fun - to be glued to the ancestral rock like a lot of old limpets....And it should preserve us from being snobs," she added.

"Snobs?"

"The 'I will maintain' sort, as Aileen puts it."

"Don't quote that dreadful child to me. I haven't an atom of snobbery in my composition. I reserve the right to know whom I please, and to exclude from my house people to whom I cannot accustom myself. Why I know quite a number of people at Burlingame. I dined there informally last night."

"Yes, because it has the fascination for you that wine has for the clergyman's son." Alexina once more yielded to temptation. "But the only people you really know at Burlingame except Mrs. Hunter are those of the old set, what you would call the pick of the bunch, if you were one of us. They went there to live because they were tired of being moss-backs. Why don't you follow their example and go the whole hog? They - and their girls - have a ripping time."

"At least they have not picked up your vocabulary. I seldom see the young people. And I have never been to the Club. I am told the women drink and smoke quite openly on the verandah."

"You may bet your sweet life they do. They are honest, and quite as sure of their position as you are. But tell me about father. How did mother come to marry him? If he was such a naughty person I should think she would have exercised the sound Ballinger instincts and thrown him down."

"Mother met him in Washington. Grandfather Ballinger was senator at the time - "

"From Virginia or California?"

"It is shocking that you do not know more of the family history. From California, of course. He had great gifts and political aspirations, and realized that there would be more opportunity in the new state - particularly in such a famous one - than in his own where all the men in public life seemed to have taken root - I remember his using that expression. So, he came here with his bride, the beauty of Richmond - "

"Oh, Lord, I know all about her. Remember the flavor in my mother's milk - "

"Well, you'd look like her if you had brown eyes and a white skin, and if your mouth were smaller. And until you learn to stand up straight you'll never have anything like her elegance of carriage. However....Of course they had plenty of money - for those days. They had come to Virginia in the days of Queen Elizabeth and received a large grant of land - "

"Don't fancy I haven't heard *that*!"

"Grandfather had inherited the plantation - "

"Sold his slaves, I suppose, to come to California and realize his ambitions. Funny, how ideals change!"

"His abilities were recognized as soon as lie arrived in the new community, and our wonderful grandmother became at once one of that small band of social leaders that founded San Francisco society: Mrs. Hunt McLane, the Hathaways, Mrs. Don Pedro Earle, the Montgomerys, the Gearys, the Talbots, the Belmonts, Mrs. Abbott, Tom's grandmother - "

"Never mind about them. I have them dished up

occasionally by mother, although she prefers to descant upon the immortal eighties, when she was a leader herself and 'money wasn't everything.' We never had so much of it anyhow. I know Grandfather Ballinger built this ramshackle old house - "

Mrs. Abbott sat forward and drew herself up. She felt as if she were talking to a stranger, as, indeed, she was.

"This house and its traditions are sacred - "

"I know it. Yon were telling me how mother came to marry a bad fast man."

"He was not fast when she met him. It was at a ball in Washington. He was a young congressman - he was wounded in his right arm during the first year of the war and returned at once to California; of course he had been one of the first to enlist. He was of a fine old family and by no means poor. Of course in Washington he was asked to the best houses. At that time he was very ambitious and absorbed in politics and the advancement of California. Afterward he renounced Washington for reasons I never clearly understood; although he told me once that California was the only place for a man to live; and - well - I am afraid he could do more as he pleased out here without criticism - from men, at least. The standards - for men - were very low in those days. But when he met mother - "

"Was mother ever very pretty?"

"She was handsome," replied Mrs. Abbott guardedly. "Of course she had the freshness and roundness of youth. I am told she had a lovely color and the brightest eyes. And she had a beautiful figure. She had several proposals, but she chose father."

"And had the devil's own time with him. She let out that much this morning."

"I am growing accustomed to your language." Once more Mrs. Abbott was determined to be amiable and tactful. She realized that the child's brain was seething with the excitements of the day, but was aghast at the revelations it had recklessly tossed out, and admitted that the problem of "handling her" could no longer be disposed of with home-made generalities.

"Yes, mother did not have a bed of roses. Father was mayor at one time and held various other public offices, and no one, at least, ever accused him of civic corruptness. Quite the contrary. The city owes more than one reform to his determination and ability.

"He even risked his life fighting the bosses and their political gangs, for he was shot at twice. But he was very popular in his own class; what men call a good fellow, and at that time there was quite a brilliant group of disreputable women here; one could not help hearing things, for the married women here have always been great gossips. Well - you may as well know it - it may have the same effect on you that it did on Ballinger and Geary, who are the most abstemious of men - he drank and gambled and had too much to do with those unspeakable women....

"Nevertheless, he made a great deal of money for a long time, and if he hadn't gambled (not only in gambling houses and in private but in stocks), he would have left a large fortune. As it is, poor darling, you will only have this house and about six thousand a year. Father was quite well off when Sally and I married and Ballinger and Geary went to New York after marrying the Lyman girls, who were such belles out here when they paid us a visit in the nineties. They had money of their own and father gave the boys a hundred thousand each. He gave the same to Sally and me when we married. But when you came along, or rather when you were ten, and he died - well, he had run through nearly everything, and had lost his grip. Mother got her share of the community property, and of course she had this house and her share of the Ballinger estate - not very much."

## VII

"Why didn't mother keep father at home and make him behave himself?"

"Mother did everything a good woman could do."

"Maybe she was too good."

"You abominable child. A woman can't be too good."

"Perhaps not. But I fancy she can make a man think so. When he has different tastes."

"Women are as they are born. My mother would not have condescended to lower herself to the level of those creatures who fascinated my father."

"Well, I wouldn't, neither. I'd just light out and leave him. Why didn't mother get a divorce?"

"A divorce? Why, she has never received any one in her house who has been divorced. Neither have I except in one or two cases where very dear friends had been forced by circumstances into the divorce court. I didn't approve even then. People should wash their dirty linen at home."

"Time moves, as I remarked just now. Nothing would stop me; if, for instance, I had been persuaded into marrying a member of the A. A. and he was in the way of ruining my young life. You should be thankful if I did decide to marry Mr. Dwight - mind, I don't say I care the tip of my little finger for him. I barely know him. But if I did you would have to admit that I was

Gertrude Atherton

following the best Ballinger instincts, for he doesn't drink, or dissipate in any way; and everybody says he works hard and is as steady as - I was going to say as a judge, but I've been told that all judges, in this town at least, are not as steady as you think. Anyhow, he is. His family is as old as ours, even if it did have reverses or something. And you can't deny that he is a gentleman, every inch of him."

"I do not deny that he has a very good appearance indeed. But - well, he was brought up in San Francisco and no one ever heard of his parents. He admitted to me at the table that his father was only a clerk in a broker's office. He is not one of us and that is the end of it."

"Why not make him one? Quite easy. And you ought to rejoice in what power you have left."

She rose and stretched and yawned in a most unlady-like fashion.

"I'm going to make a cup of coffee for our sentinel, and have a little chat with him, chaperoned by the great bonfire. Don't think you can stop me, for you can't. Heavens, what a noise that dynamite does make! We shall have to shout. It will be more than proper. Good night, darling."

# CHAPTER VII

## I

Gora Dwight with a quick turn of a strong and supple wrist flung a folding chair up through the trap door of the roof. She followed with a pitcher of water, opened the chair, and sat down.

It was the second day of the fire, which was now raging in the valleys north of Market Street and up the hills. It was still some distance from all but the lower end of Van Ness Avenue, the wide street that divides the eastern and western sections of the city, as Market Street divides the northern and southern, and her own home on Geary Street was beyond Franklin and safe for the present. It was expected that the fire would be halted by dynamiting the blocks east of the avenue, but as it had already leapt across not far from Market Street and was running out toward the Mission, Gora pinned her faith in nothing less than a change of wind.

Life has many disparate schools. The one attended by Miss Gora Dwight had taught her to hope for the best, prepare for the worst, and be thankful if she escaped (to use the homely phrase; one rarely found leisure for

Gertrude Atherton

originality in this particular school) by the skin of her teeth.

Gora fully expected to lose the house she sat on, and had packed what few valuables she possessed in two large bags: the fine underclothes she had made at odd moments, and a handsome set of toilet articles her brother had given her on the Christmas before last. He had had a raise of salary and her experiment with lodgers had proved even more successful than she had dared to hope. On the following Christmas he had given her a large book with a fancy binding (which she had exchanged for something she could read). After satisfying the requirements of a wardrobe suitable for the world of fashion, supplemented by the usual toll of flowers and bon-bons, he had little surplus for domestic presents.

Gora's craving for drama was far deeper and more significant than young Alexina Groome's, and she determined to watch until the last moment the terrific spectacle of the burning city. The wind had carried the smoke upward for a mile or more and pillars of fire supported it at such irregular intervals that it looked like a vast infernal temple in which demons were waging war, and undermining the roof in their senseless fury.

In some places whole blocks of houses were blazing; here and there high buildings burned in solitary grandeur, the flames leaping from every window or boiling from the roof. Sometimes one of these buildings would disappear in a shower of sparks and an awful roar, or a row of humbler houses was lifted bodily from the ground to burst into a thousand particles of flying wood, and disappear.

The heat was overpowering (she bathed her face constantly from the pitcher) and the roar of the flames, the constant explosions of dynamite, the loud vicious crackling of wood, the rending and splitting of masonry, the hoarse impact of walls as they met the earth, was the scene's wild orchestral accompaniment and, despite underlying apprehension and horror, gave Gora one of the few pleasurable sensations of her life.

But she moved her chair after a moment and fixed her gaze, no longer rapt but ironic, on the flaming hill-crests, the long line of California Street, nucleus of the wealth and fashion of San Francisco. The Western Addition was fashionable and growing more so, but it had been too far away for the pioneers of the fifties and sixties, the bonanza kings of the seventies, the railroad magnates of the eighties, and they had built their huge and hideous mansions upon the hill that rose almost perpendicularly above the section where they made and lost their millions. Some wag or toady had named it Nob Hill and the inhabitants had complacently accepted the title, although they refrained from putting it on their cards. And now it was in flames.

## II

Gora recalled the day when she had walked slowly past those mansions, staring at each in turn as she assimilated the disheartening and infuriating fact that she and the children that inhabited them belonged to different worlds.

Her family at that time lived in a cottage at the wrong end of Taylor Street Hill, and, Mrs. Dwight having received a small legacy from a sister recently deceased which had convinced her, if not her less mercurial husband, that their luck had finally turned, had sent Gora, then a rangy girl of thirteen, fond of books and study, to a large private school in the fashionable district.

Gora, after all these years, ground her teeth as she had a sudden blighting vision of the day a week later, when, puzzled and resentful, she had walked up the steep hill with several of the girls whose homes were on California and Taylor Streets, and two of whom, like herself, were munching an apple.

They had hardly noticed her sufficiently to ignore her, either then or during the previous week, so absorbed were they in their own close common interests. She listened to allusions which she barely could comprehend, but it was evident that one was to give a party on Friday night and the others were expected as a matter of course. Gora assumed that Jim and Sam and Rex and Bob were brothers or beaux. Last names appeared to be no more necessary than labels to inform the outsider of the social status of these favored maidens, too happy and contented to be snobs but quite callous to the feelings of strange little girls.

They drifted one by one into their opulent homes, bidding one another a careless or a sentimental good-by, and Gora, throwing her head as far back on her shoulders as it would go without dislocation, stalked down to the unfashionable end of Taylor Street and up to the solitude of her bedroom
under the eaves of the cottage.

On the following day she had lingered in the school yard until the other girls were out of sight, then climbing the almost perpendicular hill so rapidly that she arrived on the crest with little breath and a pain in her side, she had sauntered deliberately up and down before the imposing homes of her schoolmates, staring at them with angry and puzzled eyes, her young soul in tumult. It was the old inarticulate cry of class, of the unchosen who seeks the reason and can find none.

III

As she had a tendency not only to brood but to work out her own problems it was several days before she demanded an explanation of her mother.

Mrs. Dwight, a prematurely gray and wrinkled woman, who had once been handsome with good features and bright coloring, and who wore a deliberately cheerful expression that Gora often wanted to wipe off, was sitting in the dining-room making a skirt for her daughter; which, Gora reflected bitterly, was sure to be too long on one side if not in front.

Mrs. Dwight's smile faded as she looked at the somber face and huddled figure in the worn leather arm-chair in which Mr. Dwight spent his silent evenings.

"Why, my dear, you surely knew long before this that some people are rich and others poor - to say nothing of the betwixts and betweens." She was an exact woman in small matters. "That's all there is to it. I thought it a good idea to send you to a private school where you might make friends among girls of your own class."

"Own class? They treat me like dirt. How am I of their class when they live in palaces and I in a hovel?"

"I have reproved you many times for exaggerated speech. What I meant was that you are as well-born as any of them (better than many) only we have been unfortunate. Your father tried hard enough, but he just doesn't seem to have the money-making faculty like so many men. Now, we've had a little luck I'm really hopeful. I've just had a nice letter from your Aunt Eliza Goring - I named you for her, but I couldn't inflict you with Eliza. You know she is many years older than I am and has no children. She was out here once just before you were born. We - we were very hard up indeed. It was she who furnished this cottage for us and paid a year's rent. Soon after, your father got his present position and we have managed to get along. She always sends me a little cheque at Christmas and I am sure - well, there are some things we don't say....But this legacy from your Aunt Jane is the only real stroke of luck we ever had, and I can't help feeling hopeful. I do believe better times are coming....It used to seem terribly hard and unjust that so many people all about us had so much and we nothing, and that in this comparatively small city we knew practically no one. But I have got over being bitter and envious. You do when you are busy every minute. And then we have the blessing of health, and Mortimer is the best boy in the world, and you are a very good child when you are not in a bad temper. I think you will be handsome, too, although you are pretty hopeless at present; but of course you will never have anything like Mortimer's looks. He is the living image of the painting of your Great-great-great-grandfather Dwight that used to hang in the dining-room in Utica, and who was in the first Congress. Now, do try and make friends with the nicer of the children."

But Gora's was not a conciliating nor a compromising nature. Her idea of "squaring things" was to become the best scholar in her classes and humiliate several young ladies of her own age who had held the first position with an ease that had bred laxity. Greatly to the satisfaction of the teachers an angry emulation ensued with the gratifying result that although the girls could not pass Gora, their weekly marks were higher, and for the rest of the term they did less giggling even after school hours, and more studying.

But Gora would not return for a second term. She had made no friends among the girls, although, no doubt, having won their respect, they would, with the democracy of childhood, have admitted her to intimacy by degrees, particularly if she had proved to be socially malleable.

But for some obscure reason it made Gora happier to hate them all, and when she had passed her examinations victoriously, and taken every prize, except for tidiness and deportment, she said good-by with some regret to the teachers, who had admired and encouraged her but did not pretend to love her, and announced as soon as she arrived at home that she should enter the High School at the beginning of the following term.

IV

Her parents were secretly relieved. Even Mrs. Dwight's vision of future prosperity had faded. She had been justified in believing that her sister Eliza would make a will in favor of her family, but unfortunately Mrs. Goring had amused herself with speculation in her old age, and had left barely enough to pay her funeral expenses.

Mrs. Dwight broached the subject of their immediate future to her husband that evening. She had some time since made up her mind, in case the school experiment was not a success, to furnish a larger house with what remained of the legacy, and take boarders.

"I wouldn't do it if Gora had made the friends I hoped for her," she said, turning the heel of the first of her son's winter socks, "and there's no such thing as a social come-down for us; for that matter, there is more than one lady, once wealthy, who is keeping a boarding-house in this town. Gora will have to work anyhow, and as for Mortimer - " she glanced fondly at her manly young son, who was amiably playing checkers in the parlor with his sister, "he is sure to make his fortune."

"I don't know," said Mr. Dwight heavily. "I don't know."

"Why, what do you mean?" asked his wife sharply.

Mrs. Dwight belonged to that type of American women whose passions in youth are weak and anæmic, not to say exceedingly shame-faced, but which in mature years become strong and selfish and jealous, either for a lover or a son. Mrs. Dwight, being a perfectly respectable woman, had centered all the accumulated forces of her being on the son whom she idealized after the fashion of her type; and as she had corrected his obvious faults when he was a boy, it was quite true that he was kind, amiable, honest, honorable, patriotic, industrious, clean, polite, and moral; if hardly as handsome as Apollo or as brilliant and gifted as she permitted herself to believe.

"What do you mean?" she repeated, although she lowered her voice. It was rarely that it assumed an edge when addressing her husband. She had never reproached him for being a failure, for she had recognized his limitations early and accepted her lot. But something in his tone shook her maternal complacence and roused her to instant defense.

Mr. Dwight took his pipe from his mouth and also cast a glance toward the parlor, but the absorbed players were beyond the range of his rather weak voice.

"I mean this," he said with nothing of his usual vague hesitancy of speech. "I'm not so sure that Morty is beyond clerk size."

"You - you - John Dwight - your son - " The thin layer of pale flesh on Mrs. Dwight's face seemed to collapse upon its harsh framework with the terrified wrath that shook her. Her mouth fell apart, and hot smarting tears welled slowly to her eyes, faded with long years of stitching; not only for her own family but for many others when money had been more than commonly scarce. "Mortimer can do anything. Anything."

"Can he?" Why doesn't he show it then? He went to work at sixteen and is now twenty-two. He is drawing just fifty dollars a month. He's well liked in the firm, too."

"Why don't they raise his salary?"

"Because that's all he's worth to them. He's a good steady honest clerk, nothing more."

"He's very young - "

"If a man has initiative, ability, any sort of constructive power in his brain he shows it by the time he is twenty-two - if he has been in that forcing house for four or five years. That is the whole history of this country. And employers are always on the look-out for those qualities and only too anxious to find them and push a young man on and up. Many a president of a great business started life as a clerk, or even office boy - "

"That is what I have always known would happen to Morty. I am sure, sure, that you are doing him a cruel injustice."

"I hope I am. But I am a failure myself and I know what a man needs in the way of natural equipment to make a success of his life."

"But he is so energetic and industrious and honorable and likable and - "

"I was all that."

"Then - " Mrs. Dwight's voice trailed off; it sounded flat and old. "What do you both lack?"

"Brains."

V

Mrs. Dwight had repeated this conversation to Gora shortly before her death, and the girl in her reminiscent mood recalled it as she stared with somber eyes and ironic lips at the havoc the fire was playing with those lofty mansions which had stood to her all these intervening years as symbols of the unpardonable injustice of class.

She recalled another of the few occasions when Mrs. Dwight, who believed in acceptance and contentment, had been persuaded to discuss the idiosyncrasies of her adopted city.

"It isn't that money is the standard here as it is in New York. Of course there is a very wealthy set these late years and they set a pace that makes it difficult for the older families, like the Groomes for instance - I met Mrs. Groome once at a summer resort where I was housekeeper that year, and I thought her very typical and interesting. She was so kind to me without seeing me at all....But those fine old families, who are all of good old Eastern or Southern stock - if they manage to keep in society are still the most influential element in it....Family....Having lived in California long enough to be one of that old set....To be, without question, one of them. That is all that matters. I've come in contact with a good many of them first and last in my poor efforts to help your father, and I believe the San Franciscans to be the most loyal and disinterested people in the world-to one another.

"But if you come in from the outside you must bring money, or tremendous family prestige, or the right kind of social personality with the best kind of letters. We just crept in and were glad to be permitted to make a living. Why should they have taken any notice of us? They don't go hunting about for obscure people of possibly gentle blood. That doesn't happen anywhere in the world. You must be reasonable, my dear child. That is life, 'The World.'"

But Gora was not gifted with that form of reasonableness. She had wished in her darker moments that she had been born outright in the working-class; then, no doubt, she would have trudged contentedly every morning (excep when on strike) to the factory or shop, or been some one's cook. She was an excellent cook. What galled her was the fact of virtually belonging to the same class as these people who were still unaware of the existence of her family, although it had lived for over thirty years in a city numbering to-day only half a million inhabitants.

She was almost fanatically democratic and could see no reason for differences of degree in the aspiring classes. To her mind the only line of cleavage between the classes was that which divided people of education, refinement of mind manners and habits, certain inherited traditions, and the mental effort no matter how small to win a place in this difficult world, from commonness, ignorance, indifference to dirt, coarse pleasures. and habits, and manual labor. She respected Labor as the solid foundation stones upon which civilization upheld itself, and believed it to have been biologically chosen; if she had been born in its class she would have had the ambition to work her way out of it, but without resentment.

There her recognition of class stopped. That wealth or

family prominence even in a great city or an old community should create an exclusive and favored society seemed to her illogical and outrageous. A woman was a lady or she wasn't. A man was a gentleman or he wasn't. That should be the beginning and the end of the social code....When she had been younger she had lamented her mean position because it excluded her from the light-hearted and brilliant pleasures of youth; but as she grew older this natural craving had given place to a far deeper and more corrosive resentment.

She had no patience with her brother's ingenuous snobbery. A good-natured friend had introduced him to one or two houses where there were young people and much dancing and he had been "taken up." Nothing would have filled Gora with such murderous rage as to be taken up. She wanted her position conceded as a natural right.

Had it been in her power she would have forced her conception of democracy upon the entire United States. But as this was quite impossible she longed passionately for some power, personal and irresistible, that would compel the attention of the elect in the city of her birth and ultimately bring them to her feet. And here she had a ray of hope.

VI


Meanwhile it was some satisfaction to watch them being burned out of house and home.

Then she gave a short impatient sigh that was almost a groan, as she wondered if her own home would go. The family had moved into it eight years ago; and after Mr. Dwight's death his widow had barely made a living for herself and her daughter out of the uncertain boarders. Mortimer had paid his share, but she had encouraged him to dress well and no one knew the value of "front" better than he. After her death, three years ago, Gora had turned out the boarders and the last slatternly wasteful cook and let her rooms to business women who made their morning coffee over the gas jet. The new arrangement paid very well and left her time for lectures at the University of California, and for other studies. A Jap came in daily to put the rooms in order and she cooked for herself and her brother. So unknown was she that even Aileen Lawton was unaware that the "boarding-house down on Geary Street" was a lodging house kept by Mortimer Dwight's sister. Fortunately Gora was spared one more quivering arrow in her pride.

# CHAPTER VIII

I

There was a tremendous burst of dynamite that rocked the house. Then she heard her brother's voice:

"Gora! Gora! Where are you?"

She let herself through the trap door and ran down to the first floor.

Her brother was standing in the lower hall surrounded by several of their lodgers, competent-looking women, quite calm and business like, but dressed as for a journey and carrying suitcases and bags.

"You are all ordered out," he was saying. "A change of the wind to the south would sweep the fire right up this hill, and it may cross Van Ness Avenue again at any time. So everybody is ordered out to the western hills, or the Presidio, or across the Bay, if they can make it."

He had no private manners and greeted his sister with the same gallant smile and little air of deference which always carried him a certain distance in public. "You

100                    Gertrude Atherton

had better take out a mattress and blanket," he said. "I wish I could do it for you - for all of you - but I am under orders and must patrol where I am sent. When I finish giving the orders down here I must go back to the Western Addition."

"Don't worry about us," said Gora drily. "We are all quite as capable as men when it comes to looking out for ourselves in a catastrophe. I hear that several wives led their weeping stricken husbands out of town yesterday morning. Are you sure the fire will cross Van Ness Avenue to-night?"

"It may be held back by the dynamiting, but one can be sure of nothing. Of course the wind may shift to the west any minute. That would save this part of the city."

"Well, don't let us keep you from your civic duties. You look very well in those hunting boots. Lucky you went on that expedition last summer with Mr. Cheever."

Mortimer frowned slightly and turned to the door. The brother and sister rarely talked on any but the most impersonal subjects, but more than once he had had an uneasy sense that she knew him better than he knew himself. His consciousness had never faced anything so absurd, but there were times when he felt an abrupt desire to escape her enigmatic presence and this was one of them.

II

The lodgers were permitted by the patrol to cook their luncheon on the stove that had been set up in the street, the orders being that they should leave within an hour. After their smoky meal they departed, carrying mattresses and blankets.

Gora had no intention of following them unless the flames were actually roaring up the block between Van Ness Avenue and Franklin Street. She felt quite positive that she could outrun any fire.

The last of the lodgers, at her request, shut the front door and made a feint of locking it, an unnecessary precaution in any case as all the windows were open; and as the sentries had been ordered to "shoot to kill," and had obeyed orders, looting had ceased.

# CHAPTER IX

## I

Gora went up to the large attic which, soon, after her mother's death, she had furnished for her personal use. The walls were hung with a thin bluish green material and there were several pieces of good furniture that she had picked up at auctions. One side of the room was covered with book shelves which Mortimer had made for her on rainy winter nights and they were filled with the books she had found in second-hand shops. A number of them bore the autographs of men once prosilient in the city's history but long since gone down to disaster. There were a few prints that she had found in the same way, but no oils or water colors or ornaments. She despised the second-rate, and the best of these was rarely to be bought for a song even at auction.

She sighed as she reflected that if obliged to flee to the hills there was practically nothing she could save beyond the contents of her bags; but at least she could remain with her treasures until the last minute, and she pinned the curtains across the small windows and lit several candles.

Between the blasts of dynamite the street was very quiet. She could hear the measured tread of the sentry as he passed, a member of the Citizens' Patrol, like her brother. Suddenly she heard a shot, and extinguishing the candles hastily she peered out of a window from behind the curtains. The sentry was pounding on a door opposite with the butt of his rifle. It was the home of an eccentric old bachelor who possessed a fine collection of ceramics and a cellar of vintage wine.

The door opened with obvious reluctance and the head of Mr. Andrew Bennett appeared.

"What you doin' here?" shouted the sentry. "Haven't all youse been told three hours ago to light out for the hills? Git out - "

"But the fire hasn't crossed Van Ness Avenue. I prefer - "

"Your opinion ain't asked. Git out."

"I call that abominable tyranny."

"Git out or I'll shoot. We ain't standin' no nonsense."

Gora recognized the voice as that of a young man, clerk in a butcher shop in Polk Street, and appreciated the intense satisfaction he took in his brief period of authority.

Mr. Bennett emerged in a moment with two large bags and walked haughtily up the street at the point of the bayonet. Gora stood expectantly behind her curtain, and some ten minutes later saw him sneak round the eastern end of his block, dart back as the sentry turned suddenly, and when the footsteps once more receded run up the street and into his house. She laughed sympathetically and hoped he would not be caught a second time.

II

Suddenly another man, carrying a woman in his arms, turned the same corner. He was staggering as if he had borne a heavy burden a long distance.

Gora ran down to the first floor and glanced out of the window of the front room. The sentry had crossed the far end of the street and was holding converse with another member of the patrol. As the refugee staggered past the house she opened the front door and called softly.

"Come up quickly. Don't let them see you."

The man stumbled up the steps and into the house.

"You can put her on the sofa in this room." Gora led the way into what had once been the front parlor and was now the chamber of her star lodger. "Is she hurt?"

The man did not answer. He followed her and laid down his burden. Gora flashed her electric torch on the face of the girl and drew back in horror.

"Dead?"

"Yes, she is dead." The young man, who looked a mere boy in spite of his unshaven chin and haggard eyes, threw himself into a chair and dropping his face on his arms burst into heavy sobs.

Gora stared, fascinated, at the sharp white face of the girl, the rope of fair hair wound round her neck like something malign and muscular that had strangled her,

Gertrude Atherton

the half-open eyes, whose white maleficent gleam deprived the poor corpse of its last right, the aloofness and the majesty of death. She may have been an innocent and lovely young creature when alive, but dead, and lacking the usual amiable beneficencies of the undertaker, she looked like a macabre wax work of corrupt and evil youth.

And she was horribly stiff.

III

Gora went into the kitchen and made him a cup of coffee over a spirit lamp. He drank it gratefully, then followed her up to the attic as she feared their voices might be overheard from the lower room. There he took the easy chair and the cigarette she offered him and told his story.

The young girl was his sister and they were English. She had been visiting a relative in Santa Barbara when a sudden illness revealed the fact that she had a serious heart affection. He had come out to take her home and they had been staying at the Palace Hotel waiting for suitable accommodations before crossing the continent.

His sister - Marian - had been terrified into unconsciousness by the earthquake and he had carried her down the stairs and out into Market Street, where she had revived. She had even seemed to be better than usual, for the people in their extraordinary costumes, particularly the opera singers, had amused her, and she had returned to the court of the hotel and listened with interest to the various "experiences." Finally they had climbed the four flights of stairs to their rooms and he had helped her to dress - her maid had disappeared. They had remained until the afternoon when the uncontrolled fires in the region behind the hotel alarmed them, and with what belongings they could carry they had gone up to the St. Francis Hotel, where they engaged rooms and left their portmanteaux, intending to climb to the top of the hill, if Marian were able, and watch the fire.

Half way up the hill she had fainted and he had carried her into a house whose door stood open. There was no one in the house, and after a futile attempt to revive her, he had run back to the hotel to find a doctor. But among the few people that had the courage to remain so close to the fire there was no doctor. The hotel clerk gave him an address but told him not to be too sure of finding his man at home as all the physicians were probably attending the injured, helping to clear the threatened hospitals, or at work among the refugees, any number of women having embraced the inopportune occasion to become mothers.

The doctor whose address was given him not only was out but his house was deserted; and, distracted, he returned to his sister.

He knew at once that she was dead.

He sat beside her for hours, too stunned to think....It was some time during the night that the roar of the fire seemed to grow louder, the smoke in the street denser. Then it occurred to him that the inhabitants of this house as well as of the doctor's, which was close by, would not have abandoned their homes if they had not believed that some time during the night they would be in the path of the flames. And he had heard that the pipes of the one water system had been broken by the earthquake.

He had caught up the body of his sister and walked westward until, worn out, he had entered the basement of another empty house, and there he had fallen asleep. When he awakened he was under the impression for a moment that he was in the crater of a volcano in eruption. Dynamite was going off in all directions, he could hear the loud crackling of flames behind his refuge; and as he took the body in his arms once more and ran out, the fire was sweeping up the hill not a block below.

In spite of the smoke he inferred that the way was clear to the west, and he had run on and on, once narrowly escaping a dynamiting area where he saw men like dark shadows prowling and then rushing off madly in an automobile...dodging the fire, losing his way, once finding himself confronting a wall of flames, finally crossing a wide avenue...stumbling on...and on....

Gertrude Atherton

IV

Gora decided that blunt callousness would help him more than sympathy. He had recovered his self-control, but his eyes were still wide with pain and horror.

"Cremation is a clean honest finish for any one," she remarked, lighting another cigarette and offering him her match. "I should have left her if she had been my sister in that first house...."

"I might have done it - in London. But...perhaps I was not quite myself....I couldn't leave her to be burned alone in a strange country. Besides, the horror of it would have killed my mother. Marian was the youngest. I felt bound to do my best....Perhaps I didn't think at all....If this house is threatened I shall take her out to the Presidio, where I happen to know a man - Colonel Norris. Thanks to your hospitality I can make it."

"But naturally you cannot go very fast...and these sentries...I am not sure....I don't see how you escaped others...the smoke and excitement, I suppose....I think if you are determined to take her it would be better if I helped you to carry her out to the cemetery. We can put her on a narrow wire mattress and cover her, so that it will look as if we were rescuing an invalid. Out there you can put her in one of the stone vaults. Some of the doors are sure to have been broken by the earthquake."

The young man, who had given his name as Richard Gathbroke, gratefully rested in her brother's room while she kept watch on the roof. It was night but the very atmosphere seemed ablaze and the dynamiting as well as the approaching wall of fire looked very close. Finally when sparks fell on the roof she descended hastily and awakened her guest, making him welcome to her brother's linen as well as to a basin of precious water. When he joined her in the kitchen he had even shaved himself and she saw that he looked both older and younger than Americans of his age; which, he had told her, was twenty-three. His fair well-modeled face was now composed and his hazel eyes were brilliant and steady. He had a tall trim military body, and very straight bright brown hair; a rather conventional figure of a well-bred Englishman, Gora assumed; intelligent, and both more naif and more worldly-wise than young Americans of his class: but whose potentialities had hardly been apprehended even by himself. They ate as substantial a breakfast as could be prepared hastily over a spirit lamp, filled their pockets with stale bread, cake, and small tins of food, and then carried a narrow wire mattress from one of the smaller bedrooms to the front room on the first floor.

# CHAPTER X

## I

The patrol had been relieved by another, an older man, and sober. He merely reproved them for disobeying orders, glanced sympathetically at the presumed invalid, and directed them to one of the temporary hospitals some blocks farther west.

Gora, like all imaginative people, had a horror of the corpse, and averted her eyes from the head of the dead girl outlined under the veil she had thrown over it, Gathbroke was obliged to walk backward, and as both were extremely uncomfortable, there was no attempt at conversation until they reached the gates of the old cemetery the great pioneers had called Lone Mountain and their more commonplace descendants rechristened Laurel Hill.

The glare of the distant fire illuminated the silent city where a thousand refugees slept as heavily as the dead, and as they ascended the steep path they examined anxiously the vaults on either side. Finally Gora exclaimed:

"There! On the right."

The iron doors of a once eminent resident's last dwelling had been half twisted from their rusty hinges. Gathbroke threw his weight on them and they fell at his feet. He and Gora carried in the body and lifted it to an empty shelf.

"Good!" Gora gave a long sigh of relief. "Nothing can happen to her now. Even the entrance faces away from the fire and there is nothing but grass in the cemetery to burn, anyhow." She held her electric torch to the inscription above the entrance. "Better write down the name - Randolph. There's one of the tragedies of the sixties for you! An Englishman the hero, by the way. Nina Randolph is a handful of dust in there some-where. Heigho! What's the difference, anyway? Even if she'd been happy she'd be dead by this time - or too old to have a past."

Gathbroke replaced the gates, for he feared prowling dogs, and they walked down to the street and sat on the grass, leaning against the wall of the cemetery, as dissociated as possible from the rows of uneasy sleepers.

II

They slept a little between blasts of dynamite, the snoring of men and women and cries of children; finally at Gora's suggestion climbed to the steep bare summit of Calvary to observe the progress of the fire.

The unlighted portion of the city beneath them looked like a dead planet. Beyond was a tossing sea of flame whose far-reaching violent glare seemed to project it illimitably.

"Nothing can stop it!" gasped Gora; and that terrific red mass of energy and momentum did look as if its only curb would be the Pacific Ocean.

They talked until morning. He was very frank about himself, finding no doubt a profound comfort in human companionship after those long hours of ghastly comm.union down in that flaming jungle.

He was a younger son and in the army, not badly off, as his mother made him a goodish allowance. She had come of a large manufacturing family in the North and had brought a fortune to the empty treasury of the young peer she had - happily for both - fallen in love with.

He had wanted to go into business - politics later perhaps - after he left Eton, feeling that he had inherited some of the energy of his maternal grandfather, but his mother had insisted upon the army and as he really didn't care so very much, he had succumbed.

"But I'm not sure I shan't regret it. It isn't as if there were any prospect of a real war. I'd like a fighting career well enough, but not picayune affairs out in India or Africa. I can't help thinking I have a talent for business. Sounds beastly conceited," he added hastily. It was evident that he was a modest youth. "But after all one of us should inherit something of the sort. Perhaps, later, who knows? At least I can thank heaven that I wasn't born in my brother's place. He likes politics, and his fate is the House of Lords. A man might as well go and embalm himself at once. Do you know Gwynne? Elton Gwynne? John Gwynne he calls himself out here."

"I've heard of him. He's been written up a good deal. I don't know any one of that sort."

"Really? Well, don't you see? he inherited a peerage; grandfather died and his cousin shot himself to cover up a scandal. Gwynne was in the full tide of his career in the House of Commons and simply couldn't stand for it. He cut the whole business and came out here where he and his mother had a large estate - Lady Victoria's mother or grandmother was a Spanish-Californian. Of course he chucked the title. He's a sort of cousin of mine and I looked him up, and dined with him the other night. He was born in the United States, by a fluke as it were, and has made up his mind to be an American for the rest of his life and carve out a political career in this country. I'd have done the same thing, by Jove! First-class solution...although it's a pretty hard wrench to give up your own country. But when a man is too active to stagnate - there you are....I wish I had known where to find him to-day, but he lives on his ranch and I've only seen him once since. Lady Victoria took me to a ball night before last

- Good God! Was it only that?...and we were to have met again for lunch to-day."

"It is very easy and picturesque to renounce when you possess just about everything in life! If I attempted to renounce any of my privileges, for instance. I should simply move down and out."

III

He turned his head and regarded her squarely for the first time. Heretofore she had been simply a friend in need, a jolly good sport, incidentally a female. If she had been beautiful he should have noted that fact at once, for he could not imagine the circumstances in which beauty would not exert an immediate and powerful influence, however transitory.

Miss Dwight was not beautiful, but he concluded during that frank stare that her face was interesting; disturbingly so, although he was unable at the moment to find the reason. It was possible that in favorable conditions she would be handsome.

She had a mass of dark brown hair that seemed to sink heavily over her low forehead until it almost met the heavy black eyebrows. She had removed her hat and the thick loose coils made her look topheavy; for the face, if wide across the high cheek-bones and sharply accentuated with a salient jaw, was not large. The eyes were a light cold gray, oval and far apart. Her nose was short and strong and had the same cohibitive expression as the straight sharply-cut mouth - when not ironic or smiling. Her teeth were beautiful.

She had put on her best tailored suit and he saw that her "figger" was good although too short and full for his taste. He liked the long and stately slenderness that his own centuries had bred. But her hands and well-shod feet were narrow if not small, and he decided that she just escaped possessing what modern slang so aptly expressed as "class," Possibly it was the defiance in her square chin, the almost angry poise of her head, that betrayed her as an unwilling outsider.

"Bad luck!" he asked sympathetically.

She gave him a brief outline of her family history, overemphasizing as Americans will - those that lay any claim to descent - the previous importance of the Dwights and the Mortimers in Utica, N.Y. Incidentally, she gave him a flashlight picture of the social conditions in San Francisco.

He was intensely interested. "Really! I should have said there would be the complete democracy in California if anywhere. Of course no Englishman of my generation expects to find San Franciscans in cowboy costume; but I must say I was astonished at the luxury and fashion not only at those Southern California hotels, where, to be sure, most of the guests are from your older Eastern states, but at that ball Lady Victoria took me to. It was magnificent in all its details, originality combined with the most perfect taste. Of course there were not as many jewels as one would see at a great London function, but the toilettes could not have been surpassed. And as for the women - stunning! Such beauty and style and breeding. I confess I didn't expect quite all that. Miss Bascom, Miss Thorndyke, and an exquisite young thing, Miss Groome - "

"Oh, those are the haute noblesse." Gora's tipper lip curled satirically. "No doubt they lay claim that their roots mingle with your own."

"Well, we'd be proud of 'em."

"That was the Hofer ball, wasn't it! Do you mean to

say that Alexina Groome was there? Mrs. Groome, who is the most imposing relic of the immortal eighties, is supposed to know no one of twentieth-century vintage."

"I am sure of it. I danced with her twice and would have jolly well liked to monopolize her, but she was too plainly bowled over by a fellow - your name, by Jove - Dwight. Good-looking chap, clean-cut, fine shoulders, danced like a god - if gods do dance. I'm an awful duffer at it, by the way."

"Mortimer? Is it possible? And he - was he bowled over?"

"Ra - ther! A case, I should say."

"How unfortunate. Of course he hasn't the ghost of a chance. Mrs. Groome won't have a young man inside her doors whose family doesn't belong root and branch to her old set. Fine prospect for a poor clerk!"

"Jove! I've a mind to stay and try my luck. Oh!" He dropped his face in his hands. "I'm forgetting!"

"Well, forget again." Gora's voice expressed more sympathy than she felt. She deeply resented his immediate acceptance of her social alienage, even relegating her personal appearance to another class than that of the delicate flora he had seen blooming for the night against the most artful background of the season.

However...he was the first man she had ever met in her limited experience who seemed to combine the three magnetisms....Who could tell....

"I should be delighted if you would cut my brother out before it goes any further," she said untruthfully. "It will save him a heartache....Where could you meet her now? Society is disrupted here. But of course Mr. Gwynne visits down the peninsula. He could take you to any one of those exclusive abodes where you would be likely to meet the little Alexina. She is only eighteen, by the way."

"That is rather young," he said dubiously. "I don't fancy her conversation would be very interesting, and, after all, that is what it comes down to, isn't it? I've been disappointed so often." He sighed and looked quite thirty-five. "Still, she has personality. Five or six years hence she may be a wonder....I don't think I'd care about educating and developing a girl - I like a pal right away....What an ass I am, rotting like this. Tour brother has as much chance as I have. Younger sons with no prospect of succession are of exactly no account with the American mamma. I've met a few of them."

"Oh, I fancy birth would be enough for Mrs. Groome. She's quite dotty on the subject, and the people out here are simpler than Easterners, anyhow. Simpler and more ingenuous."

"How is it you know so much about it, all, if you are not, as you say - pardon me - a part of it?"

"I wonder!" She gave a short hard little laugh. "I don't know that I could explain, except that it all has seemed to me from birth a part of my blood and bones and gristle. An accident, a lucky strike on my father's part when he first came out here, and they would know me as well to-day as I know them. And then...of course...it is a small community. We live on the doorsteps of the rich and important, as it were. It would be hard for us not to know. It just comes to us. We are magnets. I suppose all this seems to you - born on the inside - quite ignominious."

"Well, my mother would have remained on the outside - that is to say a quiet little provincial - if her father hadn't happened to make a fortune with his iron works. I can understand well enough, but, if you don't mind my saying so, I think it rather a pity."

"Pity?"

"I mean thinking so much about it, don't you know? I fancy it's the result of living in a small city where there are only a few hundred people between you and the top instead of a few hundred thousand. I express, myself so badly, but what I mean is - as I make it out - it is, with you, a case of so near and yet so far. In a great city like London now (great in generations - centuries - as well as in numbers) you'd just accept the bare fact and go about your business. Not a ghost of a show, don't you see? Here you've just missed it, and, the middle class always flowing into the upper class, you feel that you should get your chance any minute. Ought to have had it long ago....I can't imagine, for instance, that if my mother had married the son of my grandfather's partner that I should have wasted much time wondering why I wasn't asked to the Elizabethan Hail on the hill. Of course I don't mean there isn't envy enough in the old countries, but it's more passive...without hope...."

He felt awkward and officious but he was sorry for her and would have liked to discharge his debt by helping her toward a new point of view, if possible.

She replied: "That's easy to say, and besides you are a man. My brother, who is only a clerk in a wholesale house, has been taken up and goes everywhere. They don't know that I even exist."

"Well, that's their loss," he said gallantly. "Can't you make 'em sit tip, some way? Women make fortunes sometimes, these days, And they're in about everything except the Army and Navy. Business? Or haven't you a talent of some sort? You have - pardon me again, but we have been uncommonly personal to-night - a strong and individual face...and personality; no doubt of that."

Gora would far rather he had told her she was pretty and irresistible, but she thrilled to his praise, never-theless. It was the first compliment she had ever received from any man but the commonplace and unimportant friends her brother had brought home occasionally before he had been introduced to society; he took good care to bring home none of his new friends.

Her heart leapt toward this exalted young Englishman, who might have stepped direct from one of the novels of his land and class...even the stern and anxious moderns who had made England's middle-class the fashion, occasionally drew a well-bred and attractive man from life....She turned to him with a smile that banished the somber ironic expression of her face, illuminating it as if the drooping spirit within had suddenly lit a torch and held it behind those strange pale eyes.

"I'll tell you what I've never told any one - but my teacher; I've taken lessons with him for a year. He is an instructor in the technique of the short story, and has turned out quite a few successful magazine writers. He believes that I have talent. I have been studying over at the University to the same end - English, biology, psychology, sociology. I'm determined not to start as a raw amateur. Oh! Perhaps I have made a mistake in telling you. You may be one of those men that are repelled by intellectual women!"

"Not a bit of it. Don't belong to that class of duffers anyway. I don't like masculine women, or hard women - run from a lot of our girls that are so hard a diamond wouldn't cut 'em. But I've got an elder sister - she's thirty now - who's the cleverest woman I ever met, although she doesn't pretend to do anything. She won't bother with any but clever and exceptional people - has something of a salon. My parents hate it - she lives alone in a flat in London - but they can't help it. My grandfather Doubleton liked her a lot and left her two thousand a year. I wish you knew her. She is charming and feminine, as much so as any of those I met at the ball; and so are many of the women that go to her flat - "

"Don't you think I am feminine?" asked Gora irrisistibly. He had a way of making her feel, quite abruptly, as if she had run a needle under her fingernail.

Once more he turned to her his detached but keen young eyes.

"Well...not exactly in the sense I mean. You look too much the fighter...but that may be purely the result of circumstances," he added hastily: the strange eyes under their heavy down-drawn browns were lowering at him. "You are not masculine, no, not a bit."

Once more Miss Dwight curled her upper lip. "I wonder if you would have said the first part of that if you had met me at the Hofer ball and I had worn a gown of flame-colored chiffon and satin, and my hair marcelled like every other woman present - except those embalmed relics of the seventies, who, I have heard, rise from the grave whenever a great ball is given, and appear in a built-up red-brown wig....And a string of pearls round my throat? My neck and arms are quite good; although I've never possessed an evening gown, I know I'd look quite well in one...my best."

He laughed. "It does make a difference. I wish you had been there. I am sure you are as good a dancer as you are a pal. But still...I think I should have recognized the fighter, even if you had been born in the California equivalent for the purple. I fancy you would have found some cause or other to get your teeth into once in a while. Tell me, don't you rather like the idea of taking Life by the throat and forcing it to deliver?"

"I wonder?...perhaps...but that does not mitigate my resentment that I am on the outside of everything when I belong on the in. I should never have been forced to strive after what is mine by natural right."

"Well, don't let it make a socialist of you. That is such a cheap revenge on society....Confession of failure; and nothing in it."

# IV

He looked at his watch: "Eight o'clock. I'll be getting on to the Presidio. Why don't you come with me?"

Gora's feminine instincts arose from a less perverted source than her social. She shook her head with a smile.

"I don't want to go any farther from my house. I shall slip down my first chance; and I have plenty to eat. Perhaps you will come to see me before you go if my house is spared."

"Rather. What is the number? And if the house goes I'll find you somehow."

He took her hand in both his and shook it warmly. "You are the best pal in the world - "

"Now don't make me a nice little speech. I'm only too glad. Go out to the Presidio and get a hot breakfast and attend - to - to your affairs. I am sure everything will be all right, although you may not be able to get away as soon as you hope."

"I don't like leaving you alone here - "

"Alone?" She waved her hand at the hundreds of recumbent forms in the cemeteries and on the lower slopes of Calvary. "I probably shall never be so well protected again. Please go."

He shook her hand once more, ran down the hill,

turned and waved his cap, and trudged off in the direction of the Presidio.

# V

She slept in her own house that night, for dynamiting by miners summoned from Grass Valley by General Funston, and a change of wind, had saved the western portion of the city. For the first time in her life Gora experienced a sense of profound gratitude, almost of happiness. She felt that only a little more would make her quite happy. Her lodgers, even her absorbed brother, noticed that her manner, her expression, had perceptibly softened. She herself noticed it most of all.

# CHAPTER XI

## I

Gathbroke met Alexina Groome again a week later.

On Saturday, when the fire was over, and she could retreat decently and in good order, Mrs. Groome, to her young daughter's secret anguish, had consented to rest her nerves for a fortnight at Rincona, Mrs. Abbott's home in Alta.

As Gora had predicted, Gathbroke found that it would have been hardly more difficult to move his sister's body, now at an undertaker's in Fillmore Street, out of the state in war-time than in the wake of a city's disaster, which was scattering its population to every point of the railroad compass. He had refused the space in the baggage car offered to him by the company; it should: be a private car or nothing; and for that, in spite of all the influence Gwynne and his powerful friends could bring to bear, he must wait.

Meanwhile Gwynne had asked him to stay with himself and his mother, Lady Victoria Gwynne, at the house of his fiancée, Isabel Otis, on Russian Hill; a massive cliff rising above one of the highest of the city's northern hills, whose old houses, clinging to its steep sides had escaped the fire that roared about its base. To-day it was a green and lofty oasis in the midst of miles of smoking ruins.

Gathbroke was as nervous as only a young Englishman within his immemorial armor can be. Gwynne, who had gone through the same nerve-racking crisis, although from different causes, understood what he suffered and pressed him into service in the distribution of government rations, and garments to the different refugee camps. But Gathbroke had the active imagination of intelligent youth, and he never forgot to blame himself for lingering in New York with some interesting chaps he had met on the *Majestic*, and afterward in Southern California, seduced by its soft climate and violent color. Unquestionably, if he had stayed on his job, as these expressive Americans put it, his sister would have been in New York, possibly on the Atlantic Ocean when San Francisco shook herself to ruin.

"But not necessarily alive," said Lady Victoria callously, removing her cigar, her heavy eyes that looked like empty volcanos, staring down over the smoldering waste. "People with heart disease don't invariably wait for an earthquake to jolt them out of life. Assume that her time had come and think of something else or you'll become a silly ass of a neurotic."

Gwynne, more sympathetic, continued to find him what distraction he could, and one day drove him down the Peninsula with a message from the Committee of Fifty to Tom Abbott; who had caught a heavy cold during those three days when he had driven a car filled with dynamite and had had scarcely an hour for rest. He was now at home in bed.

## II

The Abbott's place, Rincona, stood on a foothill behind the other estates of Alta and surrounded by a park of two hundred acres set thick with magnificent oaks. Gathbroke had never seen finer ones in England or France. Gwynne before entering the avenue drove to an elevation above the house and stopped the car for a moment.

The great San Mateo valley looked like a close forest of ancient oaks broken inartistically by the roofs of houses shorn of their chimneys. Beyond, on the eastern side of a shallow southern arm of the Bay of San Francisco, was the long range of the Contra Costa mountains, its waving indented slopes incredibly graceful in outline and lovely in color. Gwynne had pointed out their ever changing tints and shades as they drove through the valley; at the moment they were heliotrope deepening to purple in the hollows.

Behind the foothills above Rincona rose the lofty mountains which in Maria Abbott's youth had seemed to tower above the valley a solid wall of redwoods; but long since plundered and defaced for the passing needs of man.

"Great country - what?" said Gwynne, starting the car. "You couldn't pry me away from it - that is, unless I have the luck to represent it in Washington half the year. You'll be coming back yourself some day."

"I? Never. I hate the sight of its grinning blue sky after the red horror of those three days. I haven't seen a cloud as big as my hand, and in common decency it

Gertrude Atherton

should howl and stream for months."

"Well, forget it for a day. Perhaps you will be placed next the fair Alexina at luncheon - "

"Alexina...?"

"Groome. You must have met her at the Hofer ball."

"She - what - possible - "

Gwynne looked at his stuttering and flushed young cousin and burst into laughter.

"As bad as that, was it? Well, she's not bespoken as far as I know. Wade in and win. You have my blessing. She is almost as beautiful as Isabel - "

"She's quite as beautiful as Miss Otis."

"Oh, very well. No doubt I'd think so myself if I hadn't happened to meet Isabel first, and if I were not too old for her anyway."

Gwynne could think of no better remedy for demoralized nerves than a flirtation with a resourceful California girl, and if Dick annexed a living companion for his trying journey to England so much the better.

Gathbroke's excitement subsided quickly. He was in no condition for sustained enthusiasm. He felt as if quite ten years had passed since he had half fallen in love with Alexina Groome in a ball room that was now a charred heap in the sodden wreck of a city he barely could conjure in memory.

Besides, he had half fallen in love so often. And she was too young. He had really been more drawn to that strange Miss Dwight; upon whom, however, he had not yet called.

He felt thankful that the girl *was* too young for his critical taste. He wanted nothing more at present in the way of emotions.

# CHAPTER XII

## I

Rincona had been named in honor of Rincon Hill, where Tom Abbott's grandmother had reigned in the sixties; a day, when in order to call on her amiable rival, Mrs. Ballinger, her stout carriage horses were obliged to plow through miles of sand hills, and to make innumerable détours to avoid the steep masses of rock, over which in her grandson's day cable car and trolley glided so lightly until that morning of April eighteen, nineteen hundred and six.

When her husband, in common with other distinguished citizens, bought an estate in the San Mateo Valley, she named it Rincona, to the secret wrath of other eminent ladies who had not thought of it in time.

The house had as little pretensions to architectural beauty as others of its era, but it was a large compact structure of some thirty rooms, exclusive of the servants' quarters, and with as many outbuildings as a Danish, farm. Long French windows opened upon a wide piazza, whose pillars had disappeared long since under a luxuriant growth of rose vines and wistaria. At its base was a bed of Parma violets, whose fragrance a westerly breeze wafted to the end of the avenue a quarter of a mile away. All about the house, breaking the smooth lawns, were beds and trees of flowers, at this time of the year a glowing exotic mass of color; but in the park that made up the greater part of the estate exclusive of the farms, the grass under the superb oaks was merely clipped, the weeds and undergrowth removed. The oaks had been evenly shorn of their lower branches, which gave them a formal and somewhat arrogant expression, as of cardinals and kings lifting their skirts.

Alexina hated the enormous rooms with their high frescoed ceilings and heavy Victorian furniture; but Maria Abbott loved and revered the old house, emblem that it was of a secure proud family that had defied that detestable (and disturbing) old phrase: "Three generations from shirt sleeves to shirt sleeves." The Abbotts, like the Ballingers and Groomes and Gearys and many others of that ilk, had not come to California in the fifties and sixties as adventurers, but with all that was needed to give them immediate prestige in the new community; and, among those that still retained their estates in the San Mateo Valley, at least, there was as little prospect of their reversion to shirt sleeves as of their conversion to the red shirt of socialism. Their wealth might be moderate but it was solid and steadfast.

II

The entertaining of the Abbotts, Yorbas, Hathaways, Montgomerys, Brannans, Trennahans, and others of what Alexina irreverently called the A.A., had always been ostentatiously simple, albeit a butler and a staff of maids had contributed to their excessive comfort. In the eighties, evening toilettes during the summer were considered immoral; but by degrees, as time tooled in its irresistible modernities, they gradually fell into the habit of wearing out their winter party gowns at the evening diversions of the country season. Burlingame, that borough of concentrated opulence founded in the early nineties as a fashionable colony, began its career with a certain amount of simplicity; but its millions increased to tens of millions; and what in heaven's name, as Mrs. Clement Hunter, a leader and an individual, once remarked, is the use of having money if you don't dress and entertain as you would dream of dressing and entertaining if you didn't have a cent?

Mrs. Hunter, who had formed an incongruous and somewhat hostile alliance with Mrs. Abbott, knew that her valuable friend, like others of that "small and early" band, resented the fact that their standards no longer counted outside of their own set. Mrs. Abbott had turned a haughty shoulder to Mrs. Hunter for a time, for she remembered her as, in their school days, the socially obscure Lidie McKann; now, however, her husband turning all he touched to gold, she had, incredibly, become one of the most important women in San Francisco and Burlingame.

When Maria Abbott finally succumbed she assured herself that curiosity to see the more ambushed glitter of that meretricious faubourg had nothing to do with it; it was easy to persuade herself that she hoped, being an indisputably smart woman herself, gradually to impose her simpler and more appropriate standards upon these people who sorely threatened the continued dominance of the old régime.

Mrs. Hunter soon disabused her of any such notion, and during the early days of their acquaintance, after Mrs. Abbott came to one of her luncheons attired in a pique skirt and severe shirtwaist, impeccably cut and worn, but entirely out of place in an Italian palace, where forty fashionable women, some of whom had motored sixty miles to attend the function, were dressed as they would be at a Newport luncheon, Mrs. Hunter attended the next solemn affair at Rincona so overdressed and made up that the outraged Altarinos (as Alexina irreverently called them) were reduced to a horrified silence that was almost hysterical.

But one morning Mrs. Abbott caught Mrs. Hunter digging in her private vegetable garden behind the palace, and wearing a garment that her second gardener's wife would have scorned, her unblemished face beaming under a battered straw hat. Both women had the humor to laugh, and their intimacy dated from that moment, Mrs. Hunter confessing that stuff on her face made her sick; but adding that she adored dress and thought that any rich woman was a fool who didn't.

After that there was a compromise on both sides. Mrs. Hunter lunched or dined at Rincona in her simplest frocks and Mrs. Abbott wore her best when honoring Mrs. Hunter and others at Burlingame. She even went so far as to have some extremely smart silk voiles (the fashionable material of the moment) and linens made, and when asked to a wedding, a garden party, or a great function given to some visitor of distinction, complimented the occasion to the limit of her resources.

# III

Mrs. Hunter, in white duck, a sailor hat perched above her angular somewhat masculine face, was sitting on the Abbott verandah as the two Englishmen drove up. She waved her cigarette and cried gayly in her hearty resonant voice:

"Two men! What luck! And in time for lunch. I've hardly seen a man since the first day of the fire. Leave your car anywhere and come in out of the sun. I'll call Maria, and, incidentally, mention whiskey and soda."

"The whiskey and soda is all right," said Gwynne mopping his brow; Nature, having wreaked her worst on California, seemed determined to atone by unseasonably brilliant weather, and the day under the blazing blue vault was very hot.

Mrs. Abbott appeared in a few moments, smiling, cool, in immaculate white, the collar of her shirtwaist high and unwilted. Her weather-beaten face looked years older than Mrs. Hunter's, who, although plain by comparison with the once beautiful Maria Groome, had treated her clean healthy skin with marked respect.

But as the butler had preceded her with whiskey and soda and ice, Mrs. Abbott might already have achieved the mahogany tints of her mother and she would have been regarded as enthusiastically by two hot and dusty men.

"Of course you will stay to luncheon," she said as naturally as she had said it these many years, and as two hospitable generations had said it on that verandah before her. She turned to young Gathbroke with a smile, for Mrs. Hunter, who was in her confidence, had detained her for a moment with a few sharp incisive words. "I have a very bored little sister, who will be glad to sit next to a young man once more."

And although Gathbroke almost frowned at this fresh reminder of the callow years of the girl whose sheer loveliness had haunted his imagination, he went off with a not disagreeable titillation of the nerves, at Mrs. Abbott's suggestion, to find her in the park and bring her back to luncheon in half an hour.

# CHAPTER XIII

I

He was light of step and made no sound on the heavy turf; he saw her several minutes before she was aware of his presence and stood staring at her, feeling much as he had done during the progress of the earthquake.

She was standing under one of the great oaks whose lower limbs had been trimmed so evenly some seven feet above the ground that they made a compact symmetrical roof above the dark head of the girl, who, being alone, had abandoned the limp curve of fashion and was standing very erect, drawn up to her full five feet seven. Alexina had no intention of being afflicted with rounded shoulders when the present mode had passed.

But her face expressed no guile as she stood there in her simple white frock with a bunch of periwinkles in her belt, her delicate profile turned to Gathbroke as she gazed at the irregular majesty of the Coast Range, dark blue under a pale blue haze. He had retained the impression of starry eyes and vivid coloring and eager happy youth, a body of perfect slenderness and grace,

Gertrude Atherton

whose magnetism was not that of youth alone but personal and individual.

Now he saw that although her fine little profile was not too regular, and as individual as her magnetism, the shape of her head was classic. It was probable that she was not unaware of the fact, for its perfect lines and curves were fully revealed by the severe flatness of the dusky thickly planted hair, which was brushed back to the nape of her neck and then drawn up a few inches and flared outward. The little head was held high on the long white stem of the throat; and the pose, with the dropping eyelids, gave her, in that deep shade, the illusion of maturity. Gathbroke realized that he saw her for the moment as she would look ten years hence. Even the full curved red lips were closed firmly and once the nostrils quivered slightly.

The narrow black eyebrows following the subtle curve of her eyelids, the low full brow with its waving line of soft black hair, seemed to brood over the lower part of the face with its still indeterminate curves, over the wholly immature figure of a very young girl.

Gathbroke surrendered then and there. This radiation of mystery, of complexity, this secret subtle visit of maturity to youth, the hovering spirit of the future woman, was unique in his experience and went straight to his head. He forgot his sister, dismissed the thought of Dwight with a gesture of contempt. He might be modest and rather diffident in manner, owing to racial shyness, but he had a fine sustaining substructure of sheer masculine arrogance.

## II

As he walked forward swiftly Alexina turned; and immediately was the young thing of eighteen and of the early twentieth century. Her spine drooped into an indolent curve, her soft red lips fell apart, her black-gray eyes opened wide as she held out her hand to the young Englishman.

"How nice! I never really expected to see you again. I understood Lady Victoria to say you were merely passing through."

Alexina had not cast him a thought since the night of the ball but she was hospitable and feminine.

"I was detained."

She noted with intense curiosity that his bright color paled and his sparkling hazel eyes darkened with a sudden look of horror; but the spasm of memory passed quickly, and once more he was staring at her with frank capitulation.

Alexina's head went up a trifle. She was still new to conquest, and although she had met more than one pair of admiring eyes in the course of the past season, and received as many compliments as the vainest girl could wish, few men had had the courage to storm the stern fortress on Ballinger Hill, or to sit more than once in a drawing-room so darkly reminiscent of funeral ceremonies that a fellow's nerves began to jump all over him.

Nor had her fancy been even lightly captured until

Mortimer Dwight, that perfect hero of maiden dreams, had swept her off her dancing feet on the most memorable night of her life.

She had quite made up her mind to marry him. The indignant silent hostility of the family (even Mrs. Ballinger, her moment of weakness passed, having been swung to the horrified Maria's point of view) had been all that was necessary to convince the young Alexina that fate had sent her the complete romance. She hoped the opposition would drive her to an elopement; little dreaming of the horror with which Mr. Dwight would greet the heterodox alternative.

Mrs. Abbott had had a valid excuse for not asking him down: provisions were scarce, and, so Tom said, he was doing useful work in town. But Olive Bascom, whose country home was in San Mateo, had invited him for the next week end, and he had accepted. Alexina was to be one of the small house party, and there were many romantic walks behind San Mateo. A moon was also due.

III

Still Gathbroke might have entered the race with an even chance, for maidens of eighteen are merely the blind tools of Nature, had not the family made the mistake of displaying too warm an approval of the eligible young Englishman. Mrs. Groome, Mrs. Abbott, Aunt Clara, reënforced even by the more worldly Mrs. Hunter, who, however, had no children of her own, treated him throughout the luncheon with an almost intimate cordiality and a lively personal interest; whereas, if Mrs. Abbott had been driven to keep her word and invite Mortimer Dwight to her historic board she would have depressed him with the cool pleasant detachment she reserved for those whom she knew slightly and cared for not at all; Mrs. Groome, automatically gracious, would have retired within the formidable fortress of an exterior built in the still more exclusive eighties; Aunt Clara would have sat petrified with horror at the desecration; and Mrs. Hunter, free from the obligations of hospitality, would have been brusque, frankly supercilious, made him as uncomfortable as possible.

All this Alexina angrily resented, not knowing that their amiability was in part inspired by sympathy, Gwynne having told them the story of his cousin's tragic experience; although they did in truth regard him as a possibly heaven-sent solution of a problem that was causing them all, even Mrs. Hunter, acute anxiety.

Young Gathbroke was handsomer than Dwight. He was younger, and his circumstances were far more romantic, if romance Alexina must have. It was plain that he was fascinated by the dear silly child, who, in her turn, would no doubt promptly forget the ineligible Dwight if the Englishman proved to be serious and paid her persistent court.

Nevertheless Gathbroke, before the luncheon was half over, felt that he was making no progress with Alexina. Subtly it was conveyed to him on one of those unseen currents that travel directly to the sensitive mind, that these amiable people knew his story; and, no doubt, in all its harrowing details. Simultaneously those details flashed into his own consciousness with a horrible distinctness, depressing his spirits and extinguishing a natural gayety and light chaff that had come back for a moment.

Moreover, to use his own expression, he was beso-ttedly in love, and knew that he betrayed himself every time his eyes met those of the girl, who, he felt with bitterness and alarm, long before the salad, was making a desperate attempt to entertain a very dull young man.

Once or twice a mocking glance flashed through those starry ingenuous orbs, but was banished by the simple art of elevating the wicked iris and revealing a line of saintly white. Alexina was quite determined to add a British scalp to her small collection, and for the young man's possible torment she cared not at all. With young arrogance she rather despised him for his surrender before battle, or at all events for hauling down his flag publicly; and her mind traveled with feminine satisfaction to the calm smiling dominance, combined with utter devotion, of the man who had won her as easily as she had conquered Richard Gathbroke. That the young Englishman's nature was hot and tempestuous, with depths that even he had not sounded, and her ideal knight's more effective mien but the expression of a possibly meager and somewhat puritanical nature; that Dwight's heart was a well-trained organ which would never commit an indiscretion, and that young Gathbroke would have sold the world for her if she had been a flower girl, or the downfall of her fortunes had sent her clerking, she was far too inexperienced to guess; and it is doubtful if the knowledge would have affected her had she possessed it. She was in the obstinate phase of first youth, common enough in girls of her sheltered class, where the opportunities to study men and their behavior are few. Having persuaded herself that she was far more romantic than she really was, and that there would be no possible happiness or indeed interest in life after youth, she had conceived as her ideal mate the dominant male, the complete master, and easily persuaded herself that she had found him in Mortimer Dwight....If she married Gathbroke he would be her slave (so little did she know him.). Dwight would be her master. (So little did she know him, or herself.)

# CHAPTER XIV

I

After luncheon, grinning amiably when Mrs. Abbott hinted that Englishmen liked to be out of doors, she led Gathbroke to the confines of the park, where they sat down under one of the oaks that reminded him of England; for which he was in truth desperately homesick, and never more so than at this moment.

Everything combined to make him realize uneasily his youth. In England a man of twenty-three was a man-of-the-world if he had had the proper opportunities; but this girl who had infatuated him, and even the far more sympathetic Miss Dwight, made him feel that he was a mere boy; and so had this entire family, however unwittingly.

II

He spoke of Miss Dwight suddenly, for Alexina, who had been duly enlightened while the men were smoking with Tom, had tactfully conveyed her sympathy, her eyes almost round with fascinated horror and curiosity.

He set his teeth and gave a rapid but graphic account of the whole dreadful episode, willing to interest her at any price; and Alexina, sitting opposite on the ground, her long spine curved, her long arms embracing her knees, listened with a breathless interest, spurring him to potent words, even to stressing of detail.

"My goodness gracious me!" she ejaculated when he paused. "I should have gone raving mad. You are a perfect wonder. I never heard of anything so gor - perfectly thrilling. And that girl, what did you say her name was?"

Gathbroke, who had purposely withheld it, said explosively:

"Dwight."

"Dwight?"

"I think she is a sister of a friend of yours." And he was made as miserable as he could wish by a crimson tide that swept straight from her heart pump up to her widow's peak.

"Dwight? Sister? I didn't know he had one. I saw him several times during the fire and he didn't mention her."

"I suspect he was too absorbed." Gathbroke muttered the words, but man's instinct of loyalty to his own sex is strong. "A city doesn't burn every day, you know."

"Still...what is she like? Like him?"

"I do not remember him at all...She? Oh, she has a tremendous amount of dark hair that looks as if falling off the top of her head and down her face. Uncommonly heavy eyebrows, and very light gray - Ah, I have it! I have been groping for the word ever since - sinister eyes....That is the effect in that dark face. She has a curious character, I should think. Not very frank. She - well, she rather struck me as having been born for drama; tragic drama, I am afraid."

"Not a bit like her brother. How old is she?"

"Twenty-two, she told me."

"What - what does she do? They are not a bit well off."

He hesitated a moment. "Well - as I recall it, she is studying something or other at the University of California."

"And of course she boards down there with her brother, who takes care of her while she is studying to be a teacher or something." Alexina having arranged it to her satisfaction dismissed the subject. She had no mind to betray herself to this good-looking young Englishman who had been sent to her providentially on a very dull day. He would, no doubt, have been frantically interesting if he had not been so idiotic as to fall head over ears the first shot.

Still...Alexina examined him covertly as he transferred his gaze for a moment to the mountains across the distant bay, swimming now in a pale blue mist with a wide banner of pale pink above them....If she had met him first, or had never met the other at all...who knew?

III

Alexina, for all her passion for romance, had a remarkably level head. She was quite aware that there had been a certain amount of deliberation in her own headlong plunge, convinced as she was that high romance belonged to youth alone, and fearful lest it pass her by; aware also that a part of Dwight's halo, aside from his looks and manners and chivalrous charm, consisted in his being a martyr to an unjust fate, and, as such, under the ban of her august family. It was all quite too perfect....But if Gathbroke had come first his qualifications might have proved quite as puissant, and no doubt Tom Abbott, who retained his school-history hatred of the entire English race, would have provided the opposition and perhaps influenced the family.

She swept her intoxicating lashes along the faint bloom high on her olive cheeks and then raised her eyes suddenly to the tormented ones opposite. She also smiled softly, alluringly, as little fascinating wretches will who know nothing of the passions of men.

"I think you should follow Mr. Gwynne's example and stay here with us." He thought of silver chimes and contrasted her voice with Gora Dwight's angry contralto: he always thought of Gora in phrases. "So many Englishmen live out here and adore it."

"I'm perfectly satisfied with my own country, thank you."

Alexina, who was feeling intensely American at the moment, curled her lip. "Oh, of course. We have had plenty of those, too. Scarcely any of them becomes naturalized. Just use and enjoy the country and give as little in return as possible."

"Really? I fancy they must give rather a lot in return or they would hardly be tolerated. No native has worked harder than Elton these last days. I understand most of them are in business or ranching and have married California girls."

"Oh, they have redeeming points." And then having satisfied her curiosity as to how hazel eyes looked when angry she gave him a dazzling smile. "We love them like brothers, and that is a proof that we are not snobbish, for most of them are not of your or Mr. Gwynne's class - just middle-class business people at home."

"Well, you are a business nation, so why not? I have met hardly any but business men out here and I feel quite at home with them. My mother's family are in trade and I enjoy myself immensely when I visit them."

"Oh!" His halo slipped....Still, what did it matter? "I suppose you told me that to let me know you didn't need to come out here in search of an heiress. But many of our most charming girls are not. Just now it seems to me that more young men in California have money than girls...but they are so uninteresting."

She looked pathetic, her mouth drooped; then she smiled at him confidingly.

He knew quite as well as if he had not been hard hit that she was flirting with him, but as long as she gave him his chance to win her she might do her transparent little best to make a fool of him.

"Have you ever been in love?" asked Alexina softly.

"Oh, about half-way several times, but always drew back in time...knew it wasn't the real thing...Youth fools itself, you know, for the sake of the sensation - or the race. Have you?"

"Oh - " Alexina lifted her thin flexible shoulders airily and this time her color did not flow. "How is one to tell...a girl in her first season...when all men look so much alike? It is fun to flirt with them, when you have been shut up in boarding-school and hardly had a glimpse of life even in vacation. My New York relatives are terribly old-fashioned. It's great fun to give one man all the dances and watch the dado of dowagers look disapproving." And once more she gave him the quick smile of understanding that springs so spontaneously between youth and youth.

"Well...you might have given all those dances to me the other night, instead of to that fellow Dwight."

"Oh, but you see, I had already promised them to him. Lady Victoria always comes so late."

"That's true enough." His spirits rose a trifle.

"When do you go - back to England, I mean? Not for a good long time, I hope. We have awfully good times down here. Janet Maynard and Olive Bascom live at San Mateo in the summer, and Aileen Lawton at Burlingame. They are my chums and we'd give you a ripping time. We'd like to have you take away the pleasantest possible memory of California instead of such a terrible one. I don't mean anything very gay of course. You mustn't think I'm heartless." And she showed the lower pearl of her eyes and looked like a madonna.

"I'm afraid I must go soon. I've had an extension of leave already, and Hofer told me just before we left to-day that he thought he could let me have his private car inside of a week. They've been using it."

IV

There was not a dwelling in sight. The quiet of that old park with its brooding oaks was primeval. Behind her was the pink and blue glory of sky and mountain. Her eyes were like stars.

He burst out boyishly: "If I only had more time! If only I could have met you even when I first came to San Francisco...before...before...I'd - I'd like to marry you. It's fearfully soon to say such a thing. I feel like a fool. But I'm not the first man to fall madly in love at first sight...and you...you...If I tell you now instead of waiting it's because there's so little time. Would you...do you think you could marry me?"

"Oh! Ah!" (She almost said Ow.) After all it was her first proposal. She was thrilled in spite of the fact that she was in love with another man, for she felt close to something elemental, hazily understood...something in her own unsounded depths rushed to meet it.

But he was too young, and too "easy," and she didn't like his gray flannel shirt; which, laundry being out of the question, he had bought in Fillmore Street almost opposite the undertaker's.

"Suppose we correspond for a year? That is, if you must really go so soon."

"I must. I want you to go with me."

His eyes had turned almost black and he had set his jaw in a way she didn't like at all. In nerving himself to go through the ordeal he had worked up his fermenting mind into a positively brutal mood.

"Oh - mercy! I couldn't do that. My people are the most conventional in the world."

The situation was getting beyond her. She had not intended to make him propose for at least a week and then he would have been abject and she majestic. She sprang to her feet with a swift sidewise movement that made her limp young body melt into a series of curves; and, standing at bay as it were, looked at him with a little frown.

He rose as quickly and she liked the set of his jaw ones less and less.

"Are you refusing me outright?" he demanded. "That would be only fair, you know, if I have no chance."

"Well....I think so. That is - "

"Do you love another man?"

Coquetry flashed back. Nevertheless, she told the exact truth little as she suspected it.

"I love myself, and youth, and life, and liberty. What is a man in comparison with all that?"

"This." And before she could make another leap he had her in his arms; and under the fire of his lips and eyes she lay inert, intoxicated, her first flash of young passion completely responsive to his.

But only for a moment.

Gertrude Atherton

She wrenched herself away, her face livid, her eyes black with fury. She beat his chest with her fists.

"You! You! How I hate you! To think I should have given that to you...to think that another man should have been the first to kiss me...I'm in love with another man, I tell you. Why don't you go? I hate myself and I never want to lay eyes on you again. Go! Go! Go!"

# CHAPTER XV

I

During the retreat from Mons and again in those black days of March, nineteen-eighteen, Gathbroke's tormented mind snapped from the present and flashed on its screen so startling a resurrection of himself during those last dreadful days in San Francisco that for the moment he was unconscious of the world crashing about him.

He saw himself in long days and nights of anguish and despair, of embittered love and baffled passion: youth enjoying one of its divine prerogatives and the fullness thereof!

Pacing the floor of his room on Russian Hill, tramping over the mountains across the Bay, doggedly awaiting that sole alleviation of mental suffering in its early stages, a change of scene.

Finally the Hofer car was placed at his disposal and he started on his four days' journey to New York; and this brief chapter, that his friends thought so gruesome, was the least of his afflictions. The memory of his twenty

Gertrude Atherton

-four hours or more of close physical association with his sister's corpse made any subsequent adventure with the dead seem tame. And at least he was leaving behind him a State which seemed to have magnetized him across six thousand miles to experience the horror and misery she had in pickle for him. He reveled in the audible rush of the train that was carrying him farther every moment from the girl who had cut down into the core of his heart and left her indelible image on a remarkably good memory.

## II

He had asked himself one day - it was his last in California and he had taken his courage in his teeth and was on his way to call on Gora Dwight at last, picking his steps through, the still smoking ruins down to Van Ness Avenue - whether it would be possible for any man to suffer twice in a lifetime as he had suffered since that hideous moment at Rincona, coming as it did on top of an uncommon and terrible experience that had racked his nerves and soul as it might not have done had he been seasoned by war or even a few years older. At all events it had left him with no reserves even in his pride to fight his failure and his loss.

In that shrieking hell of August twenty-sixth, or again when lying abandoned and gassed in a way-side hut during that ominous retreat of the Fifth Army, when he had a sudden close vision of himself, trousers tucked into a pair of Gwynne's hunting boots, swearing now and again as he stepped on a hot brick; and heard his groping ego whisper the question through his prostrate mind, he was tempted to answer aloud, to shout "No" above the shrieking of shells and the groans of men fallen about him.

He might no longer love Alexina Groome after twelve or even eight years of complete severance; and, indeed, save in flashing moments like these he had seldom thought of her after the first two or three years; but at least she had taken the edge from his power to suffer.

He had lost his mother soon after his return with the body of her youngest child, his father had died three years later, and he had accepted these griefs with the composure of maturity. Although he had had some agreeable adventures (not that he had had much time for either women or society) he had taken devilish good care not to get in too deep - even if he still possessed the power to love at all, which he doubted.

He remembered also, what he had almost forgotten, that during that walk it had come to him with the sharpness of surprise that the image of the girl who clung to his mind with the tentacles of a devil-fish, was as he had seen her standing under the oak tree while unaware of his presence: older, a more dignified and thoughtful figure, a woman old enough to be his mate in something more than youthful passion, the ideal woman of vague sweet dreams; not as the thoughtless little coquette who had tempted him to ruin his chances by acting like a cave brute.

Given a fortnight longer, during which he remained master of himself instead of a young fool with a smashed temperament, and the unfledged woman in her, whose subtle projection he had witnessed during that moment of his capitulation, would have recognized him as her mate; as for the moment she had in his arms.

Not the least of his ordeals during those last days was the inevitable call on Gora Dwight. He felt like a cad, after what she had been to him at the end of an appalling experience, to have let, nearly three weeks go by with no apparent recognition of her existence. But he had been unable to find a messenger, there was no post; and then, after his ill-starred visit to Rincona, he had forgotten her until his final visit to the undertaker; when she had seemed to stand, an indignant and reproachful figure, at the head of the casket.

III

He had a note in his pocket and hoped she would be out. But she opened the door herself, and her dark face, thinner than he recalled it, flushed and then turned pale. But she said calmly as she extended her hand: "Come in. I wondered what had become of you." "I'm sorry. But - perhaps - you can understand - it was not easy for me to come here!"

"Of course. Come up to my diggings."

He followed her up to the attic studio, where as before he took the easy chair and accepted one of her cigarettes; which he professed to be grateful for as his were exhausted and every decent brand in town had gone up in smoke.

Gora was deeply disappointed that she had received no warning of his call, for she possessed an extremely becoming and richly embroidered silk Chinese cost-ume, as red as the flames that had devoured Chinatown a few days after she had bought it at a bankrupt sale. She had put it on every afternoon for a week, hoping and expecting that he would call; and now that she had on her second-best tailored suit, and a darned if immaculate shirtwaist, he had chosen to turn, up!...But at least the lapels of the jacket had recently been faced with red, and it curved closely over her beautiful bust. Moreover, she had just finished rearranging the masses of her rich brown hair when the bell rang.

And she had him for a time, perhaps for an hour! She set out the tea things as an intimation of the refreshment he would get at the proper time....

She too had suffered during this past interminable fortnight, but Gora was far more mature than the young Englishman, upon whom life until the last few weeks had smiled so persistently. She was too complex, she had suffered in too many ways, from too many causes, not all of them elevating, to be capable upon so short a notice, even after a night of unique companionship, of such whole-souled agony and despair. In her imagination, her sense of drama, her vanity, in the fading of vague dazzling hopes of a future to which he held the key, and perhaps a little in her stormy heart, she had felt a degree of harsh disappointment, but she had already half-recovered; and as she sat looking at his ravaged face she wondered that the death of a sister, no matter how harrowing the conditions, could make such a wreck of any man.

He told her of his difficulties in finding some one to remove the body from the vault to the undertaker's, of the delay in obtaining a private car, gave her some idea of his disorganized life since they had parted, but made no mention of Alexina Groome or Rincona. Then he politely asked her if she had any new plans for the future. Nobody seemed to look forward to the same old life.

Gora shrugged her shoulders with a movement expressive of irritation. "My brother, who is engaged to Alexina Groome, insists that I give up this lodging house."

"Oh, so they are engaged?" Gathbroke lit another cigarette, and his hand did not tremble; he felt as if his nerves had been immersed in ice water and frozen.

"Yes - marvelously. The family, as might be expected, is furious. But the girl is mad about him and of age. She is just a foolish child and should be locked up. My brother is not in the least what she imagines him. She wrote me a letter. Good heaven! One would think she had captured the prince of a fairy tale, or the hero of an old romantic novel. There should be a law prohibiting girls from marrying before they are twenty-two at least....However, the thing is done. And my brother is terribly afraid they'll find out that I keep a lodging house. He's given them to understand we both board here. They are prime snobs and so is he. I never dreamed it was in him until he began to go about in society, but then you never know what is in anybody. Otherwise, he is harmless enough, and a good industrious boy, but he'll never make the money to keep up with that set, and she won't have much. It's a stupid affair all round...."

"I've refused to budge until he finds me a job. He certainly cannot support me, even if I were willing to be supported by any one. As far as I am concerned they could know I kept a lodging house and welcome. It is honest and it gives me a good living; and, what I value more, many hours of freedom. But Mortimer is not only positively terrified they'll find it out, but he is as obstinate over it as - well, as that kind of man always is. He's looking about, and I fancy my fate is stenography or bookkeeping: I took a course at a business college shortly before my mother died. I don't know that he'd like that much better; he hinted that I might be a librarian in a small town. But I'll be hanged if I fall for that."

Gathbroke smiled. "Not that. You don't belong to the country town. But I fancy you'll have to give up the lodging house. Elton Gwynne took me down the Peninsula one day, and - well - I don't fancy they would stand for it. Aristocracies are aristocracies the world over. They may talk democracy, and really modify themselves a bit, but there are certain things they'd choke on if they tried to swallow them, and they won't even try. Better give it up before they find it out and tackle you. I don't fancy you'd stand for that. It would be devilish disagreeable. You've got to know and be more or less intimate with them all - "

"I'll not be patronized by them. I don't know that I'll go near them. For years I've resented that I was not one of them, but I don't fancy tagging in after my brother, treated with pleasant courteous resignation, invited once a year to a family dinner, and quite forgotten on smart occasions."

"Quite so. I like your spunk. Have you thought of being a nurse? All work is hard and I should think that would be interesting. Must meet a jolly lot of people. You should see the becoming uniforms the London nurses wear. Prettiest women on the street, by Jove."

Her heart sank but she replied evenly: "Not a bad idea. I've quite enough saved to take the course comfortably - "

He had a flash of memory. "And that would give you time to win your reputation as a writer. Then the nursing would be merely one more resource."

"It was nice of you to remember that. I'll consider the nursing proposition, and when you have your next war I'll go over and nurse you. That part of it - a war nurse - would be mighty interesting."

The words were spoken idly, merely to avert a pause, and forgotten as soon as uttered. But as a matter of fact the next time they met was when he looked up from his cot in the hospital after he had been retrieved from the hut by two of his devoted Tommies, and saw the odd pale eyes of Gora Dwight close above his own.

# BOOK II

## CHAPTER I

I

Gora closed the door of Mrs. Groome's room as the clock struck two, the old Ballinger clock that had seemed to toll the hours on a deep note of solemn acquiescence for the past six weeks.

She crossed the hall and entered Alexina's room without knocking. Mortimer, during the past fortnight, had moved from the room adjoining his wife's to one at the back of the house, lest it should be necessary to call Alexina in the night. He worked very hard.

Alexina still occupied her old room in the front of the house where the creaking eucalyptus trees sometimes brushed the window pane. It had been refurnished and fitted in various elusive shades of pink by Mrs. Abbott as her wedding present. There was a dim point of light above a gas jet and Gora saw that Alexina was asleep. The pillows were on the floor. She was lying flat, her arms thrown out, the dusky fine mass of her hair spread over the low head board. Her clear olive cheeks were pale with sleep and her eyelashes looked like two little black clouds.

Gora watched her for a moment. Why awaken the poor child? She was sleeping as peacefully as if that tall old clock of her forefathers had not tolled out the last of another generation of Ballingers. Her soft red lips were half parted.

It was now three years since her marriage but she still looked like a very young girl. Gora always felt vaguely sorry for her although she seemed happy enough. At all events it was quite obvious that she did little thinking except when she remembered to wish for a baby.

Gora wore the white uniform of a nurse, and a little cap with wings on the coronet of her heavy hair. It was a becoming costume and made her eyes in their dark setting look less pale and cold.

She had a secret contempt for most of the old conventions but she had given her word to awaken Alexina the moment any change occurred, and she reluctantly shook her sister-in-law's shoulder.

II

Alexina sprang out of bed on the instant.

"Mother?" she cried. "Is she worse?"

Gora nodded.

Alexina made a dart for the door, but Gora threw a strong arm about her. Those arms had held more than one violent man in his bed. "Better wait," she said softly.

Alexina's body grew rigid as she slowly drew back on Gora's arm and stared up at her. In a moment she asked in a hard steady voice: "Is my mother dead?"

"Yes. It was very sudden. I had no time to telephone for the doctor; to call you. She was sleeping. I was sitting beside her. Suddenly I knew that she had stopped breathing - "

"Would you mind telephoning to Maria and Sally? Maria will never forgive herself - but mother seemed so much better - "

"I will telephone at once. Shall I call Mortimer?"

"No. Why disturb him?"

Gora, watching Alexina, saw a curious remoteness enter the depths of her eyes, and her own narrowed with something of her old angry resentment. In this hour of profound sorrow, when the human heart is quite honest, Alexina, however her conscious mind might be averted from the fact, regarded Mortimer Dwight as an outsider, an agreeable alien who had no permanent place in the immense permanency of the Ballinger-Groomes. She wanted only her own family, her own inherent sort. Sally had hastened to California as soon as her mother's illness had been pronounced dangerous, and had stayed in the house until a week ago when she had been ordered by the doctor to Santa Barbara to get rid of a heavy cold on her chest. She had telegraphed the day before that she was threatened with pneumonia, and Maria, assured that her mother was in no immediate danger, had gone down to spend two days with her.

Possibly Alexina caught a flash from the mind of this strange and interesting sister-in-law, for she added hastily:

"You know how hard Mortimer works, poor dear. And I do not feel in the least like crying. I shall write telegrams to Ballinger and Geary: my brothers, you know." (Gora ground her teeth.) "It was too sad they could not get here, but Ballinger is in South America and Geary on a diet. I must also write a cablegram to an old friend of mine who has married a Frenchman, Olive de Morsigny. She was always so fond of mother. Would you also mind telephoning to Rincona about seven?"

"I'll do all the telephoning. Go back to bed as soon as possible. It is only a little after two." As Gora turned to leave the room Alexina put her hand on her arm and summoned a faint sweet smile.

"I cannot tell you how grateful I am, Gora dear, how grateful we all are. You have been simply wonderful -"

"I am a good nurse if I do say it myself," said Gora lightly. "But you must remember there are others quite as good; and that I - ".

"I know you would do your duty as devotedly by any stranger." Alexina interrupted her with sweet insistence. "But it has been wonderful to be able to have you, all the same. It has also given me the chance to know you at last, and I shall never quite let you go again."

Gora, to her secret anger, had never accustomed herself to the unswerving graciousness of these people, and all that it implied, but her sharp mind had long since warned her that as she had neither the position nor the training to emulate it, at least she must not betray a sense of social inferiority by open resentment.

Her voice was deep and naturally abrupt but she achieved a fair imitation of Alexina's sweet cordiality. "It has meant quite as much to me, Alexina, I can assure you. And now that I am on my own and shall have a day or two between cases I know where I shall spend them. I am only too thankful that I graduated in time to take care of dear Mrs. Groome. Write your telegrams and I will give them to the doctor when he comes. I must telephone to him at once."

III

After she had gone Alexina wrote not only her telegrams and cablegrams, but the "letters to follow." It was nearly four o'clock when she finished. Old Dr. Maitland had not yet come and she put her bulletins on the table in the hall.

She heard Gora moving about her mother's room and retreated into her own. She did not want to go to her mother yet nor did she care particularly to see Gora again, although she had certainly been very nice and a great comfort to them all.

Alexina was quite unaware that her attitude to her sister-in-law was one of unconsicous condescension, of a well-bred determination never to wound the pride of a social inferior. She found Gora an "interesting personality" and quite extraordinarily efficient.

It had been the greatest relief to all the family when that very capable Miss Dwight - Gora, that is; one must remember - had been brought by Dr. Maitland to take charge of the case after Mrs. Groome's cardiac trouble became acute and she demanded constant attention.

Gora had slept in Mrs. Groome's bedroom for six weeks, relieved for several hours of the afternoon by a member of the family or one of Mrs. Groome's many anxious friends. It was her first case and it interested her profoundly. Moreover, her personal devotion placed her for the moment on a certain basis of equality with a family whose mental processes were quite transparent to her contemptuous mind. She was excessively annoyed with herself for still caring, but the roots were too deep, and there had been nothing in her life during the past three years to diminish her fierce sense of democracy as she interpreted it.

Alexina had never given a thought to her sister-in-law's psychology, although the sensitive plates of her brain received an impression now and again of a violent inner life behind that business-like exterior. But she had seen little of her until lately, and during the past six weeks her mind had been too concentrated upon her mother's sufferings and possible danger to have any disposition for analysis.

She certainly did not feel the least need of her now. She wished, indeed, that she had asked Aileen to remain in the house last night. Aileen was her own age, they had been intimate since childhood, often without the slightest regard for each other's feelings, and was more like a sister than even dear Sally and Maria.

Suddenly she determined to go to her. She had her own latch key and would disturb no one but Aileen. She dressed herself warmly and slipped down stairs and out of the house.

# CHAPTER II

I

The city below - the new solid city - was obliterated under a heavy fog, pierced here and there by steeples and towers that looked like jagged dark rocks in that white and tranquil sea.

On Angel Island and on the north shore of the bay the deep sad bells were tolling their warning to moving craft; and from out at sea, beyond the Golden Gate, the fog horn sent forth its long lugubrious groans. The bells sounded muffled, so dense was the fog, and there was no other sound in the sleeping city.

Alexina wrapped her long cloak more closely about her and pulled the hood over her head.

As she walked slowly down the steep avenue it came to her with something of a shock that she had not thought of her husband since she had expressed to Gora her reluctance to disturb him.

She was doing the least conventional thing possible in leaving the house at four o'clock in the morning to seek the sympathy of a girl friend when any other young wife she knew (unless getting a divorce) would have flown to her husband and wept out her sorrow in his arms.

And she had been married only three years, and found Mortimer quite as irreproachable as ever, always kind, thoughtful, and considerate. He assuredly would have said just the right things to her and not have resented in the least being deprived of a few hours of rest.

On the contrary, he would no doubt resent being ignored, for not only was he devoted to his lovely young wife but such behavior was unorthodox, and he disliked the unorthodox exceedingly.

Well, she didn't want him and that was the end of it. He didn't fill the present bill. She had never regretted her marriage, for he had quite measured up to the best feats of her maiden imagination. He made love charmingly, he was manly chivalrous and honorable, and his eager spontaneity of manner when he arrived home at six o'clock every evening never varied; to whatever level of flatness he might drop immediately afterward. When they entered a ballroom or a restaurant she knew that they made a "stunning couple" and that people commented upon their good looks, their harmonious slenderness and inches, and contrasts in nature's coloring.

II

Alexina, almost unconsciously, sat down on a bench under the trees. Her mind sought the pleasant past as a brief respite from the present; she knew that that part of her mind called heart was frozen by the suddenness of her mother's death, and that her emotions would be fluid a few hours hence.

They had had a simply heavenly time together until her mother's illness. As a clerk in the family was unthinkable Mrs. Groome had lent him the insurance on one of her burned buildings and he had started a modest exporting and importing house, that being the only business of which he had any knowledge. Judge Lawton and Tom Abbott had suggested that he open an insurance office, or start himself in any business where little capital besides office furniture was needed; as Mrs. Groome's advisors they were averse to launching any of her moderate fortune on a doubtful venture. But Dwight had insisted that he was more likely to succeed in a business he understood than in one of which he knew nothing, and Mrs. Groome had agreed with him. Judge Lawton and Abbott paid over the insurance money with the worst grace possible.

And then Mortimer had a piece of the most astounding good luck. His aunt Eliza Goring had left stock in a mine which had run out of pay ore soon after her investment, and shut down. It had recently been recapitalized and a new vein discovered. Mrs. Goring's executor had sold her stock for something under twenty thousand dollars, delivering the proceeds, as directed in her will, to two of her amazed heirs, Mortimer and Gora Dwight.

Gora had been opposed to her brother leaving the firm of Cheever Harrison and Cheever, where, beyond question, he would be head of a department in time and safely anchored for life; but he had taken the step, and she reasoned that he must have a considerable knowledge of a business with which he had been associated for fourteen years, she knew his energy and powers of application, and she resented the attitude of "the family." Appreciating what his triumph would mean to him she had consented to invest her inheritance in his business and enable him to make immediate restitution to Mrs. Groome. As a matter of fact his "stock did go up" with the family, particularly as he seemed to be doing well and had the reputation of working harder than any young man on the street. As he had anticipated, a good deal of business was thrown his way.

He had accepted as a matter of course Mrs. Groome's invitation to live with her, paying, as he insisted upon it, a stipulated sum toward the current expenses. He thought her offer quite natural; not only would she be lonely without the child of her old age, but she must desire that Alexina continue to live in the conditions to which she was accustomed; the sum Mrs. Groome consented to accept would not have kept them in a fashionable family hotel, much less an apartment with several servants.

Moreover, housing room was scarce; they might have been obliged to live across the Bay; and, in his opinion, the duty of parents to their offspring never ceased.

Alexina at that time thought every sentiment he expressed "simply great," and had continued to feed from her mother's hand even in the matter of pin money. Mortimer felt it to be right, so he told her, to put his surplus profits back in his business; all he could spare he needed for "front," to say nothing of pleasant little dinners at restaurants to their hospitable young friends; who thought it no adequate return to be asked to dine on Ballinger Hill.

Moreover, he often gave her a far handsomer present than he should have done, considering the "hard times;" or at least she would have preferred that he give her the combined values in the form of a monthly allowance; she would have enjoyed the sensation of being in a measure supported by her husband.

However, she and her mother assured each other that he was bound to make a fortune in time, and then she would have an allowance as large as that of Sibyl Thorndyke, who had married Frank Bascom.

It had been like playing at marriage. Alexina put it into concrete words. Subconsciously she had always known it. She had had no cares, no responsibilities. She had merely continued to play, to keep her imagination on that plane sometimes called the fool's paradise.

## III

She realized abruptly that here was the secret of her longing for children. They would have been the real thing, given a serious translation to life.

But she had enjoyed the gay life of her little world, nevertheless, and with all the abandon of a youth which had just closed its first long chapter in that silent room on top of the hill. And no one could have asked for a more delightful companion to play with than Morty, when his working hours were over.

Mortimer loved society. It had been simply delicious, poor darling, to watch his secret delight, under his perfect repose, the first time they spent a week-end in Mrs. Hunter's magnificent "villa" at Burlingame. Even Aileen had treated his initiation as a matter of course; and they had spent the afternoon at the club, where he drank whiskey and soda on equal terms with many millionaires.

IV

It was doubtful if he enjoyed similarly his first visit to Rincona during their engagement: after all the powwow was over and the family had grimly surrendered to avoid the scandal of an elopement.

Alexina recalled that dreadful day. They had all sat on the verandah on the shady side of the house: her mother, Aunt Clara Groome, Maria, Susan Belling and Grace Montgomery, Tom Abbott's sisters, whose homes were in Alta, and Coralie Geary, born Brannan, of Fair Oaks (now Atherton) who had married a nephew of Mrs. Groome. All these were as one united family. They met every day, wandering in and out at all hours, and although they had many healthy disagreements they agreed on all the fine old fundamentals, and they stood by one another through thick and thin.

The hair of all looked freshly washed. Their complexions had perished asking no quarter. Mrs. Montgomery and Mrs. Geary were as slim and smart as Mrs. Abbott, but the others were expanding rapidly, and Aunt Clara, who was only a year older than Mrs. Groome, was shamelessly fat, and her face was so weather-beaten that the freckled skin hung as loosely as her old wrapper.

All wore white, the simplest white, and all sewed quietly for the new refugee babies; all except Alexina who talked feverishly to cover the awful pauses, and young Joan, who had crawled under the table and stuffed an infant's flannel petticoat into her mouth to muffle her giggles.

Tom had escaped to the golf links. Mortimer sat in the midst of the Irregular circle and smoked three cigars. He smiled when he spoke, which was seldom, and appeared appreciative of the determined efforts to be "nice" of these ladies who had called him Mortimer as soon as he arrived, and who made him fed more like a poor relation whose feelings must be spared, every moment.

Finally Alexina, who was on the verge of hysteria, dragged Joan from under the table, and the two carried him off to the tennis court.

In subsequent visits, now covering a period of three years, their gracious civil "kind" attitude had never varied, save only when their consciences hurt them for disliking him more than usual, and then they were not only heroic but fairly effusive in their efforts to be nice.

Nevertheless, it was quite patent to Alexina that he enjoyed smoking his after-dinner cigar on that old verandah whose sweet-scented vines had been planted in the historic sixties; or under the ancient oaks of the park where he dreamed aloud to her of sitting under similar oaks of England, the guest of Lady Barnstable or Lady Arrowmount, belles of the eighties who faithfully exchanged letters once a year with Maria Abbott and Coralie Geary.

From the family there was always the refuge of the tennis court and he played an excellent game. He also seemed to enjoy those dinners given them in certain other old Peninsula mansions, and if they were dull he was duller.

# V

Alexina had admitted to herself some time since (never to that wretch, Aileen Lawton) that he *was* rather dull, poor darling.

For a long time the aftermath of the earthquake and fire had supplied topics for conversation. For quite two years there had been an acutely painful interest in the Graft Prosecution, which, beginning with an attempt merely to bring to justice the political boss, his henchman the mayor, and his ignorant obedient board of supervisors, had unthinkably resolved itself into a declaration of war, with State's Prison as its goal, upon some of the most prominent capitalists in San Francisco.

The prosecution had been started by a small group of eminent citizens, bent upon cleaning up their city, notorious for graft, misgovernment, and the basest abuses of political power. They had assumed as a matter of course that those of their own class, who for years had expressed in private their bitter resentment against paying out small fortunes to the board of supervisors every time they wanted a franchise, would be only too glad to expose the malefactors.

But it immediately transpired that they had no intention whatever of admitting to the world that they had been guilty of corruption and bribery. They might have been "held up," forced to "come through," or renounce their great enterprises; helpless, in other words; but the law had technical terms for their part in the shameful transactions, and so had the public.

All solemnly vowed that they had neither been approached by the city administration for bribe money, nor paid a cent for franchises, some of which the prosecution knew had cost them no less than two hundred thousand dollars. Therefore did the prosecutors change their tactics. Supervisors, by various means, were induced to confess, and the Grand Jury indicted not only the boss and the mayor, but a large number of eminent citizens.

Society was riven in twain. Life-long friends cut one another, and now and again they burst into hysteria as they did it. Mrs. Ferdinand Thornton, at a dinner party, left the room as Mrs. Hofer entered it, and Mrs. Hofer gave a magnificent exhibition of Celtic temperament.

The editor who supported the prosecution with the full strength of his historic sheet was kidnapped. The prosecuting attorney was shot in the court room by a former convict who afterward was found dead in his cell. There were moments when it looked as if excited mobs would reinstitute the lynch law of the fifties.

Nothing came of it all but such a prolonged exposure of general vileness that it was possible to effect a certain number of reforms later by popular vote. The system remained inviolate, even during the mayorship of a fine old citizen too estimable to build up a rival machine; and the men of the prosecution, after many bitter harassed months, when they walked and slept with their lives in their hands, resigned themselves to the fact that no San Francisco jury would ever convict a man who had the money to bribe it.

All this had given Mortimer abundant material for conversation and he had entertained Mrs. Groome and

Alexina night after night with a report of the day's events and the gossip of the street. Mrs. Groome had been intensely interested, for this upheaval reminded her of personal episodes in the life of her husband and father, the latter having been a member of the vigilance committees of the fifties.

She had been so delighted with the efforts of the prosecuting group to bring the boss and the mayor to justice that she had permitted Alexina to invite the Hofers to dinner; but when men of her own proud circle were accused of crimes against society and threatened with San Quentin, nothing could convince her of their guilt; and she asked Alexina to follow the example of Maria and cut that Mrs. Hofer.

Alexina had never been interested in the details of the prosecution; the large moments of the drama and the social convulsions were enough for her. She refused to cut Mrs. Hofer, although she ceased to call on her, as her mother and her husband made such a point of it; but she gave little thought to the sorrows of that ambitious young matron. She had other fish to fry.

Two great hotels whose interiors had been swept by the fire were renovated and furnished and their restaurants and ballrooms eagerly patronized. The Assembly balls were resumed. There were dinners and dances in the Western Addition, where many of the finest homes in the city had been built during the past ten or twenty years; and entertaining Down the Peninsula had not paused for more than two months after the disaster.

Nevertheless, she had exulted in the fact that the husband of her choice was able to please and entertain her mother-no easy feat. Moreover, as time went on and interest in the Graft Prosecution wore thin, it was evident that Mortimer had established himself firmly in his mother-in-law's graces. He was not only the perfect husband but the son of her old age.

She had lost Ballinger and Geary in her comparative youth, and Tom was rarely in the house when she visited Rincona. But Mortimer was as devoted to her in the little ways so appreciated by women of any age as he was to his wife, and he was noiseless in the house and as prompt as the clock. During her illness his devotion touched even Mrs. Abbott, although Mrs. Groome was the only member of the family he ever won over.

VI

Poor Morty. In a way he was a failure, after all. The men of her set did not seem to care any more for him than they did before her marriage, although they were always polite and amiable; and the promise of those old family friends to throw business in his way seemed to be forgotten as time went on.

No doubt they had thought he was able to stand on his own feet after a while, but he had often looked depressed during the panic of nineteen-seven and the long period of business drought that had followed. Still, he had managed to hold his own, and his constitutional optimism was unshaken. He *knew* that when times changed he would soon be a rich man, and Alexina shared his faith. Not that she had ever cared particularly for great wealth, but he talked so much about it that he had excited her imagination; after all money was the thing these days, no doubt of that, and she had heard "poor talk" all her life and was tired of it.

Moreover, nothing could be more positive than that if Morty's father had made a fortune in his own day, and the son inherited and administered it with the canny vigilance which distinguished the sons of rich men to-day from the mad spendthrifts of a former generation, he would be as logically intimate with those young capitalists who were the renewed pillars of San Francisco society, as she was with the most aloof and important of her own sex.

She had heard Judge Lawton and other men say that if a man were still a clerk at thirty he was hopeless. The ruts were packed with the mediocre whose destiny was the routine work of the world, whatever might be their secret opinions of their unrecognized abilities and their resentment against a system that anchored them.

The young man of brains and initiative, of energy, ambition, vision and balance, provided he were honorable as well, and temperate in his pleasures, was the man the eager world was always waiting for.

Alexina knew that the United States was almost as prolific in this fine breed of young men as she still was in opportunities for the exceptional of every class.

And it was possible that Mortimer was not one of them.

Once more she put a fact into bald words. She knew that her butterfly youth had come to an end with her mother's death, and for a year she should be very much alone, to say nothing of her new burden of responsibilities. Thinking during that period was inevitable. She might as well begin now.

Mortimer had some of those gifts. He worked like a dog, he was ambitious and temperate and he was the soul of honor. But although his brain was clear enough, the blindest love would, perceive in time that it lacked originality.

Did it also lack initiative, resource, that peculiar alertness and quick pouncing quality of which she had heard? She wished she knew, but she had never discussed her husband with any one. Certainly he had stood still. Or was that merely the fault of the hard times? She had heard other men complain as bitterly.

"Fate handed you a lemon, old girl."

Alexina could almost hear Aileen's mocking voice. She even gave a startled glance down the quiet avenue. Well, she would never discuss him with Aileen or any one else.

Did she love him any longer? Had she ever loved him? What was love? She had been quite happy with him in her own little way. What did girls of eighteen know of love? Deliberately in her youthful arrogance and unlicensed imagination she had manufactured a fool's paradise; and, a hero being indispensable, had dragged him in after her.

Perhaps she still loved him. She had read and seen enough to know that love changed its character as the years went on. She respected his many admirable qualities and she would never forget his devotion to her mother.

She certainly liked him. And the family attitude roused her obstinate championship as much as ever. At least she would always remain his good friend, helping him as far as lay in her power. She had deliberately selected her life partner and she would keep her part of the contract. He filled his to the letter, or as far as in him lay. If he were not the masterful superman of her dreams, at least he was quite obstinate enough to have his own way in many things, in spite of his unswerving devotion to her charming self. He was whitely angry when she received Bob Cheever one afternoon when she was alone, and had forbidden her ever to receive a man in the daytime again. If men wanted to call on a married woman they could do so in the evening. She no longer danced more than twice with any man at a party, and he refused to read her favorite books, new or old, and chilled any attempt to discuss them in his presence.

## VII

Well, after all, what did it matter? She had dreamed her dream and he was better than most. She sprang to her feet and ran down the hill and across the street to the house of Judge Lawton.

# CHAPTER III

## I

Gora waited until her brother had finished his bath and returned to his room. When she was admitted he had a brush in either hand polishing his pale brown immaculately cut hair. He turned to her, startled, his good American gray eyes showing no trace of sleep. He always awoke with alert mind and refreshed body.

"What is it? Not - "

Gora nodded. "At two this morning. Alexina wouldn't let me call you - "

His wide masculine eyebrows met. It was correct to be angry and he was. "I never heard of such a thing - "

"She was not a bit overcome and wrote letters to her brothers and friends for at least two hours. It really wouldn't have been worth while to disturb you - I must say I was astonished; thought she'd go to pieces - but you never know."

"I'll go to her at once."

"I'd dress first. Aileen Lawton is with her."

Gora knew that Alexina had gone out at four in the morning and returned half an hour since, but the cat in her was of the tiger variety and never descended to small game.

"Oh, of course!" Mortimer gave a groan of resignation as he hunted out a pair of black socks. "I like Aileen well enough, but she has altogether too much influence over Alexina. She'd have more than myself if I didn't keep a close watch."

"I have an idea that no one will have much influence over Alexina as time goes on. She hasn't that jaw and chin for nothing. They mean things in some people."

He gave her a quick suspicious glance, but her pale gray eyes were fixed on the windmill beyond the window, that odd old landmark in a now fashionable quarter of San Francisco.

"I shall always control her," he said, setting his large finely cut lips. "I wish her to remain a child as long as possible, for she is quite perfect as she is. She is bright and all that, but of course she has no intellect - "

Gora forgot her message of death and laughed outright.

"Men - American men, anyhow - are really the funniest things in the world. Even intellectual men are absurd in their patronizing attitude toward the cleverest of women; but when it conies to mere masculine arrogance...don't you really respect any woman's brains?"

"I never denied that some women were clever and all that, but the best of them cannot compare with men. You must admit that."

"I admit nothing of the sort, but I know your type too well to waste any time in argument - "

"My type?"

She longed to reply: "The smaller a man's brain the more enveloping his mere male arrogance. Instinct of self-defense like the turtle's shell or the porcupine's quills or the mephitic weasel's extravasations." But she never quarreled with Morty, and to have shared with him her opinion of his endowments would have been to deprive herself of a good deal of secret amusement.

"Oh, you're all alike," she said lightly, and added: "Don't be too sure that Alexina hasn't intellect-the real thing. When she emerges from this beatific dream of youth she has almost hugged to death for fear it might escape her, and begins to think - "

"I'll do her thinking."

"All right, dear. You have my best wishes. But keep on the job....I'll clear out; you want to dress - "

"Wait a moment." He sat down to draw on his socks. "I'm really cut up over Mrs. Groome's death. She was my only friend in this damn family, and I coveted her money so little that I wish she could have lived on for twenty years."

"I wondered how you liked them as time went on."

He brought his teeth together and thrust out his jaw. "I hate the whole pack of superior patronizing condescending snobs, and it is all I can do to keep it from Alexina, who thinks her tribe perfection. But, by God!" - he brought down his fist on his knee - "I'll beat them at their own game yet. I simply live to make a million and build a house at Burlingame. They really respect money as much as they think they don't; I've got oil to that. When I'm a rich roan they'll think of me as their equal and forget I was ever anything' else."

"Well, don't speculate," said Gora uneasily. "Remember that luck was left out of our family."

"My luck changed with that legacy. I am certain of it. I have only to wait until this period of dry rot passes - "

"But you're not speculating?"

He looked at her with eyes as cold as her own.

"I answer questions about my private affairs to no one."

"They are my affairs to the extent of half your capital."

"You have received your interest regularly, have you not?"

"Yes."

"Then you have nothing to worry about. I understand business, as well as the man's opportunities, and you do not."

"I did not ask out of curiosity, but because I shall be

glad when you are doing well enough to let me have my eight thousand - "

"What do you want of it? Where could you get more interest?"

"Nowhere, possibly. But some day I shall want to take a vacation, a fling. I shall want to go to New York and Europe."

"And you would throw away your capital!"

"Why not? I have other capital in my profession; and, although you will find this difficult to grasp, in my head. I have practiced fiction writing for years. It is just ten months since I tried to get anything published, and I have recently had three stories accepted by New York magazines: one of the old group and two of the best of the popular magazines."

He looked at her with cold distaste, which deepened in a moment to alarm. "I hope you will not use your own name. These people who think themselves so much above us anyhow, look upon authors and artists and all that as about on a level with the working class - "

"I shall use my own name and ram it down their throats. They worship success like all the rest of the world. Their fancied distaste for people engaged in any of the art careers - with whom they practically never come in contact, by the way - is partly an instinctive distrust of anything they cannot do themselves and partly because they have an Elizabethan idea that all artists are common and have offensive manners."

"I don't like the idea of your using your own name.

Ladies may unfortunately be obliged to earn their own living - and that you shall never do when I am rich - but they have no business putting their names up before the public like men."

Gora looked at his rigid indomitable face; the face of the Pilgrim fathers, of the revolutionary statesmen, which he had inherited intact from old John Dwight who had sat in the first congress; the American classic face that is passing but still crops out as unexpectedly as the last drop from a long forgotten "tar brush," or the sly recurrent Biblical profile.

"We will make a bargain," she said calmly. "I will ask you no more questions about your business for a year - when, if convenient, I should like my money - and you will kindly ignore the literary career I mean to have. It won't do you the least good in the world to formulate opinions about anything I choose to do. Now, better concentrate on Alexina. You've got your hands full there. See you at breakfast." And she shut the door on an indignant worried and disgusted brother.

# CHAPTER IV

I

When Mortimer, after tapping on his wife's door, was bidden to enter he found her sitting with Aileen over a breakfast tray, the belated tears running down into her coffee. Aileen, promising to return after she had given her father his breakfast, made a hasty retreat; and Dwight took his wife in his arms and soothed the grief which grew almost hysterical in its reaction from the insensibility of the morning.

"You won't leave me for a moment?" she sobbed, in this mood finding his sympathy exquisite and necessary. "You'll stay home - until - until - "

"Of course. I'll telephone Wicksam after breakfast. He can run the office for a day or two. By the way Maria will be here this evening; Sally is better. Joan and Tom and the rest will be here in about an hour. Tom and I will attend to everything. You are not to bother, not to think."

"Oh, you are too wonderful - always so strong - so strong - how I love it. But I'll never get over this - poor old mommy!"

But the paroxysm passed, and just as Mortimer was on the verge of morning starvation and too polite to mention it, she grew calm by degrees and sent him down to breakfast. The emotional phase of her grief was over.

# CHAPTER V

I

It was three months later that Aileen, once more sitting in Alexina's bedroom, after her return from Santa Barbara, where she had gone with her father for the summer, said abruptly: "Dad is terribly cut up, dear old thing. He'd known your mother since they were both children, in the days when there were wooden side-walks on Montgomery Street, and Laurel Hill was called Lone Mountain, and they had picnics in it. Odd they both should have had young daughters. Another link - what? as the English say. Well - anyhow - he told me to tell you that he was just as fond of your father as of your mother, and that you must try to imagine that he is your father from this time forth, and come to him when you are in doubt about anything."

Alexina looked her straight in the eyes. "I have sometimes thought uncle daddy didn't like Mortimer."

"On the contrary, he rather likes him. He respects a capacity for hard work, and persistence, and a reputa-tion for uncompromising honesty. But of course Mortimer is young - in business, that is; and father

Gertrude Atherton

thinks - but you had better talk with him."

"No. Why should I? But I don't mind you. At least I could not discuss Mortimer with any one else. I am furious with Tom Abbott. He wants me to put my money in trust, with himself and uncle daddy as trustees - ignoring Mortimer, whom he pretends to like. He says Maria's fortune has been kept intact, that he has never touched a cent of it, but that men in business are likely to get into tight places and use their wife's money. Nothing would induce Mortimer to touch my money, but he would feel pretty badly cut up if I let any one else look after my affairs. Of course I wouldn't even discuss the matter with Tom. And if Morty does need money at any time I'll lend it to him. Why not? What else would any one expect me to do?"

"Of course Tom Abbott went to work the wrong way, the blundering idiot. No one doubts Mortimer's good faith, but the times are awful, money has paresis; and when you are obliged to take any of your own out of the stocking in order to keep business going, it is easily lost. Dad hopes you will hang on like grim death to your inheritance. You see - the times are so abnormal, Mortimer hasn't had time to prove his abilities yet; he's just been able to hold on; and if things don't mend and he should lose out, why - if you still have your own little fortune, at least you'll not be any worse off than, you are now. Don't you see?"

"Yes, I see. But Mortimer has told me of other panics and bad times. They always pass, and better times come again. And if he has been able to hold on, that at least shows ability, for others have gone under. Of course we shall live here and run the house - as mother did. I couldn't bear to live anywhere else, and Morty adores it too."

"Oh, rather. I couldn't imagine you anywhere else."

"Geary and Ballinger sent me ten thousand dollars for a wedding present and Morty bought some bonds for me, but I'm going to sell a few and refurnish the lower rooms. I love the old house but I like cheerful modern things. The poor old parlors and dining-room do look like sarcophagi."

"Good. I'll help. We'll have no end of fun."

II

There was a pause and then Alexina said: "Mortimer is so determined to be a rich man and thinks of so little else and works so hard, that he is bound to be. Otherwise, such gifts would be meaningless."

She made the statements with an unconscious rising inflection. Aileen did not answer and turned her sharp revealing green eyes on the eucalyptus grove which concealed Ballinger House from the vulgar gaze, and incidentally shut off a magnificent view.

"I don't know whether I like Gora Dwight or not," she remarked.

"Neither do I. But I admire her. She is a wonder."

"Oh, yes, I admire her, and I've a notion she's got something big in her, some sort of destiny. But those light eyes in that dark face give me the creeps. It isn't that I don't trust her. I believe her to be insolently honest and honorable - and just, if you like. But - perhaps it's only the accident of her queer coloring - she gives me the impression that while she might go to the stake for her pride, she'd murder you in cold blood if you got in her way."

"Poor Gora! You make her all the more interesting."

"Did she ever tell you that she corresponds with that Englishman who was out here at the time of the earthquake and fire and had that ghastly adventure with his sister? We all met him at the Hofer ball - Gathbroke his name was."

Alexina was staring at her with an amazed frown. "Correspond - Gora?...I remember now he told me she helped him to carry his sister's body out to the old cemetery. Is he interested in her?"

"I shouldn't wonder. They've corresponded off and on ever since. I walked, home with her one afternoon before I went south - she interests me frantically - and she invited me up to her quite artistic attic in Geary Street, where she still lives, and gave me the most vivid description of that night. It made me crawl. She stared straight before her as she told it. Her eyes were just like gray oval mirrors in which it seemed to me I saw the whole thing pass....

"Then she showed me a photograph he had recently sent her - stunning thing he is, all right, and looks years older than when he was here. She also alluded to things he had said in a letter or two. So my phenomenally quick wits inferred that they correspond. Perhaps they are engaged. Pretty good deal for her."

III

Alexina, to her surprise, felt intensely angry, although she had the presence of mind to cast up her eyes until the white showed below the large brilliant iris and she looked like a saint in a niche.

She had kept Gathbroke out of her thoughts for nearly four years, deliberately. For a time she had hated him. Mortimer's love-making had seemed tame in comparison with that primitive outburst, and never had she felt any such fiery response to the man she had loved and chosen as during those few moments when she had been in that impertinent, outrageous, loathsome young Englishman's arms. At first she had wondered and resented, loyally concluding that it was her own fault, or that of fate for endowing her with such a slender emotional equipment that she used it all up at once on the wrong man. Finally, she found it wise not to think about it at all and to dismiss the intruder from her thoughts.

Now she felt outraged in her sense of posse-ssion....Unconsciously she had enshrined him as the secret mate of her inmost secret self...a self she was barely conscious of even yet...lurking in her subconsci-ousness, the personal and peculiar blend of many and diverse ancestors....Sometimes she had glimpsed it...wondered a little with a not unpleasant sense of apprehension....

But for the most part Circumstance had decreed that she abide on the abundant surface of her nature and enjoy a highly enjoyable life as it came. Now, she had experienced her first grief, which at the same time was her first set-back. She did not go out at all. She saw much of Mortimer and little of any one else. It was the summer season and all her friends were in the country or in Europe.

She had given Mortimer her power of attorney (largely a gesture of defiance, this) and he had attended to all details connected with her new fortune. Between the inheritance tax, small legacies, and depreciations, she would have a little over six thousand dollars a year; which, however, with Mortimer's contribution, would run the old house, and keep her wardrobe up to mark after she went out of mourning. She knew nothing of the value of money, and was accustomed to having little to spend and everything provided. But her mind regarding finances was quite at rest. Even if Mortimer remained a victim of the hard times, they would be quite comfortable.

The cares of housekeeping were very light. She discussed the daily menus with James, but he had run Ballinger House for years, little as Mrs. Groome had suspected it. Mortimer, shortly after his mother-in-law's death, and while Alexina was passing a fortnight at Rincona, had given James orders to collect all bills on the first of every month and hand them to him, together with a statement of the servants' wages. Mrs. Dwight was not to be bothered.

Alexina, when she returned, had made no protest. The details of housekeeping did not appeal to her. But the arrangement left her without occupation, and much time for thought. After a long walk morning and afternoon she had little to do but read. She was an early riser and her mind was active.

IV

Dwight had not the least intention of using his wife's money, for he had perfect confidence in his change of luck, and in his ability to do great things with his business as soon as the period of depression had passed. But he had no faith in any woman's ability to invest and take care of money, he had fixed ideas in regard to a man being master in his own house, and he had asked Alexina for her power of attorney more to flaunt her confidence in him and to annoy her damnable relatives than because there might possibly be a moment when he should have need of immediate resources. Like many Americans he chose to keep his wife in ignorance of his business life, and it would have annoyed him excessively to go to her with an explanation of temporary difficulties and ask for a loan.

Moreover, he wished to keep Alexina young and superficial, ignorant of money matters, indifferent to the sordid responsibilities of life. Not only was the present Alexina no embarrassment whatever to a man full of schemes, aside from the slow march of business, for getting rich, but she was infinitely alluring.

He detested business women, intellectual women, women with careers; they tipped the even balance of the man's world; moreover, they had no accepted place in the higher social scheme. For women wage-earners he had no antipathy and much sympathy and consideration, although he underpaid them cheerfully when circumstances would permit. It was an abiding canker that his sister was obliged to support herself; he was not ashamed of it, for nursing was an honorable (and altruistic) profession, and several young women in his new circle bad taken it up; but he hated it as a man and a brother. As for her turning herself into an authoress, however, he only hoped he would make his million before she got herself talked about.

As for Alexina she was the perfect flower of a system lie worshiped and nothing should mar or change her if his fond surveillance could prevent it.

On the whole he was quite happy at this time, despite his passionate desire for wealth and his natural resentment, at the attitude of the Abbotts and their intimate circle of old friends who were so like them that he always included them in his mind when speaking of "the family." Although he was making barely enough to pay his sister the monthly interest on her money, the salaries of his employees, and, until recently, a monthly contribution to the household expenses, he had a comfortable and delightful home with not a few of the minor luxuries, an undisputed position in the best society, an honorable one in the business world, and a beautiful wife. Now that the conventions forced them to live the retired life, they could economize without attracting attention; as he paid the bills Alexina would not know whether he still contributed his share or not; (in time he meant to pay the whole and give his wife, with the grand gesture, her entire income for pin money) and, with Alexina's cordial assent, he had sold the old carriage, and the horses, which were eating their heads off, dismissed the coachman-gardener, and found a young Swede to take care of the garden and outbuildings.

Later, they would have their car like other people, but there was no need for it at present, and it was neither the time nor the occasion to exhibit a tendency to extravagance. In the matter of "front" he knew precisely where to leave off.

In a certain small anxious bag-of-tricks way he was clever. But not clever enough. He knew nothing of Alexina beneath her shining surface. If he had he would have sought to crowd her mind with the details of the home, encouraged her to join in the frantic activities of some one of the women's clubs he held in scorn, persuaded her to play golf daily at the fashionable club of which they were members, even though she ran the risk of talking, unchaperoned by himself, with other men.

He never would have left her to long hours of idleness, with only books for companions (and Alexina cared little for novels lacking in psychology, or in revelations of the many phases of life of which she was personally so ignorant); and only his own companionship evening after evening.

But he had known all the Alexina he was ever to know. Such flashing glimpses as he was destined to have later so bewildered him that he reacted obstinately to his original estimate of her,...just a child under the influence of her family or some of those friends of hers who had always hated him...erratic and irresponsible like all women...a man never could understand women because there was nothing to understand...merely a bundle of contradictions....

In some ways his mental equipment was an enviable one.

# VI

Some of all this Alexina guessed, and although she was nettled at times that he took no note of her maturing mind and character, she was, on the whole, more amused.

Indulgent by nature, and somewhat indolent, she had been more than willing that Morty should enjoy his new authority, should even delude himself that he was footing all the bills, poor dear; and she listened raptly to his evening visions of their future life in Burlingame, alternated with visits to New York and England, the while she puzzled over the intricacies of some character portrayed by a master analyst.

Sometimes he did not talk at all, utterly fagged by a strenuous day in which he had accomplished precisely nothing. But the more transparent and truncated and dull he grew the more spontaneous the "niceness" and almost effusive courtesy of his wife. Insensibly she was veering to the family attitude, but he had tagged her once for all and never saw it.

Until this moment, however, when Gathbroke had been jerked from his deep seclusion within her ivory tower by Aileen's unwelcome news, she had never had a moment of complete self-revelation....She knew instantly that she had never loved her husband: he was not her mate and Gathbroke was. She had had three years of rippling content and light enjoyment with Mortimer, they had never quarreled seriously, and they had never taken their parts in one moment of real drama.

If she had married Gathbroke they would have quarreled furiously, they would have thrown courtesy and behavior to the winds often enough, particularly while they were young, for neither would have been in the least apprehensive of wounding the rank-pride of the other, and such mutual and passionate love as theirs naturally gave birth to a high state of irritability; they would have loved and hated and made constant discoveries about each other...there would have been depths never to be fully explored but always luring them on...and the perfect companionship...the complete fusion....

How Alexina knew all this after less than three hours' association with Gathbroke, let any woman answer. She was not so foolish as to imagine herself the victim of a secret passion, or that she had ever loved the man, or ever would. She had merely had her chance for the great duodrama, and thrown it away for a callow dream. She had no passing wish, even in that moment of visualizing him interlocked with her own wraith in that sacred inner temple where even she had never intruded before, to meet him again. She had no intention of passing any of her abundant leisure in dreaming dreams of him and the perfect bliss. But he had been hers...and utterly...he had loved her...he had wanted her...he had precipitately begged her to marry him...he had offered her the homage of complete brutality.

Something of him would always be hers.

And even though she renounced all rights in him because she must, she did not in the least relish that any one so close to her as Gora Dwight should have him. She might have heard of his marriage to a girl of his own land and class with only a passing spasm, but his continued and possibly tender friendship with her sister-in-law shook her out of the last of her jejunity and its illusions....She was not exactly a dog in the manger...she was a maturing woman looking back with anger and dismay not only upon the fatal mistake of her youth, but upon the inexorable realities of her present life....

The reaction was a more intense feeling of loyalty to Mortimer than ever. She was entirely to blame. He not only had been innocent of conscious rivalry, even of pursuit - for she could quite easily have discouraged him in the earlier stages of his courtship - but he was dependent upon her in every way: for his happiness, for the secure social position that meant so much to him, for the greater number of his valuable connections, for even his comfort and ease of living.

Something of this had passed through her stunned mind on the morning of her mother's death. Now it was all as sharply outlined as the etching at which she was raptly gazing, and she vowed anew that she would never desert him, never deny him the assistance of the true partner. She had signed a life contract with her eyes open and she would keep it to the letter.

Only she hoped to heaven that Gathbroke was not serious about Gora. She wished never to be reminded of his existence again.

And, as Aileen talked of Santa Barbara, she wondered vaguely why there was not a law forbidding girls to marry until they were well into their twenties....until they had had a certain amount of experience....knew their own minds....Maria had been right....

# CHAPTER VI

## I

The darkness had come early with the high rolling fog that shut out the stars. The fog horn and the bells were silent but the wind had a thin anxious note as if lost, and the long creaking eucalyptus trees angrily repelled it as if irritated beyond endurance by its eternal visitations.

Alexina, who had been reading in her bedroom, realized that it must be quite half an hour since she had turned a page. She lifted her shoulders impatiently. She was in no humor for reading.

It was only eight o'clock. Far too early for bed. Mortimer had gone to Los Angeles on business. He had been gone a week, and she admitted to herself with the new frankness she had determined to cultivate - that she might meet, with the clearest possible vision, whatever three-cornered deals Life might have in store for her - that she had not missed him at all. His absence had been a heavenly interlude. She and Aileen had gone to the moving pictures unescorted every night (a performance of which he would have disapproved profoundly), and they had lunched downtown every day until Alexina had suddenly discovered that she had no more money in her purse; and, knowing nothing whatever even of minor finance, was under the impression that having given Mortimer her power of attorney she would not be able to draw from the bank.

Aileen had gone down to Burlingame to visit Sibyl Bascom for a few days. Alexina had declined to go, although it was a quiet party; it would be embarrassing not to tip the servants.

The wind gave a long angry shriek as it flew round the corner of the house and fastened its teeth in its enemies, the eucalyptus trees; who shook it off with a loud furious rattle of their leaves and slapped the window severely for good measure.

Alexina was used to San Francisco in all her many moods, but to-night, the wind and the high gray fog shutting out the stars, the silent house - silent that is but for the mice playing innocently between the walls - her complete solitude, made her restless and a little nervous.

What could she do?

She knew quite well that she had wanted to go to see Gora for a week. She had not indulged in any silly dreams about Gathbroke but she was curious to see his photograph. She remembered that it had crossed her mind that April day under the oak tree that if he had been older, if he had outgrown his hopelessly youthful curve of cheek, his fresh color, and the inability to conceal the asinine condition to which she had immediately reduced him, she might have given him an equal chance with Morty.

Aileen had said that he looked older. She had a quite natural curiosity to decide for herself if, had he been born several years earlier, he would have proved the successful rival in that foundational period of their youth....Or perhaps she was the reason of his rather sudden maturity. After all there was no great chasm between twenty-three and twenty-six and three-quarters. She looked little if any older. Neither did Morty, nor any one she knew.

This idea thrilled her, and, grimly determined upon no compromise or evasion, she admitted it.

Moreover, she wanted to sound out Gora.

Somehow she had no real belief that he had transferred his affections to her dissimilar sister-in-law, but her interest in Gora was growing. She wanted to know her better.

Besides, although she had often invited her to tea on her free afternoons, and to dinner whenever possible, and had occasionally dropped in to see her while she was still in the hospital, she had never called on her in her home. As Gora only slept there after a killing day's or night's work, visitors were anything but welcome; nevertheless she felt that she had been negligent, rude - three years! - and as Gora was not on a case for a day or two, now was the time to atone.

Moreover, she had never been out quite alone at night, except to run down the avenue and across the street to Aileen's. It was a long way down to Geary Street, and Fillmore Street at night was "tough." Mortimer would be furious.

She hastily changed her dinner gown to a plain walking suit of black tweed and pinned on a close hat firmly, prepared to defy the wind and thoroughly to enjoy her little adventure. Not since she had stolen out to go to forbidden parties with Aileen had she felt such a sense of altogether reprehensible elation.

# CHAPTER VII

I

Fillmore Street, its low-browed shops dark, but with great arcs of white lights spanning the streets that ran east and west, long shafts of yellow light shining across the sidewalk from the restaurants, the candy stores and the nicolodeons - where the pianola tinkled plaintively - was thronged with saunterers. Alexina darted quick curious glances at them as she walked rapidly along. In front of every saloon was a group of young men almost fascinatingly common to Alexina's cloistered eyes, their hats tilted over their foreheads at an indescribable angle, rank black cigars in the corners of their mouths, or cigarettes hanging from their loose lips, leering at "bunches" of girls that passed unattended, appraising them cynically, making strident or stage-whispered comments.

A great many girls had cavaliers, and these walked with their heads tossed, unless drooping toward a padded, shoulder; and they wore perhaps a coat or two less of make-up than their still neglected sisters. These were vividly earmined, although most of them were young enough to have relied on cold water and a rough towel; their hair was arranged in enormous pompadours and topped with "lingerie" or beflowered hats. Their blouses were "peek-a-boo" and cut low, their skirts high; slender or plump, they wore exaggerated straight front corsets, high heels and ventilated stockings. They practiced the débutante slouch and their jaws worked automatically.

Not all of them were "bad" by any means. Fillmore Street was a promenade at night for girls who were confined by day: waitresses, shop girls of the humbler sort, servants, clerks, or younger daughters of poor parents, who would see nothing of life at all if they sat virtuously in the kitchen every night.

The best of them were not averse to being picked up and treated to ice-cream-soda or the more delectable sundae. A few there were, and they were not always to be distinguished by the kohl round their eyes, the dead white of their cheeks, the magenta of their lips, who, ignoring the "bums" and "cadets" lounging at the corners or before the saloons, directed intent long glances at every passing man who looked as if he had the "roll" to treat them handsomely in the back parlor of a saloon, or possibly stake them at a gaming table. The town, still in its brief period of insufferable virtue, was "closed," but the lid was not on as irremovably as the police led the good mayor to believe; and these girls, who traveled not in "bunches" but in pairs, if they had not already begun a career of profitable vice, were anxious to start but did not exactly know how. Fillmore Street was not the hunting ground of rich men; but men with a night's money came there, and many "boobs" from the country.

Alexina had heard of Fillmore Street from Aileen, who

investigated everything, escorted by her uxorious parent, and had been informed that many of these girls were "decent enough"; "much more decent than I would be in the circumstances: work all day, coarse underclothes, no place to see a beau but the street. I'd go straight to the devil and play the only game I had for all it was worth."

But to Alexina they all looked appalling, abandoned, the last cry in "badness." She was not afraid. The street was too brilliant and the great juggernauts of trolley cars lumbered by every few moments. Moreover, she could make herself look as cold and remote as the stars above the fog, and she had drawn herself up to her full five feet seven, thrown her shoulders back, lifted her chin and lowered her eyelids the merest trifle. She fancied that the patrician-beauty type would have little or no attraction for the men who frequented Fillmore Street. Certainly the bluntest of these males could see that she was not painted, blackened, dyed, nor chewing gum.

Moreover she was in mourning.

But she had reckoned without her youth.

## II

"Say, kid, what you doin' all alone?"

A hand passed familiarly through her arm.

Her brain turned somersaults, raced. Should she burst into tears? Turn upon him with a frozen stare? Appeal for help?

Then she discovered that although astonished she was not at all terrified; nor very much insulted. Why should she be? A casual remark of the sophisticated Aileen flashed through her rallying mind: "When a man is even half way drunk he doesn't know a lady from a trollop, and ten to one the lady's a trollop anyhow."

She heartily wished that Aileen were in her predicament at the present moment. What on earth was she to do with the creature?

She had accelerated her steps without speaking or making any foolish attempts to shake him off; but she knew that her face was crimson, and one girl tittered as they passed, while another, appreciating the situation, laughed aloud and cried after her: "Don't be frightened, kid. He's not a slaver."

Irrepressible curiosity made her send him a swift glance from the corner of her eye. He was a young man, thick set, with an aggressive nose set in a round hard face. His small, hard, black eyes were steady, and so were his feet. He did not look in the least drunk.

"I think you have made a mistake," she said quietly,

and with no pretense at immense dignity (she could hear Aileen say: "Cut it out. Nothing doing in that line here"). "I, also, have made a mistake - in walking at night on this street. Would you mind letting go my arm? I think I'll take a car."

"No, I think you'll stay just where you are," he said insolently. "You don't belong here all right, but you've come and you can stand the consequences. You're just the sort that needs a jolt and I like the idea of handing it."

Alexina gave him a coldly speculative glance. "I wonder why?"

"You would? Well, I'll tell you. Never been out alone at night before, I'll bet, like these other girls, that ain't got no place on earth to have any fun but the streets. Never even rubbed against the common herd? Generally go about in a machine, don't you?"

"It is quite true that I have never been out alone at night before. I certainly shall not go again."

"No, you don't have to! That's the point, all right. And if you weren't such a beauty, damn you! I'd hate you this minute as I hate your whole parasite class."

"Oh, you are a socialist!" Alexina looked at him with frank curiosity. "I never saw one before."

He was obviously disconcerted. Then his face flushed with anger. "Yes, I'm a socialist all right, and you'll see more of us before you're many years older."

"You might tell me about it if you *will* walk with me. I

am a long way from my destination, and that would be far more interesting than personalities."

"I've got more personalities where those came from. It makes me sick to see the difference between you and these poor kids - ready to sell their souls for pretty clothes and a little fun. There's nothing that has done so much to inflame class hatred as the pampered delicate satin-skinned women of your class, who have expensive clothes and 'grooming' to take the place of slathers of paint and cheap perfume. Raised in a hot house for the use of the man on top. It's the crowning offense of capitalism, and when the system goes, they'll all be like you, or you'll be more like them. You'll come down about a thousand pegs, and the ones down below will be shoved up to meet you."

Alexina stood still and faced him.

"Are you poor?" she asked.

"What a hell of a question. Have I been talkin' like a plutocrat?"

"Oh, there are, still, different grades. I was wondering if you would be so inconsistent as to earn a little money from me and two friends of mine. We have read socialism a bit, but, we don't understand it very well. I am in mourning and it would interest me immensely."

He had dropped her arm and was staring at her.

"You are not afraid of me, then?" His voice was sulky but his eyes were less hostile.

"Oh, not in the least. I fully appreciate that you merely

wished to humiliate me, not to be insulting, as some of these other men might have been. My name is Mrs. Mortimer Dwight. I live on Ballinger Hill - do you know it? That old house in the eucalyptus grove?"

"I know it, all right."

"Then you probably know, also, that I am not rich and never have been. My husband is a struggling young business man."

"That cuts no ice. You train with that class, don't you? You're class yourself, reek with it. You had rich ancestors or you wouldn't be what you are now."

"Well, we can discuss that point another time. One of my friends is a daughter of Judge Lawton - "

"Hand in glove with every rich grafter in 'Frisco."

Alexina shuddered. "Please say San Francisco. I am positive you never heard a word against Judge Lawton's probity, nor that he ever rendered an unjust decision."

"He's a wise old guy, all right. But it would be wastin' time tryin' to make you understand why I have no use for him."

"Of course you would have no use for the husband of my other friend, Mrs. Frank Bascom."

She fully expected that the young millionaire's name would be the final red rag and that her escort would roar his opinion of him for the benefit of all Fillmore Street. But he surprised her by saying reluctantly:

"He's dead straight, all right. He's not a grafter. I've nothing against him personally, but he's part of a damnable system and I'd clean him out with the rest."

"Well, there you have three of us to your hand. Who knows but that you might convert us? Why not give us the chance? If you will give me your address I will write to you as soon as my friends come back to town."

"I don't know whether I want to do it or not. You may be makin' game of me for all I know."

"I am quite sincere. You interest me immensely. And we might teach you something too - what it means to have a sense of humor. I know enough of socialism to know that no socialist can have it. May I ask what your occupation is?"

"I'm just a plain working-man - housebuilding line."

"Then you could only come in the evening?"

"Not at all; I get off at five. You don't have your dinner until eight in your set, I believe," This with a sneer that curled his upper lip almost to the septum of his nose.

"Seven. My husband works until nearly six. He rarely has time for lunch and comes home very hungry."

Once more he looked puzzled and disconcerted, but his small steady eyes did not waver.

"My name's James Kirkpatrick." He found the stub of a pencil in his pocket and wrote an address on the flap of an envelope. "I'll think it over. Maybe I'll do it. I dunno, though."

"I do hope you will. I'm sure we can learn a good deal from each other. Now, would you mind putting me on the next car? Or don't the socialist tenets admit of gallantry to my sex?"

"Socialism admits the equality of the sexes, which is a long sight better, but I guess there's nothing to prevent me seeing you onto your car."

He even lifted his hat as she turned to him from the high platform, and as he smiled a little she inferred that he was congratulating himself on having had the last word.

# CHAPTER VIII

I

Gora, to whom she had telephoned before leaving home, was standing on the steps of her house, looking anxiously up the street, as her young sister-in-law left the car at the corner.

Gora walked up to meet her guest. "Where on earth have you, been?" she demanded. "I supposed of course that you'd take a taxi. You should not go out alone at night. Mortimer would be wild. He has the strictest ideas; and you - "

"Haven't. Not, any more. I'm tired of being kept in a glass case - being a parasite." She laughed gayly at Gora's look of amazement. "I've had an adventure. Almost the first I ever had."

She related it as they walked slowly down the street and up the steps and stairs to the attic.

Gora looked very thoughtful as she listened. "Shall you tell Mortimer?"

Gertrude Atherton

"Oh, I don't know. Possibly not. Why agitate him? The thing is done."

"But if you study with this man?"

"There is no necessity to explain where I met him. I look upon myself as Morty's partner, not as his subject. We have never disputed over anything yet, but of course as time goes on I shall wish to do many things whether he happens to like it or not. Possibly without consulting him."

"You've had time to think these past three months for the first time in your life," said Gora shrewdly. "Here we are. I hope you don't hate stairs. I do when I come home dog-tired, but somehow I can't give up the old place....And I've lit the candles in your honor."

II

"Oh, but it is pretty! Charming!"

Thought Gora: "I do hope she's not going to be gracious. I've never liked her so well before."

But Alexina was too excited to have a firm grip on the Ballinger-Groome tradition. She had had an adventure, an uncommon one, in a far from respectable night district; she had done something that would cause the impeccable Mortimer the acutest anguish if he knew of it; and she had caught sight immediately of Gathbroke's picture framed and enthroned on the mantelpiece.

She walked about the room admiring the hangings and prints, the old Chinese lanterns that held the candles.

"I am going to refurnish our lower rooms," she said. "If you have time do help me. Heavens! I wish I could work off some of that old furniture on you. I like the Italian pieces well enough, but there are too many of them. That rather low Florentine cabinet in the back parlor would just fit in this corner...."

She gave a little girlish exclamation and ran forward.

"Isn't that young Gathbroke, who was out here at the time of the earthquake and fire...or an older brother, perhaps?"

She had taken the photograph from the mantel and was examining it under one of the lanterns. Her alert ear detected the deeper and less steady note in Gora's always hoarse voice.

"It is the same. Did you meet him?...Oh, I remember he told me he met you at the Hofer ball. He rather raved over you, in fact."

"Did he? How sweet of him. I met him again, I remember. Mr. Gwynne brought him down to Rincona one day."

"Oh?"

And Alexina, knew that he had never mentioned that visit.

"But he looks much much older."

"He did before he left. That horrible experience of his seemed to prey on him more and more.

"Oh."

He had not looked a day over twenty-three on that afternoon at Eincona, two weeks after the fire.

Alexina replaced the picture, then turned to her sister-in-law with a coaxing smile. "Are you engaged? It would be too romantic. Do tell me."

"No," said Gora, shortly. "We are not engaged. Good friends, that is all, and write occasionally."

"Well, he must be very much interested - and you must be a very interesting correspondent, Gora dear! Is he? Interesting, I mean. What does he do, anyhow? I have a vague remembrance that he said something about the army."

"He was in the army, the Grenadier Guards. But he has resigned and gone into business with a cousin of his in Lancashire. He wrote me - oh, it must be nearly two years ago - that if there should be a war he would enlist as a matter of course, but as there was no prospect of any, and he was sick of idleness - his good middle-class energetic blood asserting itself, he said, - he was going to amuse himself with work, incidentally try to make a fortune. His mother left a good deal of money, but there are several children and I guess the present earl needs most of it to keep up his estates, to say nothing of his position. Fotten law, that - entail, I mean."

Alexina came and sat down on the divan beside Gora, piling the cushions behind her. "Are you a socialist?"

"I am not. I believe in sticking to your own class, whether you have a grudge against it or not, or even if you think it far from perfection."

She shot a quick challenging glance at her admittedly aristocratic sister-in-law, but Alexina had lifted the lower white of her eyes just above their soft black fringe and looked more innocent than any new born lamb. As she did not answer Gora continued:

"I remember that night I sat out with Gathbroke on Calvary he said something about socialism...that it was a confession of failure. I may feel so furious with destiny sometimes that I could go out and wave a red flag, or even the darker red of anarchy, but what always sobers me is the thought that if I had the good luck to inherit or make even a reasonable fortune I'd have no more use for socialism than for a rattlesnake in my bed. Why are you interested?"

"Only as in any subject that interests a few million people. I haven't the least intention of being converted, but I don't want to be an ignoramus. Aileen and Sibyl and I did start Marx's *Das Kapital* - in German! We nearly died of it. But I felt sure that this man, Kirkpatrick, had studied his subject, if only because his language changed so completely when he talked about it. It was as if he were quoting, but intelligently. Of course the poor man had little or no education to begin with. Somehow he struck me as a pathetic figure. Perhaps when every one is educated - and there must be many thousands of naturally intelligent men in the working class whose brains if trained would be mighty useful in Washington - well, all having had equal opportunities they would surely arrive at some way to improve conditions without struggling for anything so hopeless as socialism. I know enough to be sure that it is hopeless, because it antagonizes human nature."

"Rather. The trend under all the talk is more and more toward individualism, not self-effacing communism. As for myself I like the idea of the fight - for public recognition, I mean; and I don't think I'd be happy at all if things were made too smooth for me; if, for instance, in a socialized state it were decided that I could devote all my time to writing, and that the state would take care of me, publish my work, and distribute it exactly where it was sure to be appreciated. I haven't any of the old California gambling blood in me, but I guess the hardy ghost of those old days still dominates the atmosphere, and I have not been one of those to escape."

"It's in mine! Not that I care for gambling, really, like Aileen and Alice. But I've always been fascinated by the idea of taking long chances, and I have had inklings that I'll be rather more than less fascinated as I grow older....When are your stories to be published? I am simply expiring to read them."

"Are you?"

III

Alexina had thrust her slim index finger unerringly through Gora's bristling armor and tickled her weakest spot. The fledgling author smiled into the dazzling eyes opposite and a deep flush rose to her high cheek bones,

"Rather!"

"Then..." Gora rose and took a magazine from the table beside her bed. She spread it open on her lap, when she had resumed her seat, and handled it as Alexina had seen young mothers fondle their first-born.

"It's here. Just out."

"Oh!" Alexina. gave a little shriek of genuine anticipation. "Read it to me. Quick. I can't wait."

Gora led a lonely life outside of her work, a lonely inner life always. She had never had an intimate friend, and she suddenly reflected that there had been a certain measure of sadness in her joy both when her manus-cripts were accepted and to-day when for the first time she had gazed at herself in print....She had had no one to rejoice with her....She felt an overwhelming sense of gratitude to Alexina.

But she gave this young wife of her brother whom she knew as little as Alexina knew her, another swift suspicious glance....No, there was nothing of Alexina's usual high and careless courtesy in that eager almost excited face.

"I'd love to have your opinion....I read very badly....Make allowances...."

"Oh, fire away. If I'd written a story and had it accepted by that magazine I'd read it from the housetops."

Gora read the story well enough, and Alexina's mind did not wander even to Gathbroke. It was written in a pure direct vigorous English. A little less self-consciousness and it would have been distinguished. The story itself was built craftily; she had been coached by a clever instructor who was a successful writer of short stories himself; and it worked up to a climax of genuine drama. But this was merely the framework, the flexible technique for the real Gora. The story had not only an original point of view but it pulsed with the insurgent resentful passionate spirit of the writer.

Alexina gave a little gasp as Gora finished.

"Many people won't like that story," she said. "It shocks and jars and gives one's smugness a pain in the middle. But those that do like it will give you a great reputation, and after all there are a few thousand intelligent readers in the United States. How on earth did that magazine come to accept it?"

Gora was staring at Alexina with an uncommonly soft expression in her opaque light eyes. She felt, indeed, as if her ego would leap through them and make a fool of her.

"The editor wrote me something of what you have just said. He wanted something new - to give his conservative old subscribers a shock. Thought it would be good for them and for the magazine. You - you - have said what I should have wanted you to say if I could have thought it out....I think I should have hated you if you had said, 'How charming!' or 'How frantically interesting!'"

"Well, it's the last if not the first. Aileen will say that and mean it. I'll telephone to the bookstore the first thing Monday morning and get a copy. Now I must go. It's late."

# IV

"Let me telephone for a taxi."

Alexina laughed merrily. "You'll never believe it, but I've just thirty cents in my purse. I forgot to ask Morty for something before he left....You see, I happened to find quite a bit in mother's desk and so I've never thought to ask him for an allowance. But I shall at once."

"An allowance? But you have your own money? Or is it because the estate isn't settled? What has Morty to do with that?"

"I believe we get the income from the estate until it is settled. But I gave my power of attorney to Morty."

"Oh! But if there is money on deposit in the bank you can draw on it."

"Could I? Well! I'll just draw a round hundred on Monday at ten A.M."

"Why did you give your power of attorney to Morty?"

"Oh...why...he asked me to...I know nothing about business, and he naturally would attend to my affairs."

"But you are not going away. No one needs your power of attorney. And the executors are Judge Lawton and Mr. Abbott. You are here to sign such papers as they advise....Don't he angry, please. I am not insinuating anything against Morty. He's never bad a dishonest thought in his life...has always been, the squarest...but..."

"Well?"

Alexina's head was very high. It was quite bad enough for Tom Abbott and Judge Lawton...but for his sister...

"It's this way, Alexina. People in this world, more particularly men, are just about as honest as circumstances will permit them to be. Some are stronger than Life in one way or another, no doubt of it; but they make up for it by being weaker in others....I am talking particularly of the money question, the struggle for existence, which the vast majority of men are forced to make....

"Men fight Life from the hour they leave their homes, when they have any, to force success - in one way or another - out of her until the hour they are able to lay down the burden....Some are too strong and too firm in their ideals ever to do wrong; they would prefer failure, and generally they are strong enough to avoid it, even to succeed in their way against the most overwhelming odds....Many are too clever not to find some way of compromising and circumventing....Others just peg along and barely make both ends meet....Others go under and down and out.

"Morty, like millions of other young Americans, had good principles and high ideals inculcated from his earliest boyhood and took to them as a duck takes to water. Nor is he weak. But although he is a hard and steady worker he is also visionary. He speculated on the stock market before he was married. Probably not now as the market is moribund. He is frantic to get rich...for more reasons than one."

"But he never would do anything dishonorable."

"No. Nothing he couldn't square with his conscience if it turned out all right. But the most honest man, when in a hole, finds little difficulty in arriving at the conclusion that what is, illogically, the possession of the women of his family, is his if he needs it.

"Moreover, no doubt you have discovered that Morty is the sort of man who looks upon women as man's natural inferiors, that if there is any question of sacrifice the woman is not to be considered for a moment...especially where no public risk is involved. That sort of man only thinks he is too honest to refrain from taking some unrelated woman's money, but as a matter of fact it is because she would send him to State's Prison as readily as a man would. One's own women are safe.

"I lent Morty my small inheritance with my eyes open. But he knows a good deal of that particular business, and I did not dream the times were going to be so bad....I doubt if I ever see it again....But you must not run the risk of losing yours. I want you to promise me that on Monday morning you will go down to the City Hall and revoke your power of attorney. And as much for Morty's sake as for your own. He will lose your money if he keeps it in his hands, and then he will suffer agonies of remorse. He will be infinitely more miserable than if he merely failed in business. That is honorable. It would only hurt his pride. Then he could get a position again, and you would have your own income."

"But do you mean to say that if I did revoke my power of attorney and he asked me later for money to save his business that I should not give it to him?"

"Yes, I mean just that. Morty will never take any of the prizes in the business world. He may hold on and make a living, that is all. He has plenty to start with, and tells me he is doing fairly well, in spite of the times. But he would do better in the long run as a clerk. In time he might get a large salary as a sort of general director of all the routine business of some large house - "

Alexina curled her lip. "I do not want him to be a clerk."

"No, of course you don't! But you'd like it still less if he cleaned you out. You - would have to sell or rent your old home and live on a hundred and fifty dollars a month in a flat in some out-of-the-way quarter. You might have to go to work yourself,"

"I shouldn't mind that so much, except that I'm afraid I'd not be good for much. Perhaps it was snobbish of me to object lo Morty's being a clerk. But...well, I'm not so sure that it is snobbish to prefer what you have always been accustomed to - I mean if it is a higher standard. And after all I married him when he was only a clerk."

"You are surprisingly little of a snob, all things considered; but you are a hopeless aristocrat."

"What do you mean by that?"

"I think the line between the aristocratic and the snobbish attitude of mind is almost too fine to be put into words. But they are often confused by the undiscriminating. Will you revoke that power of attorney on Monday?"

"Shouldn't I wait until Morty is home?...tell him first? It seems rather taking an advantage...and he will be very angry."

"That doesn't matter."

"What excuse shall I give him?"

"Any one of a dozen. You are bored and want to take care of your money...intend to learn something of business, as all women should, and will in time....Ring in the feminist stuff...wife's economic indepen- dence...woman's new position in the world....That will make Morty so raving angry that he will forget about the other. Will you do it?"

"Yes, I will. I believe you are right. So were the others...there must be something in it."

She told Gora of the advice of Tom Abbott and Judge Lawton. Gora nodded.

"They meant more than they said. And merely because they are men of the world, not because they like and trust Morty any the less."

Alexina did not hear her. She was staring hard at the floor....A year ago...three months ago...she couldn't have done this thing. She had been still under the illusion that she loved her husband, that her marriage was a complete success. She would have sacrificed her last penny rather than hurt his feelings. Now she only cared that she didn't care....She had admitted to herself that she did not love her husband but that was different from committing an overt act that proved it....She felt something crumbling within her....It was the last of the fairy edifice of her romance...of her first, her real, youth....What was to take its place? The future smugly secure on six thousand a year and an inviolate social position...a good dull husband...not even the prospect of travel....

V

She sprang to her feet and turned away her head.

"Why don't you come and live with us?" she asked abruptly. "Why should you keep this on? There are so many vacant bedrooms up there. You could have one for your study. I'd love to have you. You'd have the most complete independence. Do."

Gora shook her head. "I've always this to fall back on."

"Fall back on?"

"Oh! I never meant to let that out. However....Perhaps it is as well....Morty - you know his pride - everybody has his prime weakness and that is his. Transpose it into snobbery if you like....We did not board down here. I kept a lodging house for business women. It paid well, but Morty, when he became engaged to you, insisted that I give it up. He was afraid you'd be outraged in your finest sensibilities! Well, I did. One of my lodgers resigned from her job and took it over. I entered the hospital, but kept on my room as I had to have one somewhere. Eight months later she married, and I took it back. I found I could run it as well as ever with the aid of a treasure of a Chinaman she had discovered. But I never told Morty."

Alexina laughed. "Better not. But you could run it and live with us all the same."

"No. I have too little time. I'd waste it coming back and forth, for I must be here some time every day....Besides..."

"Your own precious atmosphere?"

"You do understand!"

"Well, come to see me often. I shall need your advice."

"You bet. And now, I'll see you to your car; stay with you until you are safely transferred to the Fillmore car. And don't assert your independence in just this way again. All those loafers on Fillmore Street are not spiteful socialists."

As Gora put on her hat at the distant mirror Alexina turned to Gathbroke's picture with a scowl. She even clenched her hands into fists.

"Oh...you...you....Why weren't you....Why didn't you...."

# CHAPTER IX

## I

Mortimer arrived on Tuesday evening, looking immaculate in spite of his day on the train, and with that air of beaming gallantry that he could always summon at will, even when all was not well with him.

To-night, however, he was quite sincere. His visit to Los Angeles had been a success; he had actually put through a deal that had translated itself into a cheque for a thousand dollars. He had, through a mistaken order, been overstocked with a certain commodity from the Orient that the retail merchants of San Francisco bought very sparingly; but he had found in Los Angeles a firm that did a large business with the swarming Japanese population and was glad to take it over at a reasonable figure.

# II

It was after dinner; his taut trim body was relaxed in evening luxury before the wood fire of the back parlor, and he was half way through a cigar when Alexina rose and extended one arm along the mantelpiece. She looked like a long black poplar with her round narrow flexible figure and her small head held with a lofty poise; as serene as a poplar in France on a balmy day. But she quaked inside.

She glanced at her happy unsuspecting husband with an engaging smile. "I'm afraid you will be rather cross with me," she said softly. "But I went down to the City Hall yesterday and revoked my power of attorney to you."

"You did what?" The slow blood rose to Dwight's hair. He mechanically took the cigar from his mouth. It lost its flavor. He had a sensation of falling through space...out of somewhere....

Alexina repeated her statement.

He recovered himself. "Tom Abbott has been at you again, I suppose. Or Judge Lawton."

"Neither. Really, Morty, you must give me credit for a mind of my own. I did it for several reasons. Sibyl was here Sunday. She motored up from Burlingame with Aileen on purpose to talk to me. She has induced Mrs. Hunter and some other of the more intelligent women down there - those that read the serious new books and go to lectures when there are any worth while - to join a class in economics. One of the professors at Stanford is going to teach us. Aileen has lost frightfully at poker lately and wants a new interest; she put Sibyl up to it - who was delighted with the suggestion as she hasn't been intellectual for quite a while now, and really has a practical streak; so that studying economics appealed to her.

"I jumped at the idea. It was a God-send. I have had so little to do. I don't care for poker and one can't read all the time....But after they left I reflected that I should cut a rather ridiculous figure studying economies in the abstract if I didn't have sense and 'go' enough to manage my own affairs. Why, I was so ignorant I thought I couldn't draw any money from the bank because I had given you my power of attorney. Aileen has an allowance and the Judge makes her keep books. She usually comes out about even at poker in the course of the month, and if she doesn't she pawns something. I've been with her to pawn shops and it's the greatest fun. I don't mind telling you, as I know you never betray a confidence. The Judge would lock poor dear Aileen up on bread and water.

"Sibyl manages those two great houses herself. Frank gives her some stupendous sum a year and she is proud of the fact that she never runs over it. You know how she entertains.

"I should never dare admit to them - or to the professor if he asked my opinion on that sort of thing and it had to come out - that I was too lazy and too incompetent to manage my own little fortune. So I went down first thing Monday morning and revoked my power of attorney. I simply couldn't wait. When the estate is settled and turned over to me I shall attend to everything and not bother you, Morty dear."

III


Morty dear looked at her with a long hard suspicious stare. Alexina thoughtfully turned up her eyes and changed promptly from a poplar into a saint.

"I don't like it. I don't like it at all."

Words were never his strong point and he could find none now adequate to express his feelings.

"I may be old-fashioned - "

"You are, Morty. That is your only fault. You belong to the old school of American husbands - "

"There are plenty of old-fashioned people left in the world."

"So there are, poor dears. It's going to be so hard for them - "

"Are you trying to be one of those infernal new women?"

"Well, you see, I just naturally am a child of my times, in spite of my old-fashioned family. I'd be much the same if I'd never taken any interest in all these wonderful modern movements."

"It's those chums of yours - Aileen, Sibyl, Janet. I never did wholly approve of them."

"Neither did mother and Maria, but it never made any difference."

"Do you mean to say that you intend to ignore me...disobey me?"

"Oh, Morty, I never promised to obey you. You know the fun we all had at the rehearsal. You haven't noticed, these three years, that I've had my way, in pretty nearly everything, merely because it happened to be your way too. We've been living in a sort of pleasure garden, just playing about, with mother as the good old fairy. But everything has changed. We must look out for ourselves now, and I cannot put the whole burden on your shoulders - "

"I do not mind in the least. That is where it belongs."

Alexina shook her wise little head. "Oh, no. It isn't done any more. No woman who has learned to think is so unjust as to throw the whole burden of life on her husband's shoulders. You have your own daily battle in the business world. I will do the rest."

"What damned emancipated talk."

"What a funny old-fashioned word. We don't even say advanced or new any more."

"It's nonsense anyhow. You're nothing but a child."

"You may just bet your life I'm not a child. Nor have I awakened all of a sudden. In one sense I have. But not in this particular branch of modern science. I have read tons about it, and Aileen and I are always discussing everything that interests the public; I have even read the newspapers for two years."

"Much better you didn't. There is no reason whatever

for a woman in your position knowing anything about public affairs. It detracts from your charm."

"Maybe, but we'll find more charm in Life as we grow older."

His memory ran back along a curved track and returned with something that looked like a bogey.

"May I ask what your program is? Your household program? I had got everything down to a fine point....It seems too bad you should bother...."

"Bother? I've been bored to death, and feeling like a silly little good-for-nothing besides. The trouble is, it's too little bother. James and I have had a long talk. Housekeeping will be reduced to its elements with him, but at least I shall begin to feel really grown up when I pore over monthly bills and 'slips' and sign cheques."

She hesitated. "You mustn't think for a minute that I want to make you feel out of it, Morty. It. is only that I *must*. The time has come,...Of course, you have been paying half the bills anyhow. We could simply go on along those lines. I will tell you what it all amounts to, shortly after the first of the month, and you'll give me half."

## IV

Dwight stared at the end of his cigar. His was not an agile brain but in that moment it had an illuminating flash. He realized that this sheltered creature, with whom her mother had never discussed household economics, and from whom he had purposely kept all knowledge of his business, took for granted that he could pay his share of the monthly expenses, merely because all the men she knew did twice as much, however they might grumble. For the matter of that she never saw Tom Abbott that he did not curse the ascending prices, but there was no change whatever in his bountiful fashion of living. Alexina knew that the times were bad and that her husband was having something of a struggle, and, as a dutiful wife, was anxious to help him out for the present, but it was simply beyond her powers of comprehension to grasp the fact that he was in no position to pay half the expenses of their small establishment.

If he told her...tried to make her understand...even if she did, how would he appear in her eyes?

Of all people in the world he wanted to stand high with Alexina...he had never taken more pains to bluff the street when things were at their worst than this girl who was the symbol of all he had aspired to and precariously achieved. He had longed for riches, not because she craved luxury and pomp, but because she would be forced to look up to him with admiration and a lively gratitude. He had, in this spirit, given her; in the most casual manner, handsome presents, or brilliant little dinners at fashionable restaurants, in all of which she took a fervent young pleasure. He had dipped into his slender capital, but of this she had not even a suspicion...he had made some airy remark about celebrating a "good deal"...no wonder...he had her too well bluffed.

For an instant he contemplated a plain and manly statement of fact. But he did not have the courage. Anything rather than that she should curl that short aristocratic upper lip of hers, stare at him with wide astonished eyes that saw him a failure, even if a temporary one. He set his teeth and vowed to go through with it, to make good. This thousand would last several months, even if he made no more than his expenses meanwhile.

He shrugged his shoulders and lit another cigar. The first had died a lingering and malodorous death.

"Have your own way," he said coldly. "I only wished to keep you young and carefree. If you choose to bother with bills and investments it is your own look-out."

"Thank you, Morty dear."

She felt that it would be an act of wifely self-abnegation to defer the announcement of her interest in socialism and Mr. Kirkpatrick. Aileen and Sibyl had hailed her plan as even more exciting than the study of economics with an exceedingly good-looking young professor (who had been tutoring in Burlingame), and she had already dispatched a note to him whom Aileen disreputably called her Fillmore Street mash.

# CHAPTER X

## I

Kirkpatrick sat before a crescent composed of Mrs. Mortimer Dwight, Mrs. Francis Leslie Bascom and Miss Aileen Livingston Lawton.

His reasons for coming to Ballinger House - which even he knew was inaccessible to the common herd - were separate and tabulated. Alexina had fascinated him against his best class principles; but he not only jumped at the chance of meeting her again, he was excessively curious to understand a woman of her class, to watch her in different moods and situations. He was equally curious to meet other women of the same breed; he had never brushed their skirts before, but he had often stood and gazed at them hungrily as they passed in their limousines or driving their smart little electric cars.

He was also curious to see several of those "interiors" he had read so much about, and hoped his pupils would meet in turn at their different homes. He was a sincere and honest socialist, was Mr. Kirkpatrick, and he had a good healthy class-consciousness and class-hatred. But he also had a large measure of intelligent curiosity. He had never expected to have the opportunity to gratify it in respect to "bourgeois" inner circles, and when it came he had only hesitated long enough to search his soul and assure himself that he was in no danger of growing compliant and soft. Moreover he might possibly make converts, and in any case it was not a bad way, society being still what it was, of turning an honest penny.

But in this the first lesson he was as disconcerted as a socialist serene in his faith could be.

The three girls had curved their slender bodies forward, resting one elbow on a knee. At the end of each of these feline arches was a pair of fixed and glowing eyes. No doubt there were faces also, but he was only vaguely aware of three white disks from which flowed forth lambent streams of concentrated light. They looked like three little sea-monsters, slim, flexible, malignant, ready to spring.

He exaggerated in his embarrassment, but he was not so very far wrong.

"The little devils!" he thought in his righteous wrath. "I'll teach 'em, all right."

As it was necessary to break the farcical silence he said in a voice too loud for the small library. "Well, what is it about socialism that you don't just know? Mrs. Dwight told me you had read some."

"There is one thing I want to say before we begin," said Aileen in her high light impertinent voice, "and that is that if there is one thing that makes us more angry than another it is to be called *bourgeois*."

"And ain't you?"

"We are not. I suppose your Marx didn't know the difference, although he is said to have married well, but *bourgeois* for centuries in Europe had meant middle-class. Just that and nothing more. Marx had no right to pervert an honest historic old word into something so different and so obnoxious."

"To Marx all capitalists were in the same class. I suppose what you mean is that you society folks call yourselves aristocrats, even when you have less capital than some of them that can't get in."

"Sure thing. Take it from me."

He gazed at her astounded, and once more had recourse to his rather heavy sarcasm.

"Even when they use slang."

"Oh, we're never afraid to - like lots of the middle-class - bourgeois. Too sure of ourselves to care a hang what any one thinks of us."

Alexina came hastily to the rescue, for a dull glow was kindling in Mr. Kirkpatrick's small sharp eyes. She didn't mind baiting him a little, but as he was in a way her guest he must be protected from the naughtiness of Aileen and the insolence of Sibyl Bascom, who had taken a cigarette from a gold bejeweled case that dangled from her wrist and was asking him for a light. He gave her measure for measure, for he lifted his heavy boot and struck a match on the sole.

"You must not be too hard on us, Mr. Kirkpatrick." Alexina upreared and leaned against the high back of her chair with a sweet and gracious dignity, "We are really a pack of ignoramuses, full of prejudices, which, however, we would get rid of if we knew how. We are hoping everything from these lessons."

"Do *you* smoke?"

"No, I don't happen to like the taste of tobacco, but I quite approve of my friends smoking - unless they smoke their nerves out by the roots, as Miss Lawton does. Don't give her a light. But I'm sure you smoke. I'll get you a cigar."

She pinched Aileen, glared at Sibyl, and left the room.

## II

Mortimer was smoking furiously, trying to concentrate his mind on the evening paper.

"Give me a cigar, Morty dear."

"A cigar? What for?"

"It would be too mean of those girls to smoke unless Mr. Kirkpatrick did too, and I am sure we couldn't stand his tobacco. Even a whiff of bad tobacco makes me feel quite ill."

"I'll be hanged if I give my cigars to that bounder. The kitchen is the place for him."

"But not for us. And our minds are quite made up, you know. We are going to study with him just to find out what these strange animals called socialists are like. He is queer enough, to begin, with. And the knowledge may prove useful one of these days....If you won't give me one I'll send James out - "

Mortimer handed over one of his choice cigars with ill grace, and Alexina returned to the library. Aileen was informing Mr. Kirkpatrick how intensely she disliked Marx's beard, not only as she had seen it in a photograph, but as she had smelt it in Spargo's too vivid description.

He rose awkwardly as she entered, but he rose. She handed him the cigar and struck a match and held it to one end while he drew at the other. Their faces were close and she gave him a smile of warm and spontaneous friendliness.

Thought Mr. Kirkpatrick: "Oh, Lord, she's got me. I'd better make tracks out of here. If she was a vamp like that Bascom woman she wouldn't get me one little bit. Plenty of them where I come from. But she's plain goddess with eyes like headlights on an engine."

Perturbed as he was, however, he resumed his seat and drew appreciatively at the finest cigar that had ever come his way. It had the opportune effect of causing his class-hatred to flame afresh. No fear that he would be made soft by teaching in the homes of these pampered cats. For the moment he hated Alexina, seated in a carved high-back Italian chair like a young queen on a throne.

"Well," he growled. "Let's get to business. I've brought Spargo. Marx is too much for me. He's terrible dull and involved. He was so taken up with his subject, I guess, that he forgot to learn how to write about it so's people without much time and education could understand without getting a pain in their beans. Of course I've heard him expounded many times from the platform, but there must have been about fifty Marxes, for I've heard - or read - just about that many expounders of him and no two agree so's you'd notice it. That, to my mind, is the only stumbling block for socialism - that we have a prophet who's so hard to understand.

"So, I've settled on Spargo. He has the name of being about the best student of Marx and of socialism generally - it's split up quite a bit - and he's easy reading. I fetched him along."

He produced "Socialism" from his hat and hesitated. "I

don't know noth - a thing about teaching."

"Oh, don't let that worry you," drawled Sibyl Bascom in her low voluptuous voice and transfixing him with narrow swimming eyes; then as he refused to be overcome, she continued more humanly: "We've been to lots of classes, you know. There are all sorts of methods. Suppose one of us reads the first chapter aloud and then you expound. That is, we'll ask you questions."

"That's fine," said Mr. Kirkpatrick with immense relief. "Fire away."

And Alexina, who always read prefaces and introductions last, began with "Robert Owen and the Utopian Spirit."

# BOOK III

## CHAPTER I

I

Mr. Kirkpatrick realized his ambition to see with his own sharp puncturing little eyes (Aileen said they reminded her of a sewing-machine needle playing staccato) several of the most flagrant examples of capitalistic extravagance where parasitic femalehood idled away their useless lives and servitors battened. In other words the extremely comfortable or the shamelessly luxurious homes built for the most part by still active business men whose first real period of rest would be in a small stone residence in a certain silent city Down the Peninsula.

Several were already occupied by their widows. In a climate where a man can work three hundred and sixty-five days of the year the temptation to do so is strong, and not conducive to longevity.

The Ferdinand Thorntons, Trennahans, Hofers and others who had lost their city homes on Nob Hill had not rebuilt, but lived the year round in their country houses at Burlingame, San Mateo, Alta, Menlo Park, Atherton, or "across the Bay," using the hotels when they came to town for dances, but motoring home after the theater.

Fortunately the finest and all of the newest mansions had been built in the Western Addition and escaped the fire. Sibyl Bascom's father-in-law had erected, shortly before his death, a large square granite palace more or less in the Italian style, and as his widow preferred to live in Santa Barbara, Frank Bascom had taken it over for himself and his bride.

Olive had carried her millions to France and found her marquis. (As he was wealthy himself they contributed little to the current gossip of San Francisco.)

Janet Maynard lived with her mother, another widow of unrestricted means, in a large low Spanish house with a patio, built by a famous local architect with such success that Rex Roberts when he married Polly Luning, had bought the nearest vacant lot and ordered a romantic mansion as nearly like that of his wife's intimate friend as possible. He would live in it as soon as the idiosyncrasies of The Architect and Labor would permit,

Mrs. Clement Hunter had another pale gray stone palace, supported in front by noble pillars and commanding a superb view of the Bay, the Golden Gate, and Mount Tamalpais.

Aileen and her father lived in an old wooden house with a modern facade of stucco, and surrounded by a garden filled with somewhat blighted geraniums, fuchsias, sweet alicias, heliotrope, mignonette, and other nineteenth-century posies beloved of Mrs. Lawton in her romantic and innocent youth.

Sibyl and Alice Thorndyke's father had left his girls a square bow-windowed mansard-roofed double house, built in eighteen-seventy-eight, and unreclaimed. With it went a moderate income, and Alice lived on under the ugly old roof chaperoned by an aunt, who had been chosen from a liberal assortment of relatives because she was almost deaf, quite myopic, and so terrified of draughts that her absence when convenient could always be counted on.

# II

All of these young women belonged to Alexina's personal set, and joined the class in socialism, as they joined anything the stronger spirits among them suggested; and they attended as regularly as could be expected of "parasites" who were mainly interested in society, dress, poker, and some absorbing creature of the other sex.

Mr. Kirkpatrick hated them all with the exception of Alexina, Aileen, Mrs. Price Ruyler, the half-French wife of a New Yorker, recently adopted by California, and Mrs. Hunter, who had joined out of curiosity, having read a certain amount of socialism, but never met a socialist.

She confided to Mrs. Thornton that she was not acutely anxious to meet another, and Mrs. Thornton replied tartly:

"What do you want to belong to such a class for? It's rank hyprocrisy to pretend interest in a question we all hate the very name of, and to give the creature money that he no doubt turns over to the 'cause' with his tongue in his cheek. I'd never give one of them the satisfaction of knowing that I recognized his existence."

Said Maria Abbott firmly: "Exactly. We should ignore them, just as we ignore envious and spiteful and ill-bred outsiders of any sort."

"But we may not be able to ignore them," said Mrs. Hunter. "Their organization is the best of any party even if their numbers are not overwhelming. If they are content to advance slowly and by purely political methods there is no knowing who will own this or any government fifty years hence. For my part I'd rather they all turn raging anarchists; then we could turn machine guns on them and clean 'em out. I hate them, for I was too long getting where I am now, and I want to stay. But I don't make the mistake of ignoring them, and I rather like having a squint at them at close quarters. Kirkpatrick has taken us to several socialist meetings...we borrow the servants' coats and mutilate our oldest hats....Socialism seems to me rather more endurable than the socialists, and of these Kirkpatrick is about the sanest I have heard. They rant and froth, contradict themselves and one another, wander from the point and never get anywhere....That would give me hope if it were not for the fact that poor California is a magnet for the cranks of every fad as well as for the riff-raff and derelicts....My other hope is that even they - that is to say the least unbalanced of them - will come in time to realize that socialism is economically unsound - "

"Do you mean to say," cried Mrs. Abbott, "that Alexina has gone to socialist meetings?"

"Rather. She's very keen - "

"Believes in it?"

"Rather not. But she is naturally thorough - has a really extraordinary tendency, for a San Franciscan of her sex and status, to finish anything she has begun. Sometimes when she is arguing with Kirkpatrick she sticks out that chin of hers so far that you notice how square it is. She has him pretty well tamed though.

When he is ready to eat the rest of us alive she can smooth him down like a regular lion tamer."

"Well, you're nothing but a lot of parlor socialists," said Mrs. Thornton disgustedly. "And just as ridiculous as any other hybrids. But I'm relieved that it hasn't spoiled your taste for the simpler pleasures of life. Maria, as you don't play poker we'll have a game of bridge, Ladie, ring for cocktails, will you - or would you rather have a gin fizz? Don't look so horrified, Maria. We're better than socialists, anyhow; if they did win out you'd have farther to fall than we, for you're a moss-backed old conservative who hates change of any sort, while we not only love change of all sorts but are regular anarchists: do as we please and snap our fingers at the world. Here we are."

The three were in Mrs. Thornton's Moorish palace half way between San Mateo and Burlingame, a situation that symbolized the connecting bridge between the old and new order for Mrs. Abbott. Mrs. Thornton was a lineal descendant of the Rincon Hill of the sixties and had made her début with Maria Groome in the eighties. But she had married an immoderately rich man and had a barbaric taste for splendor that formed the proper setting for her own somewhat barbaric beauty, and imperious temper. Her dark and splendid beauty was waning, for in the matter of giving aid to nature with secrecy or with art she was faithful to the old tradition. But she was always an imposing figure and as close to being the first power in San Francisco society as that happy-go-lucky independent class would ever tolerate.

Gertrude Atherton

III


Kirkpatrick liked Mrs. Hunter, regarding her as "an honest plain-spoken dame without any frills." This estimate applied not only to her temperament but to her costumes. He admired her severe tailored suits (although he sensed their cost) and her smart, plain, hard, little hats.

The "frills and furbelows" of the younger "spenders" irritated the group of nerves appropriated by his class-consciousness almost beyond endurance; but he managed to stand it by reminding himself that irritation of all such was a healthy sign and vastly preferable to insidious tolerance.

Mrs. Hunter was also as regular in her attendance as Mrs. Dwight, Miss Lawton and Mrs. Price Ruyler, and asked fairly intelligent questions. The others floated in and out, and one by one dropped from the class, until toward the middle of the second winter none remained but Alexina, Aileen, Mrs. Hunter and Hélène Ruyler, who, like Aileen, found in the "frantic interest" of the materialistic creed which antagonized every instinct in them, a distraction from the excessive gambling which had threatened to wreck their nerves, purses, and peace of mind. They confided this artlessly to Mr. Kirkpatrick, who replied dryly that they were the best argument he had in stock.

But if the major part of his fashionable class deserted him in due course he had meanwhile seen the inside of their homes; and in each case, Alexina, who divined his interest, arranged to have him shown over the house from the kitchens and pantries straight up to the servants' quarters.

These he found unexpectedly comfortable and complete. In fact, they were so much more modern and adorned than the little cottage in the Mission where he lived with his mother that he longed for the immediate installation of a system that would teach these workers what real work was. What enraged him further was their "airs." They too obviously looked upon him as an alien intruder, whereas their mistresses, until socialism bored them, were, for the most part, as charmingly courteous as his one reliable friend, Mrs. Mortimer Dwight.

IV

During the first winter and spring while his pupils were still fairly regular in their attendance, he was both incensed and grimly amused by their various idiosyncrasies. He soon became accustomed to their vanity boxes and their public application of powder and lip stick, the frank crossing of their knees that exhibited more diaphanous silk than he had ever seen in his life before, the polite excitement that any new article of attire worn by one seemed to induce in all, the wicked but on the whole good-natured baiting of Aileen Lawton and Polly Roberts, the alternate insolence and Circean glances of Mrs. Bascom, who amused herself "practicing on him," and the constant smoking of most of them.

But what he could neither understand nor accept was their attitude toward one another. They would all rush at the hostess of the day as they entered, or at late comers, with the excited enthusiasm of loved and loving intimates who had not met for months; and Kirkpatrick, who missed nothing, knew that they met once a day if not oftener.

In spite of their intimacy their warm enraptured greetings carried a patent measure of admiration and even respect. It was always at least fifteen minutes before they would settle down for "work" and meanwhile they chattered about their common interests, but always with the air of relating long-delayed information and a frank desire to give of their best. He could have understood "gush," and sentimentalism, but this attitude of which he had neither heard nor read bothered him until one day he had a sudden, flash of enlightenment.

# V

"Is it class-consciousness?"

He asked the question of Gora, who dropped in upon a class at Alexina's or Aileen's sometimes on a free afternoon, and with whom he was walking down to the trolley car.

"Something like that. Caste they would call it if they thought about it at all, which to do them justice they don't....It used to be the fashion in San Francisco for everybody to 'knock' everybody else. Then came a revulsion and everybody began to praise and boost. You see it in all circles, but the way it has taken that crowd is to show their intense loyalty to one another by a constant reminder of it in manner, and in refraining from criticism of one another, no matter how much they may gossip about others outside of their particular set. Once, just to try my sister-in-law, I told her that in my nursing I had stumbled across evidence of an illicit love affair going on between one of her friends and a married man, the husband of my patient. My sister became so remote that I had the impression for a few moments that she really wasn't there. Once it would have infuriated me, but I have improved my sense of humor and developed my philosophy, so I merely turned the conversation, as she wouldn't speak at all. She had quite withdrawn - still further into the sacred preserves, I suppose....

"They are not only loyal but really seem to have the most exalted admiration for one another because they are all of the same heaven-born stock....That is not all, however. The truth of the matter is that they get so bored out here they would go frantic if they did not cultivate as many kinds of excitement and indigenous admirations as their wits are equal to. When they can, they vary the monotony of life with summers in Europe and winters in New York - or Santa Barbara, where they meet many interesting people from the East or England; but some of them won't leave their busy husbands or the husbands won't be left; or parents are not amenable; so they try to create an atmosphere of high spirits and sheer delight in youth and one another, and the result is almost a work of art. I rather respect them, but I envy them a good deal less than before I knew them so well."

"Oh, you envied them? They should envy you."

"Well, they don't! Yes, I envied them because it is my natural right to be one of them and fate slammed the door before I was born. It embittered my first youth, and it might have become an obsession after my brother married into society if I had not found the right kind of work. That and the boring Sundays I've spent at Rincona, and the experiences I have had with that young set, who are always at Mrs. Dwight's more or less; besides a profound satisfaction in accomplishing literary work that not one of them could do to save their lives - all this has routed a good deal of my old bitterness of spirit. I am not sorry that I had it and indulged it, however. Discontent and resentment put spurs on the soul. Anything is better than smugness,"

"It's made you different enough from these others, all right. Even from Mrs. Dwight, who is different herself....I'd rather you'd stayed discontented. The whole scheme's all wrong and you know it. You've suffered from it. You should be the last to tolerate it.

When they're jabbering away about their ninny affairs they pay as little attention to you as they do to me. They forget our existence. We don't belong, as they say. There isn't, one of them except Mrs. Dwight that I wouldn't give my eye teeth to see hanging out the wash or running a machine in a factory.'"

Gora turned to him with a smile. At this time she was as nearly happy as was possible for that insurgent too aspiring spirit.

"Nevertheless, they've made you over in a way - Oh, don't flame! I don't mean your principles...other ways that won't hurt you in the least. You cut your hair differently. You wear better shoes. You have your clothes pressed - the suit you wear up here anyhow. You've reformed your speech somewhat, and you know a good deal more about many things than you did a few months ago. I am expecting any day to see you wearing a 'boiled' shirt."

"Oh, no, not that! It'd never do. It's true enough I got to feeling self-conscious about my rough clothes and boots, especially after I met that dude brother of yours one day in the hall and he gave me a once-over that made me feel like a tramp."

"Oh!...But he was snubbed himself not so very long ago, and I suppose it gives him a certain pleasure to snub some one else, I am ashamed of him....But tell me, don't you like them rather better than you expected? Find them rather a better sort? You must see that there is practically no leisure class as far as the men are concerned - "

"They have time enough to go chicken chasing - "

"Well, aside from that? At least they do work. And the younger women? You knew before that they were frivolous because they had too much money and too few responsibilities. Many of the older women have a serious and useful side, even if they do waste an unholy amount of time at cards."

"Well, if you ask me, their manners, when they remember to use 'em, are better than I expected. Only that Miss Thorndyke is cold and haughty, but perhaps that's because she's poor (for her), or is covering up something, or is just plain stupid....Mrs. Dwight's manners are always perfect. She's my idea of a lady - just! And in the new system there'll be a long sight more ladies than is possible now, only no aristocrats....Yes, they're decent enough considering they're rotten poisoned by money and thinkin' themselves better'n the mass; and I like their affection for one another. But they could be all that in the socialist state and more too. They'd have to cut out drink and gambling, and a few other diversions some of 'em'll drift into, if one or two of 'em haven't already - just through being bored to death."

"Do you honestly think socialism means universal virtue?"

"No, I don't. I'm no such greenhorn; though there's some that does, or pretends to....But I mean there'd be no *drifting* into vice like there is now, no indulgence of any old weakness because temptation was always following them about or just round the corner. That's the trouble now....But in the most perfect state some would be watching out for their chance, just because the old Adam was too strong in spite of the fact that all the old reminders had disappeared."

"More likely they'd all murder one another because they were some ten thousand times more bored than that poor little group whose brains you are addling."

"I don't like to hear you talk like that, Miss Gora. You ought to give that pen of yours to socialism. There would be all the revenge you could want - and it's what you're entitled to. Then I could call you Comrade Gora."

"Call me Comarade by all means if it hurts you to say Miss to a fellow worker....You admit then that envy of a society you were not born into and which refuses to acknowledge you as an equal, is the secret of your desire to pull it down?"

"Partly that." he admitted cooly. "Not that I'd change places with any of those fat millionaires I see shuffling down the steps of the Pacific-Union Club - although I'll admit to you what I wouldn't to these young devils in my class, that I know some socialists who would. I hate the sight of 'em. But I want to do away with class-rights and class-distinctions, not only because I just naturally have no use for them but because I want to put an end to the misery of the world."

"You mean the material misery. What would you do with the other seven hundred different varieties?"

"Well....I guess each case would have to take care of itself. Perhaps we'd get round to it after a while. Get power and class-envy out of the world, and some genius, like as not, would invent a post-graduate course of colleges for human nature. All things are possible."

"You are an optimist! Here's our car. Come home with me and share the supper that I pay for with the tainted money of a plutocrat. Only we haven't any real plutocrats in San Francisco. Only modest millionaires. Will you?"

"Yes." said Mr. Kirkpatrick. "And thank you kindly." He even smiled, for he was developing a latent heavily overlain seed of humor; inherited from the full bay tree that had flourished in his grandfather, born in County Clare, where men sometimes indulged in rebellion but did not take themselves too seriously withal.

# CHAPTER II

## I

That winter and the following seasons for the next few years passed very rapidly for Alexina. Besides her classes and the constant companionship of her friends (to say nothing of the excitement of helping one or two of them out of not infrequent scrapes), she had for a time the absorbing interest of refurnishing the best part of her house.

The square lower hall which had been scantily furnished with the grandfather's clock, a hat-rack, and a settee, and whose walls were covered with "marble paper," was painted, walls and wood, a deep ivory white, and refurnished with light wicker furniture, palms, and growing plants. The hat-rack was abolished, and the small library on the left of the entrance turned into a men's dressing-room. The folding doors were removed from the great double parlors, the "body brussels" replaced by hardwood floors, the walls tinted a pale gray as a background for the really valuable pictures (including the proud and gracious and beautiful Alexina Ballinger, dust long since in Lone Mountain), and the splendid pieces of

Gertrude Atherton

Italian furniture which had always seemed to sulk and bulge against the dull brown walls. The rep and walnut sets were sent to the auction room and replaced by comfortable chairs and sofas whose colors varied, but harmonized not only with one another but with the rugs that Alexina under Gora's direction had bought at auction. In fact she bought many of her new pieces at auction and with Aileen found it vastly exciting to pore over the advertisements and then go down to the crowded rooms and bid.

The billiard room behind the former library she left as it was. Her mother's large bedroom upstairs she turned into a library with bookcases to the ceiling on three sides, and one of the carved oaken tables against an expanse of Pompeiian red relieved by one painting (a wedding gift from Judge Lawton, who believed in patronizing local art) that had despoiled a desert of its gorgeous yellow sunrise.

The carpet and curtains were red without pattern. The coal grate had been removed and a fireplace built for logs. It was to be her own den for long rainy winter afternoons, or the cold and foggy days of summer when she remained in the city.

The dining-room was also given a hardwood floor and a Japanese red and gold wall paper as a compliment to her martial ancestors; but as the sideboards were built into the wails end could be replaced only at great cost; they remained as a brooding reminder of the solid sixties, and no doubt exchanged resentful reminiscences at night with the chairs which had been merely recovered.

As a matter of course modern bathtubs were installed

and gas replaced by electricity.

All this made a "hole" in Alexina's bonds, the wedding-present of her brothers, but Mortimer offered no objection, knowing as he did that to achieve his ambition of being master of a house to which fashionable people would come as a matter of course the outlay was imperative. Moreover, entertaining at home would be far cheaper for him than at the restaurants.

He was doing fairly well at this time, for he had learned what commodities the retail men were likely to buy of a firm as small as his, and he had got into touch with one or two foreign markets not monopolized by the older houses. Moreover, he had been speculating a little in the new Nevada mines, and successfully. He presented Alexina with a Victrola which included the music for all the new dances, and a long coat of baby lamb lined with her favorite periwinkle blue. To his sister he returned a thousand dollars of her money.

Alexina knew nothing of these speculations and felt that her original faith in him was justified. He did not offer even yet to pay all the monthly expenses of the house, explaining casually that the greater part of his profits went back into the business; but he handed over his share promptly, and such fleeting doubts and anxieties as may once have visited his still inexperienced wife faded and finally disappeared.

II

They began to entertain a little during the second winter, Mrs. Groome having been dead nearly two years. The new floor of the large drawing-room had been laid for dancing, and their friends formed a habit, when there was "nothing on" elsewhere, of telephoning and announcing they were coming up to take a whirl. This led to more telephoning, and some twenty couples would dance in the long-silent old house at least once and often three times a week.

The new order delighted James, who felt young again, and his hastily improvised suppers were models of unpretentious succulence. There were always sherry and whiskey in the handsome old decanters on the sideboards; and, at the equally perfect little dinners, for a time, two bottles of Alexander Groome's favorite brand of champagne (which he had remembered with satisfaction on his deathbed that he had not outlived) were brought up from the cellar by the beaming James.

When, almost with tears, he informed his mistress' husband that the last bottle had been served Mortimer could do no less than order up a case. He had not the courage either to give his guests the excellent native claret where they had formerly enjoyed imported champagne or to appear a "piker" in the eyes of the far from democratic family butler.

He consoled himself with the reflection that it was "good business." Nearly all the young men, married or otherwise, that came to his house (Alexina subtly encouraged him to call it his house) were of more or less importance or standing in the world of business and finance (two were lawyers in their first flight, Bascom Luning and Jimmie Thorne), and the more prosperous he appeared to be (they knew to a dollar the extent of Alexina's income) the more apt would business be to flow his way, the less likely they would be to suspect him of playing the stock market. At all events it enhanced his standing and gave him intense pleasure.

Moreover, as time passed it became evident to his sensitive ego that he was no longer looked upon as an outsider. He was accepted as a matter of course. He was one of them. Neither men nor women (not even Aileen) continued to ask themselves whether they liked him or not. He was there and to stay and that was the end of it. They had always liked his manners; he made a charming host, and, as ever, he danced like "a god with wings on his heels."

Quite naturally in due course some one offered to put him up at the most exclusive and the most expensive club west of New York, a club to which every Californian with any pretence to fashion or importance belonged as a matter of course. Old men whose names had once been potent in the great banks or firms of the valleys below, sat and gazed with sad and rheumy eyes down upon the new city in which there was barely a familiar landmark to remind them of their youth or the years of their power and their pride. They sat there all day long, day after day; and tourists went away with the impression that the imposing brown stone mansion on the sacred crest of Nob Mill was a sumptuously endowed retreat for the incurably aged.

But the majority of its members were very much alive and still well-padded; and, far from being on a pale diet, were deeply appreciative of the famous culinary resources of the chef, and showed it.

When the offer was made to Mortimer he accepted with a bright: "Oh, thanks, old chap. I'd like it immensely," But when, on the first day of his membership, he stood in one of the front windows and gazed out at the ruins opposite - the Pacific Union Club and the Fairmont Hotel were still two oases in the rubbled waste of Nob Hill - he felt so exultant and so happy that he dared not open his lips lest he betray himself. He could mount no higher socially. All that he had to strive for now was his million - or millions. When he had half a million he would build a house at Burlingame that could be enlarged from time to time.

Only with the "Rincona crowd" he had made no headway. Maria did not hesitate to comment on the extravagance of doing the house over, the membership at the club with all it entailed, Alexina's little electric car, and above all the constant entertaining. A moderate amount was due Alexina's position; but open house - nothing made money fly so quickly. Prices were getting higher every day (there came a time, in the wake of the great war, when she looked back with sad amazement at the morning of her discontent) and rich people were getting richer while poor people like themselves (she meant what Alexina still called the A. A.) were growing poorer.

Tom Abbott had not put Mortimer up at the club. He happened to know that although his brother-in-law was doing fairly well he was not making a fortune, and suspected that he dabbled in stocks. But he said nothing of this to his wife, and as he knew that Alexina had long since revoked her power of attorney (she had given him to understand that this was done at Mortimer's suggestion) he believed that her money at least was safe.

# CHAPTER III

## I

Alexina, although she would have found it impossible, even if she had so desired, to relapse into the incognitance of the years preceding her mother's death, had nevertheless locked and sealed and cellared her ivory tower, those depths of her nature where, she suspected, her true ego dwelt. It was an ego she had forfeited the right to indulge, nor had she at this time any desire to know more of herself than she did. Life after all was very pleasant; she managed to fill it with many little and even a few absorbing interests; and once she spent a month at Santa Barbara chaperoning Janet Maynard, where her duties sat lightly upon her and she would have responded naturally if addressed as Miss Groome, so completely did Mortimer fade into the background. In the summer of nineteen-thirteen Judge Lawton and Aileen overcame all protests and took her with them to Europe, where, after a month in Paris, she visited Olive de Morsigny in her renaissance château on the Loire. The memory of Gathbroke revisited her and she half-wished the Judge would go to England, but the climate did not agree with him, and after a few more enchanted weeks, in Italy and Spain, she returned to Mortimer, who was distinctly duller than ever.

But she had reconciled herself long since to the dullness of her life-partner; he could not help it and she had willfully married him in the face of as imposing a phalanx of family and friendly opposition as ever attempted to stand between a girl and her fate.

Nevertheless, immediately after her return from Santa Barbara in the late autumn of nineteen-eleven, and wholly without, analysis or pondering, she made a significant change in the order of her life. Mortimer, who had, during her absence, occupied a large room at the back of the house visited by the afternoon sun, found himself invited to retain it....They must avoid the least possibility of a family until they were better off....She had been hearing the subject discussed...the most economical baby cost fifty dollars a month. With a permanent trained nurse, and of course they would have one, the cost would easily be doubled...thousands were required for the proper education of a child...even if she had girls she should wish them to go to college; she was not half educated herself...and boys, with their extravagances, their debts, they cost a mint; it was better for children to be born outright in the humbler classes than to be born into a rich set without riches themselves...it all put her in a panic every time she thought of it....Morty was so sensible and had such a high sense of responsibility, of course he under-stood...children, even when small, would hamper him fearfully, especially as he had not even begun to make his million....As for herself she would be more economical than ever and help him like the good pal she was.

Mortimer had the sensation of being trussed up with invisible but inflexible silken thongs. His thoughts need not be recorded.

## II

Alexina refurnished her bedroom in her favorite periwinkle blue; a low graceful day-bed with a screen before the stationary washstand helped to create the atmosphere of a boudoir. It had an intensely personal atmosphere in which man, more particularly a lawful husband, had no place.

When Alexina stood on the threshold and surveyed this room, chaste, cool, proud, and exquisitely lovely, she lifted her hand and blew off a kiss, out of the window, wafting away the memory of the room as it had been. She had remarkable powers of obliteration, a sort of River of Lethe among the backwaters of her mind, where she held below the surface all she wished to forget until it ceased to struggle. She never again gave a thought to her early relationship with her husband; not even to the indifference or distaste which had followed so quickly upon her curiosity and her determination to feel romantic at all costs.

III

Subtly she felt she was happier than she had ever been even in those first weeks, when she had barred the gates of her fool's paradise behind her; she felt as free and happy as the birds skimming over the beds of periwinkle below her window, and (miraculously finding her second youth quite as productive as her first) took no pains to conceive of anything better. She looked neither forward nor back, and all was well.

She even flirted a little, that being the fashion, and, having had enough of business men, encouraged the devotions of Bascom Luning and Jimmie Thorne. She saw them when they chose to call in the daytime, and regaled the glowering Mortimer at the dinner table with scraps of their sapience.

Mortimer had resigned himself long since to the sacrifice of several of his bourgeois ambitions, among them to be master in his own house; but not an iota of his convictions. Although it would not have occurred to him to distrust his wife if she had chosen to sit up all night with a man, he made frozen comments upon the impropriety of a woman having men in the house when her husband was not there, sitting out dances with men, taking long tramps through Marin County with three men and no one for chaperon but Alice Thorndyke and Janet Maynard - shocking flirts - whole Sundays - with lunch heaven knew where, and himself, who hated tramping, not included.

But these grim remonstrances were met in so gay a spirit of badinage that he felt ridiculous, particularly as no powers of badinage or of repartee had been included in his own mental equipment; and he usually relapsed into a polite and bored silence.

He never had had much to say at the dinner table when they were alone, and, as time went on, his comments on the day were exhausted before the soup had given place to the entrée, and Alexina fell into the habit of bringing her Italian text-book to the table - the study of Italian just then being the rage in her set - and whatever interesting book she had on hand. Mortimer made no protest. His brain was fagged at night. It was a relief not to be expected to talk when they dined alone; those long silences had been oppresive even to him; he rather welcomed the books.

# CHAPTER IV

I

This complete new freedom, and personal privacy, entailed in time a result which Alexina would have been the last to anticipate even if she had disposed of her husband by death or divorce.

Owing to the thoroughness of her mental methods she was psychologically free, the legal tie mattered as little as if Mortimer had been transposed by some beneficent law to the status of a brother. The will when it is strong enough can control acts, and, when favored by bias, thought; but it has no command whatever over the sub-consciousness, and in that mysterious region are the subtle inheritances of mind and character, the springs and the direction, of all functional life; a fate with a thousand threads on her wheel, filaments from the souls and the bodies, the minds and the acts, of every ancestor straight back to that vast impersonal ocean where, unthinkable millions of years ago proemial life awaited the call of the worlds.

This aged untiring fate at the wheel battles unceasingly with the conscious mind above, for age is prone to live by law and rote. These fates, the oldest daughters of the Earth-Mother, Nature, know nothing of morals or manners, assume that men and women are as naïve in their normality as the denizens of forest and field. And so they are while children.

II

The eternal pull between civilizing Mind (Oh, centuries yet from being civilized!) and the memoried but obstinate old lady at the wheel (who laughs when a man of powerful will and too active mind "wills" sleep; forcing him finally to choose between the horrors of insomnia, the insidious tyranny of drugs, and the doubtful and wearisome alternative of psychotherapeutics) - this pull, automatic in people of low estate, becomes bitter and often appalling where the mind is highly developed and attuned besides to the codes and customs of the best that civilization has so far accomplished.

The most vital of all these functions, for without it Mother Earth would be like an ant hill without ants, and all these ancient norms of daughters as homeless as the rest of the fates, is what man in a spirit of social compromise has labeled an instinct - the sex-instinct. It is no more an instinct than recurring sleep, lymphatic action, hunger, thirst, alimentation. It is a primal function for which Mind, wisely foreseeing the consequences of too much Nature, long since created laws both civil and social to curb. There are many impulses, Inherited, from ten thousand ancestors and constantly jogged by Earth's busy agent, human nature, that may logically be called instincts (their roots lying in the ancient social groups and their struggle to exist) but not a function that governs the law of reproduction, as appetite governs the law of renewing the vital necessities of the body.

III

In the Latin races the conscious war between the brain above and the sub-ego below, with the latter's constant reminders that mind is a mere excrescence, often warped or ill-directed, at the apex of the perfect body, is almost negligible. Even, when moral their lack of reticence, their practical logic, their habit of facing every fact pertaining to life, psychical and physical, as squarely as they face a simple question of hunger and thirst, above all their almost complete lack of that modern, development, called romance, which has given birth to a peculiar form of personal imagination, too often without foundation or logic - all these preclude that most active of all mental aids to the matter of fact needs of the body - glamour.

But it is far otherwise with the English-speaking races - loosely called Anglo-Saxon, They are powerfully sexed; their feelings and sentiments go deeper than is possible to those of more ebullient temperament but fatal clarity of vision; refinement of mind and habit and manner is perhaps the most precious of their achievements, and they have established a code which not only demands rectitude of act but suppression of thought and desire where there is no lawful outlet.

Nothing, possibly, has more infuriated the old lady at the methodically performing wheel than this. She takes her revenge and squirts poison into the physical structure of the brain, obscures the soul with dark and brooding clouds, and subtly reduces the blood system to such a state that any germ is welcome.

Gertrude Atherton

IV

Once more Mind uses its highest faculties and outwits her, having no intention that civilization shall drop below the plane to which it has been raised through long laborious centuries of time. Life becomes more diverse, more complex. The middle classes work harder to live; they have little leisure for thoughts, for introspection. Punishment is dire....Those that have leisure and yet not enough to command the more brilliant and special forms of distraction are supplied with public libraries, gymnasiums, free medical advice regarding the laws of hygiene in places where they cannot fail to see it, new forms of cheap amusement; they are subtly encouraged to take up useful work or study; or there are increasing pressures which may force even this semi-leisure class to work for luxuries if not for bread. Tens of thousands of women are led into the passionate diversions of club life. For them, too, politics with its fierce championships and hatreds and frictions; the necessity of concentration of thought on the impersonal plane if only in the matter of getting the best of rivals within the fold; and if hair flies souls are saved.

Over the Oldest Profession Mind still scratches its head in vain. It is ever hopeful, and hamstrings a sovereign patron, like alcohol, now and again; but the lady at the wheel smiles, for here, in addition to the unquenchable maternal instinct, the ignorance of the poor, and the glamour that the men of certain races have learned to give to love, she has her clearest field.

Aside from the women of commerce there are, of course, many secret rebels - now and then only does one make her exit from society through the courts. The vast majority of Anglo-Saxons in whatever clime or capital, suppress their "unrefined" appetites or vagrant fancies - which are vibrations from the wheel; sometimes hard jerks when the presiding genius is more than commonly out of patience - and rise to serene heights or grow morbid and irritable according to the strength or the meagerness of their equipment; or the nature of their resources. A cultivated resource is a persistent fiction that life is as it ought to be, not as it is, and it is no plan of theirs to read books or witness plays that might carve and populate a new groove in their brains.

Let no one imagine that this class will become more "enlightened," "broader," as time goes on. Not for a century at least. Mind has made too great a success of this product; she has practically achieved a complete triumph over the lady at the wheel. It is this class that has made civilization progress, the solid thing it is to date. The excrescences, the deserters from the normal, scintillating or subtle, may be tolerated for the spice they give to life but they will never rule,

Possibly they do not mind. Life Is made up of compromises and compensations.

# V

American women in youth, of the visibly reputable world, may be freely divided into two classes, the oversexed and those that seem cold to themselves and others until they are well into the period of their second youth - between twenty-four and thirty; and a not inconsiderable number are so and permanently. In the first case they either precipitate themselves into matrimony or have one or more intrigues until they find the man they wish to marry, when they settle down and make excellent wives. The others, if they are imaginative and high-minded, fall in love romantically and marry far too soon; or they capitalize their youth or beauty and marry to the best advantage; or they elect to live a life of serene spinsterhood like Alexina's Aunt Clara, and bring up the family children. A not inconsiderable number take their fling late.

When the American girl of the super-refined class, and whose baleful norm in the crypt was asleep at the wheel in her first blind youth, finds herself disappointed in the most intimate partnership that exists, the complaisance, voluntary at the beginning, drifts into habit, more and more grimly endured. Some have the moral courage to put an end to it as they would to any false situation, but if individuals were not rare in this world we should have chaos, not a civilization of sorts which is a pleasant place to plant the feet, however high into the clouds the head may poke its investigating nose.

It is natural that with such women during the period of endurance all love should seem distasteful, and the mind dwell upon any other subject. But remove the cause of sex-inertia and there is likely to be the stir and awakening of spring after a long monotonous winter of hard frost and blanketing snow. Or a homelier simile: remove the cause of chronic indigestion and the appetite becomes fresh and normal.

Thus Alexina.

# CHAPTER V

## I

San Francisco, commencing in September, has three or four months of perfect weather. The cold fogs and winds cease to pay their daily visits, the rainy season awaits the new year. The skies are a deep and cloudless blue, the air is warm and soft and alluring, never too hot, although the overcoats of summer are discarded.

The city lies bathed in golden sunlight or the sharp jeweled light of stars, when the moon is not blazing like a crystal bonfire. Then Mount Tamalpais and other mountains across the Bay and behind the city take on a chiseled outline that, particularly at night, makes them look curiously new, as if but yesterday heaved from the deep, and Nature too busy to provide them with a background and the soft blurs of time for centuries to come. This primeval look of bare California mountains on clear nights has something sinister and menacing in its aspect as if at any moment they might once more brood alone over the earth.

## II

Alexina returned from abroad early in November and stood one morning outside her eucalyptus grove, revolving slowly on one heel, schoolgirl fashion, as she gazed up at the steep densely populated hill that rose from the street below her own private little hill, and cut off her view of the hills of Berkeley and the mountains beyond; at the broad crowded valleys on the south; the range of hills that hid the Pacific Ocean, and included Mount Calvary with its cross and the symmetrical mass of Twin Peaks; the bare brown mountains of the north piling above the green sparkling bay with its wooded and military islands.

Like a good and valiant Californian she was assuring herself that she had seen nothing like this in Europe, and that she really preferred it to art galleries and dilapidated old ruins. But as a matter of fact she had returned to California with dragging feet and was merely staving off the disheartening moment when her ruthless candor would force her to admit it.

San Francisco was all very well, and in this dazzling light that compact mass of houses swarming over the city's hills and valleys, with sudden palms in high gardens and a tree here and there, produced the impression that all were white with red roofs, and looked not unlike Genoa. But it seemed quite unromantic and uninspiring to a girl who had just paid her first brief visit to the old world, an interval, moreover, that had been without a responsibility, cut her off so completely from her general life that when variously addressed "Mademoiselle," "Signorina," "Señorita," she ceased almost at once to feel either surprised or flattered. If she had not forbidden herself to dream she would still have been Alexina Groome with a future to sketch with her own adventurous pencil; and to fill in at her pleasure.

But although she was free in a sense she was not free to live in Europe. She was a partner with a partner's obligations. To desert Mortimer would not only be to banish him from Ballinger House to dreary bachelor quarters, with none of the comforts and little luxuries he intensely loved, but it would also deprive him of his surest social prop. People had accepted him and liked him as well as they liked the totally uninteresting of the good old stock; but many would drift into the habit of not inviting him to anything but large dances, if his wife were absent. Alexina knew that her invitations to all important and many small dinners, not avowedly bridge or poker parties, were as inevitable as crab in season; but there were too many young men whom girls would infinitely prefer to enliven the monotony of crab à la poulette, to any married man, particularly one who had as little to say as poor Morty. She had known dèbutantes who flatly refused to dance with married men or even to be introduced to them.

California was her fate. No doubt of that. She might never see Europe again, for while it was all very well to be a guest once it would be quite impossible another time. She certainly could not afford it herself and keep Ballinger House open, even for brief summer visits; as she might if her home were in New York.

Of course Mortimer might make his million, but then again he might not. Certainly there were no present signs of it and she had never seen him so depressed, not even during the panic of nineteen-seven. His eyes were as lifeless as slate, his voice was flat, although for that matter he was almost dumb. When at home he sat brooding heavily by the open western windows of the drawing-room, or moved restlessly about. To all her questions he replied shortly that the times were bad again, worse than ever; that he was holding his own, but was tired, tired out. As she had not been there he had not cared to take a cottage by himself, and had paid few week-end visits. He had nothing to talk to women about and the men talked of nothing but the business depression....Alexina had shrugged her shoulders and concluded that his attitude was a subtle reproach for leaving him to the dull cares of business while she enjoyed herself in Europe.

She was not in the least sorry for Mortimer. He had been perfectly comfortable; he had had his friends; she had left him a sum of money which with the monthly rents from the flats would pay her share in the household expenses; he could spend his free afternoons at the golf club by the ocean, and his evenings, when not invited out, at the temple of his idolatry on Nob Hill. James was a better housekeeper than she was and it was now two years that Mortimer bad been living the life of a luxurious bachelor at the back of the house with an always amiable companion at breakfast and dinner.

III

Alexina, as she stood shading her eyes from the brilliant sunlight and watching a great liner drift through the Golden Gate, wondered if Morty had consoled himself, and if his Puritanical conscience were flaying him. She hoped that he had, for she was quite willing that he should be happy in his own way, poor thing, so long as he secluded his divagations from the world - and she could trust him to do that! Now that she had ceased to be the complaisant bored wife with dull nerves and torpid imagination she would be the last to condemn him. Human Nature was an ever opening book to her these days, and she wondered what would happen to herself if any of several men she liked were capable of making her love him, whipping up a personal storm in those emotional gulfs which had slowly and inflexibly intruded themselves upon her consciousness.

She had pondered long and deeply on this subject, particularly in the old world where bonds seem looser to the mere observer whether they are or not, and where life looks to the American the quintessence of romance....She had concluded that the most satisfactory experience that could come to her would be a mad love affair "in the air" with a man who posse-ssed all the requirements to induce it, but who would either be the unsuspecting object, or, reciprocating, would continue to love her with the world between them.

For she shrank from the disillusionments of secret libertinage; she did not, indeed, believe that love could survive it, although passion might for a time. Passion was unthinkable to her without love, and when she recalled the mean and sordid devices to which two of her friends were put to meet their lovers she felt nothing but disgust for the whole drama of man and woman.

Alexina had been reared on the soundest moral principles of church and society, to say nothing of the law, but the norm at the wheel has often laughed in her amiable way at church and society and law when circumstances have conspired to help her. But against fastidiousness even the blind urge of the race seldom has availed her; she can only go on sullenly feeding the fires, heaping on the fuel, hoping grimly for the astrological moment.

IV

Alexina shrugged her shoulders impatiently and went into the house. She would go down to the bank and clip her coupons. She cultivated assiduously the practical side of life, making the most of it, delighted when repairs were needed on her flats, regretting that the greater part of her income came from ground rents, collected, as ever, by Tom Abbott, and bonds, from which she still experienced a childish pleasure in cutting the coupons. Her flats, which were in a humbler part of the western division of the city, she had never visited, but she received a call every month from the agent, who brought her the rents and complaints.

She had made a heroic effort to turn herself into a business woman but the material had been too slender; and she sometimes wished for a large independent fortune that would tax her powers to the utmost. But she never even had any surplus to invest. Her wardrobe was no inconsiderable item; living prices rose steadily; there were repairs both on her own house and the flats to be anticipated every year, to say nothing of the fiendish sum that must be set aside for taxes. But she managed to save the necessary amount; and if they lived somewhat extravagantly, at least she had never disturbed her capital.

On the whole she knew they had managed very well for young people who lived so much in the world, and she had no intention of economizing further. They had no children. Her husband was young and energetic and healthy. Her own little fortune was secure. She purposed to enjoy life as best she could; and as she could not have done this quite selfishly and been happy, she included among her yearly expenditures a certain admirable charity presided over by her equally admirable sister, and even visited it occasionally with her friends when a serious mood descended abruptly upon them....She was now on the threshold of her second beautiful youth, and found herself and life far more interesting than when, a silly girl of eighteen, she had believed that all life and romance must be crowded into that callow period. She had no idea of sacrificing this new era vibrating with unknown possibilities (it was on the cards that she might resurrect Gathbroke from his ivory tomb; lie would do admirably for her present needs, and when she found it difficult to visualize him after so long a period, she could pay Gora a sisterly visit) to a penurious attempt to increase her capital. At the same time she had no intention of diminishing it. To quote Tom Abbott (when Maria was elsewhee): She might be a fool, or even a -- fool, but she was not a -- fool.

V

She dressed herself in a black velvet suit made by her New York tailors. She had spent, a fortnight with her brother Ballinger on her way home, and he had given her a set of silver fox: a large muff and two of those priceless animals head to head to keep a small section of her anatomy at blood heat in a climate never cold enough for furs.

The day was hot. It was the sort of weather which on the opposite side of the continent arrives when spring is melting into summer and fortunate woman arrays herself in thin and dainty fabrics. But women everywhere with a proper regard for fashion rush the season, and autumn is the time to display the first smart habiliments of winter. No San Francisco woman of fashion would be guilty of comfortable garments in the glorious spring weather of November if she perished in her furs.

The coat, bound with silk braid, was lined with periwinkle blue, and there was a touch of the same color in her large black velvet hat. Nothing could make the great irises of her black-gray eyes look blue, but they shone out, dazzling, under the drooping brim; and if she was, perchance, too warm above, her scant skirt, her thin silk stockings and low patent leather shoes struck the balance like a brilliant paradox.

Alexina nodded approvingly at her image in the pier glass, found the key of her safe deposit box in the cabinet where she had left it, and went down to the smart little electric car which the gardener had brought to the door.

# CHAPTER VI

I

Alexina stood alone in the strong room of the bank leaning heavily against the wall with its endless rows of compartments from one of which she had taken the dispatch box in which she had kept her bonds.

The box had fallen to the floor. If there had been any one in the room with her he would have started and turned as the box clanged with a hollow echo on the steel surface.

The box was empty.

It was a large box. It had contained forty thousand dollars' worth of bonds, nearly a third of her fortune. The securities were among the soundest the country afforded, for Alexander Groome, wild as he may have been when relieving the monotony of life with too many diversions, not the least of which was specu-lation, never made a mistake in his permanent investments; and others had been bought with equal prudence by Judge Lawton or Tom Abbott.

But the bonds had been negotiable. She recalled Tom Abbott's warning to keep them always in her safe deposit box and the key hidden. They might be traced if stolen, but State's Prison for the thief would be cold comfort if the bonds had been cashed and the money spent.

She had always had one of the lighter Italian pieces in her bedroom, a beautiful cabinet of carved and gilded oak nearly black with age. Like all such it had a secret drawer and here she had kept her keys, and her jewels during the winter.

Who knew of this secret drawer, which opened by pressing a certain little gilded face on the panel?...All her friends, of course: Aileen, Sibyl, Alice, Olive, Janet, Hélène....Unthinkable to have a secret drawer in an old Italian cabinet which had belonged to some Borgia or other, and not exhibit it to one's chosen friends.

She had even shown it to Gora, but to no one else but Mortimer. She had kept his love letters in it for a time, written while the family was applying the polite methods of the modern inquisition at Rincona, They had remained there, forgotten, until her mother's death, when she had remembered the secret drawer as a safe hiding place for her keys and jewels; which, with her mother's, had formerly reposed in the safe under the stairs.

It was a deep drawer and when she was in town held the few valuable stones, reset, that she had inherited from her mother, besides the fine pieces she had received as wedding-gifts; when all the old friends of the family out-did themselves, and not a few of the less distinguished but more opulent, whose floors Alexina had graced while her mother slept. Her pearl necklace had been the present of her more intimate group of friends.

Alexina was not a little proud of her collection of jewels, although she seldom wore anything but her pearls. She had left it when she went abroad, in the safe deposit vault, and she sent a quick terrified glance in the coffer's direction like that of a cornered rat.

But her attention riveted itself once more on the empty box at her feet. A third of her fortune, and gone beyond redemption. Her stunned mind grasped that fact at once. No one stole bonds to keep them. But who was the thief?

Not any of her old friends. They might gamble, or drink, or deceive their legal guardians, but they drew the line at stealing. Certain sins lie within the social code and others do not. Women of her class, unless kleptomaniac, did not steal. It wasn't done. With reason or unreason they classed thieves of any sort with harlots, burglars, firebugs, embezzlers, forgers, murderers, and common people who overdressed and drank too much in public; and withdrew their skirts.

Moreover, Aileen had been with her in Europe. Olive lived there. Janet and Sibyl had more money than they could spend. The Ruylers were ranching, and Hélène was in Adler's Sanatorium with a new baby. Alice had gone to Santa Barbara before she left and had not returned.

It was insulting even to pass them in review, but the mind works in erratic curves under shock.

Gertrude Atherton

Gora had taken the thousand dollars Mortimer had returned to her and gone first to Lake Tahoe and then to Honolulu to write a novel. She would return on the morrow.

Mortimer.

It was incredible. Monstrous. She was outrageous even to link his name with such a deed. He was the soul of honor. He might not be a genius but no man had a cleaner reputation. She had lived with him now for over six years and she had never...never...never...

And she knew, unconsentingly, infallibly, that Mortimer had stolen the bonds.

# CHAPTER VII

I

Alexina drew the jewel coffer from the depths of the compartment and opened it with fingers that felt swollen and numb. But the jewels were there, and she experienced a feeling of fleeting satisfaction. They were no part of her fortune, for she believed that only want would ever induce her to sell them, but at least they were her own personal treasure and a part of the beauty of life.

She returned the fallen box to its place and locked the little cupboard, then took herself in hand. Neither the keeper outside the door of the vault nor those she met above must suspect that anything was wrong with her. What she should do she had no idea at the moment, but at all events she must have time to think.

She left the bank with her usual light step and her head high, and then she motored down the Peninsula. As she passed the shipyards she saw crowds of men standing about; some of them turned and scowled after her. They were on strike and took her no doubt for the wife or daughter of a millionaire; and in truth there was never any difference superficially in her appearance from that of her wealthier friends. She had one ear instead of several hut it was perfect of its kind. Her wardrobe was by no means as extensive as Sibyl's or Janet's or a hundred others, but what she had came from the best houses, that use only the costliest materials. Her face was composed and proud. There was not a signal out, even from her brilliant expressive eyes, of the storm within.

Her mind was no longer stunned. It was seething with disgust and fury. How dared he? Her own, her exclusive property, inherited and separate....She felt at this moment exactly as she would have felt if her jewel coffer instead of the dispatch box had been rifled; it was the instinct of possession that had been outraged. What was hers was hers as much as the hair on her head or the thoughts in her mind...an instinct that harked back to the oldest of the buried civilizations...she wondered if any socialist really had cultivated the power to feel differently. She was quite certain that if Kirkpatrick should see a thief fleeing with his purse he would chase him, collar him, and either chastise him then and there or drag him to the nearest police station.

And the thief was her husband, the man of her choice. Alexina felt that possibly if a brother had stolen her money she would have been less bitter because less humiliated; one did not select one's brothers....And if she had still loved Mortimer it would have been bad enough, although no doubt with the blindness of youthful passion she would immediately have begun to make excuses for him, reeling a blow as it would have been. But the one compensation she had found in her matrimonial wilderness was her pride in the essential honor of her chosen partner, and her complete trust. If there had been any necessity for giving a power of attorney when she went to Europe she would have drawn it in his favor without hesitation, so completely had she forgotten her earlier incitements to precaution....If she had, no doubt she would have returned to find herself penniless.

Whether he had stolen the money to speculate with or to extricate himself from some business muddle she did not pause to wonder. He had lost it; that was sufficiently evident from his depression. When his powers of bluff failed him matters were serious indeed.

He had stolen and lost. The first would have been unforgivable, but the last was unpardonable.

And he had taken her money as he would have taken Gora's, or his parents' had they been alive, because however they might lash him with their contempt, his body was safe from prison, his precious position in society unshaken. She knew him well enough to be sure that if he had had forty thousand dollars of some outsider's money under his hand it would have been safe no matter what his predicament. He would have accepted the alternative of bankruptcy without hesitation.

But with the women of his family a man was always safe. She remembered something that Gora had once said to the same effect....Yes, she could have forgiven the theft of an outsider, for at least she would be spared this sickening suffocating sensation of contempt. It was demoralizing. She hated herself as much as she hated him. Moreover there would have been some compensation in sending an outsider to San Quentin.

And there was the serious problem of readjusting her life. Two thousand dollars out of a small income was a serious deficit. Simultaneously she was visited by another horrid thought. Mortimer had heretofore paid half the household expenses. No doubt he was no longer in a position to pay any. They would have to live, keep up Ballinger House, dress, pay taxes, subscribe to charities, maintain their position in society, pay the doctor and the dentist...a hundred and one other incidentals...out of four thousand dollars a year. Well, it couldn't be done. They would have to change their mode of living.

However, that concerned her little at present. The ordeal loomed of a plain talk with Mortimer. It was impossible to ignore the theft even had she wished; which she did not, for it was her disposition to have things out and over with. But it would be horrible...horribly intimate. She had always deliberately lived on the surface with her family and friends, respected their privacies as she held hers inviolate. As her mind flashed back over her life she realized that this would be the first really serious personal talk she would ever have held with any one. Or, if her family, and occasionally, Mortimer, had insisted upon being serious she had maintained her own attitude of airy humor or delicate insolence.

She had no shyness of manner but a deep and intense shyness of the soul. Some day...perhaps...but never yet.

II

She turned her car after a time, for she feared that her
batteries would run down. The strikers were still
lounging and scowling; and this time having relaxed
her mental girths she looked at them with sympathy.
She knew from the liberal education she had received
at the hands of Mr. James Kirkpatrick, and the
admissions of Judge Lawton and other thoughtful men,
that the iniquities of employers and labor were pretty
equally divided; greed and lack of tact on the one hand,
greed and class hatred and the itch for power on the
part of labor leaders; and a stupidity in the mass that
was more pardonable than the short-sighted stupidities
of capital....But what would you? A few centuries
hence the world might be civilized, but not in her time.
Nothing gave her mind less exercise. One thing at least
was certain and that was that when strikes lasted too
long the laborers and their families went hungry, and
the employers did not. That settled the question for her
and determined the course of her sympathy. (It was not
yet the fashion to recognize the unfortunate "public,"
squeezed and helpless between these two louder
demonstrators of sheer human nature.)

But her mind did not linger in the shipyards. She had
problems of her own....The chief of her compensations,
having made a mess of her life, had been taken from
her: her pride and her faith in the man to whom she
was bound. The death of love had been so gradual that
she had not noticed it in time for decent obsequies; she
had not sent a regret in its wake....She had had enough
left, more than many women who had made the same
blind plunge into the barbed wire maze of
matrimony....And now she had nothing. She would

have liked to drive right out on to a liner about to sail through the Golden Gate...but she would no doubt have to live on...and on...in changed, possibly humble, conditions...despising the man she must meet sometime every day....Yes, she did wish she never had been born.

# CHAPTER VIII

I

She concluded, while she dressed for dinner, that she must be a coward.

Alexina was far from satisfied with herself as she was; she would have liked to possess a great talent like Gora, or be an intellectual power in the world of some sort. She was far from stultification by the national gift of complacence, careless self-satisfaction - racial rather than individual...qualities that have made the United States lag far behind the greater European nations in all but material development and a certain inventiveness; both of which in some cases are outclassed in the older world.

A California woman of her mother's generation had become a great and renowned archæologist and lived romantically in a castle in the City of Mexico. She bad often wished, since her serious mental life had begun, that this gift had descended upon her - the donee had also been a member of the A. A., and this striking endowment might just as well have tarried a generation and a half longer.

She was by no means avid of publicity - people seldom are until they have tasted of it - but she would have enjoyed a rapid and brilliant development of her mental faculties with productiveness of some sort either as a sequel or an interim. It was impossible to advance much farther in her present circumstances.

No, she was far from perfect, and willing to admit it; but she had always assumed that courage, moral as well as physical, was an accompaniment of race, like breeding and certain automatic impulses. But her hands were trembling and her cheeks drained of every drop of color because she must have a plain and serious talk with a guilty wretch. She had nothing to fear, but she could not have felt worse if she had been the culprit herself. What was human nature but a bundle of paradoxes?

At least she had the respite of the dinner hour. Only a fiend would spoil a man's dinner - and cigar - no matter what he had done. That would make the full time of her own respite about an hour and twenty minutes.

In a moment of panic she contemplated telephoning to Aileen and begging her to come over to dinner. She also no doubt could get Bascom Luning and Jimmie Thorne. Then it would not be possible to speak to Mortimer before to-morrow as he always fell asleep at ten o'clock when there was no dancing....To-morrow it would be easier, and wiser. One should never speak in anger....

But she was quite aware that her anger had burnt itself out. Her mind felt as cold as her hands. Better have it over. She put on a severe black frock, not only suitable to the occasion but as a protection from disarming compliments. Mortimer, who dressed so well himself that it would have been as impossible for him to overdress as to be rude to a woman, disliked dark severity in woman's attire. He never criticized his wife's clothes, but when they displeased him he ignored them with delicate ostentation.

II

Alexina had begun to feel that she should scream in the complete silence of the dining-room when Mortimer unexpectedly made a remark.

"Gora arrives to-morrow. Will you meet her? I shall not have time."

"Of course. I shall be delighted to see her again. It would have been an ideal arrangement if I could have left her here with you when I went to Europe."

"Yes. She was here for a week. I missed her when she left."

"W-h-at? When was she here? You never told me."

"I forgot. It was soon after you left. The ship was disabled - fire, I think, - and put back. I asked her to stay here until the next sailing."

"How jolly."

Again there was a complete silence. But Alexina did not notice it. Her brain was whirling. After all, she might be mistaken! Mortimer! He might be inno-cent....To think of Gora as a thief was fantastic...was it?...Was she not Mortimer's sister?...Why he rather than she?...And what after all did she know of Gora?...She inspired some people with distrust, even fear....That might be the cause of Mortimer's depression....He knew it....

At all events it was a straw and she grasped it as if it

had been a plank in mid-ocean. With even a bare chance that Mortimer was innocent it would be unpardonable to insult and wound him....Nor was it quite possible to ask him if his sister were a thief. She must wait, of course.

And if Gora had taken the bonds they might be recovered. It would be like a woman to secrete them in a reaction of terror after having nerved herself up to the deed.

She wished that Gora had gone to Hong Kong. Bolted. Then she could be certain. But at least she had a respite, and she felt so ebullient that she almost forgot her loss, and swept Morty over to the Lawtons after dinner; and the Judge took them all to the movies.

# CHAPTER IX

## I

Alexina would listen to no remonstrance. Gora might send her trunks to Geary Street if she liked, but she must come home to Ballinger House and spend at least one night with her brother and sister, who had missed her quite dreadfully. Gora wondered how Alexina could have missed her so touchingly in Europe, but accepted the invitation, as a note from the surgeon to whom she had written by the previous steamer asked her to hold herself in readiness for an operation a week hence.

Gora was looking remarkably well, and Alexina assumed it was not only the six months of mountain life and the three months in the tropics. She had an air of assured power, rarely absent in a woman who has found herself and achieved a definite place in life. Besides being one of the best nurses in San Francisco, in constant demand by the leading doctors and surgeons, her short stories had attracted considerable attention in the magazines, although no publisher would risk bringing them out in book form. But they were invariably mentioned in any summary of the year's best stories, one had been included in a volume of selected short stories by modern authors, and one in a recent text-book compiled for the benefit of aspirants in the same difficult art. The remuneration had been insignificant, for her stories were not of the popular order, and she had not yet the name that alone commands the high reward; but she had advanced farther than many another as severely handicapped, and she knew through her admiring sister-in-law and Aileen Lawton that her stories were mentioned occasionally at a San Francisco dinner table and even discussed! She was "arriving." No doubt of that.

## II

"When will the novel come out? I can't wait."

"Not until the spring."

They were sitting in Alexina's room and Gora had been placed directly in front of the cabinet, which she did not appear even to see. She had taken off her hat and coat and was holding the heavy masses of hair away from her head.

"Do you mind? I feel as if I had a twenty-pound weight...."

"What a question! Do what you want."

Gora took out the pins and let down her hair. It was not as fine as Alexina's, but it was brown and warm and an unusual head of hair for these days. It fell down both sides of her face, and her long cold unrevealing eyes looked paler than ever between her sun-burned cheeks and her low heavy brows.

Alexina knew that she had an antagonist far worthier of any weapons she might find in her armory than poor Morty, but she believed she could trap her if she were guilty....And she must be...she must....

"Didn't you find it too hot in the tropics for writing?"

"I only copied and revised. The book was finished before I left Lake Tahoe-an ideal place for work. Some day I shall have a log cabin up there. May I smoke?"

"Of course."

"It is almost a shame to desecrate a flower....I used to come in here sometimes and look round...the week I spent here....The room is a poem...like you....Or rather the binding of the prose poem that is Alexina."

"I'd love it if you made me the heroine of one of your novels."

"You'll have much more fun living it yourself."

"Fine chance. I don't suppose I'll ever get out of California again....I am afraid that Morty is doing quite badly."

Gora shrugged her strong square shoulders. "I never expected anything else. I asked him for another thousand dollars of my money when I was here and he looked as if he had forgotten he owed me any. Just like a man and Morty in particular. Then he said he expected to make an immense profit on something or other he had ordered from the Orient and would pay me off when I returned. Has he condescended to tell you anything about his affairs?"

"Not a word. Did you need the money badly? If I had been here I could have lent it to you."

"Thanks. I am sure you would. But I dislike the idea of borrowing. It must be so depressing to pay back....I was in no particular need of it, for of course I've saved quite a bit. I merely have a natural desire for my own and thought it was a good opportunity to strike Morty....I suppose he's been speculating. Fortunes have been made in Tonopah, but he would be sure to buy at the wrong time or in the wrong mine....Has he ever asked you for money?"

"Never. He knows, too, that I have quite a sum in bonds that I could convert into cash at once."

"Well, take my advice and hold on to them - to every cent you have. Where do you keep them?"

"In the bank...in a safe-deposit vault - Oh, how careless of me! I've left the key out on the table! I usually keep it...you remember...in the secret drawer of the cabinet."

"How I wish I had the courage to write a story about a secret drawer of an old Italian cabinet!...I wouldn't leave it lying about; although, of course, no one could use it without a pass also."

"A what?"

"They use every precaution. I know, because when I nursed old Mrs. Beresford for eight months, I was sent down to the vault twice."

Alexina's head was whirling. The blood burned and beat in her face.

"Even with her signature I couldn't get by the keeper the first time because he didn't know me. I had to be identified by her lawyer."

"I like to feel so well taken care of. What shall you do if your novel is a great success? Of course it will be. You would never go on being a nurse."

"I am not so sure it will be a success. Neither is my

publisher. He wrote me a half-whimsical half-complimentary letter saying that I must remember the average reader was utterly commonplace, with no education in the higher sense, no imagination, had an extremely limited vocabulary and thought and talked in ready-made phrases, composed for the most part of the colloquialisms of the moment. Style, distinction of mind, erected an almost visible wall between the ambitious writer and this predominant class. If they found this sort of book interesting-which as a rule they did not - they felt a sullen sense of inferiority; and if there were too many unfamiliar words they pitched it across the room with the ultimate adjective of their disapproval - 'highbrow.' But it is more the general atmosphere they resent - would resent if the book were purposely written with the most limited vocabulary possible."

"Our national self-sufficiency, I suppose. Also the fetish of equality that still persists. We are the greatest nation on earth, of course, but it isn't democratic for any one of us to be greater than the other."

"Exactly. I don't say I wouldn't write for the mob if I could. Nice stories about nice people. Intimate life histories of commonplace 'real Americans,' touched with a bit of romance, or tragedy-somewhere about the middle - or adventure, with a bad man or woman for good measure and to prove to the highbrows that the author is advanced and knows the world as well as the next, even if he or she prefers to treat of the more 'admirable aspects of our American life.' Unluckily I cannot read such books nor write them. I was born with a passion for English and the subtler psychology. I should be hopeless from any editor's or publisher's standpoint if I didn't happen to have been fitted out with a strong sense of drama. If I could only set my stage with commonplace, people no doubt I'd make a roaring hit. But I can't and I won't. Who has such a chance as an author to get away from commonplace people? Fancy deliberately concocting new ones!"

"Not you! But you'll have some sort of success, all the same."

"Yes, there are publics. Perhaps I'll, hypnotize one of them. As for the financial end what I hope is that the book will give me a position that will raise my prices in the magazines."

"You could live abroad very cheaply." Alexina raised her eyes a trifle and looked as guileless as her words.

"Oh, be sure I'll go to Europe and stay there for years as soon as I see my way ahead. I should find color in the very stones or the village streets."

"I am told that you can find most comfortable quarters in some of those English village inns, and for next to nothing. By the way, do you still correspond with that Englishman who was here during the fire?"

"Gathbroke? Off and on. T send him my stories and he writes a humorous sort of criticism of each; says that as I have no humor lie feels a sort of urge to apply a little somewhere."

"How interesting. He didn't strike me as humorous."

"I fancy he wasn't more than about one-fifth developed when he was here. Men like that, with his advantages, go ahead very rapidly when they get into their stride.

He has already developed from business into politics - he is in Parliament - and that is the second long stride he has taken in the past seven years."

"How interesting it will be for you two to meet, again." Alexina spoke with languid politeness.

Gora shrugged her shoulders, "If we do." She might not be able to show the under-white of her eyes arid look like a seraph, but she had her voice, her features, under perfect control, and she had never been quick to blush. She did not suspect that Alexina was angling, but the very sound of Gathbroke's name was enough to put up her guard.

"You must have had several proposals, Gora dear. Your profession is almost as good as a matrimonial bureau. And you look too fetching for words in that uniform and cap."

"I've had just two proposals. One was from an old rancher who liked the way I turned him over in bed and rubbed his back. The other was - well, a nice fellow, and quite well off. But I'm not keen on marrying any one."

"Still, if it gave you that much more independence and leisure...travel...a wider life...."

"I'd only consider marrying for two reasons: If I met a man who had the power to make me quite mad about him, or one who could give me a great position in the world and was not wholly obnoxious. Otherwise, I prefer to trot alone. Why not? At least I escape monotony; I have what after all is the most precious thing in life, complete personal freedom; and if I succeed with my writing I can see the world and attain to position without the aid of any man. If I don't, I don't, and that is the end of it. I'm a bit of a fatalist, I think, although to be sure when I want a thing badly enough I forget all about that and fight like the devil."

Alexina looked at the square face of her strange sister-in-law, so unlike her brother; at the high cheek bones, the heavy low brows over the cold light eyes, the powerful jaw, the wide firm but mobile mouth.

"Have you any Eussian blood?'" she asked. "'Way back?"

"Not that I know of. But after all I know little about my family, outside of the one ancestor that anchors us in the Revolutionary era. He or his son or his son's son may have married a Russian or a Mongolian for all I know. Perhaps some one of my old aunts may have worked out a family tree in cross-stitch, but if so I never heard of it. Well, I'm off to clean up for dinner."

Alexina for the first time in their acquaintance flung her arms round Gora's neck and kissed her warmly. Truth to tell her conscience was smarting, although she was able to assure herself that not for a moment had she really believed her sister-in-law to be guilty; she had merely grasped at a straw. Gora returned the embrace gratefully and without suspicion. As ever, she was a little sorry for Alexina.

# CHAPTER X

I

Alexina felt only an intolerable ennui. Gora had gone in the morning; she sat alone in her room. Of course she must have that explanation with Mortimer, but any time before the first of the month would do. She was far less concerned with that now than with the problem: what to do with her life. How was she to continue to live in the same house with him? Perhaps in far smaller quarters than these? For she could not leave him. She had no visible excuse, and no desire to admit to the world that she had made woman's superlative mistake.

She scowled at the lovely room in which she had expected to find compensation in dreams, the setting for an unreal and enchanted world.

Dreams had died out of her. For the first time in her sheltered existence she appreciated the grim reality of life. She was no longer sheltered, secluded, one of the "fortunate class." Ways and means would occupy most of her time henceforth. And it was not the privations she shrank from but the contacts with the ugly facts of life; a side she had found extremely picturesque in novels, but knew from, occasional glimpses to be merely repulsive and demoralizing.

And of whom could she ask advice! She must make changes and make them quickly. Four thousand dollars a year!...and taxes - besides the new income tax - to be paid on the downtown property, the fiats, the land on which her home stood, Ballinger House itself and all its contents.

She knew vaguely that many girls these days were given special training of some sort even where their parents were well off; but more particularly where the father was what is known as a high-salaried man; or even a moderately successful professional or business man - all of whose expenses arid incomes balanced too nicely for investments.

Not in her set! Joan, bored after her third season with dancing in winter and "sitting round Alta" in summer, had asked permission to become a trained nurse like Gora, or go into the decorating business, "any old thing"; and Maria Abbott had simply stared at her in horror; even her father had asked her angrily if she wished to disgrace him, advertise him as unable to provide for his family. No self-respecting American, etc.

But something must be done. She wished to live on in Ballinger House if possible, not only because she loved it, or to avoid the commiserations of the world; she had no desire to live in narrow quarters with her husband....And she knew nothing, was fit for nothing, belonged to a silly class that still looked upon women workers as de-classed, although to be sure two or three whose husbands had left them penniless had gone into business and were loyally tolerated, if deeply deplored.

The day after her return from Europe Alice Thorndyke had come into this room and thrown herself down on the couch, her long, languorous body looking as if set on steel springs, her angelic blonde beauty distorted with fury and disgust, and poured out her hatred of men and all their ways, her loathing for society and gambling and all the stupid vicious round of the life both public and secret she had elected to lead....She had had enough of it....After all, she had some brains and she wanted to use them. She wanted to go into the decorating business. There was an opening. She had a natural flair for that sort of thing. See what she had managed to do with that old ark she had inherited, and on five cents a year....When she had asked her sister to advance the money Sibyl had flown into one of her worst rages and thrown a gold hair brush through a Venetian mirror. Didn't she give her clothes by the dozen that she hadn't worn a month? Did any girl have a better time in society? Was any girl luckier at poker? Was any girl more popular with men - too bad it was generally the married ones that lost their heads....Better if she stopped fooling and married. By and by it would be too late.

But she didn't want to marry. She was sick of men. She wanted to get out of her old life altogether and culti-vate a side of her mind and character that had stagnated so far...also to enjoy the independent life of a money-earner...life in an entirely different world...something new...new...new.

Alexina had offered to lend her the capital, for Alice had a hard cool head. But she had refused, saying she

Gertrude Atherton

could mortgage her old barrack if it came to that...but she didn't know...it would he a break....Sib might never speak to her again...people were such snobs...and she mightn't like it...she wished she had been born of poor but honest parents and put to work in a canning factory or married the plumber.

She had done nothing, and Alexina wondered if she would have the courage to go into some sort of business with herself...they could give out they were bored, seeking a new distraction...save the precious pride of their families.

She leaned forward and took her head in her hands. If she only had some one to talk things over with. It was impossible to confide in Gora, in any one. If she broached the subject to Tom Abbott, to Judge Lawton, even in a roundabout way, they would suspect at once. Aileen and Janet and the other girls did not know enough. They would suspect also. But her head would burst if she didn't consult some one. She was too horribly alone. And after all she was still very young. She had talked largely of her responsibilities, but as a matter of fact until now she had never had one worth the name.

Suddenly she thought of James Kirkpatrick.

## II

The lessons in socialism had died a natural death long since. But Alexina and Aileen and Janet had never quite let him go. Whenever there was a great strike on, either in California or in any part of the nation, they invited him to take tea with them at least once a week while it lasted and tell them all the "ins." This he was nothing loath to do, and waived the question of remuneration aside with a gesture. He was now a foreman, and vice-president of his union, and it gave him a distinct satisfaction to confer a favor upon these "lofty dames," whom, however, he liked better as time went on. Alexina he had always worshiped and the only time he ceased to be a socialist was when he ground his teeth and cursed fate for not making him a gentleman and giving him a chance before she was corralled by that sawdust dude.

He had also remained on friendly terms with Gora, who had cold-bloodedly studied him and made him the hero of a grim strike story. But as he never read polite literature their friendship was unimpaired.

III

He came to tea that afternoon in response to a telephone call from Alexina. She had put on a tea gown of periwinkle blue chiffon and a silver fillet about her head, and looked to Mr. Kirkpatrick's despairing gaze as she intended to look - beautiful, of course, but less woman than goddess. Exquisite but not tempting. She was quite aware of the young workman's hopeless passion and she managed him as skillfully as she did the more assured, sophisticated, and sometimes "illuminated" Jimmie Thorne and Bascom Luning.

She received him in the great drawing-room behind the tea-table, laden with the massive silver of dead and gone Ballingers.

"I've only been home a week," she said gayly. "See what a good friend I am. I've scarcely seen any one. Did you get my post cards?"

"I did and I've framed them, if you don't mind my saying so."

"I hoped you would. I picked out the prettiest I could find. They do have such beauties in Europe. Just think, it was my first visit. I was wildly excited. Wouldn't you like to go?"

"Naw. America's good enough for me. 'Fris - oh, Lord! San Francisco - for that matter. I'd like to go to the next International Socialist Congress all right - next year. Maybe I will. I guess that would give me enough of Europe to last me the rest of my natural life."

"I met a good many Frenchmen, and I have a friend married to a very clever one. He says they expect a war with Germany in a year two - "

"There'll never be another war. Not in Europe or anywhere else. The socialists won't permit it."

"There are a good many socialists - and syndicalists - in France, and it's quite true they're doing all they can to prevent any money being voted for the army or expended if it is voted; but I happen to know that the Government has asked the president of the Red Cross to train as many nurses as she can induce to volunteer, and as quickly as possible. My friend Madame Morsigny was to begin her training a few days after I left."

"Hm. So. I hadn't heard a word of it."

"We get so much European news out here! America first! Especially in the matter of murders and hold-ups. Who cares for a possible war in Europe when the headlines are as black as the local crimes they announce?"

"Sure thing. Great little old papers. But don't let any talk of war from anywhere at all worry you. And I'll tell you why. At the last International Congress all the socialists of all the nations were ready to agree that all labor should lay down its tools - quit work - go on a colossal strike - the moment those blood-sucking capitalists at the top, those sawdust kings and kaisers and tsars - or any president for that matter - declared war for any cause whatsoever. All, that is, but the German delegates. They couldn't see the light. Now they have. When we meet next August the resolution will be unanimous. Take it from me. You've read of your last war in some old history book. Peace from now on, and thank the socialists."

"I should. But suppose Germany should declare war before next August?"

"She won't. She ain't ready. She'd have done it after that there 'Agadir Incident' if she'd dared. That is to say been good and ready. Now she's got to wait for another good excuse and there ain't one in sight."

"But you believe she'd like to precipitate a war in Europe for her own purposes?"

"She'd like it all right." And he quoted freely from Treitschke and Bernhardi, while Alexina as ever looked at him in wonder. He seemed to be more deeply read every time she met him, and he remained exactly the same James Kirkpatrick. "What an adventitious thing breeding was! Mortimer had it!"

"Well, I am glad I spoke of it. You have relieved my mind, for you speak as one with authority....There is something else I want to talk to you about....A friend of mine is in a dilemma and I don't quite know how to advise her....We're all such a silly set of moths - "

"No moth about you!" interrupted Mr. Kirkpatrick firmly. "Some of them - those others, if you like. The only redeeming virtue I can see in most of them is that they are what they are and don't give a damn. But you - you've got more brains and common sense than the whole bunch of women in this town put together."

"Oh, dear! Oh, dear! I'm afraid I've addled my brains

trying to cultivate them, and what I'm more afraid of is that I've addled my common sense." She spoke with such gayety, with such a roguish twinkle, and curve of lip, that neither then nor later did he suspect that she was the heroine of her own tale.

"Well, fire away. No, thanks, no more. I only drink tea to please you anyway. Tea is so much hot water to me."

"Well, smoke." She pushed the box of cigarettes toward him. "I know you smoke a pipe, but I won't let my husband smoke one at home. It's bad for my curtains....This is it - One of my friends, poor thing, has had a terrible experience: discovered that her husband has stolen the part of her little fortune whose income enabled them to do something more than keep alive. You see, it's a sad case. She believed in him, and he had always been the most honest creature in the world; and that's as much of a blow as the loss of the money."

"What'd he do it for?"

"Oh, I know so little about business...he wanted to get rich too quickly I suppose...speculated or something...perhaps got into a hole. This has been a bad year."

"Poor chap!" said Kirkpatriek reflectively.

"You're not commiserating *him*?"

"Ain't I, just? He done it, didn't he? He's got to pay the piper, hasn't he? Women don't know anything about the awful struggles and temptations of the rotten

Gertrude Atherton

business world. He didn't do it because he wanted to, you can bet your life on that. He's just another poor victim of a vicious system. A fly in the same old web; same old fat spider in the middle!. Not capital enough. Hard times and the little man goes under, no matter if he's a darn sight better fellow than the bloated beast on top - "

"You mean if we were living in the Socialistic Utopia no man could go under?"

"I mean just that. It's a sin and a shame, A fine young fellow - "

"Remember, you don't know anything about him. He's not a bad sort and has always been quite honest before; but he's not very clever. If he were he wouldn't have got himself into a predicament. He had a good start, far better than nine-tenths of the millionaires in this country had in their youth."

"Oh, I don't care anything about that. If all men were equally clever in chasing the almighty dollar there'd be no excuse for socialism. It's our job to displace the present rotten system of government with one in which the weak couldn't be crowded out, where all that are willing to work will have an equal chance - and those that ain't willing will have to work anyhow or starve....One of the thousand things the matter with the present system is that the square man is so often in the round hole. In the socialized state every man will he guided to the place which exactly fits his abilities. No weaker to the wall there,"

"You think you can defy Nature to that extent!"

"You bet."

"Well. I'm too much distracted by my friend's predicament to discuss socialism....I rather like the idea though of the strong man having the opportunity to prove himself stronger than Life...find out what, he was put on earth and endowed with certain characteristics for...rather a pity all that should atrophy....However - what shall my friend do? Continue to live with a man she despises?"

"She's no right to despise him or anybody. It's the system, I tell you. And no doubt she's just as weak in some way herself. Every man jack of us is so chuck full of faults and potential crime it's a wonder we don't break out every day in the week, and if women are going to desert us when the old Adam runs head on into some one of the devilish traps the present civilization has set out all over the place, instead of being able to sidestep it once more, well - she'd best divorce herself from the idea of matrimony before she goes in for the thing itself. Would I desert my brother if he got into trouble? Would you?"

"N - o, I suppose you are right, and I doubt if she would leave him anyway. However...there's the other aspect. What can a woman in her position do to help matters out? You have met a good many of her kind here. Fancy Miss Lawton or Mrs. Bascom or Miss Maynard forced to work - "

"I can't. If I had imagination enough for that I'd be writin' novels like Miss Dwight."

"I believe they'd do better than you think. Well, this friend isn't quite so much absorbed in society and poker and dress. She's more like - well, there's Mrs. Ruyler, for instance. She was very much like the rest of us, and now we never see her. She's as devoted to ranching as her husband."

"There was sound bourgeois French blood there," he said shrewdly. "And she wasn't brought up like the rest of you. Don't you forget that."

"Then you think we're hopeless?"

"No, I don't. Three or four women of your crowd - a little older, that's all - are doin' first-rate in business, and they were light-headed enough in their time, I'll warrant. And you, for instance - if you came up against it - "

"Yes? What could I do?" cried Alexina gayly. "But alas! you admit you have no imagination."

"Don't need any. You'd be good for several things. You could go into the insurance business like Mrs. Lake, or into real estate like Mrs. Cole - people like to have a pretty and stylish young lady showin' 'em round flats. Or you could buy an orchard like the Ruylers - that'd require capital. If we had the socialistic state you'd be put on one of the thinking boards, so to speak. That's the point. You've got no training, but you've got a thinker. You'd soon learn. But I'm not so sure of your friend. Somehow, you've given me the impression she's just one of these lady-birds."

"I'm afraid she is," said Alexina with a sigh. "But you're so good to take an interest....Suppose you had the socialistic state now - to-morrow, what would you do with all these - lady-birds?"

"I'd put 'em in a sanatorium until they got their nerves patched up, and then I'd turn 'em over to a trainer who'd put them into a normal physical condition; and then I'd put 'em at hard labor - every last one of 'em."

"Oh, dear, Mr. Kirkpatrick, would you?"

"Yes," he said grimly. "It 'ud be their turn."

# CHAPTER XI

I

She walked down the avenue with him, listening to his angry account of the great coal strike in West Virginia, where the families of miners in their beds had been fired on from armored motor cars, and both strikers and civilians were armed to the teeth.

"That's the kind of war - civil war - we can't prevent - not yet. No wonder some of us want quick action and turn into I.W.Ws. Of course they're fools, just poor boobs, to think they can win out that way, but you can't blame 'em. Lord, if we only *could* move a little faster. If Marx had been a good prophet we'd have the socialized state to-day. Things didn't turn out according to Hoyle. Lots of the proletariat ain't proletariat any longer, instead of overrunning the earth; and in place of a handful of great capitalists to fight we've a few hundred thousand little capitalists, or good wage earners with white collars on, that have about as much use for socialism as they have for man-eating tigers. I'm thinking about this country principally. Too much chance for the individual. Trouble is, the individual, like as not, don't know what's good for him and goes under, like the man you've been telling me about."

"There's only one thing I apprehend in your socialistic state," said Alexina, who always became frivolous when Kirkpatrick waxed serious, "and that is universal dissolution from sheer ennui. Either that or we'll go on eternally rowing about something else. Earth has never been free from war since the beginning of history, and there is trouble of some sort going on somewhere all the time - "

"All due to capitalism."

"Capitalism hasn't always existed."

"Human greed has, and the dominance of the strong over the weak."

"Exactly, and socialism if she ever gets her chance will dominate all she knows how. Remember what you said just now about forcing the pampered women to work when they were the underdog. But the point is that Nature made Earthians a fighting breed. She must have had a good laugh when we named another planet Mars."

"Well, we'll fight about worthier things."

"Don't be too sure. We fight about other things now. All the trouble in the world isn't caused by money or the want of it. And what about the religious wars - "

III

It was at this inopportune moment that they met Mortimer. If Alexina had remembered that this was his homing hour she would have parted from her visitor at the drawing-room door; but in truth she had dismissed Mortimer from her mind.

He halted some paces off and glared from his wife's diaphanous costume to the workman in his rough clothes and flannel shirt. As the avenue sloped abruptly he was at a disadvantage, and it was all he could do to keep from grinding his teeth.

Alexina went forward and placed her hand within his arm, giving it a warning pressure.

"Now, at last, you and Mr. Kirkpatrick will meet. You've always so snubbed our little attempts to understand some of the things that men know all about, that you've never met any of our teachers. But no one has taught, me as much as Mr. Kirkpatrick, so shake hands at once and be friends."

Mortimer extended a straight and wooden hand. Kirkpatrick touched, and dropped it as if lie feared contamination, Mortimer ascended a few steps and from this point of vantage looked down his unmitigated disapproval and contempt. Kirkpatrick would have given his hopes of the speedy demise of capitalism if Alexina had picked up her periwinkle skirts and fled up the avenue. His big hands clenched, he thrust out his pugnacious jaw, his hard little eyes glowed like poisonous coals. Mortimer, to do him justice, was entirely without physical cowardice, and continued to look like a stage lord dismissing a varlet.

Kirkpatrick caught Alexina's imploring eyes and turned abruptly on his heel, "So long," he said. "Guess I'd better be getting on."

IV


"I won't have that fellow in the house," said Mortimer, in a low tone of white fury. "To think that my wife - my wife - "

"If you don't mind we won't talk about it."

Alexina was on the opposite side of the avenue and her head was in the air. She had long since ceased to carry her spine in a tubercular droop and when she chose she could draw her body up until it seemed to elongate like the neck of a giraffe, and overtop Mortimer or whoever happened to have incurred her wrath.

Mortimer glowered at her. He had many grievances. For the moment he forgot that she might have any against him.

"And out here in broad daylight, almost on the street, in that tea gown - "

"I have often been quite on the street in similar ones. Going over to Aileen's. You forget that the Western Addition is like a great park set with the homes of people more or less intimate."

Mortimer made no further remarks. He had never pretended to be a match for her in words. But the agitating incident seemed to have lifted him temporarily at least out of the nether depths of his depression, for although he talked little at dinner he appeared to eat with more relish. As he settled himself to his cigar in a comfortable wicker chair on the terrace and she was about to return to the house he spoke abruptly in a faint firm voice.

"Will you stay here? I've got something to say to you."

"Oh?"

She wheeled about. His face was a sickly greenish white in the heavy shade of the trees.

"It's - it's - something I've been wanting to say - tell you...as well now as any time."

"Oh, very well. I must write just one letter."

She ran into the house and up the stairs and shut herself in the library, breathless, panic-stricken. He was going to confess! How awful! How awful! How could she ever go through with it? Why, why, hadn't she spoken at once and got it over?

She sat quite still until she had ceased trembling and her heart no longer pounded and affected her breathing. Then she set her teeth and went downstairs.

# CHAPTER XII

I

Mortimer was walking up and down the hall.

"Come in here," he said. He entered the drawing-room, and Alexina followed like a culprit led to the bar. Nevertheless, it crossed her mind that he wanted the moral support of a mantelpiece.

She almost stumbled into a chair. Mortimer did not avail himself of the chimneypiece toward which he had unconsciously gravitated, but walked back and forth. Two electric lights hidden under lamp shades were burning, but the large room was rather somber.

Alexina composed herself once more with a violent effort and asked in a crisp tone: "Well? What is this mystery? Are you in love with some one else? Been, making love - "

"Alexina!"

He confronted her with stricken eyes. "You know that I am literally incapable of such a thing. But of course you were jesting."

"Of course. But something is so manifestly wrong with you, and...well...of course you would be justified."

"Not in my own eyes. Besides, I shall never give up the hope of winning you back again. I live for that...although now!...that is the whole trouble....How am I going to say it?"

"Well, let me help you out. You took the bonds."

"You've been to the bank! I wanted to tell you first...the day you came back....I couldn't...."

"There is only one thing I am really curious about. How did you get in? Of course you knew where I kept the key, but - "

"I - " His voice was so lifeless that if dead men could speak it must be in the same flat faint tones. "I had the old power of attorney."

"But I revoked it."

"I mean the instrument - the paper. You did not ask for it. I did not think of it either....I trusted to the keeper taking it on its face value, not looking it up. He didn't. You see - " He gave a dreadful sort of laugh. "I am well known and have a good reputation."

"Why didn't you cable and ask me to lend you the money?"

"There wasn't time. Besides, you might have refused. I was desperate - "

"I don't want to hear the particulars. I am not in the least curious. What I must talk to you about - "

"I must tell you the whole thing. I can't go about with it any longer.Then, perhaps, you will understand."

His voice was still flat and as he continued to walk he seemed to draw half-paralyzed legs after him. Alexina set her lips and stared at the floor. He meant to talk. No getting out of it.

"I - I - have only done well occasionally since the very first. It didn't matter so long as your mother was alive, and for a little while after. But when you took things into your own hands...after that it was capital I turned over to you nearly every month - hardly ever profits."

"What? Why didn't you tell me?"

"I hadn't the courage. I was too anxious to stand well with you. And I always hoped, believed, I would do better as times improved. I had great hopes of myself and I had a pretty good start. But as time went on I grew to understand that my abilities were third-rate. I should have done all right with a large capital - say a hundred and fifty thousand dollars - but only a man far cleverer than I am could have got anywhere in that business with a paltry sixteen thousand to begin on. I got one or two connections and did pretty well, off and on, for a time; but if I hadn't made one or two lucky strikes in stocks my capital would simply have run away in household expenses long ago."

"Then why did you join that expensive club?"

"It was good business," he said evasively. "I meet the

right sort of men there. That's where I got my stock pointers."

"Did you take the bonds to gamble with?"

"No. I'd never have done that. I gambled in another way, though. I thought I saw a chance to sell a certain commodity at that particular time and I plunged and sent for a large quantity of it. It looked sure. I have a friend over there and got it on credit. I banked on an immediate sale and a big profit. But something delayed the shipping in Hong Kong. When it arrived the market was swamped. Some one else had had the same idea. I had to pay for the goods, as well as other big outstanding bills, or go into bankruptcy. So I took the bonds. It wasn't easy. But there was nothing else to do....There were about ten thousand dollars left and I tried another coup. That failed too."

"How is it possible to go on with the business?"

"It isn't. I have closed out. But I have escaped bankruptcy. People on the street think that I wanted to get into the real estate business - with Andrew Weston, a young man who has recently come here from Los Angeles. He's doing fairly well and has a good office. He wanted a hustler and a partner who had good connections. But it is slow work. There are the old firms, again, to compete with. I wouldn't have looked at it if I'd had any choice, but it was a case of a port in a storm."

"Well? Is that all? There is another matter to discuss. Our future mode of living."

"No, it isn't all. I wish you would tell Gora something.

I can never go through this again. While she was away - in Honolulu - that lawyer of my aunt sent out ten thousand dollars' worth more of stock, that had been looked upon as so much waste paper, but suddenly appreciated - some little railroad that was abandoned half finished, but has since been completed. This had been left to Gora alone. We had some correspondence and he sent it to me as Gora was traveling. It came at the wrong time for me...on top of everything else....I plunged in a new mine Bob Cheever and Baseom Luning were interested in. It turned out to be no good. We lost every cent."

## II

Alexina sat cold and rigid. Once she pinched her arm. She fancied it had turned to stone.

He dropped into a chair and leaning forward twisted his hands together.

"If you knew...if you knew...what I have been through....At first it was only the anxiety and excitement. But afterward, when it was over...when there was nothing left to speculate with...then I realized what I had done...I...a thief...a thief....I had been so proud of my honor, my honesty. I never had believed that I could even be tempted. And I went to pieces like a cheaply built schooner in its first storm. There's nothing, it seems, in being well brought up, when circumstances are too strong for you."

Alexina forebore the obvious reply. "Of course you were a little mad," she said, rather at a loss.

"No, I wasn't. I'd always been a cool speculator, and I'd never taken long chances in business before. It all looked too good and I got in too deep. But if I could have repaid it all I'd feel nearly as demoralized. That I should have stolen...and from women...."

Again Alexina restrained herself. The dead monotonous voice went on.

"I thought once or twice of killing myself. It didn't seem to me that I had the right to live. I had always had the best ideals, the strictest sense of right and wrong...It does not seem possible even now."

Alexina could endure no more. Another moment and she felt that she should be looking straight into a naked soul. She felt so sorry for him that she quite forgot her own wrongs or her horror of his misdeeds. She wished that she still loved him, he looked so forlorn and in need of the physical demonstrations of sympathy; but although she was prepared to defend him if need be, and help him as best she could, she felt that she would willingly die rather than touch him....She wondered if souls in dissolution subtly wafted their odors of corruption if you drew too close....

"Well, what is done is done," she said briskly. "I'll tell Gora and engage that she will never mention it. You have suffered enough. Now let us discuss ways and means. Does this new business permit you to contribute anything to the household expenses?"

"I'm afraid not. It takes time to work up a business."

"Then we must live on what I have left, and you know what taxes are. I suppose I had better look for a job."

"What?" He seemed to spring out of his apathy, and stared at her incredulously. "You?"

"Yes. We must have more money. I could sell the flats and go into the decorating business."

"And advertise to all San Francisco that I am a failure! Do you think I could fool them then!"

"Are you sure you have fooled them now! They must know you would have stuck to the old business if it had paid."

"It isn't the first time a man has changed his business. But if you go out to earn money - why, I'd be a laughing stock."

"Then we shall have to give up the house. The city has long wanted this lot - "

"That would never do, either. Everybody knows how devoted you are to your old home...and after fixing it up...."

"Well, what, do you suggest? You know perfectly well we can't go on."

"My brain seems to have stopped. I can't do much thinking. But...well...you might sell the flats and we could go on as before until my business begins to pay."

"Sacrifice more of my capital? That I won't do. Why don't you see if you can get back with Cheever Harrison and Cheever? I know that Bob - "

"I won't go back to being a salaried man. You can't go back like that when you've been in the other class." He beat a fist into a palm. "Why couldn't Bob Cheever have left me alone? So long as I didn't know anything about Society I never thought about it. Why couldn't your family have let me stay where I was? I should have been head clerk with a good salary by this time, and we would have arranged our expenses accordingly when your mother died. Why can't men give a young fellow a better chance when he goes into business for himself? Every man trying to cut every other man's throat. "What chance has a young fellow with a small capital?"

"Do you know that you have blamed everybody but yourself? However...perhaps you are right....Mr. Kirkpatrick puts it down to the system. I feel more inclined to trace it straight back to old Dame Nature - all the ancestral inheritances down in our sub-cellars. We are as we are made and our characters are certainly our fate. I suppose you will at least resign from the club?"

He set his lips in the hard line that made him look the man of character his ancestor, John Dwight, had been when he legislated in the first Congress. "No, I shall not resign. It would be bad business in two ways: they would know I was hard up, and I should no longer meet in the same way the men who can give me a leg up in business."

"Are you sure those are the only reasons?"

To this he did not deign to reply, and she asked: "Do you mean that you shall go on speculating?"

"I've nothing to speculate with. I mean that the men I cultivate can help me in business."

"They don't seem to have done much in the past. However...At least I'll send in our resignations to the Golf Club. As we use it so seldom no one will notice. Now I'm going upstairs to think it all over. To-morrow I shall do something. I don't know what it will be, yet."

He stood up. "Promise me," he said with firm masculine insistence, "that you will neither go into any sort of money-making scheme or sell this house." His tones had distinctly more life in them and he had recovered his usual bearing of the lordly but gallant male. His eyes were as stern as his lips.

Alexina stared at him for a moment in amazement, then reflected that apparently the stupider a man was the more difficult he was to understand. She nodded amiably.

"No doubt I'll think of some other way out. Will let you know at dinner time. Don't expect me at breakfast. Good-night."

Gertrude Atherton

# CHAPTER XIII

I

Alexina was driving her little car up the avenue at Rincona on the following morning when she saw Joan running toward her through the park and signaling to her to stop.

"What is it?" she asked in some alarm as Joan arrived panting. "Any one ill?"

"Not so's you'd notice it. Leave your car here and come with me. Sneak after me quietly and don't say a word."

Much mystified, Alexina ran her car off the road and followed her niece by a devious route toward the house. Joan interested her mildly; she had fulfilled some of her predictions but not all. She did not go with the "fast set" even of the immediate neighborhood; that is to say the small group called upon, as they indubitably "belonged," but wholly disapproved of, who entertained in some form or other every day and every night, played poker for staggering stakes, danced the wildest of the new dances, made up brazenly, and found tea and coffee indifferent stimulants. Two of

Joan's former schoolmates belonged to this active set, but she was only permitted to meet them at formal dinners and large parties. She had rebelled at first, but her mother's firm hand was too much for her still undeveloped will, and later she had concluded "there was nothing in it anyhow; just the whole tiresome society game raised to the nth degree." Moreover, she was socially as conventional as her mother and her good gray aunts, and although full of the mischief of youth, and longing to "do something," no prince having captured her fancy, enough of what Alexina called the sound Ballinger instincts remained to make her disapprove of "fast lots," and she had progressed from radical eighteen to critical twenty-one. She worked off her superfluous spirits at the outdoor games which may be indulged in California for eight months of the year, rode horseback every day, used all her brothers' slang she could remember when in the society of such uncritical friends as her young Aunt Alexina, and bided her time. Sooner or later she was determined to "get out and hustle," - "shake a leg." That would be the only complete change from her present life, not matrimony and running with fast sets. She wanted more money, she wanted to live alone, and, while devoted to her family, she wanted interests they could not furnish, "no, not in a thousand years."

II

Joan's slim boyish athletic figure darted on ahead and then approached the rear of the house on tiptoe. Alexina followed in the same stealthy fashion, feeling no older at the moment than her niece. The verandah did not extend as far as the music room, which had been built a generation later, and the windows were some eight feet from the ground. A ladder, however, abridged the distance, and Alexina, obeying a gesture from Joan, climbed as hastily as her narrow skirt would permit and peered through the outside shutters, which had been carefully closed.

The room was not dark, however. The electricity had been turned on and shone down upon an amazing sight.

Clad in black bloomers and stockings lay a row of six women flat on the floor, while in front of them stood a woman thin to emaciation, who was evidently talking rapidly. Alexina's mouth opened as widely as her eyes. She had heard of Devil Worship, of strange and awful rites that took place at midnight in wickedest Paris. Had an expurgated edition been brought to chaste Alta - plus Menlo - plus Atherton, by Mrs. Hunter or Mrs. Thornton, or any of those fortunate Californians who visited the headquarters of fashion and sin once a year? They would do a good deal to vary the monotony of life. But that they should have corrupted Maria...the impeccable, the superior, the unreorientable Maria! Maria, with whom contentment and conservatism were the first articles of the domestic and the socio-religious creed!

For there lay Maria, extended full length; and on her calm white face was a look of unholy joy. Beside her, as flat as if glued to the inlaid floor, were Mrs. Hunter, Mrs. Thornton, Coralie Geary, Mrs. Brannan, another old friend of Maria, and - yes - Tom's sister, Susan Delling, austere in her virtues, kind to all, conscientiously smart, and with a fine mahogany complexion that made even a merely powdered woman feel not so much a harlot as a social inferior.

What on earth...what on earth....

The thin loquacious stranger clapped her hands. Up went six pairs of legs. Two remained in mid-air, Mrs. Geary's and Mrs. Brannan's having met an immovable obstacle shortly above the hip-joints. Three bent backward slowly but surely until they approached the region of the neck. Maria's flew unerringly, effortlessly, up, back, until they tapped the floor behind her head. Alexina almost shouted "Bravo." Maria was a real sport.

Six times they repeated this fascinating rite, and then, obeying another peremptory command, they rolled over abruptly and balanced on all fours. Alexina could stand no more. She dropped down the ladder and ran after Joan, who was disappearing round the corner of the house.

III

"Well, I never!" she exclaimed. "Maria! Your mo - "

"She gained three pounds, for the first time in her life, and you know her figure is her only vanity. This woman came along and the whole Peninsula is crazy about her. She's taken the fat off every woman in New York, and came out with letters to a lot of women. Mother fell for her hard. I nearly passed away when I peeked through that shutter the first time. Mother! She's the best of the bunch, though. But they're all having a perfectly grand time. New interest for middle-age - what?"

"Don't be cruel. Heavens, how hot they all looked! I could hear them gasp. Hope their arteries are all right. Are they going to stay to lunch?"

"No. There's a big one on in Burlingame. Mother's not going, though. It's at that Mrs. Cutts', new Burlingame stormer, that Anne Montgomery coaches and caters for and who gives wonderful entertainments. Mother and Aunt Susan won't go, but nearly all the others do."

"Anne Montgomery. I haven't seen her since mother died."

"You look as if an idea had struck you. She's useful no end, they say; is now a social secretary to a lot of new people, and sells the 'real lace' and other superfluous luxuries of some of our old families for the cold coin that buys comforts."

"Fine idea. But I'm glad your mother will be alone. I've

come down to have a talk with her."

"Thanks. I'll take the hint."

# CHAPTER XIV

I

Alexina went up to Joan's room to remain until the gong sounded for luncheon, when she drifted down innocently and kissed the somewhat furtive-looking Maria, who was in chaste duck and fresh from a bath.

"So glad to see you, darling," she murmured almost effusively. "I hope you haven't waited long. A number of my friends have a lesson every Thursday morning, and meet at one house or another."

"Irregular French verbs, I suppose. So fascinating, and one does forget so. I thought I'd never brush up my French."

Not for anything would she have forced Maria into the most innocent equivocation, and she rattled on about her wonderful summer as people are expected to do after their first visit to Europe.

No time could have been more propitious for this necessary understanding with Maria, who was feeling amiable, apologetic, as limber as Joan, and almost as warm. She had also lost two-thirds of a pound.

## II

Alexina began as soon as Joan left them alone on the shady side of the wide piazza.

"I have a lot of things to tell you," she said nervously. "I have to make certain economies and I want the benefit of your advice."

Mrs. Abbott looked up from her embroidery. "Of course, darling. I was afraid you were going a little too fast for young people."

"That is not it. I always managed well enough....You know we've never gone the limit: polo at Burlingame and Monterey, gambling, big parties and all the rest of it. I've never run into debt or spent any of my capital. But..."

Maria began to feel anxious and took off the large round shell-rimmed spectacles that enlarged stitches and print. "Yes?"

"You know I had bonds - about forty thousand dollars' worth - those that mother left: I spent those that Ballinger and Geary gave me on the house and one thing and another."

"Yes?" Mrs. Abbott was now alarmed. She had a very keen sense of the value of money, like most persons that have inherited it, and was extremely conservative in its use.

"Well, you see, I thought I saw a chance to treble it - we never really had enough - and I speculated and lost it."

Alexina was a passionate lover of the truth, but she could always lie like a gentleman.

Maria Abbott readjusted her spectacles and took a stitch or two in her linen. She was aghast and did not care to speak for a moment. She was no fool and Tom had told her that Mortimer had changed his business and might bluff the street, but could never bluff him. She knew quite as well as if Alexina had confessed it that Mortimer had lost the money, either in his business or in stocks; although of course she was far from suspecting the whole truth.

III

"That is dreadful," she said finally. "I wish you had consulted Tom. He understands stocks as he does everything else."

"I thought I had the best tips. However - the thing is done, and the point is that I must make great changes. Mortimer is not making as much as he was, either; he came to the conclusion that he couldn't get anywhere in that business on so small a capital, and has gone into real estate. It will be some time before he makes enough to keep things going in the old way. I made all my plans last night and came down to ask you if you could take James. He has been with us so long; I can't let him go to strangers. Then I shall turn out all those high-priced servants and get a woman to do general housework. Alice says her aunt always gets green ones from an agency and breaks them in. They are quite cheap. I shall help her, of course, and if she doesn't know much about cooking I know a little and can learn more. I shall shut up the big drawing-room, put everything into moth balls, and give out that the doctor has ordered me to rest this winter, to go to bed every night at eight. That will stop people coming up three or four times a week to dance. And I can sell the new clothes I brought from Paris and New York to Polly Roberts. She's just my height and weight. Of course I must tell the girls the truth - that I'm economizing; but wild horses wouldn't drag it out of them. I don't care tuppence, but Morty says it would hurt his business. I rather like the idea of working. I'm tired of the old round, and would like to get a job if Morty wasn't so opposed - says it would ruin him."

"I should think so. At least let us wash our dirty linen at home....I have been thinking while you talked. I've only spent two whole winters in town since I married, end I've always thought I'd love to live in the old house. I've rather envied you, Alexina, dear...it is so full of happy memories for me. I did have such a good time as a girl...such a good, simple time....I'm wondering if Tom wouldn't rent it for the winter and spring. He's been doing splendidly these last two or three years, and he owned some of the property west of Twin Peaks that is building up so fast. I know he sold it for quite a lot....And I sometimes wonder if he doesn't get as tired of living in the same place year after year as I do. He could play golf at the Ingleside....I am sure he will....It would be the very best thing all round. Then we could run the house, and you and Mortimer would pay something - never mind what....People would think it was the other way, if they thought anything about it. Families often double up in that fashion."

"Maria! I can't believe it. It would be too perfect a solution, provided of course that we pay all we cost. I should insist upon keeping the slips as usual. You are an angel."

"We Groomes and Ballingers always stand by one another, don't we? The Abbotts, too. Besides, it will certainly be no sacrifice on any of our parts. It will mean a great deal to me to spend six months in town, and I know that Tom has grown as tired of motoring back and forth every day as be used to be of the train."

"It will be heavenly just having you." Alexina spoke with perfect sincerity. She had not faltered before the prospect of work, but that of Mortimer's society unrelieved for an indefinite time had filled her with something like panic. It had been the one test of her powers of endurance of which she had not felt assured.

"That will give us time, too, to get on our feet again. Morty is very hopeful of this new business. I shall go out very little, and as Joan will be the natural center of attraction it will be understood that her friends, not mine, have the run of the house."

Maria nodded. "It's just the thing for Joan. Really a godsend. She worries me more than all three of the boys. They are east at school for the winter and of course don't come home for the Christmas holidays. If you want to be housekeeper you may. I don't know anything I should like better than a rest from ordering dinner, after all these years."

"Perfect! I'll also take care of my room and Morty's. Then I'd be sure I wasn't really imposing on you. You're a dead game sport, Maria, and I'd like to drink your health."

# CHAPTER XV

I

Mortimer looked nonplussed when Alexina informed him at dinner of the immediate solution of their difficulties. He detested Tom and Maria Abbott; there were certain things he could forget in his aristocratic wife's presence, far as she had withdrawn, but never in theirs. Moreover he feared Abbott. He was as keen as a hawk; an unconsidered word and he might as well have told the whole story. Well, he never talked much anyhow; he would merely talk less.

When Alexina asked him if he had any better plan to propose he was forced to shrug his shoulders and set his lips in a straight line of resignation. When she told him what her original plan had been he was so appalled, so humiliated at the bare thought of his wife in a servant's apron (to say nothing of the culinary arrangements) that he almost warmed to the Abbotts.

Gertrude Atherton

II

Ten days later, on the eve of the Abbotts' arrival, the equanimity of spirit he was striving to regain by the simple process of thinking of something else when his late delinquencies obtruded themselves, received a severe shock. Alexina handed him a cheque for ten thousand dollars and asked him to place it to Gora's account in the bank where she kept her savings.

"Where did you get it?" he asked stupidly, staring at the slip of paper so heavily freighted.

"Anne Montgomery sold some of my things to a good-natured ignoramus whose husband made a fortune in Tonopah. She doesn't know how to buy and Anne advises her."

"What did you sell? Your jewels?"

"Some. I never wear anything but the pearls anyhow; and it's bad taste to wear jewels unless you're wealthy. I had some old lace that is hard to buy now, and real lace isn't the fashion any more. New rich people always think it's just the thing. I also sold her two of the biggest and clumsiest of the Italian pieces. She is crazy about them. Anne told her that they were as good as a passport."

Mortimer sprang to the only, the naïve, the eternal masculine conclusion.

"You do love me still!" The dull eyes of his spirit flashed with the sudden rejuvenation of his heavy body. "I never really believed you had ceased to care....you were capricious like all women...a little spoilt. I knew that if I had patience...Only a loving wife would do such a thing."

Alexina made a wry face at the banality of his climax, although the fatuous outburst had barely amused her.

"No, I don't love you in the least, Mortimer, and never shall. Make up your mind to that. Love some one else if you like....I did this for two reasons: I did not have the courage to tell Gora the truth - and that I was too unjust and penurious to restore the money you had taken; and as your wife it would have hurt my pride unbearably."

"And you are not afraid to trust me with this money?" he asked, his voice toneless.

"Not in the least. There's no other way to manage it and I fancy you know what would happen if you didn't hand it over. There is such a thing as the last straw."

# CHAPTER XVI

I

It was a week later. Alexina was changing her dress. Maria had asked a number of her girlhood friends in for luncheon, and they were to exchange reminiscences in the old house over a table laden as of yore with the massive Ballinger silver, English cutglass, and French china. Alexina was about to take refuge with Janet Maynard.

Her door opened unceremoniously and Gora entered.

Alexina caught her breath as she saw her sister-in-law's eyes. They looked like polar seas in a tropical storm.

"Why, Gora, dear," she said lightly. "I thought you were on an important case."

"Man died last night. I have just been to see Mortimer. When I got his note - just three lines - saying that he had received a cheque from Utica and deposited it to my account I knew at once - as soon as I had time to think - there was something wrong. The natural thing would have been to call me up - couldn't tell me the good news too soon....And there was a hollow ring about that note....Well, as soon as I woke up to-day I went straight down to his office. I had to wait an hour. When he came in and saw me he turned green. I marched him into a back room and corkscrewed the truth out of him - the whole truth. Then I blasted him. He knows exactly what one person in this world thinks of him, what everybody else would think of him if he were found out. I gathered that you had let him down easy. Your toploftical pride, I suppose. Well, I must have a good plebeian streak in me somewhere and for the first time I was glad of it. When I left him he looked shrunken to half his natural size. His eyes looked like a dead fish's and all the muscles of his face had given Way. He looked as if he were going to die and I wish he would. Faugh! A thief in the family. That at least we never had before."

"Don't be too sure. Remember nobody else knows about Morty, and everybody'll go on thinking he's honest. Half our friends may be thieves for all we know, and as for our ancestors - what are you doing?"

II

Gora had taken a roll of yellow bills from her purse. She counted them on the table; ten bills denominating a thousand dollars each.

"I won't take them." said Alexina stiffy. "I think you are horrid, simply horrid,"

"And do you imagine I would keep it? I What do you take me for?"

"I am in a way responsible for Mortimer's debts - his partner."

"That cuts no ice with me - nor with you. That is not the reason you sold your jewels and laces and those superb - Oh, you poor child! If I'm furious, it's more for you than on any other account. You don't deserve such a fate - "

"I don't deserve to have you treat me so ungratefully. I can't get my things back. I wanted you to have the money more than I eared for those things, anyhow. I have no use for the money. I don't owe anything and the rent Tom pays me for six months will help me to run the house for the rest of the year and pay taxes besides. So, you just keep it, Gora. It's yours and that's the end of it."

"This is the end of it as far as I'm concerned." She opened the secret drawer of the cabinet and stuffed in the bills. "They're safe from any sort of burglars there. But not from fire. Bank them to-morrow."

"I'll not touch them."

"Nor I either."

III

Gora threw her hat on the floor and sitting down before the table thrust her hands into her hair and tugged at the roots. "I always do this when I'm excited - which is oftener than you think. What dreams I had that first night - I got his note late and was too tired to reason, to suspect....I just dreamed until I fell asleep. I'd start for England a week later - for England!"

Goose flesh made Alexina's delicate body feel like a cold nutmeg grater. "England?"

"Yes!...ah...you see, it's the only place where literary recognition counts for anything."

"Oh? I rather thought the British authors looked upon Uncle Sam in the light of a fairy godfather. Our recognition counts for a good deal, I should say. I never thought you were snobbish."

"I'm not really. Only London is a sort of Mecca for writers just as Paris is for women of fashion....Just fancy being feted in London after you had written a successful novel."

"I'd far rather receive recognition in my own country," said Alexina, elevating her classic American profile. She was not feeling in the least patriotic, however. "You'd see your friend Gathbroke, though. That would be jolly. Do take the money, Gora, and don't be a goose."

"That subject's closed. Don't let me keep you. James told me that Maria is having a luncheon, and I suppose that means you are going out. I'll rest here for awhile if you don't mind."

Gertrude Atherton

# CHAPTER XVII

## I

Mortimer went off that night and got drunk. It was the first time in his life and possibly his last, but he made a thorough job of it. He took the precaution to telephone to the house that he was going out of town, but when he returned two days later he experienced a distinct pleasure in telling Alexina what he had done. Alexina, who still hoped that she would always be able to regard Life as God's good joke, rather sympathized with him, and assured him that he would have nothing to apprehend from Gora in the future: she had no more fervent wish than to keep out of his way.

## II

He found himself on the whole very comfortable. Maria was always most kind, Alexina polite and amiable, and Tom "decent." Joan liked him as well as she liked anybody, and when the family spent a quiet evening at home he undertook to improve her dancing and she was correspondingly grateful; it had been her weak point. The fiction was carefully preserved that the Dwights were conferring a favor on the Abbotts and that all expenses were equally shared. In time he came to believe it, and his hours of deep depression, when he had pondered over his inexplicable roguery, grew rarer and finally ceased. After all he had had nothing to lose as far as Alexina was concerned; one's sister hardly mattered (Did women matter much, anyhow?); and his sense of security, which he hugged at this time as the most precious thing he had ever possessed, at last made him a little arrogant. He had done what he should not, of course, but it was over and done with, ancient history; and where other men had gone to State's Prison for less, he had been protected like an infant from a rude wind. He knew that he would never do it again and that his position in life was as assured as it ever had been.

III

He spent a good many evenings at the club, and Maria found him a willing cavalier when Tom "drew the line" at dancing parties. Alexina, who had sold her car to Janet and her new gowns to Polly, had announced that she was bored with dancing and should devote the winter to study. She spent the evenings either in her library upstairs or with her friends. Mortimer saw her only at the table.

He wondered if Tom Abbott would rent the house every winter. A pleasant feeling of irresponsibility was beginning to possess his jaded spirit. He made a little money occasionally, but he was no longer expected to hand anything over when the first of the month came round - a date that had haunted him like a nightmare for four long years. Pie could spend it on himself, and he felt an. increasing pleasure in doing so.

# CHAPTER XVIII

## I

Gray naked trees; orchards of prune and peach and cherry, mile after mile. Orange trees in small wayside gardens heavy-laden with golden fruit. Tall accacias a mass of canary colored bloom. Opulent palms shivering against a gray sky. Close mountains green and dense with forest trees, their crests filagreed with redwoods. Far mountains lifting their bleak ridges above bare brown hills thirsting for rain.

The heavy rains were due. It was late in January. Alexina and several of her friends were motoring back to the city through the Santa Clara Valley, after luncheon with the Price Ruylers at their home on the mountain above Los Gatos. As it was Sunday there was an even number of men in the party, and Alexina, maneuvered into Jimmie Thorne's roadster, was enduring with none of the sweet womanly graciousness which was hers to summon at will, one of those passionate declarations of love which no beautiful young woman out of love with her husband may hope to escape; and not always when in. Alexina had grown skillful in eluding the reckless verbalisms of love, but

Gertrude Atherton

when one is packed into a small motor car with a determined man, desperately in love, one might as well try to wave aside the whirlwind.

Jimmie Thorne was a fine specimen of the college-bred young American of good family and keen professional mind. He has no place in this biography save in so far as he jarred the inner forces of Alexina's being, and he fell at Château-Thierry.

II

Alexina lifted her delicate profile and gave it as sulky an expression as she could assume. She really liked him, but was annoyed at being trapped.

"I don't in the least wish to marry you."

"Everybody knows you don't care a straw for Dwight. You could easily get a divorce - "

"On what grounds! Besides, I don't want to. I'd have to be really off my head about a man even to think of such a thing. Our family has kept out of the divorce courts. And I don't care two twigs for you, Jimmie dear."

"I don't believe it. That is, I know I could make you care. You don't know what love is - "

"I suppose you are about to say that you think I think I am cold, and that if I labor under this delusion it is only because the right man hasn't come along. Well, Jimmie dear, you would only be the sixteenth. I suppose men will keep on saying it until I am forty - forty-five - what is the limit these days? I know exactly what I am and you don't"

"I'm not going to be put off by words. Remember I'm a lawyer of sorts. God! I wish I'd been here when you married that codfish, instead of studying law at Columbia, Do you mean to tell me I couldn't have won you!"

"No. Almost any man can win a little goose of eighteen if circumstances favor him. Twenty-five is another! matter. Oh, but vastly another! Even if I'd never married before I'm not at all sure I should have fallen in love with you."

"Yes, you would. You're frozen over, that's all."

Alexina sighed, and not with exasperation. He was very charming, magnetic, companionable. He was handsome and clever and manly. She could feel the warmth of his young virile body through their fur coats, and her own trembled a little....It suddenly came to her that she no longer owed Mortimer anything. Their "partnership" had been dissolved by his own act. If she could have loved Jimmie Thorne with something beyond the agreeable response of the mating-season (any season is the mating season in California)...that was the trouble. He was not individual enough to hold her. Life had been too kind to him. Save for this unsatisfied passion he was perfectly content with life. Such men do not "live." They may have charm, but not fascination....Perhaps it was as well after all that she had married Mortimer. Another man might not have been so easily disposed of.

"Jimmie dear, if it were a question of a few months, and I made a cult of men as some women do, it would be all right. But marry another man that I am not sure - that I know I don't want to spend my life with. Oh, no."

He looked somewhat scandalized. Like many American men he was even more conventional than most women are; he was, moreover, a man's man, spending most of his leisure in their society, either at the club or in out-of-door sports, and he divided women rigidly into two classes. Alexina was his first love and his last; and as he went over the top and crumpled up he thought of her.

"I wouldn't have a rotten affair with you. You're not made for that sort of thing - "

"Well, you're not going to have one, so don't bother to buckle on your armor." She relented as she looked into his miserable eyes, and took his hand impulsively. "I'm sorry...sorry....I wish...you are worth it...but it's not on the map."

# CHAPTER XIX

## I

Gora's novel was published in February. Aileen Lawton, Sibyl Bascom, Alice Thorndyke, Polly Roberts, and Janet Maynard organized a campaign to make it the fashion. They went about with copies under their arms, on the street, in the shops, at luncheons, even at the matinée, and "could talk of nothing else." Sibyl and Janet bought a dozen copies each and sent them to friends and acquaintances with the advice to read it at once unless they wished to be hopelessly out of date: it was "all the rage in New York."

As a matter of fact, with the exception of Aileen and possibly Janet, the book almost terrified them with its pounding vigor and grim relentless logic, even its romantic realism, which made its tragedy more poignant and sinister by contrast; and, again with the exception of Aileen, they were little interested in Gora. But they were loyally devoted to Alexina and obeyed, as a matter of course, her request to help her make the book a success. They worked with the sterner determination as Alexina in her own efforts was obliged to be extremely subtle.

Besides, it, was rather thrilling not only to know a real, author but almost to have her in the family as it were. Their industrious sowing bore an abundant harvest and Gora's novel became the fashion. Whether people hated it or not, and most of them did, they discussed it continually, and when a book meets with that happy fate personal opinions matter little.

## II

Maria thought the book was "awful" and forbade Joan to read it. Joan thought (to Alexina) that it was simply the most terribly fascinating book she had ever read and made her despise society more than ever and more determined to light out and see life for herself first chance she got. Tom Abbott thought it a remarkable book for a woman to have written; a man might have written it. Judge Lawton read it twice. Mortimer declined to read it. He had not forgiven Gora; moreover, although his social position was now planetary, it annoyed him excessively to hear his sister alluded to continually as an author. Even the men at the club were reading the damned book.

III

Bohemia stood off for some time. It was only recently they had learned that Gora Dwight was a Californian. They had read her stories, but as she had been the subject of no publicity whatever they had inferred that, like many another, she had dwelt in their midst only long enough to acquire material. When they learned the truth, and particularly after her inescapable novel appeared, they were indignant that she had not sought her muse at Carmel-by-the-Sea, or some other center of mutual admiration; affiliated herself; announced herself, at the very least. There was a very sincere feeling among them that any attempt on the part of a rank outsider to achieve literary distinction was impertinent as well as unjustifiable....It was impossible that he or she could be the real thing.

When they discovered that she was affiliated more or less with fashionable society, nurse though she might be, and that those frivolous and negligible beings were not only buying her book by the ton but giving her luncheons and dinners and teas, their disgust knew no bounds and they tacitly agreed that she should be tabû in the only circles where recognition counted.

IV

But Gora, who barely knew of their existence, little recked that she had been weighed, judged, and condemned. Her old dream had come true. Society, the society which should have been her birthright and was not, had thrown open its doors to her at last and everybody was outdoing everybody else in flattering and entertaining her.

Not that she was deceived for a moment as to the nature of her success with the majority of the people whose names twinkled so brightly in the social heavens. She more than suspected the "plot" but cared little for the original impulse of the book's phenomenal success in San Francisco and its distinguished faubourgs. She was square with her pride, her youthful bitterness had its tardy solace, her family name was rescued from obscurity. She knew that this belated triumph rang hollow, and that she really cared very little about it; but the strength and tenacity of her nature alone would have forced her to quaff every drop of the cup so long withheld. Even if she had been desperately bored she would have accepted these invitations to houses so long indifferent to her existence, and as a matter of fact she welcomed the sudden lapse into frivolity after her years of hard and almost unremitting work. She had played little in her life; and a year later when she was working eighteen hours a day without rest, in conditions that seemed to have leapt into life from the blackest pages of history, she looked back upon her one brief interval of irresponsibility, gratified vanity, and bodily indolence, as at a bright star low on the horizon of a dark and terrible night.

# V

There was one small group of women, Gora soon discovered, that stood for something besides amusement, sharply as some of them were identified with all that was brilliant in the social life of the city. They read all that was best in serious literature and fiction as soon after it came out as their treadmill would permit, and they gave somewhat more time to it than to poker. It was this small group, led by Mrs. Hunter, that in common with several wealthy and clever Jewish women, with intellectual members of old families that had long since dropped out of a society that gave them too little to be worth the drain on their limited means, and with one or two presidents of women's clubs, made up the small attendance at the lectures on literary and political subjects, delivered either by some local light, or European specialist in the art of charming the higher intelligence of American women without subjecting it to undue fatigue.

This small but distinguished band discussed Gora separately and collectively and placed the seal of approval upon her. With them her arrival was genuine and permanent.

It was hardly a step from their favor to the many women's clubs of the city, and she was invited to be the luncheon or afternoon guest at one after another until all had entertained the rising star and she had learned to make the little speeches expected of her without turning to ice.

VI

The local intelligenzia, those that assured one another how great were each and all, and whose poems or stories found an occasional hospitality in the eastern magazines, who toiled over "precious" paragraphs of criticism or whose single achievement had been a play for the mid-summer jinks of the Bohemian Club; these and their associates, the artists and sculptors, still held aloof, more and more annoyed that Gora Dwight should have had the bad taste to be discovered by the Philistines, and should be flying across the high heavens in spite of their tabû.

Gora had gradually become aware of their existence, and their attitude, which both amused and piqued her. She knew now that if she had been one of them they would have beaten the big drum and proclaimed to the world (of California) that she was "great," "a genius," the legitimate successor of Ambrose Bierce, whom she remotely resembled, and Bret Harte, whom she did not resemble at all. This they would have done if only to prove that California no longer "knocked" as in the mordant nineties, nor waited for the anile East to set the seal of its dry approval before discovering that a new volcano was sending forth its fiery swords in their midst.

But it was extremely doubtful if society and upper club circles would have taken any notice of her. Both had acquired the habit, however unjustly, of regarding their local intelligenzia (with the exception of the few who kept themselves wholly apart from all groups) as worshipers of small gods, and preferred to take their cues from London or New York. They plumed themselves upon having discovered Gora Dwight and sometimes wondered how it had happened.

But Bohemia is hardly a trades union; it is indeed anarchistic and knows no boss. Gora might not be invited to Carmel this many a day, nor yet to Berkeley, nor to sundry other parnassi, but there was one club in San Francisco whose curiosity got the better of it, and she was invited to be the guest of the evening at the home of the Seven Arts Club on the twentieth of April in the fateful year of nineteen-fourteen.

VII

The Seven Arts Club had been organized by a group of painters, architects, authors, sculptors, musicians, actors and poets, most of whom had long since found various degrees of fame and moved to New York, Europe, or the romantic wilderness.

It still had seventy times seven votaries of the seven arts on its list and few had found fame as yet outside their hospitable state - where log-rolling is as amiable as the climate - but all save the elders were expecting it and many made a fair living. They met once a week, and a part of the evening pleasure of the literary wing was to "place" authors. They were willing to swallow the British authors whole (they did in fact "discover" one or two of them, as the musical critics had discovered such a rara avis as Tetrazzini, or the dramatic critics many a now famous player); but they were excessively critical of all who owed their origin to the United States of America, and particularly of those who had loved and lost the sovereign state of California.

Naturally all were more or less radical (except the cynical and now somewhat anæmic elders who gave up hope for a world that had ceased to hold out hope to them). The artists were disturbed by futurism and cubism, although as neither paid they were forced to devote the greater part of their inspiration to the marketable California scenery.

But the writers: potential or locally arrived novelists, playwrights, poets, essayists, were the real intelligenzia! They went about with the radical weeklies of the

East (or Berkeley) under their arms and discoursed under their breath (when foregathered in small and ardent groups) upon The Revolution, the day of Judgment for all but honest Labor, and hissed their hatred of Capital. And if they had much in common with those "intellectuals" to be found in every land who caress the chin of radicalism with one hand and plunge the other into the pocket of capital as far as permitted, who shall blame them? One must live and one must have something to excite one's intellect when sex, the stand-by, takes its well-earned rest.

Several of these ardent ladies and gentlemen, with the sanction of the Club's President, a business man whose contributions were the financial mainstay of the Seven Arts, and who sincerely envied the gifted members, denying them nothing, invited James Kirkpatrick to be the guest of an evening and deliver an address on Socialism and the Proletariat. He replied that he would come and spit on them if they liked but that he had as much use for parlor socialists as he had for damned fools and posers of any sort. Life was too short. As for Labor it knew how to take care of itself and had about as crying a need of their "support" as a healthy human body had of lice and other parasites.

They were not discouraged however, merely pronouncing him a "creature," and were not at all flattered or surprised when Gora Dwight accepted their invitation and asked permission to bring her friends, Mrs. Mortimer Dwight and Miss Aileen Lawton.

# CHAPTER XX

## I

The wildflowers were on the green hills: the flame-colored velvet skinned poppy, the purple and yellow lupins, the pale blue "babyeyes," buttercups, dandelions and sweetbrier, fields of yellow mustard. The gardens about the Bay and down the Peninsula were almost licentious in their vehement indulgence in color. Every flower that grows north, south, east, west, on the western hemisphere and the eastern, was to be found in some one of these gardens of Central California; the poinsettia cheek by jowl with periwinkle and the hedges of marguerite; heavy-laden trees of magnolia above beds of Russian violets. Pomegranate trees and sweet peas, bridal wreath and camellia, begonia, fuchsias, heliotrope, hydrangea, chrysanthemums, roses, roses, roses....Little orchards of almond trees, their blossoms a pink mist against a clear blue sky....The mariposa lily was awake in the forests; infinitesimal yellow pansies made a soft carpet for the feet of the deer and the puma....In the old Spanish towns of the south, the Castilian roses were in bloom and as sweet and pink and poignant as when Rezánov sailed through the Golden Gate in the April of eighteen-six, or Chonita Iturbi y Moncada, the doomswoman, danced on the hearts of men in Monterey....From end to end of the great Santa Clara Valley the fruit trees were in bloom, a hundred thousand acres and more of pure white blossoms or delicate pink. Bascom Luning took Alexina over it one day in his air-car, as she called it, and from above it looked like a scented sea that was all foam.

But no such riot and glory had come to San Francisco. This was the season for winds that seemed to blow from the four points of the compass at once and of ghostly fogs that stole up and down the streets of the city, abandoning the hills to bank in the valleys, as if seeking warmth; abruptly deserting the lowlands to prowl along the heights, always searching, searching, these pure white lovely fogs of San Francisco, for something lost and never found.

II


"I hope they're not too artistic to keep their rooms warm," said Aileen, as they drove from her house where Gora and Alexina had dined, down to the Club of the Seven Arts. "I have smoked so much, intending to prove in public how really virtuous a society girl is, in contrast to Bohemia, that I'm nearly frozen."

"Keep your wrap on," said Alexina. "Who cares? I have always been wild to get into real Bohemian circles, meet authors and artists. We do lead the most provincial life. All circles should overlap - the best of all, anyhow. That is the way I would remold society if I were rich and powerful - "

"Good heavens Alex, you are not idealizing this crowd we are going to meet to-night? They're just a lot of second and third raters - "

"What do you know about them?"

"I keep my feet on the ground and my head out of the clouds. I know more or less what it must be. Besides, the last time I was in New York I was taken several times to the restaurants and studios of Greenwich Village. I could only convey my opinion of it in many swear words. This must be a sort of chromo of it....Gora, are you as wildly excited as Alex is? I know she is because her spine is rigid; and she is probably colder than I am."

"Well, anyhow," said Alexina defiantly, "it will be something I never saw before."

"It will, darling. Well. Gora, what do you anticipate?"

Gora laughed. "I wonder? I don't think I've thought much about it. The circumstances of my life have developed the habit of switching off my imagination except when I am at my desk. I've also formed the habit of taking things as they come. I'll manage to extract something from this, one way or another."

III

The car stopped before a narrow house in the rebuilt portion of the city. The door was opened immediately and the three guests of honor, apparently very late, as a large room beyond the vestibule appeared to be crowded, were marshaled up a narrow stair into a dressing-room under the eaves.

"Looks like the loft of a barn," grumbled Aileen. There was no attendant to hear. "Well, I'm not going to leave my cloak, for several reasons - only one of which is that if this room is a sample my ill-covered bones will rattle together downstairs."

She wore a gown of black chiffon with a green jade necklace and a band of green in her fashionably done fair hair. Alexina's gown was a soft white satin that fitted closely and made her look very tall and slim and round, the corsage trimmed with the only color she ever wore. Her hair was done in a classic knot and held with a comb - a present from Aileen - designed from periwinkles and green leaves and sparkling dew-drops.

Gora shook out the skirt of her only evening-gown, a well-made black satin, very severe, but always relieved by a flower of some sort. To-night she wore a poinsettia, whose peculiarly vivid red brought out the warm browns of her skin and hair. She had a superb neck and shoulders and bust, and the skin of her body was a delicate honey color that melted imperceptibly into the deeper tones of her throat and face.

"Alexina," she said, "let us perish but exhibit all our

points. Your arms and hands were modeled for some untraced Greek ancestress and born again. Your neck is almost as good as mine, if not quite so solid...."

She had a spot of crimson on her high cheek bones and admitted to the discerning Aileen that she was the least bit excited. After all, the keenest brains of San Francisco might be down in that long raftered room they had glimpsed, and in any case she was about to be judged by a new standard.

"Oh, don't let that worry you," Aileen began.

A door at the end of the room opened abruptly and a small woman came forward almost panting. "I just ran up those stairs," she cried. "But I was bound to be the first. I used to go to school with your mother down on Bush Street - dear Minnie Morrison!"

She was a woman of fifty or sixty, with a nose like an inflamed button, eyes that watered freely, and a shabby black hat somewhat on one side.

"But my mother never went to school in San Francisco," said Gora stiffly, and eyeing this first precipitate member of the intellectual world with profound disfavor.

"Oh, yes, she did. We were the most intimate friends. To think that dear Minnie's daughter - "

"Her name was not Minnie Morrison - "

'Oh, yes, it was - "

"Don't mind her so much, Gora dear." Aileen did not

Gertrude Atherton

trouble to lower her voice. "She's drunk. Let's go down."

Another woman entered the same door almost as hastily, but she was a stately and rather handsome woman of forty, who gave the intruder such a withering look from her serene blue eyes that the unrefined member of the Seven Arts slunk out and could be heard stumbling down the stairs.

"I followed as soon as some one told me that Miss Skeers had come up here," she said apologetically. "She is not always herself, poor thing. Once she was quite distinguished as a local magazine writer, but...well, you know...all people do not have the good fortune to have their genius universally recognized, and the results are sometimes disastrous. We are so proud to welcome you to-night, Miss Dwight, and - and - your charming friends. I am Jane Upton Halsey." She appeared to think no further explanation necessary.

"Oh, yes," murmured the bewildered Gora. "It was you who wrote to me."

"Exactly. I am chairman of the reception committee." She looked expectant, then piqued, and added hastily: "Will you come downstairs? What lovely gowns. I should like to paint you all."

She herself was a symphony in pink ("dago pink," whispered Aileen wickedly), and she wore a small pink silk turban, apparently made from the same bolt as the gown.

"Perhaps we should have worn hats," said Gora

nervously. "I didn't know - I thought..."

"You are just all right. Anything goes here. We wear what's becoming, what we can afford, and what is our own idea of the right thing. Nobody criticizes anybody else."

"Now, this is life!" said Alexina to Aileen. "You will admit we never found anything like that before."

"Just you watch and catch them criticizing us....Rather effective - what?"

They were descending a staircase that led directly into the crowded room below, and they looked down upon a mass of upturned expectant faces, Gora was ahead with Miss Halsey, and as she reached the floor the faces changed their angle; it was apparent that they were not interested in her satellites.

"Let's stop here for a moment and watch," said Alexina. "It's too interesting. They look as if they'd eat her alive."

The whole company seemed to be seething about Gora, and as they were rapidly presented by Miss Halsey and passed on they produced the effect, in the inner circles, of a maelstrom. On the outer edge the women frankly stood on chairs to get a better look at the new lion, or pushed forward with frenzied determination to the fixed center of the whirlpool, whose gracious smile was becoming strained.

"Poor Gora!" said Aileen. "We do it better. A few picked souls at a time; or, even when it's a tea, just casual introductions at decent intervals, and not too

Gertrude Atherton

many references to the immortal work."

"It's simply great for Gora, anyhow; for, big or little, they're her own sort. And they're not snobs, They don't care tuppence for us."

"You're right there. I went to a big reception of all the arts in Paris once and the only people any one kowtowed to were two disgustingly rich New York women who had never done anything. But no one can be blamed for national characteristics. Heavens! What an olla podrida!"

Some of the men were in evening dress, but the greater number were not. They were of all ages, shaves, neckties and haircuts. The women wore every variety of hat, from an immense sailor perched above an immense fat face, above an immense shirtwaist bust, to minute turbans and waving plumes. They wore tailored suits, high "one piece" frocks of any material from chiffon to serge, symphonic confections like Miss Halsey's, and flowing robes presumably artistic. None wore full evening dress except the guests of honor. All, however, did not wear hats, and they arranged their hair as individually as Alexina.

IV

"This may be our chance to see the art exhibit," said Aileen. "They'll remember us in time, or Gora will...."

They descended into the room but had waited too long. Miss Halsey, turning the guest of honor over to the second in command, a woman of portentous seriousness, made her way hastily to the mere butterflies; who endeavored vainly to slink away under cover of the rotating crowd.

"You won't think me rude, I hope," she cried, "but I had to start things going, and it is awkward for all to introduce three people at a time."

"You were most considerate," said Alexina amiably. "But we only came to witness Gora's triumph, and we enjoy looking on, anyhow....We were about to look at the pictures...."

"You must meet some of our more brilliant members," said Miss Halsey firmly. "They would never forgive me, and have been almost as excited at meeting two such distinguished members of society as at meeting Miss Dwight herself. Now, if you...if you...that is..."

"Our names are Jane Boughton and Mamie Featherhurst," supplied Aileen, transfixing the lady with her wicked green eyes.

"Oh, yes, to be sure...there has been so much to think of...but your names are so often in the society columns...it seems to me I recall that one of you is the daughter of a famous judge - "

"Boughton. He's under indictment, you know, for graft, bribery, and corruption."

"Oh...ah...how unfortunate," Miss Halsey's jaw fell. Even she had heard - vaguely in her studio - of the scandal of Judge Boughton, and she wondered how she had been so absent-minded as to invite a member of his family to the club.

"You see," said Aileen coolly. "I am not fit to associate with your members, and as Miss Featherhurst is still my loyal friend, we'll just go over and sit in a corner - "

"Indeed you shall do nothing of the kind. You are our guests, and - please for this evening forget everything else."

"You nasty little beast," hissed Alexina into Aileen's discomforted ear. "She's worth two of you."

"So she is," said Aileen contritely, "I'll behave better."

Miss Halsey, who had been signaling several members and rounding up others, returned, Alexina blazed her eyes at Aileen, who murmured hastily to the hostess: "I was just joking. I am Judge Lawton's daughter, and this is Mrs. Mortimer Dwight, Gora's sister-in-law. I'd never have told such a whopper but I'm so nervous and shy. I didn't think I could go through the ordeal."

"Oh, you poor child. Well, you'll find we're not terrible in the least. Now, don't try to remember names. They'll remember yours - better than I did!"

Another small eddying circle formed about the luminaries from a lower sphere. This proved to be much like similar performances in any stratum of society. All murmured platitudes, or nothing. Nobody tried to be original or witty. Alexina and Aileen gradually disengaged themselves and were making their way toward the pictures that turned the four walls into a harmonious mass of color, when an old man came tottering up. He had bright, eyes and a pleasant face.

"Which is Mrs. Dwight?" he asked eagerly. Alexina bent her lofty head and smiled down upon him.

"Of course. Little Alexina. I remember you when you were a dear little girl and I used to see you playing about the house when I went up to have a good powwow with that clever grandfather of yours, Alex Groome - one of the ablest politicians this town ever had; and straight, damn straight."

"Alexander Groome was my father."

"Oh, no, he wasn't. He was your grandfather. You are the daughter...let me see...there were two or three young ladies....I remember when they came out in the eighties...and a boy or two...."

"I am sorry to be rude, but Alexander Groome was my father. I came along rather late."

"Impossible!....Well, I suppose you know best..." and he drifted off.

"This seems to be a home for incurables," said Aileen. "I am sure I don't know how I shall get through the evening. Gora has a slight sense of humor, you have quite a keen one, but mine is positively fiendish....Oh, Lord!"

Miss Halsey was trailing them, her hand resting lightly on the arm of another woman.

"Now this is something like," whispered Aileen. "Witch of Endor got up to look like Carmen."

The oncoming luminary was a singular-looking woman who may have been considerably less so in the privacy of her dressing-room; she had evidently expended much thought upon supplementing the niggardliness of Nature. Her unwashed-looking black hair was dressed very high and stuck with immense pins. Large, circular, highly colored, imitation jade rings dangled in tiers from her ear-lobes, and at least eight rows of colored beads covered the front of her loose, fringed, embroidered, beaded gown. She had a haggard face, deeply lined and badly painted, but something, an emanation perhaps, seemed to proclaim that she was still young.

"This, dear Mrs. Dwight and Miss Lawton, is Alma De Quincey Smith, with whose work you are of course familiar. She had her reception last week but was only too glad to come to-night and extend the welcoming hand of the east to our new daughter of the west."

Miss De Quincey Smith barely gave her time to finish. She darted forward and grasped Aileen's hand. "Oh, you must let me tell you how wonderful I think your unique green eyes go with that jade. I've been watching you!" She spoke with the eager unthinking impulsiveness of a child, which, oddly, made her look like a very old woman.

"Too nice of you," murmured Aileen, who was determined to behave.

"And you!" she cried, turning to Alexina. "Your eyes simply blaze. You look like a long white arum lily. And dusky hair, not merely black. Oh, I do think you are both too wonderful, and I am sure all these splendid artists here will want to paint you."

Alexina and Aileen were not accustomed to such spontaneous and unbridled admiration and they thought Miss Smith quite fascinating if rather queer. But Miss Smith did not number tact among her gifts and rushed on.

"Gora Dwight is too wonderful looking for words. We are all crazy over her. All the artists want to paint her already. Her coloring and style are unique and she suggests tragedy - with those marvelous pale eyes in that dark face - those heavy dark brows and heavy masses of hair. I have suggested that Folkes - your greatest portrait painter, you know, - paint her as Medea, or as the Genius of the Revolution, How proud you must be of her!"

"So we are," murmured Aileen. "We think she is the only woman writer in America worth mentioning. Why don't you paint her yourself?"

"I? I am not an artist - with the brush! I am an author, Alma De Quincey Smith."

"Oh!..." Aileen's voice trailed off vaguely, "What do you write? Plays? Essays?..."

"I - why, I'm one of the best - my stories appear constantly in the best magazines." Miss Smith, who had been deserted some time since by Miss Halsey, looked abject, helpless, and infuriated.

"Oh! We only read the worst. It must be wonderful to be famous. Come, Alex, we must see the pictures. They're going to have music and supper later."

# V

"Nevertheless," said Alexina, "they are real as far as they go, and they really do things, good or bad. They work, they aspire; they dream, and perhaps with reason, of a glorious future, when they will be as famous and successful as the founders of the club. Even if they fail they will have had the wonderful dream. Nothing can take that from them. I envy them - envy them!"

They were standing in a far corner of the room, after having examined three or four admirable and many passable paintings. Aileen looked at her in surprise. They had both been remarking upon the comic aspects of the intellectual life, and Alexina's outburst was unexpected. Aileen had seldom seen her vehement since they had outgrown their youthful habit of wrangling. She was still more astonished when she turned from a view of the Latin-seeming roofs of San Francisco from Twin Peaks, to Alexina's face. It looked drawn and desperate.

"Well, most of them will fail," she said lightly. "Look at these pictures! That is what is the matter with California - too much talent. You must be as individual as a talking monkey to get your head above the crowd. All these poor devils are doomed to the local reputation."

"Even so they have something to live for, mean something, do something. What do I mean to myself or anyone? What have I accomplished? The man I married is a dummy-husband; means nothing to me nor I to him. I have no children. Even my housekeeping for

Maria is a farce; James really does it all. I mean nothing to society now that I can no longer entertain it. I haven't even a decent vice. I don't smoke and gamble like you, nor have lovers like some of the others. I'm simply a nonentity - nothing!"

"You have personality...beauty...." Aileen was completely at a loss. "I hate being banal like that Smith idiot...but you are the perfection of a type. That is something. And you cultivate your mind - "

"My mind! What does it amount to? Anybody can pack a brain. I'd like one of those that gives out something, however little. But I can't help that. The point is I don't live. I don't care a hang about personality that doesn't get anywhere, and I care still less about being a finished type - that's the work of dead and gone ancestors, anyhow, not mine....I wish I could fall in love with James Kirkpatrick. I'd feel more justified in my own eyes if I were living with him over in the Mission - "

"His old mother would chase you out with a broom and use Biblical language. Of course I know you must be bored, Alex dear. Can't you manage to go abroad and live for a time?"

"No, I can't, and I don't see what difference that would make. But I'll tell you what I shall do. If Tom and Maria want to rent the house next year they can have it but I'll not live there. I'll not be 'held up' any longer. I'll stand on my own feet - in other words get a job. No - I've some loose money, I'll start in business."

"Good for you. Perhaps dad'll let me go in with you. Don't imagine I don't get sick of my racketing life; and when I have a spasm of reform I nearly take seriously to drink, I'm so bored. Would you have me for partner?"

"Wouldn't I? That is if you would be serious about it. I am, let me tell you. The whole family can perform suttee for all I care. I'm going to do something that will give me a place in the main stream of life."

"Trust me. I have been considering Bob's fifteenth proposal - Mr. Cheever has promised him a full partnership the day he marries, and it wouldn't be so bad. Bobby is a good sport, and we'd live the out-door life at Burlingame instead of the in - sports...tournaments...polo...cut out dissipation. We've both really had enough of it. But I believe business would be more interesting. After all that's what you marry for unless you want children - which I don't - to be interested. What'll we be? Decorators?"

"I suppose so. But all this has only just come to a head, although I know now that it has been slowly gathering force in my deepest deeps. If we do I'll take Alice on. She's sick of the game too and she has simply ripping ideas."

"Perfect. 'Dwight, Thorn - ', no, 'Thorndyke, Lawton and Dwight.' I'm too excited - convicts must feel like that when they tunnel a hole and get out. It will be our real, our first adventure."

# CHAPTER XXI

I

But two weeks later Aileen told Alexina that although she had cannily waited for what she believed to be the propitious moment and told her father about the great scheme, she had never seen him so upset. She stormed, argued, wept, but he was adamant. He would give her neither a cent nor his permission. When she accused him of inconsistency (he had supported woman's suffrage) he replied that women forced to work needed the franchise and no fair-minded man would withhold it; and if for no other reason he would forbid his daughter to go out and compete with women who must work whether they wanted to or not.

But that was only one point.

What did progress mean if women deliberately dropped from a higher plane to a lower? What had their ancestors worked for, possibly died for? It was their manifest duty to their class, to their family, to go up not down.

Moreover, when women had men to support them and

insisted upon forcing their way into the business world, they made men ridiculous and undermined society. It was dangerous, damned dangerous. If he had his way not a woman in any class, outside of nursing and domestic service, should work. He'd tax every male in the land, according to his income or wage, to say nothing of the rich women, and keep every last one of the unportioned in idleness rather than risk the downfall of male supremacy in the world.

He hated every form of publicity for the women of his class. If he had his way their names, much less photographs, should never appear in the public press. Society should be sacrosanct. Its traditions should be handed on, not lowered....Charity boards and settlement work, perhaps, but no further exposure to the vulgar gaze...he was glad she had never gone in for the last.

Civilization would be meaningless without that small class at the top that proved what Earth could accomplish in the way of breeding, the refinements of life, the beauty of distinction, in making an art of leisure, of pleasure - quite as much an art as writing books or painting pictures.

If the men in the younger nations had to work, at least they were able to prove to the older that the exquisite creatures they bred and protected were second to none on this planet, at least.

If women had genius that was another question. Let them give it to the world, by all means. That was their personal gift to civilization....He was not bigoted like some men, even young men, who thought it a disgrace for a lady publicly to transfer herself to the artistic plane and compete with men for laurels....But when it came to stripping off the delicate badges that only the higher civilization could confer, and struggling tooth and nail with the mob for no reason whatever - it was disloyal, ungrateful and monstrous.

He was no snob. He thought himself better than no man. (Different, yes.) But in regard to women, the women of his class, the class of his father before him, and of his father's father, he had his ideals, his convictions.

That was all.

## II

"In short, he's modern but not too modern. My twentieth-century arguments were brushed aside as mere fads. And yet there's probably not an important case tried in any court in either hemisphere that he doesn't read - learn something from if he can. He takes in the leading newspapers and reviews of America and Europe and even reads the best modern novels as carefully as he ever read Thackeray and Dickens - says they are the real social chronicles. He's a profound student of history, and the history of the present interests him just as much - he has those Balkans under a microscope; and collects all the data on every important strike here and elsewhere. And yet where women are concerned he is a fossil. An American fossil - worst sort. Some of the young ones are just as bad...I'll have to give in. I can't break his heart. I suppose I'll marry Bobby."

Gertrude Atherton

III

Alice Thorndyke also shook her head. "I'd like to, Alex, but frankly I haven't the courage. Your friends all stick to you like perfect dears when you step down and out and set up shop, and are so kind you feel like a street walker in a house of refuge. But secretly they hate it and they don't feel toward you in the same way at all. They may not know enough to express it, but what they really feel is that you have threatened the solidity of the order and lowered yourself as well as them. One day they may have more sense but not in our time, I am afraid."

Nevertheless, Alexina persisted in her determination. One could succeed alone. She would not be the first. She was by no means sure, however, what she wanted to do, and made up her mind to take no step before the following winter. When the Abbotts returned to Rincona in May they took James with them. Alexina closed Ballinger House, although Mortimer slept there and a Filipino came in every morning to make his breakfast and bed; and took a cottage in Ross with Janet Maynard whose mother had gone south to visit old lady Bascom, and who craved the wild peace of Marin County after too much San Francisco and Burlingame.

Marin, with its magnificent redwood forests on the coast, fed by the fogs of the Pacific, its ancient sunlit woods of oak and madroño and manzanita, its mountains and rocky hills and peaceful fertile valleys, is perhaps the most beautiful county in California, and its towns and villages are still almost primitive in spite of the many fashionable residents whose homes are close to or in them. The ocean pounds its western base, Mount Tamalpais is its proudest possession, it has a haunted looking lake; and a part of it embraces one of the many ramifications of the Bay of San Francisco, and commands a superb view of city and island and mountain. But it has a heavy brooding peace that seems to relax the social conscience. Entertaining is intermittent, and its inhabitants return to their winter in San Francisco deeply refreshed. It has its paradoxes like the rest of California. On a stark little peninsula, jutting out from bare hills into the Bay, is San Quentin, one of the State's Prisons, and along the edges of the marsh are Chinese hamlets and shrimp fisheries.

IV


Alexina and Janet purposed to spend the summer reading, idling in the sweet-scented garden, walking in the early morning, riding horseback in the late afternoon, taking tea at the club house at San Rafael, or Belvedere, perhaps, but "cutting out" all social dissipations. Janet was now twenty-six and beginning to feel the strain as well as seriously to consider what she should do with the rest of her life. She had great wealth, she was blasée as a result of doing everything she chose to do, in public or in private, and she was nearly two generations younger than Judge Lawton. Nevertheless, she perceived no allurement in the business world, and the only alternative seemed marriage. Not in California, however. No surprises there. She might take her fortune to London and become a peeress of the realm. When change became imperative better go up than down.

Alexina had never felt the attractions of dissipation and was not afflicted with moral ennui; but she was tired from much thinking and brooding and intimate personal contacts. She wanted the deep refreshment of the summer before girding up for the winter - before making her plunge into the world of business and toil.

But she was soon to discover that she had girded up her loins, or at all events brightened up her corpuscles and reposed her brain cells, for a far different purpose.

# CHAPTER XXII

## I

It is possible that only two people in California, barring German spies, leapt instantly to the conclusion that the Sarajevo bomb meant a European War. The Judge, because he had the historical background and knew his modern Europe as he knew his chessboard; and Alexina because she recalled conversations she had had in France the summer before with people close to the Government, to say nothing of mysterious allusions in the letters of Olive de Morsigny; who may have thought it wise not to trust all she knew to the post, or may have been too busy with her intensive nursing course to enter into particulars.

Janet shrugged her large statuesque shoulders when Alexina communicated her fears. What was war to her? England at least would have sense enough to keep out of it. Aileen came over after a convincing talk with her father looking as worried as if some nation or other were training their guns on the Golden Gate.

"Dad says it's the world war...that we'll be dragged in...that Germany has had it up her sleeve for

Gertrude Atherton

years...believes that bomb was made in Berlin...nothing under heaven could have averted this impending war but a huge standing army in Great Britain...hasn't Lord Roberts been crying out for it?....Dad and I dined at his house one night in London and the only picture in the dining-room was an oil painting of the Kaiser in a red uniform, done expressly for Lord Roberts...funny world...and now Britain's got a civil war on her hands and mutinous officers who won't go over and shoot men of their own class in Ulster....Russia hasn't built her strategic railways - all the money used up in graft....Oh, Lord! Oh, Lord! who'd have thought it?...Twentieth century and all the rest of it."

"Twentieth century...war...how utterly absurd....I don't wish to be rude...but really..."

This from every one to whom Alexina and Aileen, or even Judge Lawton, communicated their fears.

## II

One day Alexina and Aileen met in San Francisco by appointment and telephoned to James Kirkpatrick, asking him to lunch with them at the California Market. He accepted with alacrity, and laughed genially at their apprehensions. War? War? Not on your life. There'll never be another war. Socialists won't permit it. The kaiser? To hell with the kaiser. (Excuse me.) He, James Kirkpatrick, was in frequent correspondence with certain German socialists. They would declare themselves in the coming International Congress for the general strike if any sovereign - or President - dared to try to put over a war on the millions of determined socialists, syndicalists, inter-nationalists, and communists in Great Britain and Europe; he'd get the surprise of his life. Socialism was determined there should never be another war - the burden and life-toll of which was always borne by the poor man. He didn't believe any of those fool sovereigns, not even the crazy kaiser, would attempt it, knowing what they did; but if they turned out to be deaf and blind, well, just watch out for the Great Strike. That would be the most portentous, the most awe-inspiring event in history,

And then he dismissed a prospective European war as unworthy of further attention and held forth with extreme acrimony on the subject of the Great Colorado Strike; which rose to passionate denunciation of the miserable make-shift called civilization which, would permit such a horror in the very heart of a great and prosperous nation. But with the new system...the new system...there would not be even these abominable little civil wars...for that was what we had right here in our own country...no need to use up your gray matter bothering about European states....

He was so convincing that Alexina and Aileen thanked him warmly and went to their respective destinations lulled and comforted.

Nevertheless, the war made its grand début on August first, and Mr. Kirkpatrick, who had started on one of the passenger ships leaving New York for the International Socialist Congress, climbed ignominiously over the side and returned to the great ironic city on a tug.

III

Two letters came from Olive to Alexina and one to each of her other old friends, imploring them to come over and help. They could nurse. They could run canteens. Oeuvres. She wanted to show France what her friends, her countrywomen, could do.

But the war would be over in three months....Only Judge Lawton believed it would be a long war. Others hardly comprehended there was a war at all....Such things don't happen in these days. (Who in that wondrous smiling land could think upon war anywhere?)...It would be too funny if it were not for those dreadful pictures of the Belgian refugees....Poor things....Maria and other good women immediately began knitting for them...sat for hours on the verandahs, all in white, knitting, knitting...but talking of anything of war....It simply was a horrid dream and soon would be over....Their husbands all said so...three months....German army irresistible...modern implements of war must annihilate whole armies very quickly, and the Germans had the most and the best....Rotten shame (said Burlingame) and the Germans not even good sportsmen.

James Kirkpatrick, who avoided his former pupils, consoled himself with the thought that at least Britain would be licked...she'd get what was coming to her, all right, and Ireland would be free....Anyhow it would soon be over....When April nineteen-seventeen came he damned the socialist party for its attitude and enlisted: "I was a man and an American first, wasn't I?" he wrote to Alexina. "I guess your flag...oh, hell! (Excuse me.)"

Gertrude Atherton

IV

In December, nineteen-fourteen, Alexina and Alice Thorndyke (who grasped the entering wedge with both ruthless white little hands) went to France. Aileen was not strong enough to nurse so she bade a passionate good-by to her friends and engaged herself to Bob Cheever. Jimmie Thorne went to France as an ambulance driver, and Bascom Luning to join the Lafayette Escadrille. Gora sailed six months later to offer her services to England. In the case of a nurse there was much red tape to unravel.

A fair proportion of the women left behind continued to knit. As time went on branches of certain French war-relief organizations were formed, and run by such capable women as Mrs. Thornton and Mrs. Hunter, who had many friends among the American women living in France; now toiling day and night at their oeuvres.

Alexina and Olive de Morsigny, after a year of nursing, when what little flesh they had left could stand no more, founded an oeuvre of their own, and Sibyl Bascom and Aileen Cheever did fairly well with a branch in San Francisco, Alexina's relatives quite wonderfully in New York and Boston; although they were already interested in many others.

# V

Certain interests in California, notably the orchards and canneries, were violently anti-British during the first years of the war, as the blockade shut off their immense exports to Germany, and those that failed, or closed temporarily, realized the incredible: that a war in Europe could affect California, even as the Civil War affected the textile factories of England. To them it was a matter of indifference, until nineteen-seventeen, who won the war so long as one side smashed the other and was quick about it.

Owners and directors of copper mines - but let us draw a veil over the sincere robust instincts of human nature.

The Club of Seven Arts was proudly and vociferously pro-German. Not that they cared a ha'penny damn really for Germany, but it was a far more original attitude than all this sobbing over France...and then there was Reinhardt, the Secessionist School, the adorable jugendstyl. And the atrocity stories were all lies anyway. The bourgeois president resigned, but no one else paid any attention to them.

In nineteen-seventeen a few declared themselves pacifists and conscientious objectors, and, little recking what they were in for, marched off triumphantly to a military prison, feeling like Christ and longing for a public cross.

The others, those that were young enough, shouldered a gun and went to the front with high hearts and hardened muscles. Democracy über alles. The women enlisted in the Red Cross and the Y.W.C.A., and worked with grim enthusiasm, either at home or in France.

# VI

By this time California, almost on another planet as she was, with her abundance unchecked, and her skies smiling for at least three-fourths of the year, admitted there was a real war in the world, as bad (or worse) as any you could read about in history. The war films in the motion picture houses were quite wonderful, but too terrible.

They also discussed it, especially on those days when the streets echoed with the march of departing regiments in khaki, or one's own son, or one's friend's son enlisted or was drafted, or it was their day at Red Cross headquarters.

All the older women were at work now, and all but the most irreclaimably frivolous of the young ones. Even Tom and Maria Abbott made no protest against Joan's joining the Woman's Motor Corps; and, dressed in a smart, gray, boyish uniform, she drove her car at all hours of the day and night. She was not only sincerely anxious to serve, but she knew, and sheltered girls all over the land knew, - to say nothing of the younger married women - that this was the beginning of their real independence, the knell of the old order. They were freed. Even the reënforced concrete minds of the last generation imperceptibly crumbled and were as imperceptibly modernized in the rebuilding.

A good many of the women, old and young, continued to gamble furiously out of their hours of work; but the majority of the girls did not. Those with naturally serious minds were absorbed, uplifted, keen, calculating. They did not even dance. They realized that they had wonderful futures in a changing world. It was "up to them."

# VII

Mortimer was beyond the draft age, but, possibly owing to his gallant fearless appearance, it was rather expected that he would enlist. He did not, however, nor did he join the Red Cross or the Y.M.C.A., nor volunteer for some Government work, as so many of the men of his age and class were doing as a matter of course.

War news bored him excessively. He was making two or three hundred dollars a month; he lived at the Club when Maria Abbott occupied Ballinger House - Tom went to Washington - and he was extremely comfortable. In the Club he always felt like a blood, forgot for the time being that he was not a rich man, like the majority of its members, and there was always a group of nice quiet contented fellows, glad to play bridge with him in the evening. On the whole, he congratulated himself, he had not done so badly, although he had resigned all hope of being a millionaire - unless he made a lucky strike....But it did not make so much difference in California...and when Alexina had had enough of horrors they would settle down again very comfortably to the old life....There was very good dancing at the restaurants (upstairs) where one met nice girls of sorts who didn't care a hang about this infernal war...one of them...but he was extremely careful...he would never be divorced; that was positive...as for society he did not miss it particularly...the dancing at the restaurants was better and he didn't have to talk...whether people stopped asking him or not, now that his wife was away, or whether they entertained or not, didn't so much matter. He had the Club. That was the all important pivot of his life, his altar, his fetish...a lot he cared what went so long as he had that.

# BOOK IV

## CHAPTER I

I

The Embassy was a blinding glare of light from the ground floor to the upper story, visible above the wide staircase. After four years of legal tenebration it was obvious that the ambassador's intention was to celebrate the Armistice as well as the visit of his King to Paris with an almost impish demonstration of the recaptured right to extravagance, obliterate the dry economical past. The ambassador's country might be intolerably poor after the war, but like many other prudent nobles he had invested money in North and South America, and was able to entertain his sovereign out of his private purse. He had made up his mind to give the first brilliant function following the sudden end of La Grande Guerre and one that it would be difficult for even Paris to eclipse.

All Paris had burst forth into illumination of street and shop after nightfall, but Alexina had seen no such concentrated blaze as this; and her eyes, long accustomed to a solitary globe high in the ceiling of her room, blinked a little, strong as they were. She had come with the Marquis and Marquise de Morsigny, and after they had passed the long receiving line where the King in his simple worn uniform stood beside the resplendent ambassador, her friends' attention had been diverted to a group of acquaintances chattering excitedly over the startling munificence that seemed to them prophetic of a swift renaissance.

They moved off unconsciously, and Alexina remained alone near one of the long windows behind the receiving line; but she felt secure in her insignificance and quite content to gaze uninterruptedly at the greatest function she had ever seen. After the bitter hard work, the long monotonies, the brief terrible excitements, of the past four years, and the depressed febrile atmosphere of Paris during the last year when avions dropped their bombs nearly every night, and Big Bertha struck terror to each quarter in turn, this gay and gorgeous scene recalled one's most extravagant dreams of fairy-land and Arabia; and Alexina felt like a very young girl. Even the almost constant sensation of fatigue, mental and bodily, fell from her as she forgot that she had worked from nine until six for three years in her oeuvre, often walking the miles to and from her hotel or pension to avoid the crowded trains; the distasteful food; the tremors that had shaken even her tempered soul when the flashing of the German guns, drawing ever nearer, could be seen at night on the horizon.

And Paris had been so dark!

She reveled almost sensuously in the excessiveness of the contrast, quite unconcerned that her white gown was several years out of date. For that matter there were few gowns, in these vast rooms, of this year's fashion. Although Paris had begun to dance wildly the day the Armistice was declared, not only in sheer reaction from a long devotion to its ideal of duty, but that the American officers should have the opportunity to discover the loveliness and charm of the French maiden, the women had not yet found time to renew their wardrobes, and the only gowns in the room less than four years old were worn by the newly arrived Americans of the Peace Commission and the ladies of the Embassy. The most striking figures were the French Generals in their horizon blue uniforms and rows of orders on their hardy chests.

Of jewels there were few. When the German drive in March seemed irresistible, jewels had been sent to distant estates, or to banks in Marseilles and Lyons, and there had been no time to retrieve them after the ambassador sent out his sudden invitations. Alexina smiled as she recalled Olive de Morsigny's lament over the absence of her tiara. European women of society take their jewels very seriously, and there was not a Frenchwoman present who did not possess a tiara, however old-fashioned.

But the cold luminosity of jewels would have been extinguished to-night under this really terrific down-pour of light. The tall candelabra against the tapestried or the white and gold walls were relieved of duty; Paris had had enough of candlelight; the four immense chandeliers of this reception room, either of which would have illuminated a restaurant, had been rewired and blazed like suns. Suspended from the ceiling, festooned between the candelabra and the chandeliers, were clusters and loops of glass tupils and roses, each concealing an electric bulb. Alexina reflected that the soft haze of candles might be more artistic and becoming, but was grateful nevertheless for this rather tasteless fury of light, symptomatic as it was; and understood the ambassador's revolt against the enforced economies of a long war, his desire to do honor to his unassuming little sovereign.

II

The room, whose lofty ceiling was supported along the center by three massive pillars, was already crowded, and people entered constantly. Every embassy was represented, all the grande noblesse of Paris and even a stray Bourbon and Bonaparte. A few of the guests were the more distinguished American residents of Paris and their gowns were as out of date if as inimitably cut as the Frenchwomen's, for they had worked as hard. But Alexina ceased to notice them. She had become aware that two American officers, standing still closer to the window, were talking. One of them had parted the curtains and was looking out.

"By Jove," he said. "Strikes me this is rather risky. Six long windows opening on the garden, and the King standing directly in front of one of them. Fine chance for some filthy Bolshevik or anarchist."

"Oh, nonsense," said the other absently; his eyes were roving over the room. "Wish I could take to one of these French girls...feel it a sort of duty to increase the rapport and all that...but although the married women and the other sort of girls are a long sight more fascinating than ours, the upper - "

"American girls for me. But I'm still jumpy, and this sort of carelessness makes me nervous, particularly as the story is going about that the King came near being assassinated in the station of his home town when he was leaving. Man fired point blank at his face, but gun didn't go off or some one knocked up the man's arm. Did you notice that he looked about rather apprehensively when he arrived, at the station yesterday? No wonder, poor devil."

III

Alexina moved off, making her way slowly, but finally was forced to halt near the row of pillars. She was looking through the opposite door at the fantastic illuminations of the hall and reception rooms beyond, when, without a second's warning flicker, every light in the house went out.

Simultaneously the high clatter of voices ceased as if the old familiar cry of _"Alerte"_ had sounded in the street. Involuntarily, as people in real life do act, her hands clutched her heart, her mouth opened to relieve her lungs. A Frenchman whispered beside her. "The King! A plot!"

She waited to hear screams from the women, wild ejaculations from the men. But the years of war and danger had extinguished the weak and exalted the strong. Beyond the almost inaudible gasp of her neighbor Alexina heard nothing. The silence was as profound as the darkness and that was abysmal; she could not see the white of her gown.

All, she knew, were waiting for the sound of a pistol shot, or of a groan as the King fell with a knife in his back.

Then she became aware that men were forcing their way through the crowd; she was almost flung into the arms of a man behind her. Later she knew that a group of officers had surrounded their King and rushed him up the room to place him in front of the central pillar, but at the moment she believed that they were either carrying out his body, or that a group of anarchists was escaping.

IV

Then one man lit a match. She saw a pale strained face, the eyes roving excitedly above the flickering flame. Then another match was struck, then another. Those that had no matches struck their briquets, and these burned with a tiny yellow flame. One or two took down candles and lit them. All over the room, in little groups, or widely separated, Alexina saw face after face, white and anxious, appear. The bodies were invisible. The faces hung, pallid disks, in the dark.

Her attention was suddenly arrested by a face above the small steady flame of a briquet. It was a thin worn face, probably that of an officer recently discharged from hospital. His expression was ironic and unperturbed and his eyes flashed about the room exhibiting a lively curiosity. An Englishman, probably; nothing there of the severity of the American military countenance; although, to be sure, that had relaxed somewhat these last weeks under the blandishments of Paris. Nevertheless...quite apart from the military, there was the curious unanalyzable difference between the extremely well-bred American face and the extremely well-bred English face. It might be that the older civilization did not take itself quite so seriously....

# V

Obeying an impulse, which, she assured herself later, was but the sudden reaction to frivolity from the horror that had possessed her, she took a match unceremoniously from the hand of a neighbor, lit it and held it below her own face. The man's eyes met hers instantly, opened a little wider, then narrowed.

She looked at him steadily...interested...something ...somewhere...stirring. The match burnt her fingers and was hastily extinguished. At the same time she became aware of a fuller effulgence just beyond the pillars and that people were moving on, some retreating toward the hall. She was carried forward and a little later turned her head, forgetting for a moment the humorous face that still had seemed to beckon above the white disks that inspired her with no interest whatever.

Against the central pillar stood the King, and on either side of him two officers of his suite, as rigid as men in armor, held aloft each a great candelabra taken from the wall. All the candles in the branches had been lit and shone down on the composed and somewhat expressionless face of the King. The strange group looked like a picture in some old cathedral window.

The scene lasted only a moment. Then the King, bowing courteously, left the room, still between the candelabra; and, followed by his ambassador, whose face was far paler than his, ascended the staircase.

# VI

A Frenchman beside Alexina cursed softly and she learned the meaning of the dramatic finale to a superb but rather dull function. There had been no attempt at assassination. A lead fuse had melted; the ambassador, who had taxed his imagination to honor his King, had forgotten to give the order that electricians remain on guard to avert just such a calamity as this.

As the explanation ran round the room people began to laugh and chatter rapidly as if they feared the sudden reaction might end in hysteria. But although all the candles had now been lit, the effort to revive the mild exhilaration of the evening was fruitless. They wanted to get away. Many still believed that a plot had been balked, and that the assassins were lurking in one of the many rooms of the hotel.

Alexina met Olive de Morsigny in the dressing-room, and found her white and shaking, although for four years she had proved herself a woman of strong nerves as well as of untiring effort.

"Great heaven!" she whispered, as she helped Alexina on with her wrap. "If he had been assassinated! In Paris! I thought André would faint. His last wound is barely healed. Come, let us get out of this. Who knows?...In Paris!..."

Their car had to wait its turn. As Alexina stood with her silent friends in the porte cochère the certainty grew that some one was watching her. That officer! Who else? She flashed her eyes over the crowd about her, then into the densely packed hall behind. But she encountered no pair of eyes even remotely humorous, no face in any degree familiar....Later she whirled about again....There was a pillar...easy to dodge behind it....At this moment André took her elbow and gently piloted her into the car.

# CHAPTER II

I

Alexina in the weariness of reaction climbed the long stairs of her pension in Passy.

Sibyl Bascom, whose husband being on government duty in Washington left her free to go to France, and who rolled bandages all day long in the great hospital in Neuilly; Janet Maynard and Alice Thorndyke, who ran a canteen in the environs of Paris, and herself, had lived until the Armistice in a comfortable hotel not far from the house of Olive de Morsigny, and found much solace together. But their hotel had been commandeered for one of the Commissions; Sibyl had taken refuge with her sister-in-law, and Alexina, Janet, and Alice had found with no little difficulty vacant rooms in a second-rate pension in Passy. The food was even worse than at the hotel, the rooms were barely heated, and as trams at Alexina's hours were airless and jammed, and taxicabs in swarming Paris as scarce as tiaras, with drivers of an unsurpassable effrontery, she was forced to walk three miles a day in all weathers. It is true that she could have rented a limousine for a thousand francs a month, but it was almost a religion with workers of her class to economize rigorously and give all their surplus to the oeuvre of their devotion. Janet and Alice went back and forth in one of the supply camions of the Y.M.C.A.

## II

Alexina passed Janet's room softly. She saw a light under the door and inferred that she and Alice were playing poker and consuming many cigarettes, that being their idea of recuperation between one hard day's work and the next. She was in no mood for talking.

Her room was stuffy as well as cold; the furniture and curtains had probably not been changed since the second empire. She opened one of the long windows and stepped out on the balcony. The Seine was nearly in flood after the heavy rains, but it reflected the stars to-night and many long banners of light from the almost festive banks.

It was bitterly cold and she closed her window in a moment and moved about her room. It was too cold to undress. She was inured to discomforts and thankful that she had been brought up in San Francisco, which is seldom warm; but she longed for a few creature comforts nevertheless. During the war she had sustained herself with the thought of the men in the trenches, but now that their lot was ameliorated she felt that she had a right to what comforts she could find. The difficulty was to find them. With Paris overflowing. Generals sleeping in servants' rooms under the roof, soldiers, even officers, picking up women on the streets if only to have a bed for the night, and hotel after hotel being requisitioned for the various Peace Commissions and their illimitable suites, conditions were likely to grow worse. Olive de Morsigny had repeatedly offered hospitality, but she preferred her independence.

To leave was impossible. Her oeuvre must continue for several months. Sick and wounded men do not recover miraculously with the cessation of hostilities. No doubt she should be grateful for this refuge, and now that the war was over it might be possible to buy petrol for an oil stove.

Then she became aware that it was not only the cold that made her restless. The rigidly enforced calm of her inner life had received a shock to-night and not from the imagined assassination of a king.

She went suddenly to her mirror and looked at herself intently...shook her head with a frown. She had always been slim; she was now very thin. The roundness and color had left her cheeks. They were pale - almost hollow. Janet and Alice had rejoiced in the lack of fats and sweets, both having a tendency to plumpness had achieved without effort the most fashionable slenderness that anxious woman could wish. But she had not had a pound to lose. It seemed to her that she was almost plain. Her eyes retained their dazzling brilliancy, a trick of nature that old age alone no doubt could conquer, but there were dark stains beneath the lower lashes.

She let down her hair. It was the same soft dusky mass as ever. Her teeth were as even and bright; her lips had not lost their curves, but they were pink, not red. She was anæmic, no doubt. Why, in heaven's name, shouldn't she be? Even Olive, whose major domo, driving a Ford, had paid daily visits to the farms and brought back what eggs, chickens and other succulences the peasants would part with for coin, had lost her brilliant color and the full lines of her beautiful figure. She had rouged to-night and looked as lovely as when Morsigny had captured her, but her magnificent gown had been too hastily taken in by an elderly inefficient maid - her young one having patriotically deserted her for munitions long since, and sagged on her bones as she expressed it. Sibyl, who was in bed with the flu, had offered to lend her one of the new ones she had had the forethought to buy in New York before sailing, and was only a year old, but Olive had feared the critical eyes of French women who had not replenished their evening wardrobe since nineteen-fourteen.

Alexina did not feel particularly consoled because others had looked no better than she. Until to-night she had given little thought to her looks, but she now felt a renewed interest in herself, and the frown was as much for this revival as for her wilted beauty.

Her evening wrap was very warm and she sat down in the hard arm-chair and huddled into its folds, covering the lower part of her body with a hideous brown quilt. No doubt the sheets were damp, and she knew that she could not sleep. Why shiver in bed?

III

Was it Gathbroke? It was long since she had thought of him. She had not even seen his photograph for four or five years. If it were, he had changed even more since that photograph had been taken than after she had dismissed him at Rincona.

She was by no means sore that it was he. The light of a briquet was not precisely searching, and for the most part he had looked like more than one war-worn British officer she had seen during her long residence in Paris....It was something in the eyes...she could have vowed they were hazel...their expression had altered; it was that of a somewhat ironic man of the world, which had changed as she watched them to the piercing alertness of a man of action...but after...was it perhaps an emanation of the personality that had so impressed her angry young soul and refused to be obliterated?

But what of it? He might be married. Love another woman. All officers and soldiers during the war had looked about eagerly for love, when not already supplied, and given themselves up to it, indifferent as they may have been before....Life seemed shorter every time they went back to the front.

And if not why should he be attracted to her again! He had loved her for a moment when she had been in the first flush of her exquisite youth. That was twelve years ago. She was now thirty. True, thirty, to-day, was but the beginning of a woman's third youth, and a few weeks in the California sunshine and nourished by the California abundance would restore her looks, no doubt of that. But she would look no better as long as she remained in Paris....Nor did she wish to return to California...and beyond all question he must have forgotten, lost all interest in her long since.

Still - there had been an eager upspringing light in his eyes...was it recognition?...merely the passing impulse of flirtation over a match and a briquet?...No doubt she would never see him again.

# CHAPTER III

## I

Did she want to?

She had gone through many and extraordinary phases during these years of close personal contact with the martial history of Europe, as precisely different from the first twenty-six years of her life as peace from war.

During those months of nineteen-fifteen when she had worked in hospitals close to the front as auxiliary nurse, all the high courage of her nature which she had inherited from a long line of men who had fought in the Civil War, the Revolution, and in the colonial wars before that, and the tribal wars that came after, and all that she had inherited from those foremothers whose courage, as severely tested, had never failed either their men or their country; in short, the inheritance of the best American tradition; had risen automatically to sustain her during that period of incessant danger and horror. She had been firm and smiling for the consolation of wounded men when under direct shell fire. She had felt so profound a pity for the mutilated patient men that it had seemed to cleanse her of every selfish impulse fostered by a too sheltered life. She had bathed so many helpless bodies that she lost all sense of sex and felt herself a part of the eternal motherhood of the world. She had once thrown herself over the bed of a politely protesting poilu, covering his helpless body with her own, as a shell from a taube came through the roof.

That had been a wonderful, a noble and exalted (not to say exhilarating) period; a period that made her almost grateful for a war that revealed to her such undreamed of possibilities in her soul. She might smile at it in satiric wonder in the retrospect, but at least it was ineradicable in her memory.

If it could but have lasted! But it had not. Insensibly she accepted suffering, sacrifice, pity, as a matter of course, even as danger and death. It had been the romance of war she had experienced in spite of its horrors, and no romance lives after novelty has fled. For months nothing seemed to affect her bodily resistance to fatigue, and as exaltation dropped, as the monotony of nursing, even of danger, left her mind more and more free, as war grew more and more to seem, the normal condition of life, more and more she became conscious of herself.

## II

Life at the front is very primitive. Social relations as the world knows them cease to exist. The habits of the past are almost forgotten. It is death and blood; shells shrieking, screaming, whining, jangling; the boom of great guns as if Nature herself were in a constant electrical orgasm; hideous stench; torn bodies, groans, cries, still more terrible silences of brave men in torment; incessant unintermittent danger. Above all, blood, blood, blood. She believed she should smell it as long as she lived. She knew it in every stage from the fresh dripping blood of men rushed from the field to the evacuation hospitals, to the black caked and stinking blood of men rescued from No Man's Land endless days and nights after they had fallen.

All that was elementary in her strong nature, inherited from strong, full-blooded, often reckless and ruthless men, gradually welled to the surface. She was possessed by a savage desire for life, a bitter inordinate passion for life. Why not, when life might be extinguished at any moment? What was there in life but life? Farcical that anything else could ever have mattered.

Civilization - by which men meant the varied and pleasant times of peace - seemed incredibly insipid and out of date. It had no more relation to this war-zone than her youth to this swift and terrible maturity.

She was in many hospitals - rushed where an indomitable and tireless auxiliary nurse was most in demand - some under the direction of the noblesse division of the Red Cross, others under the bourgeois;

and in more than one were English and American girls, long resident in France, or, in the latter case, come from America like herself to serve the country for which they had a romantic passion. The majority, of course, were Frenchwomen, young (in their first freedom), middle-aged, elderly.

Of these some were placid, emotionless, extinguished, consistently noble, selfless, profoundly and simply religious, as correct in every thought and deed as the best bourgeois peace society of any land.

But others! Alexina had been horrified at first at the wanderings off after nightfall of women who had nursed like scientific angels by day, accompanied by men who were never more men than when any moment might turn them into carrion. But with her mental suppleness she had quickly readjusted her point of view. There is nothing as sensual as war. It is the quintessential carnality. Renan once wrote a story of the French Revolution, "The Abbess Juarre," in which his thesis was that if warning were given that the world would end in three days the entire population of the globe would give itself over to an orgy of sex; sex being life itself. It is the obsession of the doomed consumptive, the doomed spinster, the last thought of a man with the rope round his neck.

How much more under the terrific stimulation of war, the constant heedless annihilation of life in its flower and its maturity? Man's inveterate enemy, death, shrieking its derision in the very shells of man's one inviolable right, the right to drift into eternity through the peaceful corridors of old age. War is a monstrous anachronism and a monstrous miscarriage of justice. The ignorant feel it less. It is the enlightened, the intelligent, accustomed to the higher delights of civilization, to the perfecting of such endowments, however modest, as their ancestors have transmitted and peace has encouraged, with ambitions and hopes and dreams, that resent however sub-consciously the constant snarling of death at their heels. All the forces of mind and body and spirit become formidable in a reckless hatred of the gross injustice of a fate that individually not one of them has deserved.

But the moment remains. They compress into it the desires of a lifetime. After years of proud indivi-dualism they have learned that they are atoms, cogs, helpless, the sport of iron and steel and powder and the ambitions and stupidities of men whose lives are never risked. Very well, turn the ego loose to find what it can. If all they have learned from civilization is as useless in this shrieking hell, as impotent as the dumb resentment of the clod, they can at least be animals.

To talk of the ennobling influences of war is one of the lies of the conventionalized mind anxious to avoid the truths of life and to extract good from all evil - worthy but unintelligent. How can men in the trenches, foul with dirt and vermin, stench forever in their nostrils, callous to death and suffering, wallowing like pigs in a trough, compulsorily obscene, be ennobled? Courage is the commonest attribute of man, a universal gift of Nature that he may exist in a world bristling with dangers to frail human life; never to be commended, only to be remarked when absent. If men lose it in the city, the sedentary life, they recover it quickly in the camp. The exceptions, the congenital cowards, slink out of war on any pretext, but if drafted are likely to acquit themselves decently unless neurotic. The cases of cowardice in active warfare are extremely rare; a mechanical chattering of teeth, or shaking of limbs, but practically never a refusal to obey the command to advance. But it is this very courage which breeds callousness, and, combined with bestial conditions, inevitably brutalizes.

When good people (far, oh far, from the zones of danger) can no longer in the face of accumulating evidence, cling to their sentimental theory that war ennobles, they take refuge in the vague but plausible substitute that at least it makes the good better and the bad worse. Possibly, but it is to be remembered that there is bad in the best even where there is no good in the worst.

Indubitably it leaves its indelible mark in a collection of hideous memories, on the just and the unjust, alike; as it is more difficult (Nature having made human nature in an ironical mood) to recall the pleasant moments of life than the poignantly unpleasant, so is it far more difficult to recall the moments of exaltation, of that intense spiritual desire which visits the high and low alike, to give their all for the safety of their country and the honor of their flag. Moreover, the sublime indifference in the face of certain death often has its origin in a still deeper necessity to relieve the insufferable strain on scarified nerves, and forever. As for the much vaunted recrudescence of the religious spirit which is one of the recurring phenomena of war, it is merely an instinct of the subtle mind, in its subtlest depths called soul, to indulge in the cowardice of dependence since the body must know no fear.

If men who have been temperate and moral all their lives, or at the worst indulging in moderation, spend their leaves of absence from the front like swine, it is not a reaction from the monotony of trench life, or from the nerve-racking din of war, but merely an extension of the fearful stimulation of a purely carnal existence, even where the directing mind is ever on the alert.

The aggressors of war should be pilloried in life and in history. Men must defend their country if attacked; to do less would be to sink lower than the beasts that defend their lairs; and for that reason all pacifists, and conscientious objectors, are abject, mean, and shabby. In times of national danger no man has a right to indulge his own conscience; it merges, if he be a normal courageous man, into the national conscience. But that very fact lowers the deliberate seekers of war so far below the high plane of civilization as we know it, that they should be blotted out of existence.

As regards women Alexina was not likely to remain shocked for long at any erratic manifestations of temperament. Pride and fastidiousness and the steel armor fused by circumstances had protected her heretofore from any divagations of her own; nor had crystallized temptation ever approached her.

But her education had been liberal. Several of her intimate friends and more that she associated with daily made what she euphemistically termed a cult of men. The naïve deliberate immorality of young things not only in the best society but in all walks of life is far more prevalent than the good people of this world will ever believe. Those with much to lose seldom lose it; the instinct of self-protection envelops them as a mantle; although in small towns, where concealments are less simple, the majority of scandals are not about married women as in a less sophisticated era, but about girls.

Alexina had possessed numerous confidences, helped more than once to throw dust, amiably replaced the post. She had never approved, but she was philosophical. She took life as she found it; although the fact stood out that Aileen, who was indifferent to men, remained always her favorite friend.

An individualist, she felt it no part of her philosophy to criticize the acts of women with different desires, weaknesses, temptations, equipment from her own; all other things being equal. That was the point. These girls who made use of their most secret and personal possession as they saw fit were as well-bred as herself, honorable in all their dealings with one another and with society at large, generous, tolerant, exquisite in their habits, often highly intelligent and studious. Sex was an incident.

With the peccadillos of married women who were wives she had little tolerance as they were a breach of faith, a deliberate violation of contract, and indecent to boot. She was quite aware that Sibyl for all her posturings, and avidness for sex admiration, and "acting oriental" as the phrase went, was entirely devoted to Frank. Such of her married friends as had severed all but the nominal and public bond with their legal husbands, she placed in the same category as girls as far as her personal attitude toward them went.

IV


Therefore not only did she understand these young women driven by the horrid stimulus of war; women (or girls) heretofore sheltered, virtuous, romantic, sentimental, now merely filled with the lust of life. They were, like herself, devoted and meticulous nurses, brave, high-minded, tender; practically all, if not from the upper, at least from the educated ranks of life. But they lived under the daily shadow of death. Even when safe from the shells of the big guns, the murderous aircraft paid them daily visits, singling out hospitals with diabolical precision. They were in daily contact with young torn human bodies from which had gone forever the purpose for which one generation precedes another. Life was horror. Blood and death and shattered bodies were their daily portion. No matter how brave, they heard death scream in every shell. The world beyond existed as a mirage. No wonder they became primeval.

Alexina had met Alice Thorndyke in one of these hospitals and observed her with some curiosity. But Alice was, to use her own vernacular, the best little bourgeoise of them all. She had had her fling. Men repelled her. She never meant to marry, even for substance. When the war was over she should live the completely independent life. Nobody would care what economic liberties a woman took in the new era. The war had liberalized the most conservative old bunch of relatives a girl was ever inflicted with.

V

As Alexina sat huddled in her warm coat - the periwinkle blue to which she was still faithful - her dark fine hair, hanging about her, a mantle in itself, she recalled those days when she, too, had vibrated to that savage lust for life; those days of concentrated egoism, of deep and powerful passions whose existence she had only dimly begun to suspect after she dismissed her husband.

What had held her back? She had had a no more fastidious inheritance than most of those women, a no more cultivated intelligence, nor proud instinct of selection, nor ingrained habit of self-control.

She had put it down at first to fastidiousness, possibly a still lurking desire to be able to give all to one man; that hope of the complete mating which no woman relinquishes until toothless, certainly not in the mere zone of death.

She had concluded that it was neither of these, or at least that they had but played a part, and alone would never have won. It was a furious mental revolt at the terrific power of the body, the mind, frightened and cornered, determined to dominate; a fierce delight in the battle raging behind her serene and smiling mask to the accompaniment of that vulgar blare of war where mind over matter was as powerless in the death throe as incantations during an eruption of Vesuvius.

This internal silent warfare between her long reed-like body as little sensible to fatigue as if made of flexible steel and her extremely cold proud chaste-looking head had grown to be of such absorbing interest that the knowledge of its cessation was almost a shock. It was after a prolonged experience in a hospital where they were short of nurses and rest was almost unknown and the inroads upon her vitality so severe and menacing that she was finally ordered to Paris to rest, and there found a complete change of habit in an oeuvre founded by the equally exhausted but always valiant Olive de Morsigny, that she suddenly realized that somewhere sometime the battle had finished and mind and body were acting in complete harmony.

VI

To-night she wondered if her imagination, turned loose, stimulated, had not missed the whole point. There had been no man who had made the direct irresistible appeal. No concrete temptation....She had after all been a degree too civilized...or...romantic idealism?

There had been little to stimulate and excite since she had settled down to office work in the summer of nineteen-sixteen. Her nerves, always strong, had become too case-hardened to be affected by avions or the immense uncertainties of Big Bertha; although the light on the horizon at night during the last German Drive and the bellow of the guns had shaken her with a sort of reminiscent excitement.

But for the most part she had felt frozen, torpid, a cog in the vast military machine of France, dedicating herself like hundreds of other women to the succor of men she never saw. That extraordinary abominable experience at the front was overlaid, almost forgotten. And such news as one had in Paris was quite enough to exercise the mind....There had been the downfall of the Russian dynasty...the still more sinister downfall of the true revolutionists...the Bolshevik monster projecting its murderous shadow over all Europe, exposing the instability of the entire social structure....

## VII

Was it? Could such an experience ever be forgotten? The grass might grow over the dead on the battlefields, but the corruption fed the wheat, and the peogle of France ate the bread. This uninvited thought had intruded itself the first time she had driven by the Marne battlefields and seen the numberless crosses in the rich abundant fields.

She smiled, a small, secret, ruthless smile....That was her residue: ruthlessness. She may have left behind her in the turbulent war-zone the savage elementary lust for living at any cost, but she had ineradicably learned the value of life, its brevity at best, the still more tragic brevity of youth; she had a store of hideous memories which could only be submerged first in the performance of duty if duty were imperative; then, duty discharged and finished, in the one thing that during its brief time gave life any meaning, made this earthly sojourn bearable. If she met the man she wanted she would have him if she had to fight for him tooth and nail.

It was four o 'clock. She went to bed.

# CHAPTER IV

I

The next day Alexina found herself suddenly free of office duty, A very handsome and wealthy American woman who had not been able to visit her beloved Paris since the beginning of the World's War, and finding the State Department obdurate to the whims of pretty women, had induced Mrs. Ballinger Groome, on one of whose committees she had worked faithfully, to ask her sister-in-law to inform the Department of State that her services at the oeuvre in Paris were indispensable.

Alexina had passed the letter on to the President, Madame de Morsigny, and forgotten the incident. Olive wrote the necessary letter promptly. Not only did she believe that the time had come for Alexina to rest, but she longed for a fresh access of energy in the office that would in a measure relieve herself. Moreover, Mrs. Wallack was wealthy and had many wealthy friends. That meant more money for the oeuvre, always in need of money. Olive had given large sums herself, but the president of a charity is yet to be found who will not permit its constant demands to be relieved by the generous public. Mrs. Wallack had not only promised a substantial donation at once, but a monthly contribution. This had not been named, but Madame de Morsigny meant that it should be something more than nominal. She could do so much for Mrs. Wallack socially, now that it was possible to entertain again, that she felt reasonably confident of rousing the enthusiasm of any ambitious New Yorker. Moreover, Olive had a very insinuating way with her.

II

Mrs. Wallack presented herself at the imposing headquarters of the oeuvre, radiant, fresh, energetic, beautifully dressed. The war had interested her and commanded her sympathies to some purpose, but nothing short of personal affliction could subdue that inexhaustible vitality, and she seemed to bring into the dark and solemn rooms something of the atmospheric gayety and sunshine of a land that had done much but suffered little.

By no one was she received with more warmth of welcome than by Alexina. The sudden release made her realize sharply her lowered vitality. Moreover, the semi-yearly income which had just arrived from California was her own now and she could replenish her wardrobe and feel feminine and irresponsible once more. The reaction was so violent that after inducting Mrs. Wallack into the mysteries of her desk she remained in bed, prostrate, for two days. Then, feeling several years younger, she sallied forth in search of many things.

III

There is no such antidote to the migraines of the woman soul as clothes. Their only rival is travel and there are cases where they know none. Sometimes women remember to pity men, that have no such happy playground.

Alexina for all her ramifications, some of them too deep, had a light and feminine side. During the following fortnight she gave it full rein; she was absorbed, almost happy. She spent quite recklessly and after the years of economy and self-denial this alone gave her an intense satisfaction. In addition to her income forwarded by Judge Lawton, who had charge of her affairs, her brother Ballinger, who was as fond of her as of his own children, and very proud of her - she had received two decorations - sent her a large check with the mandate to spend it on herself.

IV

Even so, she was not always in the shops and the dressmakers' ateliers. She found much amusement in strolling up and down the arcades of the Rue de Rivoli, watching the odd throngs at which Paris herself seemed, to bend her head and stare.

Some poet had called Paris the mistress of Europe. She looked like an old trollop. She was dirty and dreary, unpainted and unwashed. The rain was almost incessant and the shop windows were soon denuded of the few attractive novelties scrambled together to meet the sudden demand after the long drought.

But under the long arcades the curious sauntering throngs were sheltered from the rain and found all things in Paris novel. Men in the American khaki, from generals to striplings, were there by the hundred; endless streams of young women in the uniform of the Red Cross, the Y.M.C.A., the Salvation Army; British and American nurses; members of the fashionable oeuvres artlessly watching this novel phase of Paris; the beautiful violet uniform of Le Bien-Être du Blessé; girls with worn faces and relaxed bodies fresh from the front, hundreds of them, arriving daily in camions and cars, thanking heaven for the sudden cessation of work, sleeping heaven knew where. The American women of the Commission, and others who, like Mrs. Wallack, had invented a plausible excuse to get to Paris and looked almost anachronistic in their smart gowns, their fresh faces, their bright, curious, glancing eyes.

There were also officers in the uniform of Britain, and

Alexina regarded them frankly, with no effort to deceive herself. The spirit of adventure was awake in her, now that the dark mood had passed, or slept. She hoped to meet the man of the embassy again, whether he were Gathbroke or another. She had liked his eyes.

She had met many charming and interesting men during the last two and a half years at Olive de Morsigny's table, especially when André, convalescent, was at home. But their eyes had said nothing to her whatever, if not for the want of trying. Alexina's imagination, torpid for many months, ran riot. This man might disappoint her, might have nothing in him for her, but she refused for more than a moment to contemplate anything so flat. Something must come of that adventure, that vital intensely personal moment when their eyes had met above flames so tiny the wonder was they could see anything but a white blur on the dark. She was as sure of meeting him again as that she trod on air after she had ordered a new gown or brought an inordinately becoming hat. She had forgotten Mortimer's existence.

# CHAPTER V

## I

One day at the Hotel Crillon she thought she had found him.

She had passed the portals of that fortress with some delay, for the American Commission protected itself as if it dwelt under the shadow of imminent assassination and theft; whereas it was merely exclusive. The sentries at the door demanded her permit, and passed her in with intense suspicion to the inner guard. This was composed of three polite but very young lieutenants in smart new uniforms with no blight of war on them, and flagrantly of the American aristocracy.

With these she had less trouble, for they recognized her social status and accepted her explanation that she had been invited for tea with one of the ladies of the Commission. Nevertheless, they knew their duty and Alexina was followed up to the door of her hostess' suite by another young guardian who watched her entrance through the sacred door as carefully as if he suspected her of carrying a bomb in her muff.

## II

The party numbered about thirty, and Alexina, after chatting with the few she knew, was standing apart by a small table drinking a cup of tea with three lumps of sugar in it and consuming cakes like a greedy boarding-school girl home for the holidays, when she caught sight of a man in the British khaki, a major by his insignia, a tall man, thin and straight, standing with his back to her at the opposite end of the room. He was talking to the host and a small group of men. She glimpsed something like half of his profile when he turned from the host for a moment. Like all men in khaki, when not pronounced brunettes, his complexion and hair looked the same color as his uniform.

Nevertheless...if she could only see his eyes...he turned his full profile...she had never glanced at Gathbroke's profile; he had given her no opportunity!...Certainly she had not the faintest idea whether the man of the embassy had had a snub nose or the thin straight feature of this man who would have attracted her attention in any ease if only because he did not carry his shoulders with the disillusioning obliquity of the British Army...why did he not turn round? Alexina felt an impulse to throw her cup straight across the room at the back of that well-shaped head.

Suddenly he shook hands with his host, nodded to the others and left the room.

III

Alexina set her cup and saucer down on the table, forebore to interrupt her hostess, who was known to talk steadily in order to avoid questions, and walked quickly and deliberately out after him. It is a primitive instinct in woman to chase the male; but civilization having initiated her into the art of permitting him to chase her, Alexina was merely bent upon giving this man his chance if the interest had been mutual and existed beyond the moment.

One lift was descending as she reached the outer corridor and the other was closed. She ran down the wide staircase as rapidly as a woman in fashionable skirts may. There was no British uniform in the hall below.

IV

She stood for a quarter of an hour under the arcade
before the Crillon waiting for a taxi, staring out into
the dreary mist of rain, at the round soft blurs of light
in the Place de la Concorde, but in no wise depressed.
What did it matter if she had not met him to-day? The
conviction that she should meet him before long was as
strong as if she were ever hopeful sixteen....That was
the real secret of her elation. She felt very young and
entirely carefree. She reflected that if she had met
Gathbroke, or whoever he might be, during the last
three years of the war she would have felt neither joy
nor elation, however interested she might have been.
To love and dream and enjoy when men were falling
every minute, writhing in agony, gasping out their life,
would have seemed to her grossly unæsthetic if
nothing worse. It was not in the picture. The primal
impulses she had experienced at the front to that harsh
music of Death's orchestra were natural enough; but
safe (comparatively!) in Paris, certainly quiet, the
romance of love would have been as incongruous and
heartless as to go out to the great hospital at Neuilly
and tango through a ward of dying men.

But now! She had done her part. She could do no
more. Men still must die, but in every comfort, with
every consolation. And there would be no more
recruits.

She was free. She was young, young, young again.

And at this moment her heart emptied itself of song
and sank like lead in her breast. She pressed her muff
against her face to hide the sudden grimace she was

sure contorted it; there had been few moments in her life when she had not been mistress of her features, but this was one of them.

Gora Dwight was walking rapidly toward her.

# CHAPTER VI

I

Gora did not see her sister-in-law for a moment and Alexina had time to recover her poise and make sharp swift observations. She had not seen Gora for four years, nor exchanged a line with her. She had almost forgotten her. The changes were more striking than in herself, who had been always slight. Gora's superb bust had disappeared; her face was gaunt, throwing into prominence its width and the high cheek bones. Her eyes were enormous in her thin brown face; to Alexina's excited imagination they looked like polar seas under a gray sky brooding above innumerable dead. There were lines about her handsome mouth, closer and firmer than ever. How she must have worked, poor thing! What sights, what suffering, what despair...four long years of it. But she had evidently had her discharge. She wore an extremely well-cut brown tailored suit, good furs, and a small turban with a red wing.

What was she in Paris for?...What...what...

Gertrude Atherton

II

Gora saw her and almost ran forward, that brilliant inner light that had always been her chief attraction breaking through her cold face...sunlight sparkling on polar seas...oh, yes, Gora had her charm!

"Alexina! It isn't possible! I was going to ask at the American Embassy for your address. I only arrived last night."

Alexina had lowered her muff and her face expressed only the warmest surprise and welcome. "Gora! It's too wonderful! But I suppose you couldn't go home without seeing Paris?"

"Rather not! It's the first chance I've had, too. Where can we have a talk?"

"It's too late for tea. Come out to my pension and spend the night. Janet and Alice have gone to Nice for a few days' rest. You'll be hideously uncomfortable - "

"Not any more than where I am - sharing a room with three others. Where can I telephone? In here?"

"Good heavens, no. Take a liberty with a duke, but with the American aristocracy, never. Come down to the Meurice. Perhaps we can find a cab there. This seems to be hopeless. Everybody comes to the Crillon in a private car or a military automobile. Taxis appear to avoid it."

# III

It only took half an hour to get the telephone connection and another to seize by force a taxi, which, however, deposited them at the Étoile. The driver explained unamiably that he wanted his dinner; and a bribe, unless unthinkable, would have been useless. In these days taxi drivers made fifty francs a day in tips, and, as a Frenchman knows exactly what he wants and calculates to a nicety when he has enough, valuing rest and nutriment above even the delights of gouging foolish Americans, Alexina knew that it would be useless to argue and did not even waste energy in announcing her opinion of him for taking a fare under false pretenses. There was no other cab in sight and they walked the rest of the way. But both were inured to hardships and took their mishap good-naturedly, trudging the long distance under their umbrellas.

IV

After a very bad dinner in an airless room as frugally lighted they made themselves comfortable in Alexina's room over the oil stove she had bought, and supplied through Olive's influence with the higher powers. She took off her street clothes and put on a thick dressing gown, giving her sister-in-law a quilted red wrapper of Janet's, which threw some warmth into Gora's pale cheeks. She looked comfortable, almost happy, as she smoked her cigarette in the arm-chair.

Alexina curled up on the bed.

"Now, Gora," she said brightly, "give an account of yourself."

Gora did not reply for a moment and Alexina examining her again came to the conclusion that she had been spared some of the horrors of the front. As a head nurse her responsibilities had been too heavy for philanderings, and having the literary imagination rather than the personal she had no doubt consigned it to a water-tight compartment and converted herself into a machine.

"I don't know that I can talk about it," she said. "I feel much like the men. It is too close. I am thankful that I Had the experience: not only to have been of actual service, indispensable, as every good nurse was, but to have been a part of that colossal drama. But I am even more thankful that it is over and if I can possibly avoid it I'll never nurse again."

"I suppose you have had no time to write?"

"I should think not! During the brief leaves of absence I spent most of the time in bed. But I have an immense amount of material. I have no idea how much fiction has been written about the war; there might have been none, so far as I have had time to discover. I've barely read a newspaper."

"The only reason I want to go back to America is to hear the news. I see a New York newspaper once in a while, and it is plain they have it all. We have next to none in Europe, in France at all events. Shall you write your stories here or go back to California? That would give you the necessary perspective, I should think."

Alexina's eyes were fixed upon an execrable print many inches above the footboard, and Gora, glancing at her, reflected that she was as beautiful as ever in spite of her loss of flesh and color. Any one would be with eyes that were like stars when they looked at you and a Murillo madonna's when she lifted them the fraction of an inch. Astute as she was she had never penetrated below the surface of Alexina, nor suspected the use she made of those pliable orbs. Alexina had such an abundance of surface it occurred to few people that she might be both subtle and deep.

"I...don't know....I rather fear losing the atmosphere...the immediate stimulation. Shall you go home, now that you are free?"

"I wonder. Could I stand it? I have longed for a rest - ached would be a better word....This last year has been full of both nervous strain and desperate monotony. Nineteen-seventeen was bad enough in another way: the internal defeatist campaign, the constant menace of mutiny, soviets in the army, strikes in the munition towns, - all the rest of it....But could one stand California after such an experience? I know they have done splendid work since we entered the war, but I know also that they will immediately subside into exactly what they were before, settle down with a long sigh of relief to enjoy life and forget that war ever was. It could not be otherwise in that climate. With that abundance. That remoteness....There seems no place out there for me. A decorator after this! What funny little resources we thought out in those days....I do not see myself fitting in anywhere. Tom wants to buy Ballinger House for Maria and I fancy I'll let him have it. I can't keep it up unaided and I might as well sell as rent it. He and Judge Lawton would invest the money and I should have quite a decent income. As for Mortimer I never want to see him again. He has not done one thing for this war - he is utterly contemptible -

"I've long since given up criticizing Mortimer. My father once sized him up. He hasn't an ounce of brain. He'd like to be quite different, but you can stretch Nature's equipment so far and no farther. He stretched his until it suddenly snapped back and found itself shrunken to less than half its natural size. Vale Mortimer. Let him rest. Why don't you divorce him? No doubt he has found some one else -

"I couldn't divorce him on that count, for I told him repeatedly to console himself. It wouldn't be playing the game. Of course there are other grounds. It would be easy enough. But our family has a strong aversion to divorce. And a unique record....Not that that would stop me if I found any one I really wanted to marry. Nothing would stop me, in fact."

Gora glanced at her quickly, arrested by something in

her voice. She had already noticed that Alexina's limpid musical tones had deepened. Just now they rang with something of the menace of a deep-toned bell.

"Have you found him?" she asked smiling. "If there are obstacles, so much the more interesting. I don't fancy that romantic streak in your nature which permitted you to idealize Mortimer has quite dried up. Once romantic always romantic - I deduce from human nature as I have studied it,"

"Well...I am rather afraid of romance. Certainly I'd never be blinded again. A man might be nine parts demi-god and if I knew - and I should know - that there was no companionship in him for me I wouldn't marry him."

"That I believe." Alexina was once more regarding the print. Gora wondered if sex would influence her at all.

"But have you met him? You were always an interesting child and you've roused my curiosity."

"No...yes...I don't know...later perhaps I'll tell you something. But I'm far more interested in you. Have you been in France all this time?"

"Oh, no. I was in Rouen for a year. Then I was in hospitals in England until the German Drive began in. March when I was sent over again. Oh, God! what sights! what sounds! what smells!" She huddled into her chair and stared at the dull flame behind the little door of the stove.

"Oh, I know them all. Think of something else. Surely you met - but literally - hundreds of officers, and some

Gertrude Atherton

must have interested you. The British officer at best is a superb creature - if he would only stand up straight. I saw one at the Crillon to-day whose good American shoulders made me stare at him quite rudely."

"Who was he?"

"Haven't the faintest idea. I only saw his back, anyway. Surely you must have been more than passing interested in one or two."

"I am not susceptible. And nursing is not conducive to romance."

"But you never were romantic, Gora dear. And you are good-looking in your odd way. And that was your great, chance."

"Well, I'm afraid I was too busy or too tired to take it. Now...perhaps...but I'm afraid I don't inspire men with either romance or passion. They like me and are grateful - that is, as grateful as an Englishman can be; they take most things for granted."

"The French are so grateful, poor dears. I loved them all. After all...Frenchmen...." Her voice grew dreamy.

Again Gora threw her an amused glance. "You must have met many of them at your friend, Madame de Morsigny's, and under far more attractive conditions than any man can hope for in a sick bed....I can't imagine any more appropriate destiny for you...you should be Madame la duchesse at the very least."

"Not money enough, and besides they've all grown so religious, or think they have, they wouldn't stand for divorce. Anyhow it would be so hard on 'The Family'!...Still....But why, Gora dear, do you depreciate yourself? It seems to me that you are just the type that a certain sort of man would appreciate - fall in love with. I've heard even American men who play about in society comment on your looks, different as you are from sport and fluff and come-hitherness; and you only need a few months' rest to look like your old self. I should think that a highly intelligent Englishman would find you irresistible, especially if you had shown your womanly side when he had holes in him. I've always had an idea that Englishmen weren't nearly as afraid of intellectual women as American men are."

"That's true enough. But I doubt if there are any men more susceptible to beauty, or quite as lustful after it, no matter how romantic they may think they are feeling. I've talked to a good many of them in the past four years, and for six months I was in charge of a convalescent hospital in Kent. I think I've pretty thoroughly plumbed the Englishman. They found me sympathetic all right, forgot their racial shyness and inadvertently gave me much valuable material. But I saw no indication that I made any sex appeal to them whatever."

"Not one? Not ever?"

Gora gave a slight withdrawing movement as if something sacred had been touched. But she answered: "Oh...some day I may have something to tell you....You said much the same thing to me a little while ago. Tell me now."

Alexina turned over on her elbow to beat up her

pillows. Then she answered lightly but firmly: "Not unless you promise to do likewise. Mine is such a little thing anyhow. I know by the expression of your face - just now - that, yours is the real thing. Is he in Paris?"

"I'm...not sure....Yes, there is something...the conditions are very peculiar...not at all what you think...there is so much more to it....No, I don't think I can tell you."

A fortnight ago Alexina could have lifted her eyes and uttered Gathbroke's name as if groping through a jungle of memories. But she could no more force his name through her lips now than she could have laid bare all that was in her tumultuous soul. It was, in fact, all she could do to keep from screaming. For a moment her excitement was so intense that she jumped from the bed and ran over and opened the window.

"This room gets intolerably stuffy. That is the worst of it - freeze or stifle."

"Oh, I have been cold so long! Please don't leave it open. That's a darling."

# V

Alexina closed it with an amiable smile. "What would you do, Gora, if you were really mad about a man? Have him at any cost? Annihilate anything that stood in your way? Anybody, I mean."

An appalling light came into Gora's pale eyes as she turned them, at first in some surprise, on her sister-in-law: "Yes, if I thought he cared...could be made to care if I had the chance...if another woman tried to get him away...yes, I don't fancy I'd stop at anything....Even if I finally were forced to believe that he never could care for me in that way, the only way that counts with men - at first, anyway...well, I believe I'd fight to the death just the same. When you've waited for thirty-four years...well, you know what you want! Better die fighting than live on interminably for nothing...less than nothing....I can't tell you any more. Please don't ask me."

"Of course not. I'll tell you my little story." And she gave a rapid vivid account of the remarkable scene at the Embassy. She concluded abruptly: "Do you think one could tell that a man's eyes were hazel - the golden-brown hazel - across a pitch dark room above the flame of a briquet?"

"Hazel?" Alexina was standing behind Gora. She saw her body stiffen.

"I could have vowed they were hazel. And that he was English. He also reminded me of some one I must have met somewhere or other...one meets so many...possibly it was only a fancy."

"You didn't see him after the lights went on again?"

"They didn't. Only candles. We were all too anxious to get away, anyhow. I fancy the King was in a hurry to get the ambassador upstairs and tell him what he thought of him - "

"Don't be flippant. You always did have a maddening habit of being flippant at the wrong time. Haven't you seen him again anywhere?"

"I've walked the Rue de Rivoli and lunched at the Ritz looking for him; but I've never had even a glimpse - unless that was his back I saw at the Crillon to-day. If I saw his eyes I'd know in a minute."

"Why should you think it was his back?"

"Some men have expression in the back of their head. And I just had an idea - fantastic, no doubt - that my particular Englishman stands up straight."

"Yours?"

"Yes, I'm feeling quite too fearfully romantic. I'm sure he's looking for me as hard as I am for him. And if I find him I'll keep him."

She saw Gora's long brown hands slowly clench until they looked like steel. She glanced at her own slim white hands. They were quite as strong if more ornamental. She yawned politely.

"I'm not so romantic as sleepy. I know that you must be dead after your journey. They say it's more trouble to travel to Paris from London than from New York.

The girls won't be back for a week. You must get your things to-morrow and come out here. I won't hear of your living in Paris discomfort with three two empty rooms."

"That is good of you. Yes, I'll come. And perhaps your landlady, or whatever they call them here, could put me up later. Now that I have come to Paris I intend to see it. I believe some of the great galleries and museums are to be reopened."

"André will arrange it if they're not. How you will enjoy it with your sensitiveness to all the arts. Take this candle in ease the bulb is burnt out. It usually is."

# VI

Gora had risen. Her face wore an expression both puzzled and grim; but she and Alexina as they said good-night looked full into each other's eyes without faltering. And Alexina had never looked more ingenuous.

Perhaps that dim idea...that she had thrown down a challenge...had come out in the open for a moment...insolently?...honestly?...She *must* be completely fagged out after that abominable trip to have such absurd fancies. She took her candle; and disposed herself in Janet's bed, between four walls that gave her an unexpected and heavenly privacy, with a deep sigh of gratitude, dismissing fantasies.

## VII

During the next ten days Alexina kept as close to Gora as was possible in the circumstances. She had made many engagements and not all of them were social; there were still gowns to be fitted, committee meetings to attend. Twice Gora appeared to have risen with the dawn, and she vanished for the day. Nevertheless, it grew increasingly evident to Alexina's alert and penetrating vision that Gora was neither peaceful nor happy; therefore it was safe to assume that she had not found Gathbroke. For some reason she had not inquired at the British Embassy. Or a letter to its care had failed to reach him. Possibly he was enjoying himself without formalities.

She took Gora twice to the Ritz to luncheon and on several afternoons to tea. But it was a mob of Americans and members of the various Commissions. A brilliant sight, but not in the least satisfactory. It was quite patent from Gora's ever traveling eyes that she sought and never found.

Therefore when Olive asked Alexina to go to one of the towns where the oeuvre had a branch and attend to an important matter that Mrs. Wallack was far too much of a novice to be entrusted with, she agreed at once. She experienced a growing desire to get away by herself - away from Paris - away from Gora. She wanted to think. What if Gora did meet him first? She would be but the more certain to meet him herself. Moreover...give Gora a sporting chance.

Janet and Alice had written from Nice that they might be detained for some time. Gora unpacked her trunk and settled down in the pension with that air of indestructible patience that had always made her formidable. She was not one of Life's favorites, but she had wrung prizes from that unamiable deity more than once.

Alexina speculated. Gora had all the brains that Mortimer lacked and commanding traits of character. She was so striking in appearance even now that people often turned and stared at her. But unless she possessed the potent spell of woman for man all her gifts would avail her nothing in this tragic crisis of her life. Did she possess it I No woman could answer. Certainly Alexina had never seen evidence of it even in Gora's youth; although to be sure her opportunities had been few. Still...when a woman possesses the most subtle and powerful of all the fascinations men are drawn to it, no matter how dark the sky or high the barriers. Nothing is keener than the animal essence. Still...she had heard that some women developed it later than others. Alexina feared nothing else.

She fancied that Gora took leave of her with a little indrawn sigh of relief. It was with difficulty that she repressed her own.

# CHAPTER VIII

## I

"Can this be Lieutenant James Kirkpatrick?"

Kirkpatrick wheeled about and snatched off his cap.

"Mrs. Dwight, by all that's holy! I never expected any such luck as this!"

They shook hands warmly in the deserted square which had been a shambles during the first battle of the Marne, and in the days of Cæsar and Attila, of Napoleon the Great and Napoleon the Little. To-day it was as gray and peaceful, its houses as aloof and haughty as if war had never been. It was a false impression, however, for it was the paralysis of war it expressed, not even the normal peace of a dull provincial town.

"I've often wondered about you," said Alexina. "But I've been working with the French Army and had no way of finding out. You don't look as if you had been wounded."

"Nary scratch, and in the thick of it. My, but it's good to see you again." He stared at her, his face flushed and his breath short. Then he asked abruptly: "When do you think we're goin' home?"

Alexina laughed merrily. "That is the first question every officer or private I have met since the Armistice has asked me. I should feel greatly flattered, but I fancy the question, being always on the top of your minds, simply babbles off."

"You bet. But - Jimminy! I'm glad to see you. You're lookin' thin, though. Been workin', too, I'll bet."

"Oh, yes - and all your old class has worked; most of them over here. Mrs. Cheever couldn't come, as her husband is in the army. But she's worked hard in California."

"I believe you. The women have come up to the scratch, no doubt of that. Although some of them! Good Lord! This isn't my usual language when speaking of them. But if some came over to do just about as they damn please, the others strike the balance, and on the whole I think more of women than I did."

"That's good news. But you mustn't blame them too severely. I mean those that really came over with a single purpose and were not proof against the forcing house of war. As for the others...well, a good many followed their men over, others came after excitement, others, as you say, to do as they pleased, with no questions asked - possibly! I shouldn't take enough interest in them to criticize them if they hadn't used the war-relief organizations, from the Red Cross down to the smallest oeuvre, as a pretext to get over, and then calmly throw us down - the oeuvres, I mean. Mine was 'done' several times. But let us be good healthy optimists such as our country loves and remind ourselves that the worthy outnumber the unworthy - and that the really bad would have gone the same way sooner or later."

"It goes. Optimism for me for ever more once I get out of France."

II

They had crossed the square and were walking down a narrow crooked street as gray as if the dust of ages were in its old walls. Alexina looked at him curiously. He had never had what might be called a soft and tender countenance, but now it looked like cast-iron covered with red rust, and his eyes were more like bits of the same metal, blackened and polished, than ever. His youth had gone. There were deep vertical lines in his face. His mouth was cynical. His bullet head, shaved until only a cap of black stiff hair remained on top, and presumably safe from assault, by no means added to the general attractiveness of his style. He was straighter, more compact, than before, however, and his uniform at least did not have the truly abominable cut of the private.

"What do you think of war as war?" she asked.

"Sherman for me. Not that I didn't enjoy sticking Germans with the best of 'em when my blood was up. But the rest of it - God Almighty!"

They stopped before a solid double door in a high wall. "Will you come and take tea with me this afternoon? I am staying here for a few days. I'm afraid I can't offer you sugar, or cakes - "

"I'll bring the sugar along. I'm in barracks just outside and solid with, the commissary."

"Heavens, what a windfall! You'll be sure to come?"

"Won't I, just? Expect me at four-thirty." He lifted his

cap from his comical head, then sainted, swung on his heel and marched off, swinging both arms from the shoulders and looking a fine martial figure of a man.

"But still the same old Kirkpatrick," thought Alexina. "I wonder if he will go Bolshevik?"

III

Her ring was answered by the old woman who toot care of the house and Alexina entered the wild garden. There was an acre of it, but it had been so long uncared for that it looked like a jungle caught between four high gray walls. It was the property of one of the French members of the oeuvre and was used as a storehouse for hospital supplies and as headquarters for Alexina when business brought her to this part of the Marne valley. She had been here several times during the siege of Verdun in nineteen-sixteen when her bed had quivered all night, and once a big gun had been trained on the city and a shell had fallen near the headquarters of the staff. Last night she had lain awake wondering if she did not miss the sound of the distant guns, as she had in Passy where there was no noisy traffic to take their place. There is a certain amount of morbidity in all highly strung imaginative minds, and although she had developed no love for Big Bertha nor for the sound of high firing guns attacking avions in the middle of the night, there had been something in that steady boom of cannon whose glare stained the horizon that had thrilled and excited her.

IV

On the right of the main hall of the house was the room she used as an office; the dining-room was opposite; the salon ran the whole length at the back. This was quite a beautiful room furnished in the style of the last Bourbons, and its long windows opened upon a stone terrace leading down into what was still a picturesque garden in spite of its neglect. There were three fine oaks, and the chestnut trees along the wall shut off the town from even the upper windows.

The oeuvre always managed to keep a load of wood in the cave and to-day the concierge had raised the temperature of the salon to sixty-five degrees Fahrenheit Alexina cleared a table and told the woman to set it for tea, then went upstairs to change her dress. As she had made her trip in one of the automobiles belonging to the oeuvre she had been able to bring her little stove, and her bedroom was also warm.

She had also brought one of her new gowns, knowing that she should receive visits from several French officers, and she concluded to put it on for Kirkpatrick. He was worth the delicate compliment; moreover it almost obliterated the ravages of war, for it was of periwinkle blue velvet edged with fur about the high square of the neck and at the wrists of the long sleeves: in these days it was wise to revert to the fashions of the centuries when palaces and houses alike were cold and gowns were made for comfort as well as fashion. To complete the proportions it had a train and the sleeves were slightly puffed. Alexina was quite aware that she "looked like a picture" in it.

Gertrude Atherton

She still wore her hair brushed softly back and coiled low at the base of her beautiful curved head. Her pearls were the only jewels she had brought to France and she always wore them. She sighed as she looked at the vision in the mirror. For Kirkpatrick! But she was used to the irony of life.

# CHAPTER IX

I

He arrived promptly at half-past four and in his capacious hands were three packages which arrested her eyes at once. He presented them one by one.

"Sugar. Loaf of white bread. Candy - I'm also solid with one of the doctors."

"I feel like pinching myself. White bread! - I've only tasted it twice in two years-both times at the Crillon. And candy - not a sight of it for more than that. I don't like the heavy French chocolates, which were all one could get when one could get anything. I shall eat at least half and take the other half back to Gora."

"Miss Dwight? She's done good work, I'll bet. Just in her line. Somehow, I don't see you - What did you do?"

He watched her hungrily as she made the tea, sitting in a gilt and brocaded chair, whose high tarnished back seemed to frame her dark head.

"Oh, Lord!" he sighed.

"What is it?"

"Don't ask me. What've you been doing? Yes, I'll drink tea to please you."

"I nursed at first - as an auxiliary, of course - what is the matter?"

"Can't bear to think of it. I hope you've not been doin' that for four years!"

"Oh, no. I've been at work with a war-relief organization in Paris most of the time. That was too monotonous to talk about, and, thank heaven, this will probably end my connection with it. I am much more interested to know how the war has affected you. Are you still a socialist?"

"Ain't I!"

"Not going Bolshevik, I hope."

"Not so's you'd notice it. I want changes all right and more'n ever, but I've had enough of blood and fury and mix-ups without copying them murdering skally-wags. That's all they are. Just out for loot and revenge and not sense enough to know that to-morrow there'll be no loot, and revenge'll come from the opposite direction. I may have been in hell but my head's screwed on in the same place,"

"I wondered...I've heard so many stories about the grievances of the soldiers."

"Every last one of 'em got a grievance. Hate their officers, and often reason enough. Hate the discipline. Hate the food. Hate the neglect in hospital when the flu is raging. Hate gettin' no letters, and as like as not no pay and no tobacco. Hate bein' gouged by the French like they were by the good Americans when they were in camp on the other side. Hate every last thing a man just naturally would hate when he is livin' in a filthy trench, or even camp, and homesick in the bargain....But as for mass-dissatisfaction - not a bit of it. Loyal as they make 'em. Laugh at Bolshevik propaganda just like they laughed at Hun propaganda. They just naturally seem to hate every other race, allied or enemy, and that makes them so all-fired American they're fit to bust. Of course there's plenty of skallywags - caught in the draft - and just waitin' to get home and turn loose on the community. But in the good old style: burglars, highwaymen, yeggs. Not a new frill. Europe hasn't a thing on the good old American criminal brand. They fought well, too. Any man does who's a man at all. But Lord! they'll cut loose when they get back. Every wild bad trait they was born with multiplied by one hundred and fifty...before I go any further I want to warn you that I'm liable to break out into bad language any minute. It gets to be a kind of habit in the army to swear every other word like."

"Don't mind me," said Alexina dryly. "After I was put out of my hotel I managed to get a room in one of the hotels on the Rue de Rivoli for two nights before I found my pension in Passy. The walls were thin. The room next to mine was occupied by two American officers and the one beyond by two more. They talked back and forth with apparently no thought of the possibility of being overheard. Such language! And not only swear words - although one of these to two of any. Such adventures as they related! Such frankness! Such plain undiluted Anglo-Saxon! Fancy a girl with all her illusions fresh, and worshiping some heroic figure in khaki, listening to such a revelation of the nether side of man's life!"

"Men are hogs, all right. I don't like the idea of your having heard such things." Kirkpatrick scowled heavily.

"Nor did I. But I had no cotton to put in my ears. I couldn't sleep in the street. Nor could I ask them to keep quiet and admit I had heard them."

"Well, I guess you can forget anything you have a mind to. You couldn't look like you do - a kind of princess out of a fairy tale and an angel mixed, if you couldn't."

"A black-haired angel! And all the princesses of legend had golden hair."

"Well, that's just another way you're different." He changed the subject abruptly. "What you goin' to do now!"

"I wish I knew."

"Goin' back to California?"

"If I knew I would tell you. But I don't. You see....Well, I shall not live with Mr. Dwight again. We had been really separated a long while before I left - and then he has done nothing for the war. That is only one reason.

What should I do there? I had thought of going into business before I left. But I shall have a good income, and what right have I to go into business and use my large connection to get customers away from those that need the money for their actual bread?"

"Not the ghost of an excuse. Farce, I call it. As long as the present system lasts women of your class better be ornamental and satisfied with that than take the bread out of mouths that need it."

"I could not settle down to the old life. It isn't that I'm in love with work. For that matter I'm only too grateful to be able to rest. But I must fill in, some way. Possibly I could do that better in France or England, where vita! subjects are always being discussed - and happening! - where I would not only be interested but possibly useful in many ways. I should feel rather a brute, knowing the conditions of Europe as I do, to go back and settle down on the smiling abundance of California. And bored to death."

"Then you think you'll stay?...You'd be wasted there - at present - sure enough."

"Sometimes I think I'll buy this house. I could for a song. Heavens! *How* I have longed for solitude in the last four years! I could have it here with my books, and go to Paris as often as I wished. It would be an ideal life. I could afford a car, and to make this house very livable. And that garden...between those gray high walls...in there...that would...."

She had forgotten Kirkpatrick and was staring through the long windows at the dripping trees and the riot of green. "There is something about the old world...in its byways like this...not in its hateful capitals...."

"Do you mean there's something you want to forget? That this place would be consolin' like?"

She met Kirkpatrick's sharp dilated eyes with smiling composure. "This war, and much that has happened - incidental to it; yes."

"You could forget it easier in California."

"I should forget too much."

"It's awful to think of you not comin' back, though I understand well enough. Europe suits you all right. But...but...."

He rose abruptly almost overturning his fragile chair.

"Good-by, and as I guess it *is* good-by I'll tell you something I wouldn't if there was any chance of my seein' you like I used to. It's this: If I'm more of a socialist than ever it's because of *you*! If my class hatred's blacker than ever *you're* the cause! *You'd* have made me a socialist if I wasn't one before. *Jesus Christ*! When I think what I might have had if we'd all been born alike! Had the same chances! If you hadn't been born at the top and I down at the bottom...common...not even educated except by myself after I was too old to get what a boy gets that goes to school long enough. I wouldn't mind bein' born ugly. There's plenty of men at the top that's ugly enough, God knows. But just one generation with money irons out the commonness. That's it! I'm common! Common! Common. *Democracy*! Oh, God!"

He caught up his cap and rushed out of the room,

Alexina ran after him and caught him at the garden door. Like all beautiful women who have listened to many declarations of love (or avoided them) she was inclined to be cruel to men that roused no response in her. But she felt only pity for Kirkpatrick.

She had intended merely to insist upon shaking hands with him, but when she saw his contorted face she slipped her arm round his neck and kissed him warmly on the cheek.

Then she pushed him gently through the door and locked it.

# CHAPTER X

I

Alexina had finished giving tea to two officers, a surgeon and a médecin major, and, enchanted almost as much by the sugar and the white bread as by their hostess, refreshingly beautiful and elegant in her velvet gown of pervenche blue, they had lingered until nearly six. As the concierge had gone out on an errand of her own Alexina had opened the garden door for them, and after they disappeared she stood looking at the street, which always fascinated her.

It was very narrow and crooked and gray. Her house was the only one with a garden in front; the others rose perpendicularly from the narrow pavement, tall and close and rather imposing. Each was heavily shuttered, the shutters as gray as the walls. The town had been evacuated during the first Battle of the Marne and only the poor had returned. The well-to-do provincials in this street had had homes elsewhere, perhaps a flat in Paris; or they had established themselves in the south.

The street had an intensely secretive air, brooding, waiting. Soon all these houses would be reopened, the dull calm life of a provincial town would flow again, the only difference being that the women who went in and out of those narrow doors and down this long and twisted street would wear black; but for the most part they would sit in their gardens behind, secluded from every eye, as indifferent to their neighbors as of old, with that ingrained unchangeable bourgeois suspicion and exclusiveness; and the façades, the street itself, would look little less secretive than now.

## II

Nowhere could she find such seclusion if she wished for it. This house was the only one in the street that belonged to a member of the noblesse, and the bourgeoisie had as little "use" for the noblesse as the noblesse for the bourgeoisie.

For the moment Alexina felt that the house was hers, and the street itself. She was literally its only inhabitant. As she stood looking up and down its misty grayness she felt more peaceful than she had felt for many days. There were certain fierce terrible emotions that she never wanted to feel again, and one of them was ruthlessness. She had done much good in the past four years; she had been, for the most part, high-minded, self-sacrificing, indifferent to the petty things of life, even to discomfort, and it had given her a sense of elevation - when she had had time to think about it. It was only certain extraordinary circumstances that brought other qualities as inherent as life itself surging to the top. It was demoralizing even to fight them, for that involved recognition. Better that she protect herself from their assaults. True, she was young, but she had had her fill of drama. All her old cravings, never satisfied in the old days of peace without and insurgence within, had been surfeited by this close personal contact with the greatest drama in history.

Why return to Paris at all? Why not settle down here at once, live a life of thought and study, and give abundant help where help was needed? There were villages within a few miles where the inhabitants were living in the ruins. (The Germans in their first retreat had been too hard pressed to linger long enough to set fire to this large town and they had not been able to reach it during their second drive.)

That had been a last flicker of romance at the embassy...a last resurgence of the evil the war had done her, as she sat in her cold room...a last blaze of sheer femininity when she discovered that Gora had come to Paris in search of Gathbroke....

She felt as if she had escaped from a bottomless pit....Assuredly she had the will and the character to make herself now into whatever she chose to be...let Gora have him if she could find him and keep him....Better that than hating herself for the rest of her life...love, far from being ennobling, seemed to her the most demoralizing of the passions...there had been something ennobling, expanding, soul-stirring in hating the brutal mediæval race that had devastated France...but in the reaction from her fierce registered vow to snatch a man from a forlorn unhappy woman no matter what her claims and have him for her own, she had shrunk from this new revelation of her depths in horror....One could not live with that....

III

A man in khaki was walking quickly down the long crooked street. As he approached she saw the red on his collar. He was a British officer. In another moment she was shaking hands with Gathbroke,

She was far more composed than he, although she felt as if the world had turned over, and there was a roar in her ears like the sound of distant guns. She had a vague impression that the war had begun again.

"You are the last person I should have expected to meet here. There is no British - "

"I came here to see you. I got your address from Madaine de Morsigny. I saw her last night at a reception and recognized her. She was at that ball in San Francisco. I introduced myself at once and asked her if you were in Paris. I was sure it was you...that night...."

"Will you come in!"

He followed her into the salon, softly lit by candles. She felt that fate for once had been kind. It was difficult to imagine surroundings or conditions in which she would look lovelier, be seen to greater advantage. But her hands were cold.

"It is too late for tea but perhaps you will share my frugal supper."

"If it won't inconvenience you too much. Thanks."

She sat down in the wide brocaded chair with its tarnished back. He stood looking at her for a moment, then took a turn up and down the long room.

Certainly she could not object to him to-day on the score of youth and freshness. His hair had lost its brightness. His face was very brown and thin and the lines if not deep were visible even in the candle light. His nose and mouth had the hard determination that life, more especially life in war time, develops; it was no casual trick of Nature with him. His eyes were still the same bright golden hazel, but their expression was keen and alert, and commanding. She fancied they could look as hard as those features more susceptible to modeling.

IV

"Smoke if you like."

"Thanks. I don't want to smoke."

Finally when Alexina was gripping the arms of the chair he began to speak.

"I feel rather an ass. I hardly know how to begin. I'm no longer twenty-three. I've lived several lifetimes since this war began, and made up my mind twice that I was going out. I should feel ninety. Somehow I don't feel vastly different from that day when I grabbed you like a brute because I wanted you more than anything on earth....

"I don't pretend that I've thought of you ever since. I've forgotten you for years at a time. But there have been moments when you have simply projected yourself into me and been closer than any mortal has ever been. You were there!

"I felt there was some meaning in those sudden secret wonderful visits of your soul to mine - I hate to say what sounds like sentimental rotting, but that exactly expresses it. They belonged to some other plane of consciousness. It takes war to shift a man over the border if only for a moment. It kept me - lately - from...never mind that now. When I saw your eyes above that tiny yellow flame...it wasn't only that your eyes are not to be matched anywhere...it seemed to me that I saw myself in them, They came as dose as that! Laugh if you like."

He stood defiantly in front of her.

"God! You look as if you never had had an emotion, never could have one. But you had once, if only for a moment!"

"I have never had one since - for any one, that is. I hear the concierge. I'll tell her to set a place for you."

V

She left the room and he stared after her. Her words had been full of meaning but her voice had been even and cold.

She returned and asked: "Are you in any way committed to Gora Dwight?"

"No...yes...that is...why do you ask me that?"

"Are you engaged to her?"

"I am not. But I came very close - that is, of course if she would have had me. She nursed me after I was wounded and gassed. She was a wonderful nurse and there was something almost romantic in meeting her again...as if she had come straight out of the past. We had an extraordinary experience as you know. I was not in the least drawn to her at that time. You filled, possessed me."

He hesitated. But it was a barrier he had not anticipated and it must go down. Moreover, it was evident that she wouldn't talk, and he was too excited for silence on his own part.

"She was there...when a man is weakest...when he values tenderness above all things...when he does little thinking on either the past or the future.

"She has a queer odd kind of fascination too, and any man must admire a woman so clever and capable and altogether fine. Several times I almost proposed to her. But there is no privacy in wards. I was sent back to

England and went to my brother's house in Hertfordshire. It was then that you began to haunt me. She had rejuvenated that California period in my mind - resuscitated it...but both express what I am trying to say. We had often talked about California and the fire. She alluded to you, casually, of course, more than once; but as I looked back I gathered that your marriage had been a mistake and that you had known it for a long time.

"She did not come to England until four months later, and then she was in charge of a hospital. I took her out occasionally - she was very much confined. I liked her as much as ever. But *I didn't want her*. It seemed tragic. There was one chance in a million that I should ever meet you again. Once I deliberately drew her on to talk of you and asked why you did not divorce your husband. She commented satirically upon the intense conservatism of your family and of your own inflexible pride. She added that you were the only beautiful woman she had ever known who seemed to be quite indifferent to men - sexless, she meant! But no woman knows anything about other women. I knew better!

"As I said it was rather tragic. To be haunted by a chimera! I liked her so much. Admired her. Who wouldn't? If she had been able to take me home, to remain with me, there is no doubt in the world that I should have married her if she would have had me....I prefer now to believe that she wouldn't. Why should she, with a great career in front of her?

"No doubt I should have loved her - with what little love I had to give. But those months had taught me that I could do without her, although I enjoyed her letters.

Even so...

"It was after she came to London that I felt I had to talk to some one and I went down, to the country to see Lady Vick-Elton Gwynne's mother. She had founded a hospital and run it, and was resting, worn out. She is a hard nut, empty, withered, arid. Nothing left in her but noblesse oblige. But there is little she doesn't know. She was smoking a black cigar that would have knocked me down and looked like an old sibyl. I told her the whole story - all of it, that is that was not too sacred. She puffed such, a cloud of smoke that I could see nothing but her hard, bright, wise, old eyes. 'Go after her,' she said. 'Find her. Divorce her. Marry her. That's where you men have the advantage. You can stalk straight out into the open and demand what you want point blank. No scheming, plotting, deceit, being one thing and pretending another, in other words ice when you are fire. Beastly rôle, woman's - ' I interrupted to remind her that it was twelve years since had seen you; that you had thrown me down as hard as a man ever got it and married another man. There was no more reason to believe that I could win you now. Then she asked me what I had come to see her and bore her to death for when she was trying to rest. 'If you want a thing go for it and get it, or if you can't get it at least find out that you can't. Also see her again and find out whether you want her or not, instead of mooning like a silly ass.'

"The upshot was I made tip my mind to go to California as soon as I could obtain my discharge. It never occurred to me that you were in Paris. Then I was sent to Paris with the Commission. I have certain expert knowledge....For some reason I didn't tell Miss Dwight....I wrote her a hurried note saying that I was obliged to go to Paris for a few weeks.

"The night after I arrived I saw you at the Embassy. That finished it. If I hadn't been sent back to England for some papers - twice - I'd have found you before this."

# CHAPTER XI

I

The concierge announced supper. Alexina had brought food with her and the little meal was good if not abundant. The dining-room was very dreary, although warmed by the petrol stove. It was a long dark room, paneled to the ceiling, and the two candles on the table did little more to define their lineaments to each other than the flames of briquet and match.

The concierge served and they talked of the Peace Conference and of the general pessimism that prevailed. Same old diplomacy. Same old diplomatists. Same old ambitions. Same old European policies. An idealist had about as much chance with those astute conventionalized brains dyed in the diplomatic wiles and methods of the centuries as an unarmed man on foot with a pack of wolves....At the moment all the other Commissions were cursing Italy....She might be the stumbling block to ultimate peace....As for the League of Nations, as well ask for the millenium at once. Human, nature probably inspired the creed: "As it was in the beginning, is now, and ever shall be," etc. "What we want" (this, Gathbroke), "is an alliance between Great Britain, and the United States. They could rule the world. Let the rest of everlastingly snarling Europe go hang." Elton Gwynne would work for that. He had already obtained his discharge and returned to America. He, Gathbroke, 'd work for it too. So would anybody else in the two countries that had any sense and no personal fish to fry.

II

When they returned to the salon he smoked. Alexina was thankful that it was cigarettes. Mortimer had made her hate cigars. If, like most Englishmen, he loved his pipe, he had the tact to keep it in his pocket.

It was she who reopened the subject that filled him.

"I feel sorry for Gora. Her life has been a tragedy in a way. Of course she has had her successes, her compensations. But it isn't quite everything to be the best of nurses, and I don't know that even writing could fill a woman's life. Not unless she'd had the other thing first. I am afraid she'll never be very popular anyhow. There are only small groups here and there in America than can stand intellect in fiction....It seems to me that she would make a great wife. I mean that. It is a great rôle and she could fill it greatly. I don't know, of course, whether she cares for you or not. I am not in her confidence. She is staying at my pension in Passy and I saw her constantly for ten days before I came here, but she did not mention your name....If she does she's the sort that would never marry any one else and her life would be spoilt. I don't mean to say she would give up, but she would just keep going. That seems to me the greatest tragedy of all....

"No! Why should there be any of this conventional subterfuge. I believe that she does care for you. I believed so long ago. I was jealous of her. I don't mean, to say that I was in love with you. I - perhaps forced myself not to be. It seemed too silly. Too utterly hopeless....Besides I knew even then the danger of letting myself go...of the unbridled imagination.

Probably love is all imagination anyhow. French marriages would seem to prove it. But we - your race and mine - have fallen into a sublime sort of error, and we'll no more reason ourselves out of it than out of the sex tyranny itself....I don't see how I could be happy with the eternal knowledge that Gora was miserable - that she would be happy if I had remained in California...."

"I have just told you that I should have gone to California as soon as I was free."

III


The air between them quivered and their eyes were almost one. But he remained smoking in his chair and continued:

"I marry you or no one. A man well and a man ill are two different beings. In illness sex is dormant. When a man is well he wants a woman or he doesn't want her. It may be neither his fault nor hers. But if she hasn't the sex pull for him, doesn't make a powerful insistent demand upon his passion, there is nothing to build on. I haven't come out alive from that shrieking hell to be satisfied with second-class emotions. I lay one night under three dead bodies, not one over twenty-five. I knew them all. Each was deeply in love with a woman....Well, I knew the value of life that night if I never did before. And life was given to us, when we can hold on to it, for the highest happiness of which we are individually capable, no matter what else we are forced to put up with. Happiness at the highest pitch, not makeshifts....The horrors, the obstacles, the very demons in our own characters were second thoughts on the part of Life either to satisfy her own spite or to throw her highest purpose into stronger relief. I'll have the highest or nothing."

"But that is not everything. There must be other things to make it lasting. Gora would make a great companion."

"Not half so great - to me - as you would and you know it. I hope you will understand that I dislike extremely to speak of Miss Dwight at all. If you had not brought her name into it I never should have done so. But now I feel I must have a complete understanding with you at any cost."

He dropped his cigarette on the table. He left his chair swiftly and snatched her from her own. His face was dark and he was trembling even more than she was.

"I'll have you...have you...."

She nodded.

Gertrude Atherton

# CHAPTER XII

## I

Gora entered her room at the pension, mechanically lit the oil stove that Alexina had procured for her, threw her hat on the bed, sat down in the low chair and thrust her hands info the thick coils of hair piled as always on top of her head. As she did so she caught sight of herself in the mirror and wondered absurdly why she should have kept all her hair and lost so much of her face. She looked more top-heavy than ever. Her face was a small oblong, her eyes out of all proportion. She thought herself hideous.

She had heard two hours before that Gathbroke was in Paris attached to the British Commission. She had met an old acquaintance, a San Francisco newspaper man, who had taken her to lunch and spoken of him casually. Gathbroke had good-naturedly given him an Interview when other members of the Commission had been inaccessible.

Gathbroke had told her nothing of a definite object when he wrote her that he was off for Paris. Nor had he mentioned it in the note he had written her after his arrival. This had been merely to tell her that he was feeling as well as he ever had felt in his life and was enjoying himself. Polite admonition not to tire herself out. He was always hers gratefully and her devoted friend.

He had written the note at the Rite Hotel, but when, assuming this was his address, she had called him up on her arrival, she had received the information that he was not stopping there, nor had been.

Gora was very proud. But she was also very much in love; and she had been in love with Gathbroke for twelve years. For the greater part of that time she had believed it to be hopeless, but it had always been with her, a sad but not too painful undertone in her busy life. It had kept her from even a passing interest in another man. She had even felt a Somewhat ironic gratitude to him and his indifference, for all the forces of her nature, deprived of their natural outlet, went into her literary work, informing it with an arresting and a magnetic vitality. She had believed herself to be without hope, but in the remote feminine fastnesses of her nature she had hoped, even dreamed - when she had the time. That was not often. Her life, except when at her desk with her literary faculty turned loose, had been practical to excess.

She would have offered her services in any case to one of the warring allies, no doubt of that; the tremendous adventure would have appealed to her quite aside from the natural desire to place her high accomplishment as a nurse at the disposal of tortured men. Nevertheless she was quite aware that she went to the British Army with the distinct hope of meeting Gathbroke again; quite as, under the cloak of travel, she would have gone to England long since had she not been swindled by Mortimer.

Until she found him insensible, apparently at the point of death, after the terrible disaster of March, nineteen-eighteen, she had only heard of him once: when she read in the *Times* he had been awarded the D.S.O.

She knew then where he was and maneuvered to get back to France. She found him sooner than she had dared to hope. And she believed that she had saved his life. Not only by her accomplished nursing. Her powerful will had thrown out its grappling irons about his escaping ego and dragged it back and held it in its exhausted tenement.

He had believed that also. He had an engaging spontaneity of nature and he had felt and shown her a lively gratitude. He was restless and frankly unhappy when she was out of his sight. He had a charming way of Baying charming things to a woman and he said them to her. But he was also as full of ironic humor as in his letters and "ragged" her. And he talked to her eagerly when he was better and she had gone with him to a hospital far back of the lines. There were intervals when they could talk, and the other men would listen...and had taken things for granted.

So had she. He had not made love to her. There was no privacy. Moreover, she guessed that his keen sense of the ridiculous would not permit him to make love to any woman when helpless under her hands.

But how could there be other than one finale to such a story as theirs? What was fiction but the reflection of life? if she had written a story with these obvious materials there could have been but one logical ending - unless, in a sudden spasm of reaction against romance, she had killed him off.

But he would live; and not be strong enough to return to the front for mouths...the war *must* be over by then....As for romance, well, she was in the romantic mood. It was a right of youth that she had missed, but a woman may be quite as romantic at thirty-four as at eighteen, if she has sealed her fountain instead of splashing it dry when she was too young to know its preciousness. Once before she had surrendered to romance, fleetingly: during the week that followed the night she had sat on Calvary with Gathbroke and watched a sea of flames.

The mood descended upon her, possessed her. She had other patients. There were the same old horrors, the same heart-rending duties; but the mood stayed with her. And after he left, for England. She knew there could, be but one ending. Her imagination had surrendered to tradition.

Moreover, she was tired of hard work. She wanted to settle down in a home. She wanted children. She must always write, of course. Writing was as natural to her as breathing. And she had already proved that a woman could do two things equally well.

II

She never thought of trying to follow him back to England, to shirk the increasing terrible duties behind the reorganized but harassed armies. The wounded seemed to drop through the hospital roof like flies.

Nevertheless when she was abruptly transferred to London she went without protest! It was then that she began to have misgivings. She was given charge of a large hospital just outside of London and her duties were constant and confining. But she managed to go out to lunch with him twice and once to dine; after which they drove back to the hospital in a slow and battered old hansom.

She returned a few weeks before the Armistice. She had not seen him for four months. He was well and expecting to be sent back to the front any day. At present they were making use of him in London.

If anything he appeared to admire her more than ever, to be more solicitous for her health. He lamented personally her exacting duties. But it was the almost exuberant friendliness of one man for another, for a comrade, a good fellow; although he often paid her quick little diagnostic compliments. If she hadn't loved him she would have enjoyed his companionship. He had read and thought and lived. Before the war he had been in active public life. He had far greater plans for the future.

He had been almost entirely impersonal. It had maddened her. Even the night they had driven through the dark streets of London out to her hospital, although he had talked more or less about himself, even encouraged her to talk about herself, there had not been one instant of correlation.

But she had made excuses as women do, in self-defense. He assumed that he might easily go back to the front just in time to get himself killed, although the end of the war was in sight....Her utter lack of experience with men in any sex relation had made her stiff, even in her letters; afraid of "giving herself away." She had no coquetry. If she had, pride would have forbidden her to use it. Her ideals were intensely old-fashioned. She wanted to be pursued, won. The man must do it all. Her writings had never been in the least romantic. Well, she was, if romance meant having certain fixed ideals.

One thing puzzled her. When she wrote she manipulated her men and women in their mutual relations with a master-hand. But she had not the least idea how to manage her own affair. What was genius? A rotten spot in the brain, a displacement of particles that operated independently of personality, of the inherited ego? Possession? Ancestors come to life for an hour in the subliminal depths? But what did she care for genius anyhow!

One thing she would have been willing to do as her part, aside from meeting him mentally at all points and showing a brisk frank pleasure in his society: give him every chance to woo and win her, to find her more and more indispensable to his happiness. But she was no woman of leisure. She could not receive him in charming toilettes in an equally seductive room. She had nothing for evening wear but an old black satin gown. After her arrival in London she had found time to buy a smart enough tailored coat and skirt, and a hat, but nothing more.

And after the Armistice was declared she only saw him once.

Then came his abrupt departure for Paris. His noncommittal note. Even then she refused to despair. It would be an utterly impossible end to such a story...after twelve years...not for a moment would she accept that.

# III

She applied for her discharge. During her long stay in the British service she had made influential friends. She had also made a high record not only for ability but for an untiring fidelity. Her vacations had been few and brief. She obtained her discharge and went to Paris. Her pride would permit her to telephone. What more natural? Nothing would have surprised him more than if she had not. She had little doubt of his falling into the habit of daily companionship. He knew Paris and she did not. He would have seen her daily in London if she had been free.

Something, no doubt of that, held him back. He was discouraged...or not sure of himself....She had assumed as a matter of course that he was at the Ritz. When she found that he was not, had not been, she realized that he had omitted to give her an address.

That might have been mere carelessness....But to find him in Paris! She had not visualized such swarms of people. She might almost have passed him on the street and not seen him. But not for a moment did she waver from her purpose. She held passionately to the belief that were they together day after day, hours on end....

Unbelievable.

IV


She had telephoned an hour ago to the hotel where he was staying with other members of the British Commission and been told that he was out of town, but might return any moment.

There was nothing to do but write him a note and wait. She was not equal to the humiliation of telephoning a third time. She wrote it at the hotel where her English friends were staying and sent it by messenger, having heard of the idiosyncracies of the Paris post.

Hastings, her newspaper friend, had been altogether a bird of ill omen. He had told her that the American market was glutted with "war stuff." The public was sick of it. Some of the magazines were advertising that they would read no more of it. She had told him that her material was magnificent and he had replied: "Can it. Maybe a year or two from now - five, more likely. I'm told over here that the war fiction we've had wished on us by the ton resembles the real thing just about as much as maneuvers look like the first Battle of the Marne, say, when the Germans didn't know where they were at; went out quail hunting and struck a jungle full of tigers....Why not? When most of 'em were written by men of middle age snug beside a library fire with mattresses on the roof - in America not even a Zeppelin to warm up their blood. But that doesn't matter. The public took it all as gospel. Ate it up. Now it is fed up and wants something else."

What irony!

And what a future if he - but that she would not face.

# CHAPTER XIII

I

She heard Janet Maynard, who had returned alone the day before from Nice, enter the next, room. She kept very still; she had no desire for conversation. But Janet tapped on her door in a moment and entered looking very important.

"I've something to tell you," she announced. "You'd never guess in a thousand years. Don't get up. 111 sit on the bed-used to any old place. Only too thankful it isn't a box, or to sit down at all. Try one of mine? Don't you feel well?"

"I've a rotten headache."

"Oh...mind my smoking?"

"Not a bit. What did you have to tell me?"

"Well, 'way back in ancient times, B.W., nineteen hundred and six, a young Englishman named Gathbroke came to California after his sister, who was ill." She was blowing rings and did not see Gora's face.

When she leveled her eyes Gora was unbuttoning her gaiters. "It seems she died some time during the fire and he had a perfectly horrid experience getting the body out to the cemetery. But that has nothing to do with the story. He met Olive and the rest of us - *and Alexina* - the night of the Hofer ball. I had forgotten the whole thing until Olive reminded me that we had joked Alex afterward about the way she had bowled him over. His eyes simply followed her, but Mortimer gave him no chance.

"Then. I remembered something else. Isabel Gwynne once told me that her husband was sure Gathbroke had proposed to Alex one day when he took him down to Eincona. He was in a simply awful state of nerves afterward. John thought he was going out of his mind. Now, here's the point. Night before last Olive was at a, ball and who should come up to her and introduce himself but Gathbroke. He's changed a lot but she recognized him. Well, he hardly waited to finish the usual amenities before he asked her plump out if Alex was in Paris, said he was positive he had seen her at that embassy ball where all the lights went out and they expected a riot. He turned white when he did it, but he was as direct as chain lightning. He wanted her address. Of course he got it. Olive was thrilled. It's safe to assume that he's with Alex at the present moment. At any rate Olive called him up this morning intending to ask him to dinner, and was told he was out of town. Now, isn't that romance for you?"

"Rather."

"Twelve years! Fancy a man being faithful all that time. Hadn't got what he wanted, that's probably why. Have you ever heard Alex speak of him? Think she'll divorce Mortimer?"

"I asked her the other night why she didn't. She said it was against the traditions of the family. But - I recall - she said - it seemed to me there was a curious sort of meaning in her voice - that if she wanted to marry a man nothing would stop her."

"And it wouldn't. Nothing would stop Alexina if anything started her. The trouble always was to start her. She's indolent and unsusceptible and fastidious. But deep and intense - Lord! Mark my words, she saw him at the Embassy. If she did and the thing's mutual she'll give poor old Maria such a shock that the war will look like ten cents."

"Possibly."

"You look really ill, Gora. No wonder you have headaches with that hair. It's magnificent - but! Go to bed and I'll send up your dinner. Got any aspirin?"

"Yes, thanks."

"Au 'voir."

## CHAPTER XIV

I

The day was fine and Alexina took advantage of the brief interval of grace and went for a walk. Gathbroke was in Paris but might come out any moment. She wore a coat and skirt of heavy white English tweed with a silk blouse of periwinkle blue. The same soft shade lined her black velvet hat.

She had a number of notes changed at the bank and struck out for one of the ruined villages. She was in a mood to distribute happiness, and only silver coin could carry a ray of light into the dark stupefied recesses of those miserable wretches living in the ruins of homes haunted by memories of their dead.

She felt a very torch of happiness herself. Her body and her brain glowed with it. The currents of her blood seemed to have changed their pace and their essence. The elixir of life was in them. She felt less woman than goddess.

She knew now why she had been born, why she had waited. As long as this terrible war had to be she was thankful for her intimate contact with the very martyrdom of suffering; never else could she have known to the full the value of life and youth and health and the power to be triumphantly happy in love. She would have liked to wave a wand and make all the world happy, but as this was as little possible as to remake human nature itself she soared into an ether of her own to revel in her astounding good fortune.

## II

The village she approached was picturesque in its ruin for it climbed the side of a hill, and although the Germans had set fire deliberately to every house the shells for the most part remained. Along the low ridge was a row of brick walls in various stages of gaunt and jagged transfiguration. They looked less the victims of fire than of earthquake.

The narrow ascending street was filled with rubble. She picked her way and peered into the ruins. At first she saw no one; the place seemed to be deserted. Then some one moved in a dark cellar, and as she stood at the top of the short flight of steps a very old woman came forward into the light. There were two children at her heels.

Alexina suddenly felt very awkward. She had always thought the mere handing out of money the most detestable part of charity. But there was nothing here to buy. That was obvious.

The old woman however relieved her embarrassment. She extended a skinny hand. The poor of France are not loquacious, but like all their compatriots they know what they want, and no doubt feel that life is simplified when they are in a position to ask for it.

Alexina gratefully handed her a coin and hurried on. Her next experience was as simple but more delicate. A younger woman had fitted up a corner of her ruin with a petticoat for roof and a plank supported by two piles of brick for counter and had laid in a supply of the post cards that pictured with terrible fidelity the ruins of her village. Alexina bought the entire stock, "to scatter broadcast in the United States," and promised to send her friends for more; assuring the woman that when the tourists came to France once more these ruined villages would be magnets for gold.

She managed to get rid of her coins without much difficulty, although comparatively few of the village's inhabitants had returned, and these by stealth. Many of them had trekked far! Others were still detained at the hostels in Paris and other cities where they could be looked after without too much trouble.

Several had set up housekeeping in the cellars in a fashion not unlike that of their cave dwelling ancestors, and a few had found a piece of roof above ground to huddle under when it rained. Some talked to her pleasantly, some were surly, others unutterably sad. None refused her largesse, and she was amused to look back and see a little procession making for the town, no doubt with intent to purchase.

In one side street less choked with rubbish small boys were playing at war. But for the most part the children looked very sober. They had been spared the horrors of occupation but they had suffered privations and been surrounded by grief and despair.

III

When she had exhausted her supplies she took refuge in the church. It was at the end of the long street on the ridge and after she had rested she could leave the village by its farther end, and by making a long detour avoid the painful necessity of refusing alms.

There was no roof on the church; otherwise it would have been the general refuge. Part of it including the steeple was some distance away and looked as if it had been blown off. The rest had gone down with one of the walls. It was a charred unlovely ruin. Saints and virgins sometimes defied the worst that war could do, but all had succumbed here. The paneless windows in the walls that still remained precariously erect framed pictures of a quiet and lovely landscape. The stone walls were intact about the farms in which moved a few old men and women in faded cotton frocks that looked like soft pastels. The oaks were majestic and serene. The hills were lavender in the distance. But the farm houses were in ruins and so was a château on a hill. Alexina could see its black gaping walls through the grove of chestnut trees withered by the fire.

She wandered about looking for a seat however humble but could find nothing more inviting than piles of brick and twisted iron. She noticed an open place in the floor and went over to it and peered down. There was a flight of steps ending in cimmerian darkness. Doubtless the vaults of the great families of the neighborhood were down there. She wondered if the spite of the Huns had driven them to demolish the very bones of the race they were unable to conquer.

IV


Suddenly she stiffened. A chill ran up her spine. She had an overwhelming sense of impending danger and stepped swiftly away from the edge of the aperture; then turned about, and faced Gora Dwight.

# CHAPTER XV

## I

"Oh," she said calmly, although her nerves still shuddered. "You must walk like a fairy. I didn't hear you."

"One must pick one's way through rubbish."

"Ghastly ruin, isn't it?"

"Life is ghastly."

Alexina made no reply lest she deny this assertion out of the wonder of her own experience. She guessed what Gora had come for and that she was feeling as elemental as she looked. She herself had recovered from that sudden access of horror but she moved still further from, that black and waiting hole.

"Are you going to marry Gathbroke?"

The gauntlet was down and Alexina felt a sharp sense of relief. She was in no mood for the subtle evasion and she had not the least inclination to turn up her eyes. She made up her mind however to save Gora's pride as far as possible.

"Yes," she said.

"You dare say that to me?"

Alexina raised her low curved eyebrows. She seldom raised them but when she did she looked like all her grandmothers.

"Dare? Did you expect me to lie? Is that what you wish?"

Gora clutched her muff hard against her throat. (Alexina wondered if she had a pistol in it.) Her eyes looked over it pale and terrible. Alexina had the advantage of her in apparent calm, but there was no sign of confusion in those wide baleful irises with their infinitesimal pupils.

"You knew that I loved him. That I had loved him for twelve years."

"I *knew* nothing of the sort. You had his picture on your mantel and you corresponded with him off and on but you never gave me a hint that you loved him. Twelve years! Good heaven! A friendship extending over such a period was conceivable; natural enough. But a romance! When such an idea did cross my mind I dismissed it as fantastic. You always seemed to me the embodiment of common sense."

"There is no such thing. It is true - that I hardly believed it then - admitted it. But I knew we should meet again. He never had married. It looked like destiny when I did meet him. I nursed him - "

She paused and her eyes grew sharp and watchful, Alexina's face showed no understanding and she went on, still watching.

"I nursed him back to life. Through a part of his convalescence. A woman *knows* certain things. He almost loved me then. If we could have been alone he would have found out - asked me to marry him. We should be married to-day. If I could have seen him constantly in London it would have been the same." She burst out violently: "I believe you wrote to him to come to Paris."

"My dear Gora! Keep your imagination for your fiction. I had forgotten his existence until I saw him, for a few seconds, at a reception. Don't forget that he came to Paris under orders from his Government."

"But you recognized him that night. You came down here to meet him, to get away from me."

"Far from coming here to meet him I had given up all hope of ever seeing him again. He found out my address and followed me. You also seem to forget that you never mentioned his name to me in Paris. How was I to know that you were still interested in him?"

"That first night...you guessed it...you threw down a sort of challenge. Deny that if you can!"

"No! I'll not deny it. I wanted him as badly as you did if with less reason. Nevertheless...believe it or not as you like...I came down here as much to leave the field clear to you as for my own peace of mind. I think...I fancy...I decided to leave the matter on the knees of the gods."

"Do you mean to tell me that if I had met him while we were together in Paris, and you knew the truth, that you would not have tried to win him away from me?"

"I wonder! I have asked myself that question several times. I like to think that I should have been noble, and withdrawn. But I am not at all sure....Yes, I do believe I should, not from noble unselfishness, oh, not by a long sight, but from pride - if I saw that he was really in love with you. I'd never descend to scheming and plotting and pitting my fascinations against another woman - "

"Oh, damn your aristocratic highfalutin pride. I suppose you mean that I have no such pride, having no inherited right to it. Perhaps not or I wouldn't be here to-day. At least I wouldn't be talking to you," she added, her voice hoarse with significance.

Once more Alexina eyed the muff. "Did you come here to kill me?"

"Yes, I did. No, I haven't a pistol. I couldn't get one. I trusted to opportunity. When I saw you standing at the edge of that hole I thought I had it."

Alexina found it impossible to repress a shiver but in spite of those dreadful eyes she felt no recurrence of fear.

"What good would that have done you? Murderesses get short shrift in France. There is none of that sickening sentimentalism here that we are cursed with in our country."

"Murders are not always found out. If you were at the bottom of that hole it would be long before you were found and there is no reason why I should be suspected. I didn't come through the village. I didn't even inquire at your house. I saw you leave it and followed at a distance. If I'd pushed you down there I'd have followed and killed you if you were not dead already."

Alexina wondered if she intended to rush her. But she was sure of her own strength. If one of them went down that hole it would not be she. Nevertheless she was beginning to feel sorry for Gora. She had never sensed, not during the most poignant of her contacts with the war, such stark naked misery in any woman's soul. Its futile diabolism but accentuated its appeal.

"Well, you missed your chance," she said coldly. Gora was in no mood to receive sympathy! "And if you hadn't and escaped detection I don't fancy you would have enjoyed carrying round with you for the next thirty or forty years the memory of a cowardly murder. Too bad we aren't men so that we could have it out in a fair fight. My ancestors were all duellists. No doubt yours were too," she added politely.

"Perhaps you are right." For the first time there was a slight hesitation in Gora's raucous tones. But she added in a swift access of anger: "I suppose you mean that your code is higher than mine. That you are incapable of killing from behind."

"Good heavens! I hope so!...Still...I will confess I have had my black moods. It is possible that I might have let loose my own devil if - if - things had turned out differently."

"Oh, no, you wouldn't! Not when it came to the point. You would have elevated your aristocratic nose and walked off." She uttered this dictum with a certain air of personal pride although her face was convulsed with hate.

"Gora, you are really making an ass of yourself. If you had taken more time to think it over you wouldn't have followed me up with any such melodramatic intention as murder. Good God! Haven't you seen enough of murder in the past four years? I could readily fancy you going in for some sort of revenge but I should have expected something more original - "

"Murder's natural enough when you've seen nothing else as long as I have. And as for human life - how much value do you suppose I place on it after four years of war? I had almost reached the point where death seemed more natural than life."

"Oh, yes...but later....There are tremendous reactions after war. Settled down once more in our smiling land my ghost would be an extremely unpleasant companion. You see, Gora, you are just now in that abnormal state of mind known as inhibition. But, unfortunately, perhaps, in spite of the fact that you have proved yourself to be possessed of a violence of disposition - that I rather admire - you were not cut out to be the permanent villain. You have great qualities. And for thirty-four years of your life you have been a sane and reasonable member of society. For four of those years you have been an angel of mercy....Oh, no. If you had killed me you would have killed yourself later. You couldn't live with Gathbroke for you couldn't live with yourself. Silly old tradition perhaps, but we are made up of traditions....That was one reason I left Paris, gave up trying to find him....I knew that I could have him. But I also knew that you had had some sort of recent experience with him, that you had come to Paris to find him, that possibly if left with a clear field you could win him. I knew - Oh, yes, I knew! - that he would know instantly he was mine if we met. But...well, I too have to live with myself. It might be that he was committed to you, that if he married you, you would both be happy enough. "When he did come nothing would have tempted me to accept him if I had still believed - "

"Did he tell you? Tell you how close he came? Tell you that I was in love with him?"

"My dear Gora, I fancy that if he were capable of that you would not be capable of loving him. I certainly should not." There was a slight movement in her throat as if she were swallowing the rest of the truth whole. She had adhered to it where she could but Gora's face must be saved. "Your name was not mentioned. I asked him no questions about his past. I am not the heroine of a novel, old style. He told me that he loved me, that he had never loved any other woman, never asked any other woman to marry him. That was enough for me. I had no place in my mind for you or any one else. Perhaps you don't know - how could you - that years ago, when he was in California, he asked me to marry him."

"Calf love! If you had not been here now - "

"He would have gone to California as soon as he could

get away. He had made up his mind to that before he came to Paris."

"What!"

Gora's arms dropped to her sides and she stared at the floor. Then she laughed, "O God, what irony! I talked of you more or Jess as was natural...and he remembered...we had recalled the past vividly enough.... Why couldn't one of those instincts in which we are supposed to be prolific have warned me?....Much fiction is like life!...Any heroine I could have created would have had it...had more sense....I have botched the thing from beginning to end."

She raised her head and stared at Alexina with somber eyes; the insane light had died out of them. They took in every detail of that enhanced beauty, of that inner flame, white hot, that made Alexina glow like a transparent lamp.

She also recalled that she had watched her pack her bags...that pervenche velvet gown...Alexina had described the quaint old salon....Her imagination, flashed out that first interview with Gathbroke with a tormenting conjuring of detail....

"Yon are one of the favorites of life," she admitted in her bitter despair. "You have been given everything - "

"I drew Mortimer," Alexina reminded her.

"True. But you dusted him out of your life with an ease and a thoroughness that has never been surpassed. Think what you might have drawn. No, you are lucky, lucky! The prixes of life are for your sort. I am one of the overlooked or the deliberately neglected. Not a fairy stood at my cradle. All things have come to you unsought. Beauty. Birth. Position. Sufficient wealth. Power over men and women. An enchanting personality. All the social graces. You have had ups and downs merely because after all you are a mortal; and as a matter of contrast - to heighten your powers of appreciation. No doubt the worst is over for you. I have had to take life by the throat and wring out of her what little I have. That is what makes life so hopeless, so terrible. No genius for social reform will ever eliminate the inequality of personality, of the inner inheritance. Nature meant for her own sport that a few should live and the rest should die while still alive."

"Gora, I don't want to sound like the well-meaning friends who tell a mother when she loses her child that it is better off, but I can't help reminding you that a very large and able-bodied fairy presided at your cradle. You have a great gift that I'd give my two eyes for; and you know perfectly well - or you will soon - that you will get over this and forget that Gathbroke ever existed, while you are creating men to suit yourself." Her incisive mind drove straight to the truth. "You will write better than ever. Possibly the reason that you have not reached the great public is because your work lacks humanity, sympathy. You never lived before. You were all intellect. Now you have had a terrific upheaval and you seem to have experienced about everything, including the impulse to murder. Most writers would appear to live uneventful lives judging from their extremely dull biographies. But they must have had the most tremendous inner adventures and soul-racking experiences - the big ones - or they couldn't have written as they did....This must be the more true in regard to women."

Gora continued to stare at her. The words sank in. Her clear intellect appreciated the truth of them but they afforded her no consolation. All emotion had died out of her. She felt beaten, helpless.

She was obliged to look up as she watched Alexina's subtly transfigured face, fascinated. It made her feel even her physical insignificance; the more as she had lost the flesh that had given her short stature a certain majesty.

"Oh, life is unjust, unjust." She no longer spoke with bitterness, merely as one forced to state an inescapable fact. "Injustice! The root of all misfortune."

"Life is a hard school but where she has strong characters to work on she turns out masterpieces. You will be one of them, Gora. And I fancy that women born with great gifts were meant to stand alone and to be trained in that hard school. It is only when women of your sort have a passing attack of the love germ that they imagine they could go through life as a half instead of a whole. When you are in the full tide of your powers with the public for a lover I fancy you will look back upon this episode with gratitude, if you remember it at all."

"Perhaps. But that, is a long way off! I have just been told that the order of fiction with which my mind is packed at present is not wanted. It has been contemptuously rejected by the American public as 'war stuff.'"

"Good heaven! That *is* a misfortune!"

For a moment Alexina was aghast. Here was the real

Gertrude Atherton

tragedy. She almost prayed for inspiration, for it lay with her to readjust Gora to life. To no one else would Gora ever give her confidence.

"I don't believe for a moment," she said, "that the intelligent public will ever reject a great novel or story dealing with the war. The masterly treatment of any subject, the new point of view, the swift compelling breathless drama that is your peculiar gift, must triumph over any mood of the moment. Moreover, when you are back in California you will see these last four years in a tremendous perspective. And no contrast under heaven could be so great. You probably won't hear the war mentioned once a month. No doubt much that crowds your mind now will cease to interest the productive tract of your brain and you will write a book with the war as a mere background for your new and infinitely more complete knowledge of human psychology. No novel of any consequence for years to come will be written without some relationship to the war. Stories long enough to be printed in book form perhaps, but not the novel: which is a memoir of contemporary life in the form of fiction. No writer with as great a gift as yours could have anything but a great destiny. Go back to California and bang your typewriter and find it out for yourself."

For the first time something like a smile flitted over Gora's drawn face. "Perhaps. I hope you are right. I don't think I could ever really lose faith in that star." She was thinking: Oh, yes! I'll go back to California as quickly as I can get there - as a wounded animal crawls back to its lair.

She would have encircled the globe three times to get to it. *Her state*.

To her it was what family and friends and home and children were to another. It was literally the only friend she had in the world. She would have flown to it if she could, sure of its beneficence.

"I shall go as soon as I can get passage," she said. "And you?"

"I must go too unless I can get a divorce here. I shall know that in a few days."

"Well, we travel on different steamers if you do go! I shall stop off at Truckee and go to Lake Tahoe. It will be a long while before I go to any place that reminds me of you. I no longer want to kill you but I want to forget you. Good-by."

Gertrude Atherton

# CHAPTER XVI

When she reached the foot of the hill she turned and looked back. Alexina was standing in one of the jagged window casements of the church. The bright warm sun was overhead in a cloudless sky. Its liquid careless rays flooded the ruin. Alexina's tall white figure, the soft blue of her hat forming a halo about her face, was bathed in its light; a radiant vision in that shattered town whose very stones cried out against the injustice of life.

Alexina, who was feeling like anything but a madonna in a stained glass window, waved a questing hand.

"The fortunate of earth!" thought Gora.

She set her lips grimly and walked across the valley with a steady stride. At least she could be one of the strong.

# Choose from Thousands of 1stWorldLibrary Classics By

Ada Leverson
Adolphus William Ward
Aesop
Agatha Christie
Alexander Aaronsohn
Alexander Kielland
Alexandre Dumas
Alfred Gatty
Alfred Ollivant
Alice Duer Miller
Alice Turner Curtis
Alice Dunbar
Ambrose Bierce
Amelia E. Barr
Andrew Lang
Andrew McFarland Davis
Andy Adams
Anna Sewell
Annie Besant
Annie Hamilton Donnell
Annie Payson Call
Annonaymous
Anton Chekhov
Arnold Bennett
Arthur Conan Doyle
Arthur M. Winfield
Arthur Ransome
Atticus
B.H. Baden-Powell
B. M. Bower
Baroness Emmuska Orczy
Baroness Orczy
Basil King
Bayard Taylor
Ben Macomber
Bertha Muzzy Bower
Bjornstjerne Bjornson
Booth Tarkington
Boyd Cable
Bram Stoker
C. Collodi
C. E. Orr
C. M. Ingleby
Carolyn Wells
Catherine Parr Traill
Charles A. Eastman
Charles Dickens
Charles Dudley Warner
Charles Farrar Browne

Charles Ives
Charles Kingsley
Charles Klein
Charles Lathrop Pack
Charles Whibley
Charles Willing Beale
Charlotte M. Braeme
Charlotte M. Yonge
Charlotte Perkins Stetson
Clair W. Hayes
Clarence Day Jr.
Clarence E. Mulford
Clemence Housman
Confucius
Cornelis DeWitt Wilcox
Cyril Burleigh
D. H. Lawrence
Daniel Defoe
David Garnett
Don Carlos Janes
Donald Keyhoe
Dorothy Kilner
Dougan Clark
Douglas Fairbanks
E. Nesbit
E.P.Roe
E. Phillips Oppenheim
Edgar Rice Burroughs
Edith Van Dyne
Edith Wharton
Edward J. O'Biren
Edward S. Ellis
Edwin L. Arnold
Eleanor Atkins
Eliot Gregory
Elizabeth Gaskell
Elizabeth McCracken
Elizabeth Von Arnim
Ellem Key
Emerson Hough
Emily Dickinson
Enid Bagnold
Enilor Macartney Lane
Erasmus W. Jones
Ernie Howard Pie
Ethel Turner
Ethel Watts Mumford
Eugenie Foa
Eugene Wood

Evelyn Everett-green
Everard Cotes
F. H. Cheley
F. J. Cross
Federick Austin Ogg
Ferdinand Ossendowski
Francis Bacon
Francis Darwin
Frances Hodgson Burnett
Frances Parkinson Keyes
Frank Gee Patchin
Frank Harris
Frank Jewett Mather
Frank L. Packard
Frank V. Webster
Frederic Stewart Isham
Frederick Trevor Hill
Frederick Winslow Taylor
Friedrich Kerst
Friedrich Nietzsche
Fyodor Dostoyevsky
G.A. Henty
G.K. Chesterton
Gabrielle E. Jackson
Garrett P. Serviss
Gaston Leroux
George Ade
Geroge Bernard Shaw
George Durston
George Ebers
George Eliot
George MacDonald
George Meredith
George Orwell
George Tucker
George W. Cable
George Wharton James
Gertrude Atherton
Grace E. King
Grace Gallatin
Grant Allen
Guillermo A. Sherwell
Gulielma Zollinger
Gustav Flaubert
H. A. Cody
H. B. Irving
H.C. Bailey
H. G. Wells
H. H. Munro

| | | |
|---|---|---|
| H. Irving Hancock | James DeMille | Louisa May Alcott |
| H. Rider Haggard | James Joyce | Lucy Fitch Perkins |
| H. W. C. Davis | James Lane Allen | Lucy Maud Montgomery |
| Hamilton Wright Mabie | James Lane Allen | Lydia Miller Middleton |
| Hans Christian Andersen | James Oliver Curwood | Lyndon Orr |
| Harold Avery | James Oppenheim | M. Corvus |
| Harold McGrath | James Otis | M. H. Adams |
| Harriet Beecher Stowe | James R. Driscoll | Margaret E. Sangster |
| Harry Houidini | Jane Austen | Margaret Vandercook |
| Helent Hunt Jackson | Jens Peter Jacobsen | Margret Penrose |
| Helen Nicolay | Jerome K. Jerome | Maria Edgeworth |
| Hendrik Conscience | John Burroughs | Maria Thompson Daviess |
| Hendy David Thoreau | John Cournos | Mariano Azuela |
| Henri Barbusse | John F. Kennedy | Marion Polk Angellotti |
| Henrik Ibsen | John Gay | Mark Overton |
| Henry Adams | John Glasworthy | Mark Twain |
| Henry Ford | John Habberton | Mary Austin |
| Henry Frost | John Joy Bell | Mary Catherine Crowley |
| Henry James | John Kendrick Bangs | Mary Cole |
| Henry Jones Ford | John Milton | Mary Hastings Bradley |
| Henry Seton Merriman | John Philip Sousa | Mary Roberts Rinehart |
| Henry W Longfellow | Jonas Lauritz Idemil Lie | Mary Rowlandson |
| Herbert A. Giles | Jonathan Swift | M. Wollstonecraft Shelley |
| Herbert N. Casson | Joseph A. Altsheler | Maud Lindsay |
| Herman Hesse | Joseph Carey | Max Beerbohm |
| Homer | Joseph Conrad | Myra Kelly |
| Honore De Balzac | Joseph E. Badger Jr | Nathaniel Hawthrone |
| Horace Walpole | Joseph Hergesheimer | Nicolo Machiavelli |
| Horatio Alger Jr. | Joseph Jacobs | O. F. Walton |
| Howard Pyle | Julian Hawthrone | Oscar Wilde |
| Howard R. Garis | Julies Vernes | Owen Johnson |
| Hugh Lofting | Justin Huntly McCarthy | P.G. Wodehouse |
| Hugh Walpole | Kakuzo Okakura | Paul and Mabel Thorne |
| Humphry Ward | Kenneth Grahame | Paul G. Tomlinson |
| Ian Maclaren | Kenneth McGaffey | Paul Severing |
| Inez Haynes Gillmore | Kate Langley Bosher | Percy Brebner |
| Irving Bacheller | Kate Langley Bosher | Peter B. Kyne |
| Israel Abrahams | Katherine Cecil Thurston | Plato |
| Ivan Turgenev | Katherine Stokes | R. Derby Holmes |
| J.G.Austin | L. A. Abbot | R. L. Stevenson |
| J. Henri Fabre | L. T. Meade | R. S. Ball |
| J. M. Barrie | L. Frank Baum | Rabindranath Tagore |
| J. Macdonald Oxley | Latta Griswold | Rahul Alvares |
| J. S. Fletcher | Laura Lee Hope | Ralph Henry Barbour |
| J. S. Knowles | Laurence Housman | Ralph Waldo Emmerson |
| J. Storer Clouston | Leo Tolstoy | Rene Descartes |
| Jack London | Leonid Andreyev | Rex Beach |
| Jacob Abbott | Lewis Carroll | Rex E. Beach |
| James Allen | Lilian Bell | Richard Harding Davis |
| James Andrews | Lloyd Osbourne | Richard Jefferies |
| James Baldwin | Louis Tracy | Richard Le Gallienne |

Robert Barr
Robert Frost
Robert Gordon Anderson
Robert L. Drake
Robert Lansing
Robert Lynd
Robert Michael Ballantyne
Robert W. Chambers
Rosa Nouchette Carey
Rudyard Kipling
Samuel B. Allison
Samuel Hopkins Adams
Sarah Bernhardt
Selma Lagerlof
Sherwood Anderson
Sigmund Freud
Standish O'Grady
Stanley Weyman
Stella Benson
Stephen Crane
Stewart Edward White
Stijn Streuvels
Swami Abhedananda

Swami Parmananda
T. S. Ackland
T. S. Arthur
The Princess Der Ling
Thomas A. Janvier
Thomas A Kempis
Thomas Anderton
Thomas Bailey Aldrich
Thomas Bulfinch
Thomas De Quincey
Thomas H. Huxley
Thomas Hardy
Thomas More
Thornton W. Burgess
U. S. Grant
Valentine Williams
Various Authors
Victor Appleton
Virginia Woolf
Walter Camp
Walter Scott
Washington Irving
Wilbur Lawton

Wilkie Collins
Willa Cather
Willard F. Baker
William Dean Howells
William le Queux
W. Makepeace Thackeray
William W. Walter
Winston Churchill
Yei Theodora Ozaki
Yogi Ramacharaka
Young E. Allison
Zane Grey